Come for me.

Caught, Reyna listened to the voice that had called her from across the stars.

Set me free.

More than a century ago, Birnam Rauth, whose voice was her father's voice, whose eyes were her father's eyes, had walked upon this soil. And now his voice pleaded through the moonlit trees.

Set me free.

Something had happened to him here. And now Reyna, Juaren and Verra walked under the same trees, opened themselves to the same danger, seen or unseen...

STARSILK

SYDNEY J. VAN SCYOC

BERKLEY BOOKS, NEW YORK

STARSILK

A Berkley Book/published by arrangement with
the author

PRINTING HISTORY
Berkley trade paperback edition/September 1984

ISBN: 0-425-07207-X

A BERKLEY BOOK ® TM 757,375
The name "BERKLEY" and the stylized "B" with design are
trademarks belonging to Berkley Publishing Corporation.

PRINTED IN THE UNITED STATES OF AMERICA

STARSILK

ONE
TSUUKA

When Tsuuka had soothed her weanlings to sleep and seen that her cubs were curled in their bower, warm in their bedding silks, she descended to the lower limbs of her tree to her solitary bower. It was the third night since she had taken song-dreams, and the barriers her mind set against the nightmares were crumbling. Dark images pressed against her eyelids, making them heavy. Painfully she stretched out on the silent-silks piled on the floor of her bower, letting the cool swaths slither across her furred limbs, and permitted herself to slip briefly into a light, dreamless sleep. Even as she dozed, she monitored the depth of her sleep, not permitting awareness to escape her entirely. Because to do so was to give herself to the nightmares that hovered at the raw edges of her fatigue.

When the moon rose and shone against the brilliant swaths that formed the walls of her bower, she shivered alert again. Rising, she pushed aside first the scarlet swath, then the amber, and stretched. Her brief sleep lingered in her limbs, a faint warmth, but fatigue still tugged at the rest of her body and the nightmares still pressed near, dark-clawed and insistent. Growling softly, she curled back into the silent-silks and groomed herself, drawing a rough tongue through her glossy chestnut fur. Carefully she cleansed away the dusty residue of the day. Moonlight made jewels of the dampness her tongue left behind.

But she could no more groom away fatigue than she had napped it away earlier. When her fur dried, the need for sleep tugged at her again, irresistibly, and she knew that this time it would not be light and dreamless. The peculiar tension that drew at her muscles was unmistakable. She knew she must take song-dreams before she slept again or she would slip into the pit of nightmare. And she hadn't even a bower-sibling to hold her as she thrashed against its black walls.

Shivering, reluctant, she rose from her bed. She slid the scarlet and amber swaths back into place, shutting out the inquiring moon, and loosened the azure songswath that was drawn tight against the framework of the bower. This was her skyswath, her bower companion, the silk she had chosen to share her closest thoughts.

The swath reached immediately for moonlight, trilling brightly, tuning its song. At the same time it uttered its ritual question, speaking softly within Tsuuka's mind. *Tsuuka? Are you Tsuuka, daughter of Mirala, sibling of Maiilin? Are you Tsuuka, mother of Dariim and Falett, Paalan and Kaliir?*

Tsuuka stretched her aching muscles, arching her fingers and toes until the black claws snicked free. *I am Tsuuka!* she cried in silent response.

Breeze caught the sky-blue swath and made it flutter, bringing rising brilliance to its audible song. Even its silent voice became more distinct. *Are you Tsuuka, hunter of the forest and the clearings? Tsuuka, who stalks so skillfully, who pounces so lightly, whose cubs and weanlings are always fat and sleek?*

I am Tsuuka! she cried again, again silently, caught between the swimming need to let her eyelids close, to let her breath grow thick and regular in her throat, and some residual resistance to the swath's induction ritual. The silk's voice was supple and sweet; it promised her what she must have. But she did not want to deliver herself to song-dreams tonight, nor any night. She did not want the helplessness they brought, however briefly.

Still what choice had she? Breeze rippled at the azure songswath, producing a softly accusing note. *If you are Tsuuka, why are my sister-silks silent? Why do you hold their harmony captive?*

At this plaint, Tsuuka's lips curled in a predator's grimace, sharp with gleaming teeth. *Why would you sing when I only want to sleep, silk? My weanlings and my cubs are in their swathings. The forest is still. Why must I free your voices when I want to rest?*

Because you know what dark things are loose among the trees, clamoring for your attention. To us they are only the thoughts that join us to the spinners and to the unseen. But to you the images they bear are nightmares, and when you grow tired they draw close around you. You must take song-dreams to rebuild the barriers of your mind.

Dark things that were only thoughts: it was the same answer she always heard, no more satisfactory tonight than on any other occasion. Irritably Tsuuka drew black claws across the captive swath. *Hear me, silk. I am Tsuuka who stretched you here, Tsuuka who can free your voice or bind it silent against the poles. Why are your thoughts nightmares to me? Why do they draw me into the pit? Why is there no way to escape but through song-dreaming? Tell me quickly, silk, before I bind you tight again.*

The silk rippled softly. *Why is the moon in the sky, my Tsuuka? Why is the wind in the trees? Do you know? Then why do our two kinds live together in the forest, you guarding the spinners from grass-pups and prickle-hides and other predators who would harm them, the spinners protecting you from the insect flyers that would sap your blood—and we delivering you from nightmares? How would you live without us? How would we live without you? This is the way of our life, as it has long been—as we have long lived it.*

The way of their life. As always there was evasion in what the silk said. There were questions left unanswered. But Tsuuka drew in her claws, reluctantly admitting the inevitability of the swath's argument. There were sithi who did not live in forest, sithi who hunted in the grasslands that stretched beyond the tall trees. They were wretched things, their bodies welted from the feeding-stings of flying insects, their coats patchy, their cubs ill-fed because the flyers so weakened them that they hunted poorly. But in the forest the spinners climbed to the flyers' high nests, where the sithi could not reach, and fed on their larvae before they could hatch. *I would not live without you and be fed upon,* she acknowledged. *I would not raise my cubs that way.*

And don't you like our songs, Tsuuka? The silk's voice had grown smug, self-satisfied. *We will sing everything that pleases you. We will sing you songs as silken as the meadows by moonlight, as majestic as the trees standing against the stars. We will sing you songs as piquant as the faces of your cubs, as soft as the fur of your weanlings. We will sing you songs to drown out the cry of your sibling as she wanders the forest.*

Tsuuka quivered unwillingly at this reminder. *My sibling doesn't live in this quarter of the forest, silk. It has been seasons since I last heard her cry in the trees. It has been seasons since I last saw her empty face and met her empty eyes.* In fact, no one but the skyswath spoke of Maiilin now. The other sithi kept silence, as if they had forgotten her name, as if they had forgotten everything about her that first day Tsuuka returned from the deep trees, crying and alone.

But Tsuuka thought of her sibling often, with aching heart. Did Maiilin listen to the silks now as she wandered the distant quarters of the forest? Did their song torment her damaged mind with loosely tethered memories of their cub days, when they had been sleek chestnut shadows darting through the meadow, laughing together, both as bright and swift and free as only Tsuuka was now? *My sibling has gone, and none of my young will be like her. All my cubs will be sleek and free,* Tsuuka protested with the insistence of fear. Because what guarantee did she have that it was true? *Sleek and free like me.*

I am sorry you grieve for your sibling still, when she bears the chains of her damaged mind in total ignorance, the silk murmured silkenly. *But we love our freedom too, Tsuuka, hunter. Hear how bright my voice is, now that you let me reach out for the light I love? Free my sisters and we will all sing for you. You are tired. The barriers of your mind have begun to crumble. We will sing songs to rebuild them, to banish the images that join us and draw you to the nightmare pit.*

Tsuuka sank back to her bed, retracting her claws. Her furred body was long, sinuous with predator grace, and her head was delicately formed, set with eyes that gleamed like yellow jewels. In them were reflected all the brilliant hues of the songswaths stretched taut upon the framework of her bower. She drew a furred hand across her eyes, acknowledging that there was no other way. She must either take song-dreams or face the nightmare pit.

Reluctantly she made her choice, the choice she always made. Then she rose and loosened the songswaths, first the scarlet and amber swaths, then the lilac and noon-yellow ones, finally the chartreuse, crimson and emerald swaths. Their voices sighed through the bower, murmuring to each other. *Sing!* she commanded, throwing herself down on the silent-silks. She closed her eyes and let her breath slowly thicken.

For a time there was only the gossiping murmur of the freed fabric, wordless, faint. Then the breeze came again, rippling at the moonwashed rainbow, and the lilac silk uttered a soft trill. The sound rose joyously, drawing response first from the yellow, then from the amber swaths. The chartreuse joined its ringing voice to theirs, and finally the darker silks, the scarlet, emerald and crimson, added their deep, clear tones.

Their sound was silken, sweet, their harmony pure. But Tsuuka snicked her claws free and drove the sharp tips into her flesh, determined to cling to some vestige of alertness. Kaliir had been restless today, her eyes too bright. She could well wake in the night. And the time was near when Dariim and Falett must choose their own tree and build their first bower. She could see encroaching maturity in the new, hard shine of their fur, in the lengthening of their limbs. Sometimes Dariim thrashed at her bedding, briefly caught in a cub-dream, faint parody of the swirling night-vortices that drew in adult sithi. If Tsuuka could not respond to her young...

But it was already too late. The rising voices had taken possession of her. Numbness began at the base of her skull and spread along nerve passageways across her shoulders and down her back, reaching for her limbs. As the paralysis touched her arms, her claws retracted involuntarily and her hands fell. With a whimper she rolled to her back. One glossy-furred leg remained flexed. The other stretched straight. Her breath came in shallow pants. Her yellow eyes remained open and staring.

The songs the rippling swaths sang her were as promised: of forest meadows and tall trees, of hot sun by day and cool breeze by night, of the distant sound of cubs playing and the nearer sound of spinners tittering over their work. The songs were of all things Tsuuka celebrated. There was no hint of discord, no lapse of harmony.

Yet as the swaths sang, Tsuuka was aware of a single, high note that was sustained through the entire chorus. It was penetrating, barely perceptible, yet insistent, inescapable. She tried to roll her head to pinpoint its source. But paralysis was complete. She could neither focus her staring eyes nor close her sagging jaw.

Did the note come from the azure swath? From the yellow? Perhaps it came from more than one. It continued, penetrating, painful, frightening in its rapidly increasing intensity. Soon it became more than sound. It became something near-tangible that flowed into the tips of her fingers and burned along the pathways of her nervous system, twisting her body in convulsions. She uttered a helpless whimper, her arms and legs thrashing, as a sudden rush of nightmare images flashed into her awareness, the contents of a hundred torturing dreams exploding into her consciousness in a single instant.

Before they could unfold, before they could scour her raw, the penetrating note flared from the realm of sound into visibility. A thin strand of intense yellow light, it laced itself through the exploding nightmare images, brilliantly illuminating them. Then the strand blossomed with visible energy, becoming so fiercely luminescent that everything else was lost in its glare. With a silent scream, Tsuuka surrendered consciousness to the song-dream.

She slept long after that. When she woke, she sprawled gracelessly across her bed-silks, her fur still matted with perspiration. Her limbs were flaccid. But the penetrating note was gone, as were the tension and fatigue of the past few days. And the nightmares which had beckoned were gone too, banished back across the renewed barriers of her mind. As she dragged herself to a sitting position, the song of the swaths caressed her, their lyric wordless, yearning and sweet, as it had always been.

As always. And yet...

But she did not want to think now of evasions, of unanswered questions, of half-glimpsed realities she could never bring to full definition. Tenderly, carefully Tsuuka groomed herself in the waning moonlight. She drew her pink tongue through her wet fur, unconscious of everything but the rainbow voices. Peace infused her as she smoothed the last rumpled patch of fur back into place.

By then the moon was setting and the voices of the swaths fell to a chorus of whispers. *You are Tsuuka,* the azure swath murmured as the others ebbed into silence.

I am Tsuuka, yes.

The moon leaves and our voices dim, my Tsuuka. Did you find our song all we promised? Did it take the nightmares from your mind?

It was everything, Tsuuka responded. *I will loose you again when next the moon comes. I will listen again. As always.*

We will sing again, the swath replied. *You are Tsuuka.*

Then their voices were gone. Tsuuka rose from her bed-silks and made her way around the circular bower, drawing the silks taut against the framework of poles. When they were secure, she pushed aside the lilac and yellow swaths to watch the moon set behind the trees.

When its last rays were gone, Tsuuka paced around the bower. Her senses possessed a ringing clarity and her muscles rippled smoothly beneath the freshly groomed fur. She was primed for the day that lay ahead, a day of hunt, of play, a day of sunning herself in the clearing when her belly was full and her cubs fed. But it was not yet dawn. It was too early to leave her tree. And there were questions in her mind that she did not want to confront.

She peered around the bower restlessly, looking for occupation, and her gaze touched the one swath she had not loosened. Stretched mute against the bower poles, it was of white silk and it shone softly even without the illumination of the moon. She never released the starswath when the other swaths sang. It could not blend its voice harmoniously with theirs. She had only to loosen it and the others fell into resentful silence, refusing to continue their song.

Yet this swath did not require moonlight to sing. The light of a single star was sufficient to tune its strange voice. And the questions it raised in her mind were enough to distract her from the other, more troubling questions that sometimes disturbed her nights. Tsuuka drew her fingers down its shimmering length. The silk seemed to respond, straining at the poles to feed on the warmth of her hand.

"Do you love your freedom, silk?" Tsuuka asked aloud. This of all the silks was deaf to her thoughts. Nor could it whisper in her mind. In fact it seldom spoke in any way she understood.

Drawn taut against the poles, the swath could make no reply.

"Do you love your freedom?" Tsuuka repeated, slowly easing the tension on the white swath.

Breeze slapped at the slackened silk, whipping a wordless note, high and trembling, from the swath. At the same time the swath spoke in a second voice which fell into a lower register. The words it uttered were incomprehensible, spoken in some alien tongue, sharply articulated, crackling with urgency.

Her eyes narrowing, Tsuuka touched the pole again, giving the swath more slack. Immediately it caught the breeze and billowed, both its voices rising, one singing wordlessly, the other speaking with a strange, crackling insistence.

"You are very poorly modulated," Tsuuka suggested, running the back of her hand down the rippling silk.

Disregarding her comment, the silk sang and spoke, its words sharp-edged, cutting in their force. Occasionally the voice uttered a spate of words Tsuuka found very nearly comprehensible, as if it spoke her own language, but with faulty emphasis, the words molded too crisply, too precisely separated into individual units. Once or twice she even caught the term "sithi-hunter," the name of her kind.

Frowning, she lounged back against her silks. The starswath was a puzzle. Its song could scarcely be so called. It held no power to soothe; its power to relieve was nonexistent. Yet she had heard the copy-master speaking by the stream one night when the spinners had tied it there to air and had wished to have one of its copies for her own. Few other sithi owned them. Their voices were too harsh, the words they spoke meaningless. But Tsuuka's nights were lonely without a sibling, and the starsilk would offer distraction.

The spinners had created the silk at her request, whispering over their stick-looms, extruding the sticky substance that formed in the special glands of their throats, joining and smoothing it into a mute, glossy sheet. When the swath was completed, they hurried away to their nests carrying the mute swath and the copy-master, securely rolled, with them. What occurred there was secret. No sithi had ever seen, but Tsuuka knew it involved moonlight and breeze and a second substance produced by the spinners' throat glands, not sticky this time but watery and acrid-smelling.

Later that night the spinners had washed the new silk in the stream and hung it to dry. Its voice had filled the moon-dappled clearing beneath the trees with an incomprehensible tension, as if the developing process had wakened some slumbering spirit who protested the wrongs of a previous existence. The new silk had spoken almost as vehemently, sung almost as harshly as the copy-master, although it had not twisted so angrily against the pole, had not strained so fiercely at the knots that bound it.

Tension—there was tension in the starvoice, impatience, a frustrated desire to communicate. And the frustration was emphasized when occasionally a few words emerged in the sithi tongue, as now. *"From beyond your sun, sithi, so far beyond your sun..."*

How had a silk learned to speak the sithi tongue? And what did it mean, from far beyond her sun? It was another puzzle that could not be resolved. She would never know why the starswath spoke both in the sithi language and in a foreign tongue. She would never guess what it wanted to tell her so urgently.

There were many things she did not understand, among them what had happened to Maiilin that day so long ago in the heart of the trees. Tsuuka growled softly to herself, wishing that memory did not press so insistently at her mind. Despite the years that had passed, she had never been able to relegate the events of that day to forgetfulness.

The day had been warm, the air a caress against their cub-fur, and there had been something in the breeze that had challenged them, something that had reminded them they would not be cubs much longer. Maiilin had wanted to go into the grasslands that day, to hunt in the brush as their most distant ancestors had. She had wanted to run in the deep grasses, she had wanted to climb the twisted, lonely trees, she had wanted to do reckless things while the wine of spring was in their veins.

Tsuuka, always the more cautious sibling, had found a dozen reasons not to do any of those things. There were flyers in the grasslands, and she did not want to be stung. Game was sparse. And what landmarks could there be in the stretching grasses? How would they find their way back if they ran too far? And what if they met the few sithi who still lived there? Would they be hostile? Perhaps they even carried disease. She had heard they were sickly and ill-fed—and too ignorant to know they would be neither if they made their home in the forest instead of the grasslands.

Finally she had prevailed. She had persuaded Maiilin not to go to the grasslands. But she had not coaxed the restlessness from Maiilin's mood. And so she had let Maiilin tease her into venturing into the heart of the forest instead, where the trees grew so densely that sunlight hardly touched the ground. There the tree trunks were not white and dry-barked but dark and mossy. Maiilin had been there alone many times, or so she said, although their mother had warned them against it. Was Tsuuka afraid to go even once? Was Tsuuka still a milk-cub, clinging to her mother, afraid to see the mysterious things Maiilin had seen? Was Tsuuka afraid to climb the oldest trees? Afraid to look into the secret places deep in their cavernous trunks, where there were things Tsuuka could not even imagine—strange, growing things with blind eyes and half-formed limbs?

Tsuuka didn't believe everything Maiilin said. She didn't believe Maiilin had done and seen everything she claimed. Certainly she had no desire to do and see those things herself. Half-formed, growing things—she shuddered, their mother's warning clear in her mind. And although she weakened eventually and went with Maiilin, she seemed to hear her mother's admonition more distinctly with every step.

"When you go to search for your own tree, cubs, you must not go near the heart of the forest. Nor must you go there in play. Listen to me. There are things no sithi must see, and that is where they live."

Things no sithi must see? Even then, before she was old enough to hear the silks' silent-talk, Tsuuka had understood that the spinners and the songsilks joined thoughts with something called the unseen. That in fact the unseen directed the activities of the spinners and decided which silks were to be created and when. Was that what no sithi must ever see—the unseen? And if so, what was it—a blind, growing thing? Why did it hide in the heart of the trees, and why must no sithi see it?

One thing was certain. If there was something she must not see, she did not want to see it. And so when they neared the place where the trees stood tallest, Tsuuka hung back, hoping Maiilin would be cowed by her own daring. Because there was something ominous in the quiet of the deep trees. There were no bright sithi bowers here. They had left those far behind. There were no sounds of activity, although several times as they made their way farther into the shadows, Tsuuka thought she heard scurrying sounds nearby. She listened anxiously, realizing she didn't even know what game lived this deep in the trees. She had heard that spinners came here. But would spinners rattle furtively in the brush, hiding from them, when the sithi were their protectors?

Finally apprehension overcame her and she refused to go farther, despite Maiilin's chuckling scorn. She hunched down and made herself small in the shadows, leaving Maiilin to go alone to the secret places she insisted she knew.

And Maiilin did go. Tsuuka shivered miserably as her footsteps faded into the trees.

It wasn't long before Tsuuka began to hear sounds—sounds she had not heard before. Rustlings, shiftings, creakings. Did she imagine them? Did she hear them only because she was alone and frightened? Or was something moving in the shadows—in the same shadows where Maiilin had disappeared? Did the very darkness move, as if it were about to rise up and reach for her?

Suddenly Tsuuka did not want to be alone. And she did not want Maiilin to be alone, no matter how boldly she had ventured into the deepness of the trees. Because there was something there. Something . . .

But before Tsuuka could summon courage to leave her hiding place, before she could make her reluctant limbs work, she heard a sudden, shrill scream that seemed to come from many throats. Terror-struck, she shrank deeper into hiding, trembling at the thrashing sounds that came after the scream—then paralyzed by a hoarser scream that was followed in turn by the longest silence she had ever known.

She cowered, hardly able to breathe, listening with every quivering nerve for another sound, terrified for her sibling. Because although she had not recognized the first volley of screams, it seemed to her that the second scream had been Maiilin's. And now there was only silence, ominous and long. She measured it by the frightened throbbings of her heart.

Finally, when there was no sound—when there was no sound at all—she crept from hiding and picked her way through the trees in the direction Maiilin had taken. Her heart leapt so wildly she could scarcely breathe. The shadows seemed to writhe lazily behind her, half-animate.

She still remembered how small Maiilin looked, silk-bound on the carpet of leaves. She still remembered how still Maiilin lay, with the sticky strands coiled around her. They seemed to have dampened her consciousness, as if they were permeated with something that paralyzed wit and will. Tsuuka approached in open-mouthed shock. Who could have bound her sibling this way, with strings of fresh silk? Certainly not the spinners. They looked to the sithi for protection. And this silk did not smell like any silk spit by spinners. It had a pungent odor.

She would never forget the awful moments when Maiilin began to stir. Because when her sibling wakened, she did not recognize Tsuuka. Her eyes were glazed, her tongue thick, her muscles slack. And she was able to answer none of Tsuuka's questions. She only looked at Tsuuka with blank lack of recognition.

Maiilin had been able to say nothing. Quick, curious Maiilin had been silenced. Tsuuka tore the drying strands of silk with her claws, careful not to let it touch her flesh. She pleaded with Maiilin to tell her where the silk had come from, why there was a swelling wound in her left flank. But when she was freed, Maiilin only took her feet and staggered away into the stuporous shadows, groaning.

There had been something agonized in that utterance, something pleading. But Tsuuka had been able to do nothing because she had not known what was to be done. She had not even been able to coax Maiilin to come back to her. And when she had run to fetch her mother and the other adult sithi, they had refused to come. They had even refused to tell Tsuuka what was happening.

Tsuuka had not learned until later that her sibling had turned into a growler. She had not even known such a thing could happen. She had thought the few growlers who wandered the forest were misborn, like Pitha's cubs, whose legs were twisted, or Manoo's weanlings, born blind. She had never learned otherwise because the sithi did not speak of the growlers. On that topic, a dread silence reigned.

And so she was solitary now, except for her cubs, deprived of the bower-sibling who should have shared her life, who should have hunted with her and sunned with her and raised cubs in kinship with hers. Tsuuka's jeweled eyes dulled, reflecting her growing sense of disturbance.

As if to emphasize her mood, a growler cried deep in the trees. The hoarse voice resonated ominously.

Tsuuka's ears came erect. She ran to the silken wall and pulled aside the noon-yellow swath. But did she want to see the growler? Did she want to see the coarseness of its features, the emptiness of its eyes? With a low growl, she stepped away, sliding the yellow swath back into place. Quickly she pulled the starswath taut, then loosened the azure songswath, her fingers trembling.

The swath caught the breeze immediately. Its voice drifted wisply into the chamber, light-starved. *Are you Tsuuka?*

I am Tsuuka and I am torn, she cried silently. *Sing, swath! Sing me glad again!*

For a moment there was only a silken fluttering. Then the breathy voice returned, faintly. *If you are Tsuuka . . .*

Tsuuka projected her demand forcefully the second time, urgent as the growler roared again from the trees. *I am Tsuuka and I command you to sing!*

But my sisters, the swath persisted, its voice plaintive. *My sisters are pulled mute, Tsuuka.*

Mine is a growler, lost in the far quarters of the forest! Tsuuka retorted fiercely. *And you know your sisters cannot sing when the moon is set. But there is light enough for you, skyswath. The moon has retreated beneath the horizon but there are high clouds to cast back the last of its light. So sing to me, soothe me, or I will tear you down and throw you away.*

The swath quivered. *I am no voiceless rag, to be thrown down and forgotten. I am your soul-silk.*

It will happen if you refuse me my song! There are nightmares making in my mind again, swath.

A light breeze sighed against the reluctant swath. *They are not the nightmares that stalked you earlier. These nightmares come from your thoughts, not ours. But loose me from my pole and I will sing to you, Tsuuka, my hunter.*

Tsuuka hesitated momentarily, then set her trembling hand to the pole.

The silken cloth furled free, its loose end fluttering away on the breeze. As the fabric danced, now dipping, now twisting, shadow played along its length in ever-changing patterns. The song it sang was sweet and subtle, a reflection of the light it gathered. When the growler cried again, Tsuuka scarcely heard.

Later, when she realized from the increasingly jubilant note of the swath's song that the sun lay just below the horizon, Tsuuka reeled in the swath, secured it and stretched out on her silent-silks to groom herself for the day.

Yet the troubling questions were still there, nibbling at the edges of consciousness. Why had Maiilin turned to a growler? Had she seen what no sithi was intended to see? What could that be, and what was the unseen? Tsuuka was an adult now, yet she knew little more than she had as a cub. The time was near when Dariim and Falett must leave her tree and find their own. If Maiilin had become a growler for no reason, why should not Dariim, who was much as Maiilin had been, be taken the same way? For no reason. And if there was no reason for that most fundamental event, was there a reason for anything? Or did the world unfold purposelessly around her? Was life no more than a randomly woven net of event, created without plan or care?

Tsuuka had never thought in that vein before, and she did not want to do so now, yet the questions were there. And so she was relieved when she heard Paalan and Kaliir waking, when they came tumbling into her bower to roll in her silent-silks with her, growling and feinting, distracting her from her thoughts for a while. She would be alone again, but not while the sun shone and her cubs demanded attention from her.

TWO
REYNA

I t was early when Reyna woke, but the narrow slot of sky visible from her window was vivid with sunlight and there was already laughter on the plaza below. Reyna lay staring at her ceiling, trying to warm herself to the day. In a few hours the first feast of the new season would begin, and at dusk it would be wood-smoke time. The women had already built pyramids of logs on the plaza, and the children were bringing sticks and twigs to add to them. Reyna could hear their shrieks when occasionally a pyre swayed or tottered under their ministrations. She could smell the festival breads too, baking in the kitchens, and she knew that in the stonehalls, her agemates were crouched over their work tables, stitching with anxious fingers. This was the year and season of their second majority, of full adulthood. Today they were permitted to add their first stitches to the family gowns, and tonight was their first night to dance while wood-fires burned.

Reluctantly Reyna pushed aside her coverlet and went to the window, leaning bare arms on the rough stone sill. Last year she and Aberra had watched the dancing together from the shadows of the plaza. They had tasted the husky fragrance of the smoke and watched their parents as they moved among the other gowned dancers, firelight glancing off the dark planes of their faces. Danior had danced too, a third tall, dark figure among the sturdy, white-haired people of the halls.

That had been last year. This year everything had changed. Danior, their brother, had gone away soon after wood-smoke night last year, and they had heard nothing from him until he returned at harvest time with a mate, a lean-limbed desert woman who wore a double-edged blade at her waist even when she sat to eat. They had stayed just long enough for Reyna to guess she would never learn to bear Tiva's black-eyed gaze easily. Then they had ridden back to the desert.

More disturbing, when Danior and Tiva had gone, her father had gone with them—and for no apparent reason. Reyna knew that he and her mother had argued. She had heard words from the chamber they shared, late at night. And there had been silences at the dining table, while they sat staring at their plates and eating little. Reyna had found it unsettling to have tension between them when each had guarded the other's interests so vigilantly for so long. Reyna had wondered uneasily if they would find some resolution to their disagreement or if they must go to Juris Minossa for mediation.

They had done neither of those things. Instead one day her father had announced that he intended to ride with Danior to visit his brother Jhaviir in the desert. He wanted to see the glass-paned city the desert people were building there, he said, where so recently there had been little but sand and scorched brush. He wanted to know more about the customs and languages of the desert clans. He wanted to see the changes his brother was bringing to the region. He would record what he saw and send messages to Reyna and Aberra often. And one day, when he had seen enough, he would return to Valley Terlath.

Those were the things he had said. But there had been something different behind his words, something he had tried carefully to conceal. Reyna had glimpsed it briefly before he rode away: some injury, some grief. Uneasily she had tried to guess its origin, without success. And since she didn't know why her father had gone, she couldn't guess when he would return. Sometimes when she glanced over the two brief messages he had sent, she thought perhaps he would not.

And if that weren't enough—

But she didn't want to think about Aberra now. The morning was warm, and it was wood-smoke day—time to put away grief. Turning quickly, Reyna pulled on her shift and hurried from the chamber.

There was no mistaking the excitement in the corridors. Sweepers wielded their brooms carelessly, laughing and jostling. Apprentices scampered aimlessly. A crew of stalklamp trimmers had left their barrow unattended. It was heaped with glowing vines. The mingled smells of festival foods baking floated in the air. Reyna nodded briefly to Nivan, her mother's personal runner, and hurried to the stairs, suddenly hungry.

She had hoped to find people in the dining hall, still breakfasting at the long tables. The empty chairs at her own table disturbed her less when other chairs were full. But this morning the hall was empty except for a clutch of herders. They addressed themselves silently to their morning meal, their faces ruddy from the sun. Reyna filled her platter from the serving table and sat watching them, her appetite slowly slipping away. Because her thoughts followed an inevitable course as she gazed at the herders.

They went to the mountain just as Aberra had gone. They went striding up its rocky flanks each spring with their herds, carrying a pike and a pack—the same things Aberra had carried. Through the grazing season, they met all the perils of the mountain. Sometimes they even met its beasts, although not intentionally. They did not seek out the breeterlik, the crag-charger, the minx, as Aberra had gone to do.

Sometimes they met them anyway. But the herders had come back for wood-smoke night. And Aberra—

Aberra had not come back. Quickly Reyna pushed back her chair, unable to sit longer at the empty table. She wasn't crying. She had finished with that days ago. But her stomach had turned sour and there was a lump in her throat—familiar manifestations. If only she could eat without looking at Aberra's empty chair, if only she could climb to the tower without listening for Aberra's footstep behind her, if only she could cipher without expecting to glance up at the sound of Aberra's voice, if only she could learn to do those things—

She had not learned yet and Aberra had been gone for nineteen days. Reyna stood, clumsily, almost spilling her drink, and bolted from the dining hall. She moved blindly through the corridors, wondering how long would it be before she could turn and not expect to see Aberra beside her? How long before she could speak and not expect Aberra to answer? And why hadn't she guessed, that morning when Aberra had failed to join her in the scribing room, that she was going to the mountain? Why hadn't she guessed, after the winter's clumsy sparring matches, after the spring evenings when Aberra had left her dinner untouched and bolted herself into her chambers, after the mornings when she had emerged looking as if she had not slept, that she was preparing herself to go? That she was preparing herself to track down one of the great beasts of the mountain and confront it with only a pike, hoping to kill it and return to the valley with all the changes of a barohna upon her?

Certainly Reyna had recognized Aberra's fear. And she had recognized the sparse preparations Aberra made for her challenge. But she had never thought ahead to the day when Aberra would conquer her fear and go.

Or had she conquered it? Perhaps it was fear that had finally driven her to go. Certainly she had left the dining table and, with no word to anyone, taken up her pike and pack, and gone. Simply gone, walking pale and remote down stone avenues, through the orchard, up the flank of the mountain. Word came swiftly back, carried by breathless orchard monitors, that the eldest daughter was going to meet her challenge. Reyna had heard and run after her, cold, disbelieving, first the stone pavement, then the soil of the orchards unreal beneath her pounding boots. Aberra had gone—without making her formal parting from their mother. Without asking Reyna to walk to the trees with her. Without imparting the things an older daughter traditionally imparted to a younger one when she left to make her challenge. Aberra had gone, abrogating every tradition of a palace daughter's leave-taking.

Reyna could not believe it. But when she reached the orchard, the children who had come to pollinate the blossoms stood staring up the flank of the mountain, their pollen brushes forgotten. Reyna looked where they looked, and far above she saw a speck of white: Aberra's shift.

Then she believed it, although at first she nourished the closely guarded hope that she was mistaken, that Aberra had not gone so abruptly, so poorly prepared, to make her challenge. That she had gone for a day's walk, not to meet her beast.

But Aberra had not returned that night or the next morning. No one had heard of her since.

Afraid of the fear, the old people had said, and Reyna recognized that it was true. Aberra had never been bold. Her spirit had been as fragile as her body. She had never liked rough games or frightening tales. Because she was afraid, she had waited seasons past the time when a palace daughter normally went to make her challenge. Finally, Reyna guessed, she had grown so oppressed by the daily terror of waking and realizing that her challenge still lay ahead that she had simply gone, impulsively, without preparation or ceremony, before she could renege.

Reyna halted, suddenly cold with a thought she had not examined before. When her time came, would the fear be the same?

When her time came? She shivered, drawing a hissing breath. She was fifteen now. This was the season of her second majority. Within a year, within two, her agemates in the stonehalls would bear their first children. When her mother was fifteen, she had held the sunthrone for two years.

Shaken, Reyna realized she had let confusion and grief blind her to one clear fact: with this year, her time had come, unless she intended to wait as Aberra had. And what would she gain from that? Turning, Reyna looked around at the people who hurried through the corridor. A few nodded to her. A few spoke. But what were they thinking? Did they already wonder among themselves when she would follow her sister? Did they ask each other what her chances were, whether she would be the next barohna of Valley Terlath?

Or did they see a lack in her? A lack as glaring as the lack she had seen in Aberra? Was that why she sometimes surprised a shadow in Juris Minossa's eyes? Because she was the only palace daughter remaining and Juris Minossa saw no strength in her? Was that why her mother had been more distant than ever since Aberra had gone?

Did she have the strength to become a barohna? Could she take stone into her heart and make herself hard with it? If she trained, could she kill her beast and return walking as tall as her mother, all the changes of a barohna upon her? Or would she die as Tanse had died, as Aberra had died? She had wondered these things before, but abstractly, with no sense of urgency.

Today they struck her with full force, and she tried to find answers. Sometimes, she realized, she felt as strong as the mountain. But other times she felt fragile, as if she would shatter in the breeze. If there were some way to know which in truth she was, weak or strong—

But there was not. No palace daughter had ever gone to the mountain knowing whether she would return. And what would it serve her to know? If she had some choice, if she could decide to spend her life differently, to serve her valley in some other way—

She could not. A palace daughter's choice was to go to the mountain and survive—or go to the mountain and die. A palace daughter had no other purpose in life and no other service to offer.

And these were not thoughts for a festival day. Reyna glanced around, suddenly oppressed by the mood of celebration around her. The contrast painted her own mood darker.

A bough for the fire—she and Aberra had always gone to the plaza before the dancing began and added boughs to the pyres. This year she must fetch boughs for them both—and one for Tanse as well.

She seized desperately at that excuse to desert the palace. She must have been pale as she hurried down stone corridors toward the plaza. Palace workers paused to glance after her. Once one of her agemates, apprenticed to the bakers, called her name, concerned. Reyna walked faster, pretending not to hear, her boots striking the flagged floor sharply.

If she had a choice, if Aberra had had a choice, if Tanse had had one— But for a palace daughter, there were no choices. By the time she reached the plaza, Reyna was running. She hardly noticed when she reached the avenues. She hardly saw the stonehalls, the sheds and storage buildings, the diked fields. She ran, not acknowledging the people she passed, not even slowing to welcome the bright sun.

She didn't slow until she reached the orchards. There she threw herself into the grass, breathless. Tiny fruits hung upon the trees, drinking sunlight and turning it to sugar. New leaves spun a lacy canopy overhead. They rustled in the morning breeze, speaking with a hundred green voices. *Aberra, Tanse*—

Reyna quickly realized she had come to the wrong place to cast off grief. The orchard held too many associations. When Tanse had gone to make her challenge, this was where she and Aberra had paused while she told Aberra all the things an older daughter traditionally passed on to her younger sister. And when Aberra had gone, this was where Reyna had stood with the children, helplessly watching.

Blinking back tears, Reyna glanced up the flank of the mountain, to the spot where she had seen Aberra's white shift that morning. If she could call that moment back, if she could reel time backward and draw Aberra back to the orchard—

Reyna caught her breath. For a moment it seemed time did flow backward. Because there was someone on the lower flank of the mountain, following the trail downward. Rigidly Reyna rose to her feet, staring up the mountain, her chest tight.

She had not been mistaken. Someone climbed down the mountain. *Aberra?* Her heart began to pound rapidly. It had been nineteen days. Had it simply taken Aberra that long to track her beast, to take it? Was she coming back now, changed, ready to harness the sun and capture its heat in the sunthrone? Was she coming back to serve as the next barohna of Valley Terlath?

Reyna did not move voluntarily through the trees toward the first rise of the mountain's flank. Her feet carried her forward without instruction. She continued to gaze up, magnetized by the figure that moved among the rocks. If it were Aberra, if she had survived—

Hardly glancing down at the uneven ground, Reyna left the orchard. She moved toward the rocky trail, holding her breath—hoping.

And then, with sharp disappointment, she saw that it was neither a barohna nor a palace daughter climbing down the mountain trail. The figure was male. He carried a bulky load on his back. And when he came nearer, she saw that he was dressed in furs, that he carried a pike in one hand.

Reyna sagged to a flat stone at the foot of the trail, tremulous with disappointment. A hunter. It was a hunter who came down the mountain, probably drawn to the valley by the prospect of feasting and dancing. She could see now that he wore a vest of breeterlik hide, that he wore both cap and trousers sewn from rock-leopard fur. He appeared young, no older than her brother Danior, and he was lean and sun-hardened. His hair flashed white by sunlight.

As he came nearer, he seemed not to notice her sitting on the stone, her knees drawn up, her eyes wet now with unshed tears. There was a distance in his gaze, as if he were so occupied with his own purposes that he didn't even notice the trail beneath his feet.

Reyna frowned, watching him with reluctant interest. He was near enough that she could see his face now and he didn't look like a man coming to the valley to celebrate. His lips were set, his brow deeply creased. He moved in an envelope of isolation, as if he were totally alone in the world, as if it held no one else but him.

He moved as if he were as alone as she felt at that moment.

Perhaps that was what it meant to be a hunter: to be alone. Or perhaps—her heart closed tight, a fist in her chest—perhaps he had come bringing news of Aberra. Perhaps he knew what beast had taken her, how it had happened. Perhaps that was why he frowned into the sun with such somber purpose.

She stood without thinking as he reached the end of the trail. "My sister—" she said, then halted, afraid she had spoken too suddenly.

But she hadn't startled him. He must have been aware of her all along, although he had given no sign. He turned slowly, examining her with guarded grey eyes. He seemed not to comprehend her half-spoken question. He seemed not to know how to respond to it. He touched his lips with his tongue and said, "Your sister?" His voice was husky, as if he had not used it for many days.

Reyna sighed, dropping back to the stone. "I thought perhaps you had seen my sister, Aberra. I thought perhaps you had news of her." When he did not respond, she said, "She went to her challenge four hands ago. No one has seen her since." It seemed to her, as he continued to study her, that he held himself carefully in her presence, as if he expected some injury from her.

What injury did he think she had to offer? And if he hadn't come to dance at the festival, if he hadn't brought news of Aberra, why had he come? Not just for the company of people, surely. Everyone knew what hunters were: aloof, solitary, self-governed.

Perhaps he had come simply to sell his furs. Carefully he set his load to the ground. "I don't know of your sister," he said.

Again Reyna noticed the unused quality of his voice. Was that why his manner was strange: stiff, guarded, and distant? Simply because he spent too much time alone? Was that why he seemed wary, as if he expected a rebuff?

"I don't suppose you've stopped to talk to any of the herders on the other slopes?" she probed. "Or to the lens tenders?"

"I haven't stopped to talk to anyone."

She nodded, bowing her head, letting go her brief hope that Aberra might still return. When she glanced up again, the hunter was peering down over the valley, studying its distant structures with the same guarded attention he had given her face a moment ago. She sighed. "Tonight is wood-smoke night," she said. Perhaps he didn't know.

Perhaps he didn't care. He didn't nod, didn't acknowledge her words. "You're the daughter of the palace below?" he asked finally, turning back to her.

"Of course." He didn't have to ask that. Her slightness, her fragility, the auburn of her hair and the amber of her eyes told him that. Who but a palace daughter looked as she did?

"And below is Valley Terlath?"

"Yes."

"Your barohna then is Khira."

"Khira is my mother." Why did he ask?

A distracted nod. "And the Arnimi quarter here. They fly their ships from here."

Reyna stiffened. The Arnimi had quartered in the western wing of the palace since her grandmother's reign. They came and went unobtrusively, observing without mingling, recording without interfering. No one had any complaint against them. But if the throne were hers, she would send them to some other valley—or back to their own distant world. And quickly, because she had never learned to like them.

"They fly from here," she said shortly. And why did that matter to a hunter? She stood again. "I must go down. If you've come for the festival, you can walk back with me." It was only civil to offer that. And, reluctantly, she was curious. She had never met a hunter before. Were they all so guarded? Were they all so tense? Or were they so only in the presence of strangers?

Who was not a stranger to a hunter? Certainly he glanced sharply at her, as if her courtesy were suspect. Abruptly he squatted and with the tip of his pike drew a random figure in the hard soil. "I'm not going down until tomorrow."

She shrugged, disowning any show of disappointment. "We will see you then," she said formally and turned to go.

She had not taken many steps before he spoke again. "Wait."

She turned, surprised. The word sounded more a plea than a request, and when she turned back, he seemed momentarily disconcerted, whether with himself for calling after her or with her for responding, Reyna couldn't guess. Quickly he bent over the load he had deposited on the ground. "I found nigh-berries this morning. And yesterday I dried fairyflowers. I have dried meat too, in my pack."

He wanted her to eat with him? She hesitated, surprised that he asked—equally surprised to find that she wanted to accept. Despite his manner, there was something in his eyes that spoke to her, although she could not name it. Perhaps it was only a kindred loneliness. "I brought nothing," she said slowly.

He frowned, his white brows drawing together sharply. "I asked for nothing."

Had she offended him so easily, just by suggesting she did not want to be entirely his guest? When they were strangers, just met? "No. You didn't," she said carefully, sinking back to the flat stone. Perhaps she would understand him better if she ate with him, although she could not think why it mattered that she understand him. "I would be pleased to share your food. I'm Reyna Terlath," she offered.

"I'm Juaren."

"And your valley?"

It was a natural question, but it brought a glint to his eyes and made his lips draw tight. "I have no valley. I'm alone."

Alone. He was just as alone as he appeared, although she could not guess why that must be. Surely a hunter was not required to renounce his valley entirely. Surely there was some hall he considered home, even if he did not go there to take wintersleep.

Reyna felt alone too as they ate. Juaren served her from his pack, laying out foods silently, making no attempt to talk with her. Occasionally she felt his glance upon her, but when she looked up, he turned quickly away, frowning and tense, as if he felt awkward in her presence.

She sat silently for a time after they had eaten, wondering if they didn't have something to say to each other—wondering what it might be. He reloaded his pack and sat staring down at the ground, drawing figures with the tip of his pike. If he wanted to talk, she decided finally, he didn't know how to do it. He didn't know how to begin. Or he was afraid to begin.

Neither did she know how to begin, when she knew so little of him. What could she say to a man who claimed no valley? A man who seemed so uneasy in her presence? A man who must have spoken to no one for days? Finally she stood. "I have to go down now. I'm taking boughs to the wood-fire."

He nodded.

"Tomorrow then."

"Tomorrow," he agreed, remotely.

But again when she had gone a distance, he called her back. "Reyna Terlath," he said.

She turned. "Yes?"

He frowned, hesitating. When he went on, the words seemed to cost him effort. "I lost my guild master when Coquel had his seventh winter rising. I have walked alone since then."

"That—that's a long time," she said, awed. She could not imagine walking half the winter alone in the mountains, while people took wintersleep in the valleys below. Certainly if she had done so, she wouldn't fall into easy conversation with the first stranger she met. It would take her many hands of days to rediscover the habits of company. "It's a very long time."

He nodded and squatted again, occupying himself over his pack. When she did not turn away immediately, he said distantly, "Tomorrow."

"Yes," she agreed, and turned back toward the orchard.

She did not glance back until she reached the trees. Then she saw that he peered intently at the sky, shielding his eyes with one hand. Puzzled, she followed the direction of his gaze and saw an Arnimi aircar spiraling over the valley, glinting in the sun. Her lips tightened and she turned away to find boughs for the fire.

That occupied only a few minutes of her time. She had the entire walk back to think of their meeting, to wonder if Juaren had come only to sell furs or for some other reason. To wonder why he seemed afraid that she would slight him. Why expect her to be arrogant just because she was a palace daughter? No one else expected it. She wondered too how he had wintered alone in the mountains, with no one to speak to, no one to share thoughts with, and survived. If she had a choice, she would never choose a hunter's life, not if it meant she must walk alone.

If she had a choice . . . but she had no more choice than Tanse had had, than Aberra had had—than her mother had once had. She shook her head impatiently and began to run.

She did not see Juaren again until night. By then tables had been set, pyres had been lit, and wood smoke floated over the plaza. Reyna hovered in the shadows, watching as her agemates appeared in their gowns, generations of embroidery weighing down the antique fabric. Tima, Maffi, Pili—she remembered when she had run down stone avenues with them, laughing. She remembered when they had watched together while spring lambs were born. She remembered the day they had tossed rocks into the drinking well and Juris Minossa had learned of it and called them to her chambers.

Bittersweet memories, because tonight Tima and Maffi and Pili danced and Reyna did not. She stood in the shadows, watching gowned figures move through the veiling smoke, smelling the sweetness of the fire, listening to the crackle of logs. Finally, when the laughter became too loud, the celebration too joyous, she slipped away into the palace.

Empty corridors, lit by the orange glow of stalklamp. Flagged floors that echoed with the sound of her boots. Tables of food, ravaged now. Empty platters and mugs everywhere, even on the floor.

Her feet led her down long corridors to the throneroom. There she hesitated under the tall arches, gazing at her mother's throne. By day, when Khira sat on the throne, the mirrors mounted high on the throne-room walls captured sunlight broadcast from the mountainside lenses and focused it upon the throne. If the barohna were upon the throne, it caught light and glowed.

Tonight the sunthrone was dark. Khira was in her chambers, or perhaps she watched the dancing from the shadowed verges of the plaza. Reyna knew she would not dance this year. Reyna's father was in the desert, and a barohna did not dance with any man who was not to be her mate, for whatever term.

But if her father didn't intend to return—Reyna gazed at the throne uneasily, then slipped away, not wanting to explore that thought.

She wandered the corridors until eventually she found herself on the plaza again, listening to the beat of drums, to the flutter of flutes, watching the ceaseless changing of partners. There would be talk of the dancing for many days. Tomorrow the elder women would begin to study genealogies, and soon there would be the pledging of mates, some for the season, some for the year, a few for even longer terms.

Reyna had never felt so alone on wood-smoke night. She had never felt so alone at all.

Then she saw Juaren near the edge of the plaza. Firelight touched his face and made his white hair gleam. He still wore his hide vest, his fur cap and trousers, and he looked as alone as she. He looked as if he walked in the high mountains, with no one near. He didn't glance at the dancers as he walked among them. He didn't pause to listen to the music, to study the gowns with their heavy embroidery. He didn't acknowledge the glances the younger women directed at him or the unspoken question of the men.

Reyna was surprised at the sharpness of her reaction. Perhaps the spice of wood smoke touched her more than she guessed. Or perhaps it was the beat of the drums. Suddenly her mouth was dry, her heart pounded, her face burned. Why had he come, when he had said he would not? Had he heard the music drifting through the trees? Had he seen the light of the fires? Had he realized, sitting alone at the foot of the trail, that he wanted to speak with her again? They had said so little the first time, but she thought that was because he had not known how to speak, because he had been alone too long. And he was walking directly toward her now and he knew no one else in Valley Terlath.

Did he know that palace daughters didn't dance? Surely he saw how she was dressed. She wore the same shift she had worn that morning, roughspun, unadorned.

He paused, finally meeting her eyes. His face was guarded, but something that might have been a question flickered in his eyes. And how many questions were there to be asked on wood-smoke night?

Only one. Reyna's stomach clutched. She didn't know whether to nod acceptance or turn away in refusal. If he were only passing through

Valley Terlath, why shouldn't he dance with a palace daughter? He was no more interested than she in choosing a mate, in making a pledge. But the drum beat was throbbing and wood smoke was sweet, and they were the only two young people not dancing. Perhaps—

He had stopped. That was all she noticed at first. He had halted, his face stiffening, his hands slowly closing at his sides. Not even his eyes moved. Suddenly they were directed toward the center of the plaza, flat and unreadable.

Slowly Reyna realized that the dancing pairs had drawn back, gazing in the same direction. The older people who gossiped at the edges of the plaza had become still. Even the music missed a beat, as if the drummers were momentarily distracted. Reyna peered from the shadows, puzzled.

Then she saw. Her mother was moving across the plaza, tall and dark in her festival gown, her hair falling dark upon her shoulders. Firelight played upon her face, upon her barohnial features—wide mouth, strong nose and brows, commanding eyes. She moved with a slow inevitability, her face telling nothing of her thoughts. Her sunstone cuffs glowed at her wrists, rings of fire.

Reyna licked her lips, recognizing that her mother moved as Juaren had moved a few moments earlier, as if she were alone, as if she saw none of the people who clustered on the flaggings. But she saw Juaren. She gazed at him and deep-buried pain flickered in her eyes.

Reyna drew a harsh breath. Why did sight of Juaren pain her mother? Reyna could not imagine. He had never visited Valley Terlath before.

But the pain was clear now. It tugged at Khira's mouth. It darkened her eyes. It showed in the set of her shoulders and the rise of her chin when finally she stood before Juaren and held out her hands.

He took an involuntary step back, white-lipped, stunned. It took him moments to find his voice. "You are—you are Khira Terlath," he said. The words were husky.

Khira's voice was clear. "I am Khira Terlath, and I will dance with you."

The words echoed, and color ebbed from Juaren's face. He grew rigid, his eyes fixed. He groped for words—words he did not find.

"I will dance with you," Khira repeated, extending her hands.

Reyna caught a stunned breath and held it, reluctantly understanding what she saw, what she heard. Khira had asked Juaren to dance and he could not refuse. No man refused the barohna. Not because she held some dreaded authority, although hers was the final word in most matters. Not because she was feared, although with her glowing cuffs she could burn any person to ash. But because she honored the man she invited to dance.

She honored him publicly, offering him the hospitality of her chambers—offering him the honor of becoming her mate, however briefly, of fathering her next daughter.

But Khira had a daughter, a daughter who stood frozen at the edge of the plaza as Juaren stepped stiffly forward and accepted Khira's hands. Khira had a daughter who watched white-faced, speechless, hardly even aware of the people who turned to glance covertly at her. She stared as Juaren and Khira fell into the familiar steps, understanding with crushing clarity what she saw.

A hunter had come from the mountains. Her mother had seen him and had invited him to be her mate—perhaps just for this one night, perhaps for the season. She had invited him to share quarters with her and to father a daughter.

Because—what other reason could she have?—she saw some lack in the daughter she already had. Because she had decided that although Reyna would go to the mountain—what choice had a palace daughter?—she would not return.

Because she feared that if she did not bear another child, there would be no barohna to warm the valley and make it live?

Yes, those were the things she thought. Her actions spoke them aloud for everyone to hear. Slowly Reyna's hand crept to her throat. There was a cry of hurt and protest lodged there. It choked off her breath. Her mother had so little faith in her that she had summoned a stranger to her chambers. She had so little faith that she intended to share her bed with a man she had not seen before tonight.

No wonder there was pain in her eyes. Khira was the only barohna on all of Brakrath to take a permanent mate. She was the only barohna to bear four children in succession to the same man. But one of those children—Danior—was male and could not assume the throne. And the other three had been lacking. So she must take another mate. She must take a stranger, as other barohnas did.

Reyna struggled for breath, groping unwillingly for the full dimension of the situation. Was that why her father had gone to the desert? Because her mother must take a new mate and he did not want to see it? Because he did not want to see her dancing on wood-smoke night with another man?

Reyna did not want to see it either. She wanted to protest. She wanted to cry out. She wanted to tell her mother, here, now, before everyone, that she needed no new daughter. That she had one who recognized her obligation, however belatedly.

But what good would that do? Reyna drew her hand from her throat and made a fist of it. Her mother had a clear duty to the people of the valley, and she had chosen tonight to fulfill it. She could not yield to words.

Instead Reyna must offer action. She must demonstrate that she was fully aware of her obligation—and fully aware that the time had come to meet it. She must choose the date for her challenge. She must announce it, and then she must train to meet it. She must work until her body was hard and her spirit unflinching. She must train until she was as strong, as hard as she sometimes felt she was. She must take stone into her heart and prepare to best any beast the mountain could offer.

How long would that take? It didn't matter. She was of age now, and she had a duty, just as her mother did. The mountain had always been her future, her choice. This was the season when she must go. She had already taken too long to waken to that.

Dancers moved across the flaggings again, her mother and Juaren among them. Wood smoke curled around them, obscuring their faces, hiding expression. Trembling, pale, Reyna turned from the plaza and fled down palace corridors to her chambers. She saw clearly what she must do, and she had to believe that the doing was possible, that she could find the stone to harden herself with. But as she threw herself across her bed, the knot in her throat was not an unuttered protest. Nor was it unshed tears. It was fear, hard and choking. It was fear, the beast she must live with day and night until she went to meet her challenge.

THREE
REYNA

The beast drove her hard over the next hands of days. Reyna trained, sometimes in the solitude of the training room, with torches casting long shadows, sometimes on the plaza, sometimes in the fields and the orchards. She did everything she knew to harden herself. She ran, she tumbled, she climbed and jumped. She called upon the fair-haired youths of the halls to spar with her and to wear the beast masks for her. She wove targets and drove her pike into them. She did things neither of her sisters had done, things she had found written in scrolls, things she had heard told in tales.

She pushed herself hard and slept the same way, tumbling into dreamless oblivion each night, forgetting everything, even the ache of her muscles. Often, as her training progressed, she woke feeling strong. She woke feeling certain, her mind clear, her body elastic, and she knew she could face her beast and win. Even so, she could not bring herself to announce the date she had set for her challenge. Because on other days her confidence ebbed and she did not feel strong at all, not even in the first quiet moments of the day.

That disturbed her because she was much aware of what went on around her. Her mother had pledged Juaren for the warmseason. He slept in her chambers, and sometimes Reyna heard them talking in low voices in the evening. Their conversations seemed passionless, formal, empty. Occasionally they danced on the plaza late at night. Reyna watched from her window and thought from the way they held themselves that neither danced with the other. They both danced alone, even when their hands touched.

They seemed alone at the dinner table too, sitting silently, hardly glancing at each other. At first Juaren looked up whenever Reyna joined them and she saw the same momentary question in his eyes she had seen on the plaza on wood-smoke night. But no matter what she understood of the way other barohnas lived, taking mates in casual succession, she could not meet Juaren's eyes when he sat in her father's chair. Nor could she bring herself to acknowledge him when she met him outside the dining hall. Not only had he taken her father's place, his very presence was public testimony to her mother's lack of faith in her. Each time she saw him, she became smaller in her own eyes. The pain of that was real, almost physical. If only her mother had spoken to her first, if only her mother had trusted her to prepare, to be strong...

Soon he no longer glanced up when she entered the dining hall. Soon he learned not to see her, at the table, in the corridors, on the plaza. Nor did he seek acquaintance among the people of the valley. He carried the isolation of the mountains with him wherever he went, a barrier, a protective shield.

Against what, Reyna wondered. Did he expect rebuff from the people of the halls too? Her father had been loved in the valley. Had Juaren heard? Did he expect everyone to feel as Reyna did?

Or did he expect to be received without welcome for some private reason? Had he been received that way elsewhere? He ate in the dining hall less and less often as the warmseason progressed. He ate alone on the plaza instead, kneeling on the flaggings, untouched by the glances of the people who passed. And he spent much time sitting cross-legged on the wall that overlooked the western plaza, watching Arnimi aircars come and go. He studied the cars with frowning attention, as if he intended to catalogue every detail of their construction, as if the people who flew them held more interest for him than anyone else in the valley.

Reyna could not blame him if he were bitter or angry, although he seemed neither. There were courtesies normally shown a guest in the valley, and she had shown him none of those. And her mother—it must be belittling to be pledged to a woman who scarcely acknowledged his presence. It must seem to him that he had emerged from the isolation of the mountains to an isolation far more grievous.

Occasionally Reyna paused in her training and took herself to task for her own conduct. On the day they met, Juaren had seemed wary that she would slight him. Now she had done so, not once but many times, and he accepted her behavior as if it were only what he had expected, as if it were exactly what he had guarded himself against.

Why? Why had he expected to be treated no better than he was treated in Valley Terlath this warmseason? And why didn't it anger him?

Perhaps it did. Or perhaps it injured him, despite his effort to remain aloof. Because occasionally she glimpsed him at a distance and realized how stiffly he held himself, how tightly he wore his lips, how carefully guarded his glance had become—even more guarded than on the first day they met. Perhaps the situation made him feel as small as it made her feel.

Reyna did not have as much time as she would have liked to think of it. Her training demanded her close attention. That and the beast-fear that chased her. *Stone*. She must have stone in her heart. That was how a palace daughter became a barohna—by having the gritty substance for it. By making herself as hard as the sunstones a barohna used to warm her valley.

Still it seemed to Reyna that her mother had not made herself so hard. The people of the valley looked to her for a successor, and she had undertaken to provide one. But each day she became more silent, more distant, more withdrawn. She moved about her public functions like a woman half-blind, speaking distractedly when she must sit to hear disputes, ruling indifferently when her word was solicited.

And Reyna knew that if she did not make her challenge on the date she had chosen, if she did not succeed in it, Juaren would be only the first of a succession of temporary mates. There would be other men living in Khira's chambers, other men for whom the honor of being a barohna's mate would turn to ashes, other men who would find themselves dancing at night with a woman who might as well have been stone.

A woman who was not stone. If she were, why did the passing days paint such a dark mood upon her?

And all needlessly.

It had to be needlessly. Reyna told herself that each day as she went to the training room. The discipline she imposed upon herself would not be wasted. She would not even consider that possibility. By the date she had chosen, she would be strong enough for any beast, and Khira would need no other daughter. Juaren could return to the cleaner loneliness of the mountains and her father could return from the desert.

Reyna repeated that vow to herself as she completed the set of calisthenics she had prescribed for herself that day and began to run around the perimeter of the training room. But what use were vows, she wondered, when she could not find courage to announce her date? Her very silence was an admission of doubt. Her mother, Juris Minossa, everyone in the valley must recognize it as such.

Troubled, she completed the circuits she had set herself, washed from the bucket and pulled on a fresh shift for dinner. The smell of roast fowl and fresh-baked bread met her when she stepped into the corridor, but the clutching in her stomach was not hunger. The date— she must announce the date.

Tonight? Could she find courage tonight? The words were so simple. All she had to do was catch her mother's attention and utter them.

If Juaren were not at the table, perhaps she would do it tonight. Perhaps she would find courage tonight. Silently she pledged herself to that as she walked down the corridor.

She held her breath when she entered the hall. Palace workers already ate at the long tables, talking quietly among themselves, laughing. Juaren was not there.

Tonight then. She shivered as her appetite deserted her.

No one looked up as she made her way to her mother's side. Sitting, Reyna studied Khira covertly, measuring her mother's strength against her own apparent fragility. Her mother's hands were long and strongly built, her own were delicate and pale. Her mother's features were prominent, her own slight. Her mother's hair was burned black by the sunlight she caught in her sunstone and dispersed across the valley. Reyna's was auburn silk. And her mother's eyes—

Eyes that see fire, valley people called a barohna's eyes, deep and distant and far-seeing. Tonight they turned upon Reyna and Reyna caught a moment's unguarded pain in them. She recoiled, startled.

"Fresh eggs, daughter?" the serving monitor asked, bending near.

"No," Reyna protested without thinking. Did it hurt her mother so much to look at her? Did she think so little of the preparation she was making for her challenge? Instinctively Reyna pressed her hands to her thighs, feeling the new strength of muscle there, trying to find reassurance in it. She was slight, but so was every palace daughter. Khira had been slight once too, before she had met her challenge.

"My mother—" she said quickly. She must give her the date now, before she lost courage.

Her mother sighed deeply and pushed back her half-eaten dinner, hardly recognizing that Reyna had spoken. "My daughter, we must have words. Come to the throneroom when you have eaten."

"Come? Yes, I will come," Reyna said slowly, her voice trailing away. What could she say when her mother had risen and was already striding away? Reyna looked after her with the same baffled foreboding she had felt when she watched Aberra walk up the mountainside. First the hurt in her mother's eyes, then the abrupt summons. What did it mean? Did her mother think she was training poorly? Did she think she had already delayed her going for too long?

"Fowl, daughter?" The serving monitor bent near again, eager to fill Reyna's empty platter.

Reyna had no appetite. "Nothing," she whispered, sliding from her chair.

There were places in the palace where she went when she was troubled: the small, enclosed northern plaza, the scribing room, the weaving chambers. Time lived in all those places, legend and reality fusing. Tonight she chose the tower. She climbed the stone stairs slowly, her face bathed in the orange glow of the stalklamp that grew upon the damp walls. When she reached the windows, she leaned on the rough stone sills, gazing out over the valley.

There was little enough to see, so soon after sunset. Moisture from the fields her mother had warmed that day rose and clouded the stars. The moons had not yet risen. The only sources of light were the sunstone slab on the plaza and the winking beacon the Arnimi had mounted on their wing of the palace.

Reyna watched it for a while, wondering distantly why Juaren watched the Arnimi with such close interest. Then, the weariness of the day's training aching in her shoulders, she descended and went to the throne-room.

She had expected to find her mother alone in the great vaulted chamber, only the darkened mirrors for company. Instead Juaren sat on the dais to the left of the throne, stitching a pelt. He raised his head as she entered and addressed her with a guarded gaze.

Stiffening, Reyna approached the throne. When she felt its warmth on her face, she said formally, "You asked me to come, my mother." At least her voice did not shake.

Her mother sighed deeply, as she had done before, and nodded. "I asked you to come. Juaren, would you send a runner for Verra? Tell her my daughter has come and ask her to join us now."

Silently Juaren put aside pelt and needles and left the throneroom. Reyna looked after him, confused. Verra? The one Arnimi her mother called friend? What had an Arnimi to do with what they must discuss? "My mother, I have set the date for my challenge," she said quickly. If they could discuss it before Juaren returned—

Something in her mother's eyes stopped her. Her mother's lips hardened. "No, my daughter, you will not go." Khira's fingers pressed the glowing arms of the throne. "That is why I have sent for Verra. To tell you why you will not go."

Not go? The words were so unexpected Reyna stared at her mother blankly. How could she not go to make her challenge? Every palace daughter did that. How else were the valley thrones to be filled, the fields warmed, the seasons tempered? No matter how many died, each sister went in turn until one returned a barohna.

And Verra—Verra was to tell her why she must not go? Reyna knew how little her mother liked the Arnimi. It surprised her that she permitted them to maintain quarters in the palace. Did she allow it just because Verra was her friend?

But her mother had done other things that were surprising too, things that made her a legend in far valleys. Not only had she met her challenge before she came of age, she had taken a starship instead of a mountain beast as her bronzing prey. She had done that, Reyna knew, because the starship had threatened to take her father from Brakrath. And later she had broken with tradition by refusing to wear the pairing stone that would have linked her to a stone mate, another barohna like herself. Instead she had taken Reyna's father as her confidant and as her permanent mate, in defiance of all custom. And he was not even Brakrathi.

He was not Brakrathi, and he no longer lived in the palace, Reyna reminded herself dully. Reyna's hands tightened as Juaren stepped back into the room. He walked lightly, as if he wished to leave no print on the polished floor, and sat beside the throne again, picking up his work without word. But she saw some stiffness in him, some guarded quality, and knew he was as aware of her presence as she was of his.

"Mother—"

' "We will talk when Verra comes."

Reyna frowned, subsiding unwillingly. "We will talk then," she agreed.

Verra was not long in arriving. She entered quietly, her boots tapping lightly on the flaggings. She was a woman in her middle years, her hair greying, fine lines webbing her eyes. Reyna was relieved to see that at least she had brought none of the other Arnimi. Reyna did not want to be in their presence tonight. There was something cold in their prominent eyes, something arrogant in the thrust of their padded bellies, something affected in their plucked eyebrows and black-painted eyelids. They had come when Khira was a child and had spent the years observing Brakrathi society, just as their parties were observing other societies scattered through the galaxies. Their intent, she knew, was to compile a history of all the races of humanity, detailing their development since Earthexodus, the period when the stars had been settled. Brakrath held particular interest because its settlers had never reached their intended destination but had been stranded here instead, cut off from outside influence for tens of centuries before their whereabouts was discovered.

Reyna could appreciate the value of the history the Arnimi proposed. She could not appreciate their methods of gathering information. It seemed as cold as their eyes, as arrogant as their bellies. Even tonight Verra wore her meters and instruments strapped to her black uniform belt, ready to ply them. Reyna glanced at them and bristled. What could they tell the Arnimi that their senses could not? It seemed to Reyna that their constant use of instruments was nothing more than an admission that their faculties were dull.

An attitude she had taken from her mother, she knew. Still Verra was not as objectionable as the others. The years had left traces of understanding upon her features and there was an animation in her eyes none of the other Arnimi had. She inclined her head formally. "Barohna."

"Friend," Reyna's mother responded. "You know why I summoned you."

Verra's gaze shifted briefly to Reyna. "The matter we spoke of three nights ago, when you called me to your quarters."

"That matter. My daughter has been training to make her challenge. I have just told her that she is not to go."

Reyna shrank as all three gazes turned upon her, her mother's distant, Verra's frowning, Juaren's guarded but probing. Her shoulders tightened. "My mother—" What could Khira mean, that she was not to go?

Her mother raised one hand, refusing to hear her objection. "You are not to go. I know it startles you that I tell you so, but there is a very good reason why you must not. I disregarded it in the case of your sisters. Now I have decided that I must not disregard it again. That's why I've called Verra here." Frowning, she stood and descended from the dais, going to stand beneath the mirrors mounted high on the walls. She gazed up for a time—but not, Reyna realized, at her own reflection. She was looking at something beyond that, something that brought pain back to her eyes. She turned sharply. "I know how little use you have for the Arnimi and their methods, daughter. You learned that from me, just as I learned it from my own mother. They go about our valleys watching and recording, using their instruments as if they were better than ears and eyes. They study all of Brakrath the same way. Recently they have even dared go to the desert and approach the clansmen.

"The Council's first impulse, when the Arnimi arrived on our world, was to send them away. But they promised to make themselves unobtrusive. And what harm could they offer, so long as they did not interfere in the governing of our valleys? So they were permitted to stay and to conduct their investigations, although they had to agree to many conditions and many restrictions.

"Seven years ago, the year after Danior first went to the desert to visit his uncle, Verra came to me and told me the Arnimi had learned to tell with their instruments which palace daughters had the substance to become barohnas—and which did not."

Reyna stared up at her mother, drawing breath sharply. The Arnimi could tell that with instruments? It was a statement that went against everything she knew. She darted a disbelieving glance at the meters Verra wore at her waist. "No," she said. "There is no way anyone can tell that." No one could guess which daughter would return from the mountain a barohna until it happened. No one had ever known, through all the centuries. Some daughters trained until they were strong and hard and died anyway. Others went carelessly and came back changed. There was no pattern, no clue. For the Arnimi to say that there was—

"I understand your disbelief," her mother said, pulling her embroidered gown close as she strode back to her throne. She looked down briefly at Juaren, who had put down his stitching and listened without expression. "I did not believe either at first, when Verra told me. Not even when she showed me the log the Arnimi had made of their study over the past fifteen years and I saw that they had predicted correctly in every case. We have always believed that there is some presence in the heart of the palace daughter who is destined to become a barohna. That there is some hardness of spirit, some governing control dormant in her. We call it stone, and we have always believed that if she trains well, the crystals will form to their full substance and guide her—in taking her beast, in learning to use the barohnial stones, in finding the wisdom she requires to govern her valley. We have believed that it is the final crystallizing of the inborn stone that causes a palace daughter to change so dramatically when she kills her beast. We have believed this is what makes her grow, body and spirit, overnight.

"But the Arnimi have discovered that what makes a barohna is a tiny cellular mass, a bundle of fibers—located not in the heart but in the brain. It lies there dormant until the adrenal stimulation of the challenge, of near-death, causes it to undergo a rapid alteration, and that produces an accompanying maturation in the entire body. The Arnimi have learned to detect the small electrical aberration that announces its presence even in its dormant state."

Reyna stepped back from the throne, instinctively rejecting what she heard. "They've discovered this with their meters, I suppose," she said in a hard voice. The Arnimi thought they had learned something centuries of barohnas had never guessed—not by using their senses or their reason but by using their instruments.

"Yes," her mother said without embellishment.

It was an answer more effective than any argument. Reyna stared at Khira for long moments, not wanting to believe, caught between confusion and the beginnings of anger as she felt herself wavering. She turned sharply to the Arnimi. "And did you bring your instrument with you tonight?" Was that what her mother had called her here for? To be examined like a head of livestock? The thought made her face burn.

Verra did not respond to the challenge in Reyna's voice, only to her words. "I have it here," she said evenly, taking a small unit from its holder at her belt. "Of course you must understand that the actual analysis of electrical activity is not a function of this particular instrument. It only serves to transmit raw data to our banks, where it is analyzed and charted. Then the appropriate response is transmitted back to the hand unit. In our initial metering of you some years ago—"

Reyna stiffened. "You've never metered me with this instrument. I've never seen it before." But she was not entirely certain that was true. She had never been able to avoid the Arnimi and their meters entirely. And the Arnimi meters were much like one another, shiny cases, dialed faces, pinpoints of vivid light—

"No, I'm sure you have not. We performed the initial metering in our quarters seven years ago, as part of a general physical examination. We used a broader range instrument at that time, since there were so many different functions to be examined. I'm sure you remember the occasion."

Reyna frowned, wishing she could deny that she did. But she had entered the Arnimi quarters only once, when she, Tanse and Aberra had been sent there by their mother. Reyna remembered clearly the smell of cold metal and the chill eyes of the Arnimi personnel who had swept sensor-wands over their bodies. "You told us we were being examined for our health," she said sharply to her mother.

"Yes, and if I had heeded what Verra told me, your sisters would be alive today. They would never have gone to their challenges. Because it was useless. There was no stone in their hearts to give them command of the sunthrone. Not the smallest crystal."

"Or to use our terms of reference, Reyna," Verra said, "the activating mass was not present in their brain tissue. There was nothing there to be stimulated to growth by the adrenal rush of the challenge. Nothing to spur change and rapid maturation. Nothing to enable them to use the sunstone, the pairing stones, any of the stones a barohna must use. Had one of your sisters by chance taken her bronzing prey, she would not have returned to the valley a barohna. She would have remained a palace daughter, never growing, never changing."

Reyna shook her head stubbornly. "No. No." Surely if what Verra said were true, there had been palace daughters who had taken their beasts and not changed. What had happened to them?

But she knew without asking. She knew what she would do if she killed her beast and found herself unchanged. She would look for another—and another after that, until finally one of them ended her quest with its claws.

But remain a palace daughter to her death? That was what her mother was suggesting. That was what her mother insisted upon, in fact, by forbidding her to go to her challenge. Reyna shrank from the suggestion, her face paling. Remain always small and fragile, with the stature of a child? Grow old that way? Uselessly, unable to command the stones—unable to fulfill any function within the structure of valley life?

Slowly she turned to stare at her mother. Was that what she was suggesting? That she simply remain in the palace, without function, without office? That she spend her life that way, while the people questioned her silently with their eyes? Her voice faltered. "If I take my prey—"

"If you take your prey," Verra said gently, "it will mean nothing, Reyna. Except that you had the courage and the agility to do it. Here—" Lightly, before Reyna could draw back, she pressed her instruments to the flesh of Reyna's temple. When she withdrew it, a small amber light glowed on its dial. "If you had the potential to become a barohna, the indicator would show red. But it does not. You can see that clearly."

Reyna glanced from her mother to the Arnimi and back again, her thoughts running so rapidly she could hardly apprehend them. *Clearly?* She could see many things clearly. There was a throne to be held. There were seasons to be tempered, fields to be warmed, a valley to be governed. Without a barohna to capture the sunlight from the barren mountainsides and store it in her stones, without a barohna to release it as it was needed, none of those things could happen. The valley would grow cold and die. "I can see that you believe an instrument before you believe me, my mother," she said with anger so tremulous she was afraid she would melt to tears. "I have done what I could for you. I have trained as Tanse did not, as Aberra did not—"

Muscles hardened in her mother's jaw and emotion flashed from the deepness of her eyes. "Yes, you have trained, and I have watched you, knowing I let your sisters die needlessly. Because I refused to believe what the Arnimi told me, although your father urged me to. Because I refused to break with the old ways in this one thing, although I have broken with them in others. Now I do believe what Verra tells me. Now I intend to do what your father begged me. I forbid you to make your challenge.

"How many daughters must I lose before I trust my friend not to lie to me?"

Reyna shrank from the hard passion of her mother's words. So Khira believed she had no stone, no hardness. No crystalline substance to call response from the barohnial stones. Why then did she feel as if her entire heart had turned to rock?

Or had it turned to ice? She felt cold as she thought of doing what her mother intended her to do: nothing. There were palace daughters who never made their challenge, of course. They lived out their lives in their mothers' palaces, child-like wraiths without place or purpose. But she could not live like that. Better to go as Aberra had gone. As Tanse had gone.

Or so her thoughts ran. At the same time her hands clenched painfully and her heart beat to a frightened rhythm. She felt as if it would leap from her chest.

Was this what Aberra had felt, she wondered, going to the mountain with her pike in hand, knowing that she would not survive whatever encounter chance brought her? Reyna wondered distractedly what beast had killed Aberra. A lumbering breeterlik, spraying acid from its belly sphincter? A minx, pink-eyed gamester that walked on two feet? Or had Aberra crawled into a sheltering cavern and died slowly, of exposure? Perhaps someday someone would find some sign of her. Then they would know. As for herself—

"If you won't let me try," she said, making her voice hard, "who is going to take the throne when you leave it?" She had never, she realized, spoken to her mother so coldly—or with such challenge. She had never dared. But tonight she had nothing to lose from it. Tonight she could speak anything.

Her mother's fingers tightened briefly on the arms of her throne. "Your sister will take the throne," she said.

Her sister? "I have no sisters."

"You have one. She will be born late next winter. She is already well enough developed that Verra can tell me that she will be the next barohna of Valley Terlath."

Reyna took a single step back, feeling time grow thick around her, binding her. It had been fewer than forty days since wood-smoke night. Her mother had already conceived? And Verra had already used her instrument on the unborn child? Reyna's thoughts, her reactions were suddenly so slowed by shock that she seemed hardly able to speak. *Her sister*—Juaren's child. Juaren's child already lived in her mother's womb, taking her place, her purpose, her life.

Because that was what she saw slipping away now: both purpose and life. Before tonight she had recognized that she might die on the mountain. Now they told her that not only must she die, her death would be for nothing. She must go without even the chance of returning.

Or she must stay and not make her challenge at all. Reyna stared helplessly at them all, her mother, Verra, Juaren. In her mother's eyes, in Verra's, she saw pain. She did not comprehend what she saw in Juaren's gaze. For one disquieting moment, it seemed almost like understanding. As if he understood better than either of the others what she felt. But why should he understand? She could find no reason.

Gradually the initial shock ebbed and her mind began to work at normal speed again, considering the possibilities that faced her. There were not many. Examining them, she fixed upon the only one she found tolerable. Did none of them understand, she wondered, that although her mother could forbid her to go to the mountain, she could not stop her? Did she propose to put a guard at her chamber door? To confine her by force?

Reyna was sure she did not. Valley Terlath was not governed that way. Her mother relied upon authority to restrain her. Just as Verra, she realized, relied upon rationality.

But authority had no power over her now. And rationality could not sustain her when everything had shattered around her. Slowly she looked down at herself, at her slight figure, at the fragility of her hands and wrists. She was slight and small, little taller than a child. How long could she live this way? A hundred years? Two hundred, trapped in an immature shell of flesh?

She answered her own question. She would live this way no longer than the day after Midsummer Fest. Then she would test the accuracy of Verra's instrument in her own way. She had already made her plans, and what had she left but those?

Certainly not hope.

Deliberately she let her eyes sweep over the three of them, Juaren, Verra, her mother. Softly she said, "I have selected the date when I will go to the mountain, my mother. And that is the date when I will go." She was surprised how little her voice shook.

She was equally surprised at the composure she mustered as she turned and withdrew from the throneroom, her boots snapping against the polished flaggings. But of course that was only external. Internally she had already begun to shake as she reached the corridor. Her legs already felt weak, her head light. Forcing herself, she continued along the corridor, spine stiff, boots striking the stone flaggings smartly.

She did not waver until she reached the upper corridor and neared her own chambers. Then she sagged against the stalk-grown wall, her throat thick with unshed tears.

"Daughter—" The hall monitor approached and spoke diffidently, his wizened face concerned.

"Nothing. It's nothing," she said, drawing herself up and entering her chambers. She stood at the center of the floor for a long time, staring at the same stone walls so many palace daughters had stared at before her. She could guess the fear they had known after announcing the dates of their challenges. Surely that was the same from generation to generation. But at least they had been spared the futile anger, the helpless bitterness she felt tonight. She lay down on her bed, tears beginning to burn hot tracks down her cheeks.

Nothing. Verra had made her nothing with her meter. Her mother had made her nothing with her command. Juaren had made her nothing by fathering the next barohna of Valley Terlath. Now it only remained for some mountain beast to make nothing of the little that remained. She would go to the mountain on the day she had chosen.

FOUR
REYNA

"Daughter! Daughter, the barohna asks for you. She has things to speak to you."

Moaning, Reyna tried to escape the insistently whispered words, the fingers that tapped at her shoulder. Her mother had things to speak? Hadn't her mother already spoken enough tonight? Reyna rolled away, squeezing her eyes shut. "No." The protest was muffled by her bed-covers.

Nivan, her mother's runner, sighed regretfully and tapped at her shoulder again. "Daughter, she has told me to bring you."

"No," Reyna repeated, but she knew it was useless. If she didn't go with Nivan, her mother would send a second runner and a third. Reyna rolled out of her covers. "It's still dark, Nivan," she said, glancing toward the window.

Nivan nodded apologetically. "Kimira's night will be here soon."

Yes, Kimira's night, the interval after both moons had set, when darkness was total; the time when once a young girl of the stonehalls had dreamed herself lost and wandering in the fields. She had awakened in her own bed, but at dawn the field workers had found the frozen droplets of her tears shining on the ground—or so it was said in the halls. Some of the people of the halls still believed their spirits deserted their bodies during Kimira's night and wandered through an elusive dimension that had neither time nor place.

Certainly Reyna's spirit felt dislocated. Shivering, she put feet to the floor and went to her window. Starlight held a special hurting brilliance tonight, when it should have been dulled by what she knew. "Tell my mother I will be with her when I have dressed."

Her fingers were stiff as she pulled on trousers and laced into boots. She stared at them as if they belonged to someone else, their very clumsiness reminding her of the choice she faced: to remain a palace daughter or to die uselessly.

Because despite her angry declaration earlier in the evening, if she went to the mountain, what use would her death be? It would not bring a moment's warmth to the valley. The sunthrone would not light because she had gone. The fruit of the orchards would not be sweeter. Grain would not grow taller in the fields.

But if she remained...

Another chill shuddered through her body. Standing, she rubbed her swollen eyelids. Then she stepped into the stalklit corridor.

She had not visited her mother's chambers since her father had gone. The room seemed more austere than she remembered. Hadn't there been small figurines on the bureau? Woven hangings on the walls? Those things were gone now. And her mother had let the stalklamp grow so thickly across the ceiling that its runners threw a bright, harsh light against the bare walls.

Her mother's face, seen by the gaudy orange light of overgrown stalks, seemed as hard-used as the walls. Beneath the stone-burn, her features were pallid. And there were clusters of deep wrinkles in the fabric of her gown, as if she had bunched it spasmodically in her fists. Juaren sat on the windowsill, his face shadowed, frowning. Looking at them, Reyna guessed neither had slept. And there was something in the atmosphere of the chamber that made her wary, a sense of words spoken in her absence, words that concerned her. She hesitated, then met her mother's gaze with a quiver of doubt. "You wanted to speak with me."

Her mother frowned, seeming to reach past some reluctance. "Yes. We must talk again. Our conversation earlier was cut short."

Her brief hesitation steeled Reyna. "No. I left without being dismissed, but there was nothing more to be said." Nothing at all.

"It was cut short," Khira repeated, finally finding conviction in the words. She swept at her hair with a strong-fingered hand. "You know custom as well as I do. I told you tonight that you are to have a sister. There were things that you should have said to me in turn, things that are traditionally said upon this occasion. You left without saying them. I've thought about it and I've decided I must hear them now."

Reyna stared at her mother disbelievingly. Was that why she had been called back at this hour? Was that why her mother had not slept? Did she really expect her to make the customary pledges—to care for and to teach a sister she would never see? A sister who would be born seasons after she died? "I can't pledge anything to this sister," she said. "You know I have already set a date for my challenge."

Khira's eyes narrowed. "And will you keep it with no thought for your sister?" she demanded. "Perhaps you don't have a full sense of the obligations of an older sister to a younger one. Aberra was too close to you in age to fulfill the usual responsibilities. But this child will be sixteen years your junior, and you are needed to tend and teach her. You are needed to supervise her through the winters, when I go to my mountain palace. You are needed to tell her the legends of our valley and to see that she learns to cipher scrolls and to conduct herself well. So long as there is an older sister, those are her obligations. Most sisters consider them privileges."

Reyna caught a sharp breath, realizing belatedly why her mother pressed the issue, angry that she did so. Did her mother think she could be so easily dissuaded from making her challenge? Did she think she would welcome any excuse to forget the date she had set? That she would seize upon this one? "I would have considered it a privilege too if you had given me this sister five years ago, when my father still shared your chambers."

For a moment she thought she had gone too far. Khira lowered her head, a frown darkening across her face. But when she spoke again, it was softly, in reluctant concession. "I knew you would answer me that way. I knew before I even spoke. I've seen myself in you since you were small, and you've given the same response I would have given. Even your tone is the same: angry."

Khira had seen herself in her? Reyna shrank from the words, wondering if Khira intended to mock her with them. "If what you and Verra say is true, I will never be like you."

Slowly Khira shook her head. "Never mind what Verra's instrument says. You know what I am. Impatient. Strong-minded. Possessive. And all too tender in certain places. You are much the same. So much so that I thought you would be the one to take the throne from me, even after what Verra reported to me seven years ago."

Reyna looked up sharply, surprised. "You thought that?" Her mother had found her impatient? Strong-minded? Possessive? From childhood? It didn't seem to her that she was any of those things, not to a significant degree. In fact it occurred to her, studying her mother's face, that if her mother had indeed seen those things in her, it had been from the simple need to see herself mirrored in one of her young. And Reyna had been the only one who could bear the reflection without wavering.

"Yes. When Tanse left, I knew she would not come back. For many years, I did not think Aberra would even find the courage to go. When she did, I knew she would not return. I knew it as well as you knew it. But you—"

"You thought that I would go—and return?" Reyna wanted to believe that much at least: that her mother had seen some strength in her. Because if her mother had seen it, despite what the Arnimi's instrument said—

"I felt you would. But I've learned from the Arnimi that my feelings can be mistaken. That they often are."

"Perhaps this time they are not," Reyna said slowly. If her mother believed that she could go to the mountain and return a barohna, despite what Verra said—

"If I go—"

Her mother's gaze shuttered. She turned abruptly and stared at the pitted stone wall. "You will not go. I have already told you that."

Reyna caught a baffled breath, anger returning. "And I have already told you that I will, on the date I have selected." But the words did not hold the same conviction they had held earlier. They were flavored with hesitation. Because if the Arnimi were indeed right and her mother wrong—

"You will not go," Khira repeated. She turned back, her eyes suddenly as hard as Reyna had ever seen them. "Because if you do, your father will never return to Valley Terlath. And I have already told you what I am: strong-minded and possessive—and tender in certain places. Your father is one of the places where I am tender. I won't spend the rest of my reign without him."

Reyna retreated involuntarily from the blaze of her mother's eyes, confused. Her father would not return? She licked her lips. "What— what has my father to do with whether or not I make my challenge?" He had never even spoken to her on the subject. Not once, and she had been far closer to her father than to her mother. In fact, she realized, the few times she had tried to speak of her challenge with him, he had turned away and begun speaking—too hurriedly—of other things.

"Do you want him to make his home in the desert permanently?"

"No." That, at least, didn't require deliberation. "But why should he? Why—"

"He has already told me that if I let you make your challenge, that if you die, he will never return to Valley Terlath. Even if you do stay he may not return, because I didn't stop Aberra. I didn't tell her. I waited too long and she went."

And her mother blamed herself for that? "Palace daughters have always gone," Reyna protested. Palace daughters had been born to that expectation from the day Niabi first drew fire from the sunstone.

Khira shook her head. "You and I understand that. We are Brakrathi. But your father is not. He honored my decision not to tell you the results of the first Arnimi examination. He honored my decision to let Tanse go.

"But her death put a distance between us. Perhaps it was only grief at first—his grief. A barohna learns to hold her daughters lightly, to keep a distance from them, no matter how deeply she cares for them. Life in the valley can't stop each time a palace daughter goes to seek her beast.

"But your father never learned to keep that distance. Finally, last year, he came to me and told me that unless I instructed Aberra to set aside any thought of making a challenge, that unless I instructed you in the same way, he could not stay. When I refused, he went to the desert. It was not his place to speak to Aberra or to you. The tradition was not his to set aside. It was yours, mine, Aberra's, but never his. All he could do was leave."

So that was why they had argued late at night. That was why they had been silent at the dinner table. Because her father had not wanted to sacrifice his daughters to tradition. And since it had not been his place to intervene, he had done the only thing he could do. He had gone.

Reyna frowned. Could she go now, knowing it meant her father would not return? Knowing it meant her mother must live alone or take a succession of mates? Torn, Reyna glanced up and saw that the hardness had gone from her mother's eyes. They were shadowed. "The Council—does the Council know about the Arnimi's tests?"

"Yes. They have elected, at least for now, to speak of them to no one."

"They know and they're doing nothing?" Reyna said incredulously.

Khira shrugged. "The matter isn't as simple as it appears, I suppose, although it appears simple enough to me. The Council feels it isn't just a matter of deciding which daughters are permitted to make their challenge and which are forbidden. The Council wants time to consider the entire fabric of our society. Time to decide how much change can be permitted without damaging that fabric—and everyone who depends upon it."

Reyna shuddered at that argument. Their own daughters—and the Council chose not to tell them. Chose to let them die as they always had, winnowing themselves in that brutal way, when the same thing could be accomplished so much more cleanly, so much more easily with a tiny instrument.

But what would the Arnimi's instrument leave those who had been turned away from the challenge? Life—but on what terms? How many would want to live out their lives as palace daughters, with no place and no pride—not even the pride of a bravely chosen death?

Confused, she raised one hand to her temple, trying to stroke her thoughts to order. What was life without pride and purpose?

What were pride and purpose without life?

"You told me," she said finally.

"Yes," her mother agreed, and said no more.

And Juaren sat on the sill listening to it all with silent attention. Reyna's hand quivered against her temple as she weighed diverse factors: tradition, her father's wishes, her mother's, the expectations of the people, her own long-held expectations. "I have to go," she said finally, knowing there had never been any other answer. To renege would rob Tanse's death, Aberra's death of all meaning. She could never think of them without guilt if she acceded to her mother's wishes. And to remain in the palace, the people questioning her silently with their eyes—

There was always the chance that the Arnimi were wrong. They had dissected and studied most Brakrathi lifeforms, but they had never dissected a barohna. And how many palace daughters had gone to their challenge since the Arnimi had begun their study? The number could not be large. There was room for error. "I have to go," she repeated, more strongly.

Juaren turned away sharply at her declaration, frowning out the window, lips tight. Her mother sighed deeply, her hands bunching her gown. Slowly she paced to the window and stared out too. "It is Kimira's night," she observed distantly.

"The moons have set," Reyna agreed. It seemed appropriate that they were gone. What did not seem appropriate was the bright, clean fire of the stars.

"And you must have your challenge."

"I must," Reyna agreed again, despite the sudden pressure of tears against her eyelids and the tightening of fear at her chest.

Her mother lingered longer at the window. Then, as if reluctantly, she turned and approached the bureau. Bending, she drew open a lower drawer and took out a carefully folded length of white fabric. She unfolded it, letting it spill through her fingers. "You know what this is."

Reyna gazed at the silken length uncertainly, frowning. It resembled a mourning sash, but the fabric slipped so smoothly, so sinuously through her mother's fingers it might have been alive. "The starsilk," she said, puzzled. "Danior brought it when he came back from the desert the first time he visited our uncle. It—it has a voice." She knew little beyond that. Danior had seldom worn the silk in the valley, although

Reyna had heard that he sometimes wore it when he rode alone in the mountains. And the voice it spoke with, if what she had heard were true—but that could not be. That, surely, was a tale. Valley Terlath was full of tales.

"Here. Listen to it speak." Her mother stepped to the window and shook the silken fabric loose into the night breeze. It reached out sinuously, twisting like something alive, starlight painting it white against the darkness.

Reyna's breath caught in her throat as the silk began to speak. Its voice was the voice she had been told the silk used—her father's. But the words were alien, sharp and pleading at once, jagged with urgency. Reyna chilled, trying to understand why her mother held the silk to the wind, why it spoke with such wrenching distress. She knew her father had come from beyond Brakrath as a child. Was this his voice speaking some language he had known before coming here? But the silk didn't speak with a child's voice. Its voice was a man's.

Reyna glanced at Juaren and saw that he had come stiffly alert. He listened to the silk with full attention, his face for once unguarded. "It's—my father's voice," she said.

Slowly Khira drew the silk in the window and coiled it. "It is—but Iahn doesn't speak this language and he never uttered these words. You've heard the term Rauthimage, haven't you? You've heard it whispered in the halls. You've heard the name Birnam Rauth?"

Reyna stiffened. "I've heard certain things," she said. They were not things she cared to give credence. "I know that my father came here in a starship as a child, that you destroyed another starship when it came to take him away, that people say he is enough like his brother Jhaviir that they might have been born to the same season." But the other things she had heard—

"Yes, Iahn and Jhaviir are alike because both are Rauthimages."

Reluctantly Reyna nodded. "I've heard the term. But what it means—"

"I'm sure you've heard what it means as well, but you refused to believe. Most valley people find it hard to accept. They understand so little of the ways of the universe beyond Brakrath, of the peoples who live there." Khira bowed her head and stroked the silken fabric. "One of the peoples is the Benderzic, a ship race. They don't inhabit a world or a land. They make their home in a series of ships that orbit a small yellow sun near Pernida's Crown. They are different from us—and from the Arnimi—in a number of ways. More ways, I'm sure, than either of us could comprehend. One of those ways is the manner in which they reproduce. They don't take mates as we do and have children as a result of the mating.

"Instead they take cell scrapings from individuals selected to be parents and grow offspring from those cells. The scrapings are placed in a growing medium and through various techniques eventually an infant, genetically identical to the parent, is formed from them." She paused, studying Reyna closely. "I'm sure you find that as repugnant as I do."

Reyna hugged herself in distaste. "I do." Repugnant and incredible at once, not something she would believe if anyone but her mother told her of it.

Her mother shrugged, unconsciously touching her abdomen. "The process is something like the one by which we propogate stalklamp from cuttings, or so the Arnimi tell me. But of course humans are not cuttings. And even more repugnant is the way the Benderzic maintain their economy. They select individuals from outside their own race and take scrapings from them, without their permission. Then they sell the offspring—the images—or exploit them in other ways.

"Well over a century ago the Benderzic encountered an explorer and scientist named Birnam Rauth. They took tissue from him without permission. Later they propogated offspring—images—from his tissue and trained and programmed them to gather certain types of data. They made them into information-gathering tools, little more than human instruments, and then set them down on various worlds. Their function was to learn about the resources of these worlds, about the dangers, about the customs and limitations of the people already living there. After a while, the Rauthimages were retrieved and the information they had gathered was sold to anyone willing to bid for it.

"Perhaps Birnam Rauth would have protested what the Benderzic did, when he learned of it. But he disappeared shortly after his encounter with them. He was traveling alone. No one knows what world he was bound for or if he reached it. He resupplied at a small port on Rignar, not far from his home world, Carynon, and was not heard from again.

"Iahn was a Rauthimage, of course, as was his brother Jhaviir—your uncle. Iahn was left here as a child, to gather information to be bid away to anyone who wanted to exploit our world. And when the Benderzic ship came to retrieve him, I did not permit it to do so."

"You made the ship your bronzing prey," Reyna said. That part of the story at least was familiar.

"Yes. I was too young to go for my challenge. I had just begun my initial training. But this challenge came to me, and I had no choice. I was a child when I went to the plain for the summer. The Benderzic ship came, I destroyed it, and I returned to the valley a barohna. And I took Iahn as my permanent mate, even though the Council disapproved."

"But the silk—" Reyna said, puzzled. Where was the tale leading them? She saw that Juaren listened closely, wondering too.

"Before Iahn came here, he lived for a short time on several other worlds. On the last of them, a star-trader crashed shortly before the Benderzic took him away. After the crash, the people he lived with looted the trader. Part of the cargo was silks similar to this one. He held one briefly in his hands and heard it speak. He didn't identify the voice as his own at that time because the silk spoke with a man's voice and he was still a child.

"Later a similar star-trader crashed on Brakrath. These ships are apparently without any sentient crew. The Arnimi think they may not even be traders, despite the goods they carry. They may be uncrewed spy ships, masquerading as traders in order to trace the movements of the Benderzic drop-ships.

"At any rate, Jhaviir found the second trader many years later and retrieved the silks it carried. He recognized the voice this one carries at once, because by then he was a man and it was his voice too. He kept the silk, as well as others that carry no human voice, and eventually gave this one to Danior. The Arnimi used their language files to translate the words it speaks.

"It carries one message, repeated over and over. *I am held here, I don't know how. They keep me bound and they feed me strange sub-*

stances. I can't speak, but the thoughts that leave me go somewhere. Somewhere, and I think they are recorded. If you hear them, come for me. Let me go. Set me free.

"*My name is Birnam Rauth and my thoughts are recorded. If you hear them, come for me.*

"*Come for me.*"

Reyna caught her breath sharply. So the silk carried a distress call—from the man her father had been taken from. "Where is he?" she demanded. "Is he still alive? Could he be?" She knew that different strains of humans had different life expectancies. And she had heard that some, on some worlds, had learned to extend their lives far beyond the span even a barohna could anticipate.

"He could be. The Carynese—and of course your father and Jhaviir are genetically Carynese, even though they've never seen Carynon—come from what Verra calls evolved stock. They live for as much as four centuries under normal circumstances."

And so Birnam Rauth might still be alive. Although why it concerned her, when she could do nothing... "Where is he being held? Do you know?"

Her mother stroked the silken fabric. "I do. You know, Reyna, that Danior is able to use a pairing stone, even though he has none of the other powers of the stones."

Reyna drew her gaze from the shimmering fabric. "Yes." Her brother was an anomaly, the first son ever brought to live birth by a barohna, the first male ever to use any of the barohnial stones, although his abilities were few and sharply limited.

"He and Keva, Jhaviir's daughter, wear paired stones. Through his, he is able to reach not only into Keva's mind but into the world the silks came from. When they sing—this is the only one that speaks; the others sing in a voice that is not human at all—he can walk on the world where the silks originated. Not physically of course, but with his senses. He's seen the surroundings, the inhabitants. He's seen the configuration of stars in the sky, and from that the Arnimi are able to calculate the location of the world."

The world where Birnam Rauth was being held? "They know—they know where the message came from?" Never mind that she could do nothing. Impulsively Reyna took the coiled silk from her mother's hand.

She went to the window and spilled the silk out to capture the wind. The sharp urgency of its voice made her draw it back immediately. "And no one has gone to see what happened? To see if he's alive?" How could anyone hear the message and not want to investigate? Certainly she wanted to know what had happened, and she had hardly heard Birnam Rauth's name before tonight.

"To our knowledge, no one has. It's been over a century since he disappeared. The Arnimi relayed this new information to the Co-Signators, but they declined to investigate. They consider the chances that he is still alive very slim. And the world the silk comes from has never been explored—except, of course, by Birnam Rauth. The only person who wants to go, who wants to see if he can learn what happened is your father."

Reyna looked up at her in surprise. But why be surprised that the urgency of the message affected her father as it affected her, especially when it was spoken in his own voice, by a man who could be called his father? She frowned at a sudden stab of apprehension. "He's not— he hasn't—" Had her father lied when he said he was going to the desert? Had he gone somewhere else instead—to search for Birnam Rauth?

"No. The Council has forbidden him to go. He still carries a Benderzic tracer."

"A tracer?" Reyna glanced at Juaren and saw that he was listening as he had before, with full attention, eyes narrowed, face unguarded.

"When the Benderzic dispatch a Rauthimage, they implant a tracer deep in his heart muscle. It enables them to locate him over great distances when they return for him. If Iahn were to leave Brakrath and encounter the Benderzic—"

Reyna felt herself suddenly breathless. "What would they do?"

"The same thing they would have done if they had taken him when they first came for him. They don't consider a Rauthimage human. They consider him a tool, to be used. And they have very specialized means of using him. They would very easily learn things we don't want known about Brakrath. Iahn has lived among us too long now to leave. We can't have what he knows auctioned away."

"Then he can't go," Reyna said, relieved. Distractedly she glanced at Juaren and saw that his thoughts had raced ahead of hers.

For the first time he left the windowsill, standing, the glint of stalk-lamp bright on his white hair. "Do I understand you, barohna? Iahn can't go—but other people can. Other people can go to learn what happened?" His eyes were narrowed, intent.

Reyna stared at him, startled by the suggestion behind his words. *Other people can go?* What other people were there? What other people cared what had happened to Birnam Rauth?

There was herself.

She examined that thought, stunned by it. The Council would not permit her father to leave Brakrath to investigate Birnam Rauth's distress call. The CoSignators, the alliance the Arnimi were pledged to, had declined to make a search. One man, lost for over a century, was of no urgent concern to them.

But this was not any man. This was the man her father had been taken from. In some essential way this man *was* her father. And she had touched the silk, she had heard its plea. She had wanted to respond.

She still wanted to, no matter how incredible the possibility.

And why, she wondered suddenly, had her mother told her any of these things? Why had she brought out the silk and let it sing? Reyna drew a careful breath, wondering if the answer that occurred to her could possibly be the correct one.

Hesitantly she tested it. "If someone—if a person decided to go to learn what happened, how would she get there? And the world—what is it like? Do you know?" Surely she was wrong. Surely her mother did not intend that she go.

But Khira did not rebuff her query. Instead she answered it with careful deliberation, as if she were picking her way through some critical negotiation—as if she were indeed proposing what Reyna thought. "Danior has seen it of course. He tells me there are beasts there, beasts as imposing as any you will find on the slopes of Terlath."

And so it was true. Her mother had brought out the silk and made it sing, she had told Birnam Rauth's story—all for one reason: to offer Reyna an alternative to going to the mountain. To offer her a choice no palace daughter had ever had. "So I could make my challenge there," she said slowly, hardly believing she spoke the words. Would she go so far? Would she place herself at risk to search for a man who was probably long dead? Only because she had heard his voice? And because her mother did not want her to go to the mountain?

She had already sworn to go to Terlath, and to no purpose. If she could not bronze, she would bring nothing from the mountain even if she took her beast.

But if she went to the place where Birnam Rauth was held, even failure would have some meaning. And if she were successful, if she found him or learned what had become of him, if she brought that news to her father—

"How could I travel there?" Would her mother have suggested the journey if there were no way she could make it?

Would she really make the journey if there were a way she could do so? The prospect was incredible. But she had wanted a choice. She had wanted a way to prove herself, to serve, without dying uselessly.

She had proposed to go to the mountain, knowing she would not return.

Khira stared briefly out the window, catching her gown in her hands, crushing it. "If you choose to go," she said finally, "the Arnimi will give you a small ship and see that you know how to use it. Or they will send someone to pilot it for you."

"You've already spoken to them?" Had she planned that far ahead?

"Only to Verra, and she has no authority. But they will do what I ask. It is little enough after all the years I have permitted them to quarter in my palace."

Reyna studied her with a sense of unreality. Her mother forbade her to go to Terlath—but she would permit a journey of this magnitude? And she would ask the Arnimi to give her a ship and teach her to use it?

She would do those things. Her tension as she waited for Reyna's response was testimony to that.

Reyna touched her lips with a dry tongue, finally realizing why Khira's mood had been so dark these past days. Not because she had taken a stranger into her chambers. Not because she would bear a daughter by him. She had chosen a hunter, after all. After this warm-season she need never see Juaren again. And her liaison with him was a matter of duty.

Her mood had grown from Reyna's activities instead. Each day she had watched her train and known it was for nothing. How had Khira described herself? Impatient, strong-minded, possessive—and tender in certain places. She had learned, as barohnas did, to keep her distance from her daughters. But she had never kept her distance from Iahn. He was her consort, her confidant, her counselor, the person she held closest. Each time she had looked out and seen Reyna training for her challenge, she had seen Iahn's self-imposed exile extending into permanence.

She had tried to turn Reyna from her challenge with reason, with command, with diversion. And finally she had offered her a choice, a challenge of another kind, one from which she could return, not as a barohna, but perhaps with some measure of pride. One which offered purpose.

The very essence of a choice, Reyna realized, watching her mother torture the fabric of her gown, was that it must be made. She must accept or decline it. And how much time did she need to weigh alternatives?

Very little. Surprisingly little. "I'll go." Although the words were bold and her decision firm, her voice wavered.

Her mother gazed at her blankly for a moment, then glanced quickly down and smoothed her gown against her thighs. "I thought you would," she said. It was hard to tell if her voice held regret or relief. Perhaps there was some measure of each. "You will need to train for this, just as you have trained for your challenge. I will speak to the Arnimi and make the other arrangements. If you do well, we will welcome you back to our valley before too many seasons." The words had the air of ceremony. With them she put a distance between them again.

"I will train," Reyna affirmed, respecting the distance. Certainly she would need to be strong to meet the challenge of a strange world, a world where silks spoke and sang, a world no one had seen except through a pairing stone. Her mind worked quickly. Plans—she must make plans. She had committed herself to an unthinkable journey. Now she must decide how to make it successful.

She must train harder and longer, of course. Then she must go to Wollar, if there were time, and ask him to teach her to track. That would be a useful skill anywhere. Although—she glanced at Juaren. He could teach her to track as well as Wollar, perhaps better, if he would—if he could overlook the slight she had given him since he had pledged himself to her mother.

Any thought of asking that service of him died when she saw his expression. If his face had been unguarded before, it was naked now— naked and white. Even his lips were pale. He touched them with the tip of his tongue and stepped forward. He looked like a man who had glimpsed an opportunity, only to see it snatched away. "Barohna, I will go too," he said.

Reyna drew a sharp breath. Juaren's eyes flickered from Khira to her, and she saw immediately that he mistook her surprise for objection. His features hardened defensively and a pulse leaped in his temple. "I will go," he repeated, a hard edge to his voice.

Khira concealed her surprise no better than Reyna had. She raised her head sharply, her pupils narrowing to pinpoints, her shoulders stiffening. "You?" she said. "Why? Why would you go, Juaren?" This certainly had been no part of her plan.

Reyna echoed her mother's question silently. Why did he want to accompany her on this journey? Birnam Rauth was no one to him, and the voyage could be perilous. But one of the first things he had asked her the day they met had concerned the Arnimi. And he had spent long hours this warmseason sitting on the wall overlooking the western plaza, watching their aircars come and go. She remembered how intently he had watched, remembered the concentrated attention he had directed at the Arnimi.

Was that what drove him? His interest in the Arnimi? But what did that stem from? What was its origin?

He drew a long breath, looking from one to the other of them. For an unguarded moment he seemed to offer some explanation. But he quickly thought better of it, shook his head, and said stiffly, "I am a hunter, barohna, and we set prices for our goods. You knew that when I offered you my furs. You knew that when you asked me to stitch them into garments for you. You knew I would ask something in return. Now I am asking it."

Khira ran a long-fingered hand through her dark hair, frowning. "It seems a large price for a bale of furs, Juaren." It was more question than statement. And strangely, Reyna saw, she seemed injured by his words. As if she really cared that he proposed to leave.

Juaren steeled himself against her frown. "Any one of those furs could have cost my life, barohna. I showed you the scar I took from the minx's claws. I told you the course of the infection that followed."

"You told me," Khira agreed slowly. "And I was concerned and asked you to remain with me until you could find an apprentice. I even asked you to come with me to my winter palace at the end of the warmseason. But you gave me no answer."

"I didn't," he said reluctantly.

"My mother—" Reyna said, startled by the direction the discussion took.

Khira raised one hand, silencing her. She spoke carefully, as if she wanted to be fully understood, as if it mattered to her. "Juaren, we have danced together, we have talked together, we have made a child together. You have had my heart for the season. I offered it for the next as well. But you ask a price instead."

Juaren's lips briefly froze. Pain touched his eyes. "I ask the price for my furs, barohna," he said. "Not for anything else. And your heart—"

Reyna glanced quickly from one to the other. Had her mother really given him her heart? She had seen no evidence of it. And neither of them had thought to ask if she wanted company on her trip.

That was as well, because she didn't know. She hadn't had time to think the question through. It was too unexpected.

"Your heart—" Juaren said again, softly. "Perhaps you think you've offered me that. But I don't believe you have it to offer. Not now. Not while your mate is in the desert. And certainly not if he returns."

Khira sighed, nodding in reluctant recognition of the truth. "Then I suppose it doesn't seem I've offered you much at all."

"An honor," he said. "And your company sometimes, when your responsibilities were not too heavy. And concern."

Khira shrugged, accepting what he said. "Then indulge my concern and tell me why you want to go on this journey. You don't have Reyna's reasons. Birnam Rauth means nothing to you. And there clearly is danger."

This time it seemed to cost him more to evade her query. Juaren stared down at the floor, biting his lip. Finally he shook his head and said simply, "I'm a hunter, barohna."

Khira's brows rose. "Then what is your prey? What do you expect to find on a strange world that you can't find here?"

"I'm a hunter," he repeated.

"And you won't tell me more than that? You ask to go with my daughter but you won't tell me why?"

"I ask the price for my furs."

They had reached an impasse. He was pale, tight-lipped, tense, and Khira was hurt, although she tried to hide it. They both turned to Reyna. "Daughter, this decision clearly isn't mine. It has to be yours," Khira said.

Hers, and she was hardly ready to make it. "I think I should go alone," she said, but without conviction. Whatever Juaren's need, it seemed as compelling as hers. And she remembered well that moment on wood-smoke night when he had walked across the plaza toward her and she had thought they might dance. She remembered the question in his eyes. She remembered the meal they had shared earlier in the day.

She remembered too the slight she had offered him since then—the unwarranted slight she had never had courage to rectify. Impulsively she said, "Juaren, on wood-smoke night—" She let the question trail away, wondering if he would guess what it had been.

"I know that palace daughters don't dance," he said, meeting her eyes squarely. His were grey, unsmiling. In their depths was the same question she had seen before. "But I thought that perhaps if we danced in the shadows, where no one would see—"

Reyna sighed, cherishing the intention as much as she might have cherished the experience. Yes, they might have danced in the shadows. But everyone would have seen and wondered what it meant. There would have been whispers and stories for days.

But of course a palace daughter was always the subject of whispers and tales. If she went on this journey, the stories would not end in Valley Terlath, and they would span years rather than days.

If she went on this journey with a hunter, a man from the mountains, the stories would be even more eagerly told. But was that her concern tonight? Reyna bowed her head. When she raised it again, she had weighed all the factors and she had decided. "Come with me," she said. There had been a question in his eyes from the beginning. She didn't know that she could answer it. Perhaps he was too wary to fully divulge it. Perhaps she didn't have the answer. But at least she could make amends for her behavior. And she would not be going to a strange world completely alone. "Come with me."

FIVE
DARIIM

Dariim and Falett clawed open a nest of sharp-snouted bark-shredders that morning and feasted in the bright midday sunlight, grinning at each other with gleaming eyes and sharp teeth. Later, while Falett napped with their mother, Dariim heard a telltale scratching near the roots of a nearby tree and cornered a fat brown treemole. Chuckling, she carried it back to share with her sibling. And later still, their mother caught a heedless grass-puppy that came tumbling right under her nose, and they all feasted again. And so Dariim curled next to her sibling that night with no thought of midnight frights. She fell asleep thinking of nothing but the day's prowess, her full stomach, and the time when she would be the swiftest and the best hunter in the woodlands, as her mother was now.

At first she slept with light contentment, her muzzle buried in Falett's fur. Then, slowly, her sleep deepened until even the moonlight that fell across her eyelids dimmed. Soon she retained only a shadowy awareness—until, abruptly, she shuddered awake at the sound of her own voice raised in a hoarse, moaning growl.

Her hands and feet twitched and her claws were working blindly at her bedding. Startled, she drew them in and stared around in waking confusion. Her heart throbbed against her chest wall, but as on every

65

other night when she had awakened this way, her distended eyes found
nothing to explain her fright. She was in her bower, Falett curled asleep
beside her, the moon shining upon them both. And they were alone.

Tremulously Dariim pressed the back of one dark-furred hand to her
sibling's muzzle. Falett stirred and curled tighter, baring her teeth in a
grin of sleeping satisfaction. Dariim gazed down at her, trying to find
reassurance in her slow, deep breath. Why had she thought there was
something here, some dark, cloying presence, when there was only
Falett?

Had it been a nightmare? At that thought, the hair at the back of her
neck rose, an instinctive response. Briefly she was tempted to nudge
Falett's shoulder, to wake her sibling to share her unease. Dariim and
Falett had suckled and tumbled together from birth; they had stalked
their first treemoles together and shared their first kill. They carried the
same scent; the smell of Falett's fur was the smell of her own, familiar
and comforting.

But what comfort could Falett offer against the nightmares, if that
was what had come in her sleep? And if the nightmares had begun
coming to her, why not to Falett?

Why should there even be nightmares, when the night was warm
and the hunting good? Only because the spinners and the songsilks and
some creature no sithi had ever seen sent silent thoughts in the air?
Why should those thoughts throw such long shadows? There were many
questions in Dariim's life. Sometimes they flashed through her mind
so brightly they might have been sugar-darters skimming at the flowers
of the clearing, the sun iridescent on their wings. She could not catch
them no matter how stealthily she approached or how fluidly she leapt.
They always whisked away from her grasping claws, then came taunting
back at her.

Now apparently there were to be more questions. She curled back
into her silks, considering them, wishing Falett shared her free-reigning
curiosity. She had learned to tell from the distracted way her mother
carried herself, from the puffiness of her eyelids and the twitch of her
nose, when the nightmares stalked her. She had slipped to her mother's
bower on those nights and seen her lying in the thrall of the swaths,
head thrown back, teeth bared. Song-dreaming that was called, when

the swaths reached out bright arms of silk and turned moonlight and breeze to song—song that drove away the nightmares.

But how did the songs drive away the nightmares? Or was it the swaths' silent-talk that did that? How would she know until she had a silk of her own, until she had heard for herself what the silks said in their silent tongue while they sang? Dariim pulled her tongue absently through her fur, wondering as she slowly groomed herself back into drowsiness.

When sleep came, drawing at her eyelids, making her breath soft and slow, a shiver of fright quickly brought her awake again. She sat, an involuntary tremor running through her body. Finally, when the cold sense of fear did not pass with the minutes, she slipped from her silent-silks and, ashamed, crept down the trunk to her mother's bower.

Tsuuka lay curled as peacefully as Falett. Her songsilks were stretched tight upon their poles: scarlet, amber, azure; lilac, yellow, emerald; crimson and chartreuse. Moonlight touched them and fell across the bower floor in a muted rainbow. Dariim padded across the bower and fingered the silks. They were slippery-smooth, cool to her touch. Just stroking them made her wonder again, and more keenly, about the songs they sang and the things they did.

But wondering would not sharpen her senses for the hunt. Only sleep would do that, and Dariim did not intend to go hungry. She curled up beside her mother, forcing her mind to be quiet. The scent of her mother's fur was distinctive, reassuring. Soon Dariim slept again.

But again moonlight dimmed and she had the sense of a dark presence. It tugged at her, trying to pull her into some spinning, whining, ill-defined blackness. She whimpered, her muscles stiffening, and struggled to drag herself away. Slowly a growl of terror grew in her throat.

The sound of her own voice woke her again. She shuddered from the silks, her fur damp with perspiration. Shaken, she blinked unhappily at her mother, wishing she could waken her and nuzzle next to her to be comforted like a weanling.

But she wasn't a weanling. She was a cub in her seventh summer. In a few seasons, she and Falett would select their own tree and choose their own silks. For Falett there would be lilac, amber and yellow, because Falett did not like bright colors and bright sounds. For Dariim there would be emerald, crimson and azure, and perhaps she would have a starswath as well, as her mother did. But she would not listen to it often. Its voice was so sharp-edged, so urgent, it made the hair rise at the back of her neck.

The thought of sleeping again made her hair rise too. Disturbed, she slipped from her mother's bed and padded to stroke the songsilks. If she had a silk of her own, she wouldn't have to fear sleeping. If she had a silk, it would chase the nightmares away, although she shivered when she remembered how her mother's arms and legs twitched when she took song-dreams.

But after song-dreaming her mother slept, and the next day no game in the woodlands was safe from her. Dariim thought of her mother's prowess and her eyes glinted. She drew her fingers across the crimson swath, counting the game she might take if she tuned her muscles well. Bark-shredders, treemoles, the tiny, juicy squabblers that hid under the fallen leaves . . . Her eyes darted around the bower. Did she dare loosen the swaths with her mother sleeping so near?

She knew she did not. But after a moment her eyes brightened and then gleamed with a hopeful thought. The spinners had been working beside the stream today, making new silks. There would be songsilks there now, drying.

Dariim toyed with this new idea and its manifold possibilities, licking distractedly at her fur. There would be no one to see if she took a silk from the streamside. The sithi slept in their bowers and the spinners had scrambled to their nests hours ago, giggling and chattering. And there were places in the woodland where she could take a silk to listen to its song.

She thought longer, her interest sharpening. She had so many questions. How was she to know if these were nightmares if she didn't try to turn them to song-dreams? If they were nightmares, was she ready to speak to the silks now, silently, as her mother did? She tried to imagine a smooth, cool azure voice sounding in her mind, tried to imagine herself speaking back to it. What would her own silent voice sound like? Would it be like her spoken voice, husky, sometimes growling? Or would it be different?

Finally it was curiosity that drove her down the tree. She was a hunter, not prey. If she could not sleep, at least she could stalk the answers to her questions, just as the dark dreams were stalking her.

The white trunks of the trees gleamed by moonlight. As Dariim darted through the grove, she heard a silken voice from somewhere overhead and peered up. A single silk curled from Misaad's bower, reaching eagerly into the moonlight. Dariim caught its amber light on the yellow surfaces of her eyes. Her tongue darted at her lips, small and pink, suddenly eager. Then she ran on.

She heard the seductive murmur of voices before she reached the stream, a rainbow chorus, some voices trilling sweet and high, others falling into a lower register. Their song was without words, without perceptible meaning. Yet it made Dariim's heart beat faster. Her mind growled with the same cub-hunger that sometimes gripped her stomach.

Hunger, even this one, challenged her, making her aware of the inborn cunning of her muscles, of the razor keenness of her senses. She was a sithi-hunter, daughter of Tsuuka, sister of Falett. She was sleek and silent, a shadow with teeth. She chuckled to herself as she ran through the grove and then slipped among the streamside trees. Reaching the water, she stared up at her prey with eager eyes.

She saw silks of every color, singing in the breeze. Their bright hues danced across the surfaces of her eyes. Drinking their brightness, she felt an involuntary stirring of the flesh of her neck, a quivering alertness.

There was no one watching. She slipped forward. Her fingers sampled individual swaths, searching for the brightest, the smoothest, the one with the sweetest song.

She had thought she wanted an azure swath like her mother's. Instead it was a clear red one that caught her attention. The song it sang was like molten sunlight, like a dancing band of energy, like a piece of her own spirit given color and substance.

The song it sang was red, and sweeter and more piercing than any other song. The red silk reached for the moon with rippling impatience, as if it intended to snatch all the silver light for itself. It was tied differently from the others, Dariim saw, wound tightly around the pole and secured with knots like none she had ever seen before. Seeing it, hearing it, she didn't hesitate. Quickly Dariim flexed to her toes and worked at the intricate knots.

The chore proved easier than expected. When she had undone the first two knots, the silk itself seemed to do the work, the slippery fabric twisting and wriggling until it shed the remaining knots. No sooner was the last knot loose than the silk twisted in Dariim's grasp, thrashing wildly. Her claws snicked free in instant response. "You have a song for me," she muttered hoarsely, clutching the slippery fabric. "You're going to sing to my dreams." Despite the gruff words, she felt a flash of alarm at the swath's unexpected strength, at the way it writhed, trying to escape her grasp. None of her mother's silks fought. Nor did any of them sing with such fire.

Quickly, before the swath could wriggle free, she tied it around her waist, using three hard knots, and tucked the free ends under. Then, with a burst of exhilaration, she dropped to all fours and ran into the trees. She kicked up her feet as she ran. She slashed the air with her claws, cutting a crooked, capering course. The silk clung to her waist like a band of hot energy.

She knew she must take it far from the bower of any sithi before she let it sing. She was a cub with no tree of her own. She hadn't yet taken her first grass-puppy, and no spinner had ever made a songsilk for a cub.

Especially not a silk so strange as this one. Even with its ends tucked securely under, it hummed impatiently every time she crossed a patch of moonlight. And when she paused and touched it, it writhed under her fingertips. Certainly none of her mother's silks behaved so.

Had she taken it from the stream too soon? The spinners extruded the silks during daylight hours, giggling over their stick-looms, drawing long strands of silk from their throat glands and coloring them with the juice of their tongues. Then they carried them to their nests during the first hours of night to let them take voice from the copy-masters they kept hidden there. Finally they washed them by moonlight in stream water and hung them to dry. Was there a final process she knew nothing about, some juice or spittle they applied to make the silks tame?

If so, she had taken her red silk before it was done. It wriggled at her waist like a thing with a will of its own.

That only made her blood beat faster with excitement. She had not stalked her first grass-puppy, but she had a songsilk like no other sithi had. And she would be the only one to hear its wild song.

There were many parts of the woodlands where no sithi claimed trees. One was deep in the heart of the grove, where the oldest trees stood. Another was at the southern reaches of this quarter, where fire had mysteriously found a footing and turned the trees to torches. That had happened years before her birth. Now brush and white-stalked saplings competed for space and sunlight, and there was no tree sturdy enough to house a bower.

Bounding, growling, chuckling, Dariim raced toward the southern arm of the grove.

By the time brush caught at her fur and scratched at her eyes, she had forgotten her nightmare. She had forgotten the questions that had sent her slipping down her mother's tree. She had forgotten everything but the exhilarating energy of the red silk at her waist.

She dodged into the scrubby bushes, searching for a sapling strong enough to resist the tug of the silk. By then the ends of the silk had already wriggled free and flapped noisily against her furred flanks.

She found one sapling taller than the others, its trunk sturdier. Biting at her lip, Dariim untied the swath from her waist, careful not to let it writhe away from her. It raised its voice as she worked, singing its red song, making her fingers clumsy with its energy.

It struggled as she secured it to the sapling, snapping angrily at her, stinging her arms. But when she pulled the triple knots tight and jumped back, the red silk reached for the moon, its voice brightening.

Dariim backed away from the sapling and sat, wrapping her arms around her drawn-up legs. *Hear me, silk,* she said silently, willing the words to reach the silk through the bright clamor of its song. *I am Dariim, daughter of Tsuuka, sister of Falett. I am the swiftest and the sleekest cub-hunter in the forest and I would speak with you.*

The silk rustled, twisting back upon itself briefly, but Dariim heard no reply.

Listen to me, red swath. You are my silk now. I want to sleep without any dreams but song-dreams. Today I took for prey a nest of bark-shredders and a treemole. Tomorrow I'll stalk a grass-puppy, so my muscles must be strong and my senses clear. I need your song-dreams.

If the swath heard, it gave no clue.

Frustrated, Dariim scooted forward, moonlight glinting fiercely from her oblique yellow eyes. *I want song-dreams from you, silk.*

Still there was no response. Dariim flicked her claws free and drove them angrily into the palms of her hands. She bared her teeth in thought. Was there a trick to silent-speaking, one she didn't know? Or was the silk not ready? Had she taken it too soon?

Perhaps it was improperly made. Perhaps if she had left it by the stream, the spinners would have seen its imperfection and dumped it into their melting vat.

No. She could not hear it sing, so much more brightly, so much more strongly than any silk she had heard before, and think there was an imperfection. If there was any imperfection, it was in her. She was too young, just a cub. She was not ready for silent-speaking and song-dreaming. Perhaps the darkness that stalked her sleep was not a nightmare at all. Perhaps it was something else entirely.

Her claws dug deeper at her palms. Now that she took time to think, she knew she should return the silk to the stream. She knew better than to snatch any other sithi's game. But some other sithi had asked the spinners to make this silk, and she had stolen it. She growled to herself miserably, rocking back and forth while the silk sang its electrifying song, yearning for the moon. Slowly, caught, Dariim drew in her claws and became quiet, listening.

The red silk spun tales she could not comprehend, its song wordless and compelling. Behind the song Dariim heard feelings alien to any she knew, feelings colored with an intelligence she did not understand. It was an old intelligence, one tempered by more years than she could imagine. But it was impatient too, vigorous and insistent and resentful.

Dariim became so lost in the strange song she did not notice that the swath had gradually worked loose from the knots she had tied. She did not realize what had happened until the silk billowed wide and fluttered away from the sapling, gliding and twisting away on waves of moonlight. Then she was so startled she could only stare, her mouth gaping. Shock fluttered uselessly in her throat and emerged as a meek growl of surprise.

Gathering wit, she drew her tongue back into her mouth and jumped up, loping after the silken fugitive. It seemed to be celebrating its freedom, swirling and spinning in the silver light, rippling back upon itself, then stretching itself full length and gliding.

It flirted through the charred area and led Dariim back to where the trees stood tall. It was like a streak of midnight sun rippling past the reaching white trunks of the trees. Dariim galloped after it, still too surprised to feel anything but a first baffled intimation of loss. Her silk—she couldn't catch her silk. It moved too quickly, too fluidly. Her legs wouldn't carry her fast enough, she couldn't leap high enough.

And it was fleeing into the deepest heart of the grove, where the trees grew so old and tall they made the air dark with shadow—the deepest heart of the grove, where her mother had told her never to go. She knew that spinners came and went here, tottering awkwardly on short pink legs, their eyes large and witless, their tiny bodies soft and vulnerable. But no sithi made bowers or hunted here. Because there was something here...

Dariim ran among the thick-trunked trees with faltering steps. The very darkness was cloying, familiar.

The very darkness was like her nightmare, black, insubstantial, smothering. Reluctantly, the hair rising along her spine, she cantered to a halt, staring after the fluttering red silk. All her muscles twisted with the pain of watching it go, until finally she could stand it no longer and dropped to fours, pursuing it again.

The sound of her running feet was sponged up by the soft ground. She ran in silence, hardly even aware of the rush of her breath and the soft flutter of her heart. As she ran, her body fell into the rhythm of the chase. Her weight rocked easily, her stride lengthened, she found new depths to her lungs.

And then she was in the darkest heart of the trees, and the silk floated buoyantly higher, higher, until it was obscured in the limbs of a moss-trunked tree larger than any Dariim had ever seen. She rocked to a halt, settling back on her haunches to stare up. Far above, where moonlight reached through the dense foliage, she could see the silk. It had tangled itself in the upper branches of the tree.

Dariim hesitated only a moment. Claws were for many things, and one of them was climbing. She unsheathed hers with a snick and leapt at the moss-furred trunk, never taking her eye from the silk.

She had climbed barely three times her own length when a sudden shrilling cry rang down from the tree. It seemed to come from dozens of throats, a sharp, penetrating screech of anger. Dariim froze, clinging to the trunk, and stared up.

Spinners lined the lower branches of the tree, their witless faces drawn with fury. They flailed their tiny arms and screamed down at her, glaring with so many fiery eyes Dariim shrank back. She had never seen spinners like this before, furious and threatening. It surprised her that anything a spinner did could frighten her. But her heart was fluttering wildly at her chest wall and her skin crawled with the instinctive desire to turn tail and run.

Why were they here, in the heart of the grove? What was in the tree that made them so angry that she trespassed? Had they come for the silk she had stolen? But how had they known it would lodge in this tree, the oldest, the tallest, the mossiest in the grove?

Why did they come and go here so much in the first place? She had never wondered before. She had never thought about the spinners at all, in fact.

She thought about them now, clinging to the damp bark, the muscles of her thighs cramping. For the first time it seemed strange to her that these tiny, reclusive creatures could create the bright silks that sang by night in the forest. It seemed strange that she could not understand the chatter that passed among the spinners but that the silks they created could speak silently to sithi in the sithi tongue. It even seemed strange that she had never wondered about any of these things before. She felt as if a new and perplexing realm of questions had opened to her.

She also felt reluctant to climb higher in the face of the shrilling spinners. Muttering to herself, she released her claws and dropped to the ground, landing on all fours. She peered up the tree again, then turned and stalked away, the spinners screaming after her, turning the shadowy air dense with their anger.

She didn't surrender her carefully assumed dignity until she was beyond sight of the tree where the spinners shrilled. Then she sat on her haunches and looked back, suddenly dejected. She was Dariim, daughter of Tsuuka. She was sleek and fast and strong. One day she would be the best hunter in this quarter of the forest. But tonight she had run as fleetly as her ancestors and she had not taken her prey. It still clung to the upper branches of the tree. She could hear its song above the fading shrill of the spinners.

Her silk. She was a cub too young to speak with a silk, and it was a silk too wild to be tamed. But it was her silk.

First, though, there were many questions to be answered, and she had nowhere to take them. Slowly she turned back in the direction of her mother's bower. After she had walked a distance, she no longer heard the shrill of the spinners or the wild song of the silk. She heard only the sound of her feet on the soft ground, and somewhere in the distance the baleful cry of a growler. Shivering, she began to run.

SIX
REYNA

There were many things Reyna had expected to feel when Brakrath fell away through the port of the shuttle, when the palace grew small and the growing fields tiny, when the workers became no more than toiling insects—when at last the clouds grew thin and the mountains became snow-capped nonentities, stripped by distance of power and legend.

Wonder at seeing Brakrath as none of her people had seen it before. Gratitude that the Arnimi had agreed to her mother's request to arrange transportation. Relief that the Council had not forbidden the journey and that it was Verra and not some other Arnimi who had been designated to accompany them. Curiosity about where Juaren had gone the day after their meeting in Khira's chambers. He had left with no word to anyone. The Arnimi had brought him back only two days before they were to leave, lean, brown, and even more a stranger than he had been the first day she had met him.

Instead of those things she stared out the port at the rapidly shrinking face of Brakrath and felt an emptiness so profound it was more like nausea. The orchards she had roamed since childhood, the mountain paths her feet knew, the familiar sky—as Brakrath diminished below, Reyna had a sudden, aching regret for all those things. She wished she had gone away too, just to feel the land beneath her feet before she left it.

In the valley every sensory clue had meaning for her: the way the shadow of the clouds moved across stone avenues; the texture of the air at Dark-morning when the first snows fell; the familiar smells of the cannery, of the kitchens, of the fields and pens. She had learned to sift and evaluate all those clues without pausing to deliberate. She knew when it was time for the children to go to the orchards with brushes to pollinate the trees. She knew when the women of the halls would release the kestries they incubated from eggs each year and let them fly over the fields to assure a successful planting. She knew when there had been drinking in the halls and when there would be singing and story-telling. She had tuned herself so finely to the ways of the valley that she gave no second thought to the customs and formalities of communal life.

Now the motion of the craft told her that everything she knew had become meaningless. Reyna shivered and clutched the arms of the couch Verra had strapped her to. The smells of the cabin were foreign, the air so dry it parched her throat. She had no way to evaluate the sounds and vibrations of the craft. She had only the sense of humming, droning disturbances just below the threshold of sound. And when they reached the carrier ship and went among the people who crewed it and who traveled upon it—and Verra had told her there would be many—she would not know how to speak to them. Even if she understood their language, what were the proper things to say? What were the courtesies? How would they respond if she inadvertently violated them?

And how many of these questions were troubling Juaren? She had tried to catch his eye, had tried to find some acknowledgement there, but his manner was distant, distracted. Was he as overwhelmed as she by the step they were taking? Or was it just a hunter's nature to become a stranger again after every parting? Was that why he had become a hunter—because of some natural aloofness that could never be entirely breached?

Reyna shivered. She had taken breakfast an hour ago in the familiar confines of the palace dining hall. Now she might never see Valley Terlath again. Bleakly she wondered how her mother had ever thought her strong-minded. She felt only cold and afraid.

"Reyna?"

She glanced toward the couch where Verra reclined. Her voice sounded lost in the small cabin. "Yes?"

"There are drugs I can give you if you're nauseated."

Reyna looked at her blankly, her words not fully registering. Nauseated? But that was only a part of the fear, a fear harsher and more consuming than any she had known before. And all the sharper because she could do nothing about the causes of it. Involuntarily she glanced at Juaren. He lay with eyes closed, his face grey. Did he feel as ill as she did? "I don't need anything," she said.

But Verra had already unstrapped and bent over her, studying her with a frown. "I think you should let me give you a derm. If your stomach is upset, you might not retain an oral."

"I'm—"

"In fact, I'm going to give you both derms. Neither one of you has ever been off the ground before. I don't want to dock aboard *Narsid* with the two of you spewing."

Reyna wanted to refuse, but when Verra returned from the tiny comfort cabin, Juaren extended his wrist silently. Reluctantly Reyna accepted the cold spray too. To her surprise, the nausea ebbed away within moments, taking the worst of her fear with it. She lay back against the couch briefly puzzled. She had thought she was nauseated because she was afraid. Could it have been the other way? Then, seeing that Juaren had unstrapped, she unbuckled her own straps and sat, carefully.

Juaren had already moved to the large viewport before she dared take her feet. She stepped across the cabin after him gingerly, half expecting her weight to disturb the balance of the small craft.

Brakrath had shrunk to a compact, cloud-swept globe below. Like a child's ball carelessly suspended in the air, it looked as if the slightest force could bounce it beyond reach forever. Reyna stared down, licking dry lips.

"It—it looks so small," she said, as much to herself as to Juaren.

Their eyes met briefly, and in his Reyna recognized a flash of her own feeling, a wish that their home looked more imposing. He nodded tensely, stepping away. "You said you would show me how the ship is operated," he reminded Verra.

The Arnimi nodded. "I did. We have an hour before we berth aboard the *Narsid*. Then perhaps three ship-days before we're placed in stasis for the long-range pod. I'll show you as much as you can see in that time." She smiled, her eyes bright with enthusiasm—something Reyna had rarely seen in an Arnimi. "But it won't be enough. It never is."

She was wrong. They saw far too much in the next few hours. Reyna had barely begun to understand what Verra told them about the operating principles of the small craft when they reached the *Narsid*. It swallowed their tiny shuttle and they stepped out into the silver-brightness of its metal belly, a place of towering shadows and echoing catwalks. Before Reyna had time to sort her impressions of that, a courier met them and guided them from the docking deck into the corridors of the carrier. There strange-suited people surged past them, their scent alien, their look barely human.

Tall people with oddly-jointed limbs and cavernous faces. Short people with glistening ebony skin. An occasional somber Arnimi, prominent eyes bulging, padded belly quivering. People who wore suits of fur and people whose fur was their own. Once a group of men and women in brilliant yellow suits ran by, laughing, their dark eyes flashing from strikingly proportioned faces. Reyna turned and stared after them, so startled she couldn't frame a question.

Verra touched her arm. "Tathem-eds," she said. "They look very much like your own people, don't they?"

Reyna nodded numbly. They were like a race of barohnas, tall, bronzed, handsome. But the mark of the sunstone wasn't upon them. Their faces were mobile, their eyes bright and laughing. And there were men among them, men dark and tall as men never were on Brakrath, except for her father and his brother. "What do they do? Are they part of the crew?"

"Oh yes. They've crewed aboard CoSignatory ships since Tathem signed the Conventions, three centuries ago. And they perform as well. You'll see them dance later in the lounges, if you want. First we have to log in and get our cabin assignments."

Logging in: a procedure conducted in a language Reyna didn't understand, involving formalities that had no apparent meaning. She learned several things from it. One was that she was to be identified while aboard the carrier by the print of her right thumb. Another was that in certain sections of the ship, where few people passed or paused, every natural scent was swept from the air by invisible equipment, leaving only a chill emptiness. Finally was that Juaren was no more at ease aboard the *Narsid* than she. She saw that in the tense set of his shoulders, in the perspiration that beaded his upper lip despite the sterile chill of the air, in the wariness of his gaze as they left the administrative section and made their way through the ship again.

Everyone seemed to have purpose in the busy corridors. Everyone seemed to understand the fast-clipped words that crackled from the walls. Everyone seemed to walk with brisk certitude, seldom pausing to nod or speak to anyone else.

By the time their blue-suited guide had conducted them to their cabins and abandoned them there, Reyna's head rang with a muffled sense of confusion, the muscles of Juaren's jaw twitched with tension, and Verra's smile had become strained. They had been assigned a suite of rooms, three small cells with beds and comfort cubicles opening off a larger room furnished with angular metal chairs and tables. Glancing around, she saw that her pack was half-hidden beneath one uncomfortable-looking chair, Verra's case and Juaren's pack piled against it.

There was no window. There was only a wall painted with a tangle of green stems, a sullen orange sun rising from one corner. Reyna stepped back and licked her lips involuntarily. Was the rendering intended to make the room seem spacious? It only made her feel that she was about to be devoured, either by green tendrils or orange sun. "Verra, the people we saw in the corridors—the people who work this ship—"

"The crew is taken entirely from the CoSignatory worlds. We try to have permanent representatives of each world aboard each ship of this class. It helps us understand each other. We consider *Narsid* and its sisters vehicles for cultural exchange." Verra confronted the angry painted sun, drawing one hand back through her hair distractedly, a faint frown settling at the corners of her mouth. "Later, if you want, I'll tell you which people originated from which worlds. And there are tapes to tell you about their cultures, if you want to screen them. Although you may prefer to screen technical tapes or entertainment tapes. You can learn almost as much about a people from their art and technology as through a more formal approach."

Where they came from, how they manufactured trade items—Reyna shook her head impatiently. That wasn't what she wanted to know about the people she had seen, although perhaps that was what an Arnimi would consider significant. She wanted to know how they reconciled themselves to the arid air of the carrier, to the false color of the walls, to the constant crackle of disembodied voices. "How long must they stay here? On the ship?"

The question seemed to touch some sensitive spot. Verra's frown deepened. "Many of them spend their entire adult lives on board. They raise their families here, in cultural enclaves set aside in the private corridors of the ship." Abruptly she turned from the muraled wall. "And I've been away from all this for a long time. It's beginning to seem almost as strange to me as it must seem to you. Perhaps Commander Bullens is right. Perhaps I've begun to assimilate to a greater extent than I've been willing to recognize."

Reyna studied the Arnimi woman, puzzled by her reference to the commander of the Arnimi party on Brakrath. Then she frowned. One of the conditions the Council of Bronze had set the Arnimi was that those who came to study Brakrath must remain until the study was completed. Communications with Arnim or any of the CoSignators were severely limited and monitored by Council members. So Verra had lived for almost thirty years on Brakrath, isolated from her own people and her own world except for the other members of the Arnimi study group. "My mother asked the Council to permit you to return to Arnim," she said impulsively. She had overheard talk of her mother's request after the Council session which had reluctantly endorsed her own trip.

"Yes, when I return you to Brakrath, I will be permitted to visit Arnim. To meet my children." Verra spoke distractedly, as if the words had little meaning for her.

"Your children?" Reyna said and was immediately sorry for the surprise that sounded so sharply in her voice. The Arnimi study group had arrived on Brakrath thirty years before. But Verra could have been little more than twenty at the time, too young to have borne children and seen them grown. Had she left them on Arnim for someone else to raise?

"My children," Verra repeated with a shrug. "I made arrangements for them before I left Arnim. I was able to give birth to the first one personally, shortly before we departed." Slowly her frown darkened, becoming something else, more painful. Abruptly she turned away. "We're all tired, Reyna. I'll request an alarm in an hour. Then we can go to the dining room and after we've eaten, we'll explore the ship." Before Reyna or Juaren could respond, she slipped into one of the cubicles and slid the door shut.

Reyna stared at the glossy-painted door, trying to make sense of what Verra had said. She had given birth to one of her children personally? How had she given birth to the others? Did the Arnimi reproduce in the same impersonal way the Brakrathi did? How old were Verra's children now? Apparently at least the first was already an adult.

And after she had escorted Reyna and Juaren back to Brakrath, she would meet them. Yet she didn't seem eager. The flatness of her words, the darkening of her eyes before she turned away—

Reyna had never considered before how little she knew about the Arnimi. She knew they came from a world they had restructured to resemble Old Earth, where all humans had once lived. But considering how long the Arnimi study group had spent on Brakrath, considering how intensively they had surveyed the land and the people, very little information had passed in the other direction. Reyna's father had commented once that the Arnimi deliberately held themselves aloof to preserve their objectivity, to prevent their personal response to the Brakrath culture from coloring their observations.

It would be easier to think they remained aloof from simple natural arrogance. Of the several dozen Arnimi Reyna knew by sight, only Verra ever paused to exchange courtesies. Only Verra ever smiled. Only Verra was friend to a barohna or to anyone of Brakrath.

Gradually Reyna became aware that Juaren was watching her, grey-eyed, somehow wary. Tired, confused, she couldn't bring herself to meet his eyes. "I'm tired," she said, as abruptly as Verra, and slid the painted metal door into the middle cell.

The bed was hard. There was no bedding and she could find no way to dim the harsh white light that glared from the ceiling. She lay rigidly for long minutes, every muscle tense, as if she could brake the *Narsid* with her own scant muscular strength.

Finally, when the light continued to glare through her closed eyelids and her muscles refused to loosen, she retrieved her pack from the main room. She set it beside her on the bed and opened it. Familiar tools, personal possessions, extra clothing—the starsilk. Sighing, she pulled out the silk and let it slip through her fingers. It gleamed softly against the roughspun of her shift.

But when she stood and held it full-length, it did not speak. There was no movement of air in the cubicle and the only light was artificial.

Holding the silk reassured her anyway. It reminded her that she had not left Brakrath casually, upon a whim. Even if she did not return from her search, she had gone for a good purpose.

Briefly she crushed the white silk in her fingers. Then she folded the silk and put it aside and lay down again. She slept immediately.

Her dreams were swift and confusing, played out against a backdrop of painted walls. She followed them to strange places, struggling to make sense of the increasingly incoherent images. She was relieved when a soft rapping at her door broke the flow.

"Reyna?" Verra's voice was muffled.

Reyna opened her door and stared at Verra in surprise. The Arnimi woman had discarded her severe black uniform. In its place she wore a richly embroidered festival gown, its soft blue folds coiling around her feet. The patterns worked upon it were intricate, finely done, incorporating many of the same symbols and devices Khira wore. But Khira's festival gowns were old, handed down over the centuries, the softly aged fabric heavy with generations of needlework. This gown had been created by a single hand.

Verra saw her confusion. "Your mother wanted to give me a gift, years ago. I asked for this," she explained. "But of course I've never been permitted to wear it. We're required to maintain uniform on-site."

To maintain uniform for thirty years? "The sun in spring," Reyna said softly. Surely that small acknowledgement of Verra's transformation was appropriate after thirty years. The lines of the gown concealed the Arnimi woman's protruding abdomen, and its color made the shades of her hair richer. To complete the effect, she had wiped the black lines from under her eyes and drawn in a delicate blue webwork.

Verra colored, obviously pleased. "The autumn sun, I'm afraid," she said. "Now—I overslept the alarm and Juaren has already gone to look around. Are you hungry?"

Juaren had gone alone? Set out into the maze of corridors and passageways with no guide? But of course he hunted the mountains that way, winter and summer—alone. And Reyna was surprised to find that she was hungry. "Yes. Do we have to call back the guide?"

"I think we can find our way. I've looked over the directory and the corridor maps. Most of the basic public units are located centrally, just as I remember from our original journey. And we'll know immediately if we wander too near the peripheral units—the enclaves and the support areas. Those zones are posted."

Posted? "The people who crew the ship—" Reyna said uncertainly.

"They don't like casual travelers wandering through their residential corridors." She glanced at Reyna's shift. "Why don't you wear your emerald coverall? It makes you look just a little taller."

It was Reyna's turn to blush. Without thinking she had undertaken the journey in a coarse-spun shift, like a girl of the stonehalls going to tend her family's sheep. Certainly she had seen no one else in the corridors that morning who looked as much the child as she did. "I'll change," she said, embarrassed.

"Wait—please don't misunderstand," Verra said quickly, touching her arm. "I'm the only person on ship who has seen a Brakrathi before today. The other passengers, the crew—they'll be curious. They'll be looking. We want to give them something to remember."

Reyna hesitated. "They—they know we're here?" No one they had passed in the corridors earlier had given any sign of interest.

"By now they do, yes. Word has passed that the Brakrathi party is aboard."

"And I look like a child."

Verra frowned at the bitterness of the words. "No. You look like a young woman—one who doesn't require physical stature to be imposing. But why detract from the effect by wearing the same clothes you would wear to the training room or to the fields? A lot of people will be watching while you're aboard *Narsid*. A lot of people wonder why the Council of Bronze has refused to permit trade between Brakrath and the CoSignators. A lot of people wonder why no intercultural exchange has been allowed, why the Council has refused even to hear a presentation of the Conventions. They wonder why there is no Brakrathi enclave on any ship of the fleet, despite the invitations that have been extended."

Reyna stiffened, her gaze flickering momentarily to the painted orange sun. Her people had been offered a place aboard the ships? They had been offered trade and exchange? But what had they to gain from those things? "Why would we want to leave Brakrath?"

"For any number of reasons," Verra said gently. "To learn more about the other races of humankind. To find new ways of doing things. To form alliances against the hostile races who prey on us all. To gain new perspectives."

Reyna frowned up at the Arnimi woman. What was she suggesting? That the Council was wrong to exclude trade from Brakrath? That the exclusion suggested they were concealing some weakness? She remembered what her mother had said about the fabric of society and all the people who depended upon it. The people of the halls were finely tuned to life in the valleys. What did other races have to offer that would serve rather than disrupt? Could they turn back the winter? Could they make the summers warm? Only the barohnas could do that. "We aren't ready to change. We don't need to change."

"No, Reyna, but you may not always have free choice in the matter. Your people lived for tens of centuries in isolation. But now the Co-Signators know Brakrath is inhabited. The Benderzic know it is inhabited and they've surely guessed that it has desirable resources. And there will be others. Ignorance won't be a defense against any of them. Neither will isolation.

"But I'm not asking you to abrogate the Council's position on exchange. I'm not asking you to do more than to understand what the Revanids, the Teyites, the Koyus, all the others will be thinking, will be wondering, when they see you in the public units of the *Narsid*."

Reluctantly Reyna nodded. The Revanids, the Teyites, the others—whoever they might be—would be wondering if the Brakrathi were reclusive because they hid some weakness. Because they were afraid of contact. Because they were ashamed. It was her place to show them that none of those suppositions were true.

She could not do that looking like a child. "I'll change," she said again.

"And let me do your eyes."

The emerald coverall had been patterned after a coverall Reyna's father wore when he first arrived on Brakrath. It was cut from the finest spun fabric and tailored to fit sleekly. It was completely free of decoration except for a vertical stripe that ran its length on either side, lending her the illusion of height. Reyna pulled it on and smoothed the fabric against her body.

When she was dressed, Verra brushed her auburn hair and secured it in an intricately convoluted roll at the crown of her head. "I wore my hair this way when I was young," she said softly, studying the effect. "And I wore these on my ears." From a small container she took a pair of clear, faceted stones. "Here—let me put them on you."

She clamped them to Reyna's earlobes and Reyna gazed at them in the tiny mirror, catching her breath. The stones caught light and shivered it into hundreds of dancing motes. Their clarity, their brilliance surpassed that of any stone from a gem master's bench. "What—what do they do?" she asked. She couldn't guess the use of such stones in the right hands.

Verra laughed, stepping back to study the effect. "Absolutely nothing, Reyna. All you can do with these stones is look like a young woman of wealth."

Gingerly Reyna touched one brilliant stone. A woman of wealth? Was that the illusion Verra was trying to create? Was that what she had been before coming to Brakrath? "When you wore them, Verra—"

"Yes. I was a woman of wealth. Or at least the daughter of people of wealth. Not in one of the larger cities, but in a rural province, where the social lines were much more clearly drawn. That's why I'm a rebel, I suppose. Because I was reared so differently from my shipmates. They grew up in certificated nurseries, but my parents took me into their home and raised me themselves, along with my brothers and sisters— a process almost guaranteed to produce deviants of one kind or another, at least on Arnim."

Verra a deviant? A rebel? Because she had learned the simple gift of friendship? Because she had set aside the arrogance of the other Arnimi?

"But I'm not a woman of wealth any longer. I decided that experience would make me richer than anything my family had to offer. And perhaps it has. I don't know—perhaps it has." She paused, frowning at the doubt she heard in her own voice. "And now the eyes. I have a green pen that should do the job. Close your eyes, Reyna."

Reluctantly Reyna obeyed. A few minutes later she stared in surprise at the effect Verra had created. She had drawn an intricate pattern of asymmetrical whorls on Reyna's lower lids, then carried it scrolling upward in a sharp sweep to her temples. Reyna gazed at herself in the mirror, hair upswept, jewels flashing from her ear lobes, her eyes peering enigmatically from their carefully rendered mask, and almost believed she was as much a woman as she looked at that moment.

No one stared as they made their way through the busy corridors. No one pointed or whispered or tried to detain them. But it was clear now that word had passed that they were aboard. As she followed Verra toward the public dining area, Reyna was aware of the quick flicker of dozens of eyes, of sharpened attention and swiftly focused gazes. And thanks to Verra's tutelage, she was aware of the questions behind the glances and the gazes.

She was instinctively aware of the responses she must make. She had learned from her mother to hold a steady gaze. When they met, the people of the halls averted their eyes and nodded formally to each other, but her mother never dropped her gaze. Even though she uttered the same ceremonial observations that the people of the halls did, she spoke the words with raised chin and unwavering eyes.

Reyna did not have a barohna's eyes, but she steeled herself as she accompanied Verra down the busy corridors and held every eye that met hers.

Dark eyes, pale eyes, narrow eyes; eyes with specialized lenses and eyes with oddly shaped lids; eyes so large and dark they seemed to have no pupil; eyes so pink and squinting it hurt to see them. She held her head erect and met them all, trying to appear as strong-minded as her mother had told her she was.

But when they reached the dining hall, she was able to eat only a few bites from the platter Verra fetched her. Then she sat so stiffly her muscles ached. She didn't even know, she realized, what meal they ate. Had they slept through the afternoon? Was this their evening meal? Or was it only midday? The harsh lights that illuminated the dining area told her nothing.

"Do you know the hour?" she asked finally, when Verra pushed back her own platter.

"Early afternoon ship time. Midafternoon our own time." Verra glanced around. "Why don't we go visit the public growing rooms? Perhaps we'll find Juaren there—or in the zoological section."

"Yes," Reyna agreed. Juaren at least would be familiar. And Juaren, of all the people on the ship, would not try to guess the mood and worth of an entire people simply from the way she carried herself.

But they did not encounter Juaren until much later. By then Reyna had almost convinced herself with her own pose. She had walked tall through so many corridors, she had met so many eyes, she had become aware of so many people who turned and glanced after her covertly, that she began to feel that she was what Verra said she was. She had almost begun to believe that she was not just a child in a woman's guise.

They visited the planting rooms and she saw vines that swayed to music and flowers that grew from seed to blossom while they watched. They visited the zoological area and she saw creatures as various as the worlds they had come from, some alert and pacing, others held in stasis except for specified hours each day. In the late afternoon they watched the Tathem-eds dance in the forward lounge, their lean, handsome bodies speaking a language even Reyna could understand. Other groups appeared after them, offering their own entertainment to passengers so various Reyna could not remember the names of all the worlds Verra told her they had come from.

So gradually she hardly recognized at first what was happening, assurance deserted her. She looked around, beginning to feel lost among the strange peoples who sat together in the lounge. Was she the only one to whom all this was new, dazzling—overwhelming? Was she the only one who found the mingling of so many scents confusing? Was she the only one whose eyes ached from the harshness of the lights?

Was she the only one who wanted only to retreat to her chamber, to her bed, to try to assimilate everything she had seen and heard?

But she had no chamber on the *Narsid*. She had only a cell. And she didn't think she could assimilate everything in just a few hours. It would take much longer.

Verra touched her arm. "It's enough, isn't it?"

Reyna nodded reluctantly. It was enough. She ached to escape the people, their scent, the lights. But she didn't want to be closed in tight quarters with the painted sun. "Is there someplace we can go that's—" What word did she want? Quiet? Private? Their quarters were quiet and private.

"There's a place I haven't shown you yet. It will be less crowded than this, especially at this hour." Verra stood.

She led the way through long corridors, quieter now than they had been earlier. Even the voices that spoke from the walls did so more quietly, with less of an emphatic crackle. Reyna followed, pressing her fingertips to her burning eyelids, trying to cool them.

Then Verra guided her through an arched portal and the entire universe pressed against her eyelids. They had stepped through a curtain of plastic chain into a large chamber with smoothly curving transparent walls. Beyond the walls lay the stars, nothing to obstruct view of them but the narrow black railing that fit itself to the contour of the transparent walls. Reyna caught her breath, startled by the brilliant display. A few steps into the chamber, even the floor fell away into transparency. She stared down, suddenly dizzy, knowing that if she stepped forward she would lose her balance and spiral weightlessly down toward—

Toward what? What world lay below the *Narsid*? If she lost her balance, if the floor opened under her feet, how long would she tumble before she touched soil again? Or would she fall among the stars forever? Had anyone ever fallen from a ship like the *Narsid*? She tried to imagine what legends might be told of the person who had.

She tried to imagine what legends would be told in the valleys of Brakrath if she were the first to fall.

"Do you want to hold the railing?" Verra suggested.

"No." Her answer was unequivocal. Because to hold the railing, she must cross the floor. She must walk on the stars. Surely no one would voluntarily take that first step.

But there were other people at the railing. She realized that gradually as she grew accustomed to the fire of the stars. A tall, spindle-limbed woman with clawed hands. A lantern-jawed man even taller. Two people garmented entirely in black, only their eyes visible. And Juaren was there, dressed in hides and furs. He turned at the sound of their voices.

A momentary flicker of his eyes suggested he was as relieved to see a known face as Reyna was. But he quickly veiled the betraying emotion, watching Reyna with guarded eyes.

She realized after a moment that he recognized her disorientation and was waiting to see what she would do. He was waiting to see if she had the courage to walk on the stars.

"You would feel much steadier at the railing, Reyna," Verra urged.

She knew she would not. But Juaren had set foot upon the void. How could she do less? Steeling herself, she crossed the brief distance gingerly, as if she trespassed upon an unstable ledge, as if she expected rock to crumble and spill her down the mountainside at any moment.

Then she gripped the railing. Instinctively she stared out, not down, and she did feel steadier. Carefully she drew a deep breath. When the ship did not rock, she loosened her painful grip on the rail and turned to Juaren. She saw with surprise that he gripped the railing even more tightly than she did, his fingers white upon it. He gazed slightly upward and to his left, his features pale, carved into stony stillness. Frowning, Reyna followed his gaze.

Intuition told her what he looked at. Her own hands tightened on the rail again. "Our sun—"

He nodded tightly, his lips pale. "There was an attendant here earlier. He pointed it out to me. If you look, you can see the shape of one triangle within another. Our sun is at the apex of the inner figure."

She studied the sky. "There?" she said uncertainly. "Near the red star? Is that Adar?" Adar was her mother's host-star, only visible from Brakrath during the darkest days of winter.

"I don't know which star is Adar. I can't tell from here. But our sun is the small one. The pale one. If you describe a line between the red star and that smaller yellow one—" He tapped at the transparent substance that separated them from the stars. "—if you draw a line, our sun lies just below it. *There*."

That was their sun? So dim? So pale? She could barely distinguish its light. "Are you sure? The attendant—how did the attendant know what star you were looking for?"

"He knew who I was. What else would I be looking for?" He spoke sharply, as if she had challenged him. And his hands, she saw, had closed even tighter on the rail. Obviously the shrinking paleness of their sun made him as anxious as it made her.

"I thought—I thought it would be larger," she said. And brighter. More prominent in the company of stars. But if this scant brilliance was all that was required to nurture the people of Brakrath, to warm their summers and bring their crops to harvest . . .

She frowned, an unwelcome thought stirring at the back of her mind. *If* this was all that was required? But if their sun was sufficient, why must her mother draw sunlight from the barren mountainsides into the valley to support the crops? Why must palace daughters offer themselves to die on the mountain? If this was all that was required, why had her sisters died? Why had her father left the valley? Why did her mother carry Juaren's child?

Was this what Verra meant by gaining new perspectives? Seeing their life-giving sun for what it was—a star pale among its brighter companions? Reyna began to feel empty again, as empty as she had that morning, when Brakrath first fell away through the port. Her chest tightened painfully. Her hands grew cold on the railing.

Something of what she felt must have shown in her face, because Verra and Juaren stared at her, Verra concerned, Juaren tight-lipped, his own face unexpectedly bleak. She recoiled from their gazes, wanting to turn away, to retreat to her cubicle. Their sun was a pale star—and what was she? A child who had put pebbles in her ears, drawn a mask upon her face, and called herself a woman. She stared out at the stars and felt herself shrinking within her emerald coverall.

She couldn't stay here. At least in her cubicle there would be no one to watch her grow small.

But some gritty pride gripped her. She drew a sharp breath, angry at her own weakness. "You've never told me why you came," she said. "My mother asked twice and you didn't answer."

"Why?" Apparently she had asked the wrong question. He was suddenly both more tense and more distant than before. "Because I made a promise. And because I'm a hunter."

What kind of answer was that? And why was he reluctant to trust her with his reasons? Because she had shown him discourtesy after he pledged to her mother? Or was there some other strain in him? She looked down at his hands, white-knuckled on the rail. It almost seemed, from the way he held himself, that he guarded some closely-held vulnerability from her. "You've come to take prey then?" she probed. It seemed important to know, to understand at least that much.

"I've come because I made a promise," he said again, his voice low, strained.

"To your master? The master of your guild?" she guessed. "But why would he send you to another world to hunt? Aren't there furs enough on Brakrath? Furs enough for all the members of your guild?"

He turned sharply, his eyes glinting. "You know nothing about my guild," he said. "You know nothing about the things my master taught me."

She shrank, confused. Had she made him angry so easily? How? Did he think she had somehow slighted his guild with her questions? "I can guess what he taught you," she said. "To track, to stalk—"

Juaren's face had grown taut, the flesh pulling tight across the bones. "Those are the least of the things a hunter learns. Why do you think there are so few of us? My master trained only me, just as his master trained only him. There aren't so many who are willing to live as a hunter does. We ask a price for our furs, but we pay a price too, you know."

She drew back, the stony bleakness of his eyes making her wonder what price he had paid, how many winters he had spent stalking prey in the mountains while the people slept below.

Just as they slept below the *Narsid* tonight. Reyna pressed her temples, her hands beginning to shake—like a child's. She tried to seize control of the reaction and could not. There was a reason for that: what else was she but a child? Why dress herself like a woman and stand trying to understand Juaren when she hardly understood herself tonight? No wonder they could only talk at cross purposes. They had traveled too far today. They had taken too long a step, from their home to the stars. He must be as anxious as she was, though perhaps for different reasons. "I'm tired," she said, bowing her head, touching her temples.

For a moment it seemed her gesture touched him. Almost involuntarily he extended one hand. But at the last moment he drew it back. "I'm tired too," he said stiffly and turned away, hurrying across the transparent floor and out the arched door. The plastic chain curtain thrashed briefly behind him and then hung still again.

Reyna looked after him in dull incomprehension. They hadn't argued, but she almost wished they had. Then perhaps he would have betrayed himself. Perhaps he would have revealed himself. How could she even guess where his tender places lay if he wouldn't let her step near? If he considered every probe something to be guarded against?

Tired, confused, she turned back to the window. But she could not look out at the blaze of stars without seeing again how small their world was, how dim their sun. Slowly the corners of her eyes filled with tears. She brushed them away angrily. "I want to go to bed," she said.

"Of course," Verra agreed. "The day has been long."

And there would be longer ones still, Reyna guessed. She had come far from home. Many long days lay between her and her return. Wiping her eyes again, she turned and followed Verra from the chamber.

SEVEN
REYNA

Reyna woke when her stomach told her it was morning and lay staring at the walls of her cubicle. She gathered nothing more from them today than she had the night before. Certainly they suggested no way she might learn to talk with Juaren. Perhaps she was wrong to think she could. She was a palace daughter, after all, raised to think only of Valley Terlath, of the service it might require of her one day. He was a hunter. He had chosen a life outside the valleys, a life of isolation. Perhaps she would never understand him. Perhaps he would never trust her.

Given that, what were they to do now? Simply maintain their distance? But they had left Brakrath together bound for the same destination. Soon they would enter stasis on the same small vessel. And soon after that they would set foot together on an unknown world. If they could only talk first, if they could only reach some understanding . . .

Perhaps if she insisted, they could talk this morning. But when Reyna stepped into the lounge they shared, Juaren's door stood open and his cubicle was vacant.

Reyna hesitated, glancing around the lounge—painted sun, coiling vines, walls that pressed relentlessly near. Wherever Juaren had gone, she didn't want to wait for him here.

Briefly she examined herself in the tiny mirror, taking her own measure. Yesterday she had dressed to answer the question of a thousand eyes and had ended by feeling small. Today her mood was different. Today, she decided, she would dress to answer her own questions.

Quickly she stepped into her shift. Then, working briskly, she pulled her hair back and fastened it into a loose braid like she sometimes wore when she trained. She examined herself again in the tiny mirror, then rubbed away the faint remnant of green ink with a damp cloth. Finally she took down the white songsilk and tied it at her waist.

She paused then, exhaling softly, letting the cool fabric spill through her fingers. There was a silken spell in the white cloth even when it was silent. It seemed to melt against her waist, to warm itself from her stroking fingers. And it reminded her that she had not come aboard the *Narsid* to be seen. She had not come to answer the unspoken questions of strangers, no matter what Verra's evaluation of the situation. She had come with one purpose: to take passage to the world the silk had come from. If there were questions to be answered aboard the *Narsid*, they were hers. And if the people in the corridors looked at her and saw a child, then that was what they saw. Surely they had seen children before.

The momentum of decision carried her forward, out the door of the suite. She did not pause when she heard Verra's door open, when she heard the Arnimi woman's surprised query.

There were many places on the *Narsid* where Verra had not taken her. Reyna discovered that by following her feet through the branching corridors. There were several small dining areas she had not seen before, the smells that came from their adjoining kitchens so cloying she didn't pause to see what was served at the tables. People ate here, she suspected, whose foods were so repugnant that other people aboard did not want to see or smell them.

There were small garden rooms, some of them cold and dry, others oppressively damp and warm. She paused in each one and sampled the air, wondering what worlds were simulated there. Later she discovered a large room lit by blazing orange lamps. Long-limbed people lay on thin mattresses on the floor, soaking up the heat, their dark skin gleaming as if freshly burnished. Once she found a room that was filled entirely with steam. She entered the first of double doors, then retreated in panic when she saw dark, moving shapes in the steam. She hurried away, embarrassed, before anyone could see how frightened she was. But perhaps other people had those nightmares too.

Twice, in remote corridors, she was challenged by blue-uniformed guards. Once, from the far end of the corridor, she heard children's voices. She turned back reluctantly, realizing that she had approached a crew enclave, wishing she could see at close quarters how the people who worked the *Narsid* lived.

At last, when the harsh lights were beginning to burn her eyes and the dry air made her throat hurt, she found a dim room where dozens of small screens were recessed into the walls. People sat before the individual screens while rapidly changing scenes appeared upon the screens. Reyna slipped quietly into the room and watched. After a while she realized that the people selected which scenes they would see by going to a central console and punching at colored buttons there.

Were these the tapes Verra had mentioned? After watching for a while longer, Reyna approached the console and casually punched a sequence upon the colored buttons. A moment later a small, opaque cube slid from a narrow chute into her hand. She looked around quickly to see if anyone were watching. But the others were too preoccupied with their own screens to notice her uncertainty. Shrugging, she approached a vacant chair and did as she had seen the others do, dropped the cube into a small chute in the chair's padded arm.

Her screen filled with color and light and a feminine voice murmured incomprehensibly near her ear. Reyna jerked, startled, but forced herself to remain seated. For a time she could not resolve what she saw into coherent patterns. Then she realized she looked at tiny flakes of living color which swam through an underwater environment. The webbed water plants they swam among were delicate, their long, trailing leaves veined with color. Periodically they seemed to be sucked erect by some force and briefly held there, immobile. Then, released, they began to dance and sway in the turbulence of the water, until finally the water was still again and the plants drooped into a second immobility.

She watched the strange dance and the swimming flecks in fascination until she realized that the tape had begun to repeat itself, and not for the first time. She had seen the same configuration of swimming flecks at least twice before, caught for a moment in a framing circle of leaves. She frowned and gazed around the room until one of her neighbors tapped at his chair arm and his screen became dark. Experimentally Reyna explored the arm of her own chair and found a control. She tapped it and her screen too immediately darkened. Then she went to the central console for a fresh tape.

She remained in the room, progressively more lost in the scenes the cubes called up for her, until she heard her name spoken behind her.

Surprised, she half-rose and looked around. There was no one behind her, but before she could sit again, her name was repeated. "Reyna Terlath. Attention, Reyna Terlath. Please proceed to the nearest ID station and identify yourself. Reyna Terlath—"

The ship's com was speaking her name from the walls, instructing her in her own language, however poorly spoken. She drew away from the chair guiltily, wondering what she had done wrong. Her first impulse, as the message was repeated, was to flee to the suite. If someone wanted to speak to her, let him approach her there. And in person, not in the form of a disembodied voice.

But she had kept no mental chart of the corridors she had followed in her odyssey through the *Narsid*. She had simply walked, relying on chance to take her back to some familiar area eventually. And so far it had not. Now, she realized, she didn't know how to return to their suite.

Nor was she entirely certain how to locate the nearest ID station. Were those the inconspicuous metal plates that appeared in the walls of the corridors at irregular intervals? She had seen other people press their hands to them.

"Reyna Terlath—"

She looked around self-consciously and was relieved that no one seemed to notice her name crackling from the walls. Quickly she deserted the screening room.

She blinked uncertainly in the brightly lit corridor and walked until she located one of the metal plates. Looking around again, catching no more than a few sidelong glances, she pressed her hand to it.

Nothing startling occurred, except that the summons from the ship's com abruptly ceased and the usual incomprehensible string of communication resumed. Reyna hesitated, looking up and down the corridor. What would happen now that she had done as instructed? Or had she? How was she to know if the metal plate was actually an ID station? She waited for a few moments beside it, then turned uncertainly back toward the screening room.

But the fascination was broken. She stood for a few moments scanning the panoply of bright scenes, then withdrew, wandering down the corridor aimlessly.

From somewhere nearby, she soon smelled food cooking. She quickened her pace and found herself at the entrance to the dining area where she and Verra had eaten the day before. As then, the area was crowded. Reyna paused, glancing around the room. She saw people she had seen before, or others very like them, but she did not see Verra or Juaren.

However there were many people eating alone. Surely she could learn how to obtain food from the tall consoles at back of the hall, just as she had learned how to screen tapes.

But before she could enter the dining hall, a blue-uniformed woman approached, holding out one hand in injunction. "Reyna Terlath, come," she said, stiffly, as if the Brakrathi syllables were strange in her mouth. "Come with me."

Reyna hesitated. Was this why she had been instructed to press the ID panel? To indicate where on the ship she was to be found? Unconsciously she stroked the songsilk, smoothing it against her leg. "Where do you want me to go?" she demanded, suspecting there would be no explanation, suspecting the woman had only learned to parrot those few words of Brakrathi.

"Come with me," the woman repeated. "Reyna Terlath, come with me."

Shrugging, Reyna went.

The woman led her past a uniformed guard and down corridors she had not seen before. The walls were painted with a geometric design of dazzling brilliance. Yet each time Reyna glanced through an open door, she saw people hunched over desks and consoles with no brightness in their eyes.

At last the woman indicated that she was to enter a door to their right. Reyna did so and found herself in a small, cluttered room furnished with shelves, table and chairs. Paper was strewn liberally in deep piles and the walls were hung with printed documents she could not read. Not knowing what else to do, she sat down and looked around. Something about the room was familiar, but she couldn't say exactly what. Its close dimensions? Its untidiness, as if the urgent press of work precluded order?

She turned at the sound of the door, then colored as Juaren stepped into the room. He glanced at her in quick surprise, hesitating before taking the chair farthest from hers. He nodded to her, then stared down at his hands tensely, saying nothing.

Nor did she find anything to say, although the situation had become even more familiar—two people shown into a small, cluttered room and left there alone. She squirmed in her chair and glanced at his guarded face. Surely he recognized what she did in the situation. He must have lived in a settled valley before going to the mountains. He knew how disagreements were mediated, how misunderstandings were rectified. Surely he saw that they had been brought here to talk.

But what were they to say? How were they to begin? "I think," she said, her voice sounding tentative, "I think that if we don't speak, Verra will come and mediate for us. She's probably already here, somewhere." In another room nearby or in the corridor, waiting to step in and assume the role of the juris if they could not talk without her.

Juaren nodded, still staring at his hands. The knuckles had grown very white. When she said nothing more, he spoke, the words low, difficult, as if they were spoken against resistance. "I don't know what we have to say to each other. It's been many days since we met."

She was not surprised at the bitter edge his words held. It had been many days—many days of silence. They had eaten at the same table but she had never offered him bread or accepted food from his hand. They had passed in the corridors but she had never spoken. She had recognized from the first that he was wary of slights, but she had offered him nothing else.

And now she demanded that they talk. "I just thought that if we could talk, if we could understand each other—" She paused, and when he made no response, she plunged ahead, letting some of her own frustration show. "All right, this is what I have to say. You know very well why I came. But when I asked why you came, you wouldn't tell me. And when I tried to learn about your guild, you answered me as if I were a child. You made me feel ignorant." That much was true, even if it did place the blame for their strained relationship on the wrong shoulders.

He shifted in his chair, glancing down at his hands again, uncomfortably. "Everyone is ignorant in something," he said finally, his voice neutral.

So at least he had put aside bitterness. But he had given her an observation, not an answer. "Of course."

He shifted again, a muscle in his jaw jumping. For a time he seemed to struggle against his own reluctance. Finally he raised his head and met her gaze directly, as if he had forced himself to a decision. As if he had forced himself to put aside doubt and trust her. "Everyone is ignorant of my guild. You think that because I call myself a hunter, I only hunt. You think that's all I've ever done. You think the crafts of hunting are all I learned from my master. And you think I do it for the price it brings."

"I—I thought so," she admitted. "But last night I heard you say that you pay a price too." Isolation. Danger. The loneliness of the mountains in winter. How must it feel to stand on the mountainside, cold and wakeful, while the people took wintersleep below? Because women of barohnial blood did not take wintersleep either, she knew what it was to wander through the halls of an empty palace during the long cold season. She knew how empty the vacant chambers were. She knew how little taste food had when she sat alone at the table. But at least she had shelter, food, and a library to read from.

He sighed deeply. With effort, he opened his hands, letting them lie palm-up on the table. His nails had bitten crescents into the skin. "I paid a price before I ever joined the guild," he said. "I was a winter-child."

The unexpected self-revelation made Reyna chill. She drew a painful breath and stared at his bleeding palms, at the sudden, unguarded bleakness of his face, and wished she hadn't heard what he said. But she was the one who had insisted he talk. She was the one who had demanded he take down the barriers he must have set around those bitter words. And—just from those few words—she understood much about him that she had not understood before. She understood why he had chosen the isolation of the mountains to life in his home valley. She understood why he guarded himself so carefully, why he withheld trust. She understood why he met slight as if he expected nothing more. "How—how did it happen?"

"How?" His voice took a hard edge. "Komas, my master, had an explanation for it. Some people, he told me, are intended to be born. There is a power—in the mountains, in the sky, perhaps in the sun itself—that intends their birth. So their two parents are drawn together. They dance at Midsummer. The tides rise, the woman drinks the ovulant, and the power has its way."

"A child is born," Reyna said softly. It was a familiar ritual and a familiar tale, time-hallowed. Most of the children of the halls could count Midsummer Fest as the date of their conception. But a winter-child was not born as a result of the Midsummer dancing. Children conceived at Midsummer were not born until late the following spring, after their mothers had wakened from wintersleep and had had time to replenish their sleep-depleted nutritional reserves. A winter-child was conceived earlier in the year, whether intentionally or by mischance. And a winter-child was born in the winter, while his mother still slept. "Was it intentional?" she asked. She knew that occasionally a woman slipped the ovulant from the storage room shelf and drank it out of season. Usually that only happened when she was in the grip of some unresolved conflict—with herself, with her mate, with her family. What she had done was quickly enough detected and the birth prevented.

"No," he said. "It was spontaneous. Some power intended me born— or so Komas insisted—and so my mother ovulated out of season. She ovulated spontaneously, without even knowing it had happened. My father had no more way of knowing than she did. And when she realized she had conceived, she concealed it. Maybe she believed in the same power Komas did. Perhaps she was only frightened of a termination. Or perhaps she was embarrassed to ask for it. Maybe she thought no one would believe the ovulation had been accidental.

"Whatever her reason, instead of going to the midwife and requesting a termination, she put on heavier skirts and laughed at the dining table about the extra reserves she was putting on for winter. No one guessed it was anything else—not until waking days, when they found me beside her. She must have wakened for the birth, because I was wrapped in the blankets with her. But she was dead and I was alive. Alive and warm."

Reyna shuddered. Alive and warm because he had passed wintersleep in his mother's womb, fattening on her reserves while she slowly starved. "If she hadn't taken the sleepleaf, if she had petitioned to be excused from wintersleep—" she said.

"Then she would have lived. Or if she had conceived me even a month later, she might have lived. It was the last month that killed her."

Yes, during the last month the unborn child went through its swiftest growth, drawing most heavily upon its mother's resources. Then the mother needed to be awake, able to feed herself, or the child would take everything, draining her. "Your father—"

Juaren shrugged. "They had pledged for a single year. By the time I was born, the year was done. He turned me back to her family and moved to another hall. When I was ten, I petitioned Juris Karnissa to call him to her chambers so we could speak. I thought—" His eyes narrowed and he knotted his hands again. "I thought there was something to be said between us, though he had never spoken to me or even nodded. I thought that if we sat together in Juris Karnissa's chambers, we would find something. I didn't have any idea what, just that it was important that it be said—and soon, or we might never speak." He shrugged again. "Of course that was what he wanted. That we never speak. He declined the petition."

And never spoke with his son. Reyna felt the same cold claw of anguish at her heart that Juaren must have felt.

But he had been born to that anguish. Not much was spoken aloud of winter births, but there were whispered tales, passed with shivers and dread. Every girl of the halls grew up with the secret fear that in some winter of her womanhood, a cold, ground-dwelling spirit would reach into her unguarded womb and leave an unnatural child there to drain away the fat she had stored for the long sleep. Every girl of the halls entertained the secret fear that some spring her family might find her pale and cold in her bed, with a rosy, fat child beside her.

To be that rosy child, to grow up with tales whispered around you, tales suggesting that you were the product of a supernatural violation, to be set apart forever, an intruder who had come without invitation, without welcome . . . how could he have lived that way and learned to trust? How could he have lived that way and learned to expect acceptance?

Reyna hugged herself miserably. "And I treated you just as your father did. I refused to speak."

"Yes." He frowned down at the table top. "After my petition was refused, I went to the mountains and never returned. I had no place in the valley. I never did have, even with my mother's people. They whispered the same stories everyone else did, no matter what they said aloud. I had only lived with them thinking one day I could earn a place. Finally I recognized that I could not." His voice fell. "And now you are in the same position. You have no place in your valley either."

She looked up sharply to see if he spoke with satisfaction. But she had never met spite from him, and she didn't meet it now.

And he was right. She had no place. Even if she found Birnam Rauth alive and brought him back to Valley Terlath, what place would she have? She would still be a palace daughter who could never become a barohna, who could never attain any semblance of womanhood. That was why, she realized, when her mother had first told her that she must not make her challenge, she had seen understanding in Juaren's eyes. He had recognized from his own experience what she was feeling.

"Neither of us has a place," she said. Restlessly, she released her hair from its braid and drew it through her fingers. "But you still haven't told me why you wanted to come."

He shrugged, trusting her now. "It was what Komas wanted."

"Your guild master? The man who taught you to hunt?"

"The man who taught me what hunters once were, in the first days," he said. "Even the hunters have forgotten, most of them, and there aren't many left now. We've been called hunters so long . . ."

"In the first days after the stranding?" she probed when he did not go on. That was how the first timers had come to Brakrath so many tens of centuries ago. They had ridden a starship that fell, stranding them.

"In the first days after the stranding. In the first years. In the first centuries," he said softly. "We were sentries then, not hunters. We stood outside the valleys and watched."

He had stopped speaking again. He seemed to be looking back, perhaps trying to picture those first settlements, before the people had adapted to Brakrath's harsh conditions. There had been no barohnas then. There had been neither stonehalls nor palaces. Sleepleaf had not been discovered. There had been only poorly prepared people struggling against the long, harsh winters and the short, inhospitable growing seasons. There had been only people starving.

And hoping. "They watched for ships," Reyna said, remembering the things she had read in the palace library. "The people thought they would be missed. They thought ships would come to find them, to take them to the world they had been bound for when their ship fell. And so they sent men to stand sentry."

"At first they thought ships would come to find them, yes. Later they feared other ships would come—to destroy them. There were rival groups leaving Earth during that time. Earthexodus they called it. Sometimes people from the different groups tried to claim the same world, and there were wars. So the first timers realized after a while that they might as readily be found by unfriendly ships as by their own."

"I don't remember that," she said slowly. But she hadn't read all the scrolls. She didn't know all the stories.

"It's true. Komas told me, just as his master told him. And there was another consideration as well. The first timers had learned that there were other races traveling among the stars too, not even human. If any of them sent down ships—"

Reyna remembered dark shapes moving in the steam and shuddered. "They wanted sentries to stand watch against that too."

"Yes, even though they might be able to do nothing to protect themselves. Sometimes when I'm in the mountains I think of that: a few thousand people, stranded, barely able to care for themselves—and the sky."

Reyna shivered. The sky, from which anything could come. She shut her eyes and saw their sun as she had seen it the night before, frail among its thousands of brighter sisters. The people of Valley Terlath had never seen what she saw or felt what she felt. They had never guessed how obscure their world was. But the first timers had known and they must have recognized that their own strength was as insubstantial as their sun's.

"Sometimes when I'm in the mountains, I like to think I'm standing sentry for one of the early settlements, taking a few furs just to occupy myself, to have something to offer for my keep when I visit the valleys. Our pledge comes from that time. Komas was the last hunter living who could repeat it in the old words—except for me." Softly Juaren recited a rhythmic strand of words.

He spoke them so softly Reyna could hear the loneliness in them—and the love. She pressed her temples, for a moment confused by that—the love. The people of the valleys had made him an outcast with their whispers and their superstition. Why should he have any tenderness for them?

But why should she care what became of the people of Valley Terlath? Her sisters had died for them and received nothing but a small place in the legends of the valley in return. She would have received nothing more for her own death. Her eyelids trembled and she pressed them tight against unwelcome tears. "What—what does it mean in modern tongue?" she demanded.

"Just that I will stand watching through every storm. That if I see danger I will approach and study it. And that then I will wake the people, so they can prepare." Again he opened his hands, frowning down at the crescent-shaped wounds in the palms. "And that is why I came."

She looked up at him, frowning. He seemed to think he had made himself clear, and in fact he had explained many things. But the critical point eluded her. "You came because—"

"The ships have come. First they brought the Arnimi. Then they brought the Benderzic. Finally they brought the starsilk. Komas saw them all, and so did I. We saw Arnimi aircars flying over the land. We visited the place where Khira stoned the Benderzic ship. We learned where your uncle found the trader and we went there.

"Komas thought at first that when we had seen all the ships, we would have fulfilled the second condition of the pledge. We would have studied the danger. But we realized when we had seen the last—the trader—that it wasn't the ships that were the danger. It was the people who sent them. They were the ones we must study."

Reyna frowned, carefully following the line of his reasoning. He had taken a pledge to watch for ships and to study them if they came.

But when he had seen the ships, when he had examined them, he had realized they were no more than shells. The danger lay with the people who flew them. "The Arnimi. The Benderzic. And whoever sent the trader," Reyna said slowly. "They're the ones you must study." And he had studied the Arnimi, sitting long hours upon the plaza wall.

"Yes, but not only them. We thought about it more and realized it was the climate beyond Brakrath we must evaluate. We must learn how our strengths measure against the strengths of other peoples. We must learn what our weaknesses are. We must learn—" He sighed. "We must learn the danger. And then we must waken the people."

He said the words as if he had said them to himself hundreds of times, trying to plumb their full meaning. *Waken the people.* Something in his voice made her shiver again. "What—what do you mean—waken the people?"

"They're sleeping," he said. "They have no interest in anything beyond Brakrath. They see the Arnimi aircars but they hardly wonder about them. They know what your mother did to the Benderzic ship, but they do no more than make tales of it. They heard the starsilk speak when your brother wore it but they don't ask themselves why it speaks. They simply shrug the question away and make more tales. They don't feel compelled to look beyond their own valleys for anything."

"Everything they need is there," Reyna protested. Yet just the night before she had wondered if it were.

"Then what if someone else—some other race—wants what we have? The Benderzic—"

Reyna drew back in her chair, frowning. *The hostile races who prey on us all,* Verra had said. There must be many such races if the Benderzic had come to gather information about Brakrath to bid away, if the Arnimi and the other CoSignators felt obliged to band together for mutual protection.

Brakrath had no such protection, beyond the strength of the barohnas. And what, she wondered uneasily, was that? Three hundred women scattered widely through the mountains, communicating only through pairing stones and messengers. The pairing stones were cut in sets of two, so that the two women who wore them could communicate with one another. But if either wanted to communicate with any other barohna, she must send a messenger on foot.

Was that good enough? And how did the sun-wielding power of the barohnas measure against the technological strength of other races? Reyna caught at the starsilk, crushing it between her fingers, and realized she didn't know. She knew nothing of the strength of other races. She only knew that they were many in numbers and various in form. She couldn't even begin to count how many different kinds of humans she had seen since she had come aboard the *Narsid*. She hadn't thought to ask Verra if the ship transported non-humans too. Nor had she thought to ask how many races of non-humans existed, how widely spread they were, what they were like in their habits and temperaments.

Juaren was right. The people of Brakrath were sleeping. And she had been sleeping too. The Arnimi had been quartered in Valley Terlath since before her birth. Yet she had never tried to learn from them the things they knew about the universe beyond Brakrath. She had had too much scorn for them to do that.

And what was her scorn based upon? Upon the fact that the Arnimi used instruments she didn't understand to measure things she considered unimportant? Or simply upon the fact that they were strange, unattractive and distant, with no place in the legends of Valley Terlath?

She had other questions too, as unwelcome as those. How, for instance, were the people to be wakened if they didn't want to wake? If the Council of Bronze didn't want them wakened? Her mother had gone against the Council in telling her she must not make her challenge. Would she go against the Council again—not just once, but time and again?

Was the Council sleeping too? Certainly they were reluctant to see change. Was that a reasoned reluctance or one no more rationally based than her own scorn for the Arnimi? The fabric of valley life—how easily might it disintegrate? And if it did disintegrate, what had they to put in its place? The people lived well now. But there had been many times in their history when they had not, when they had lived at the bare edge of survival. There had been times of disorder and hunger.

Given the intransigence of the environment, the two traveled in company—disorder and hunger. Reyna combed her fingers back through her hair, wishing she knew where to turn for answers. "Your master, Komas—" she said. "He died in the winter."

Juaren rubbed his forehead, as if stroking at some remembered pain.

He spoke without expression. "We decided last winter to come to Valley Terlath to study the Arnimi. We wanted to observe them while everyone else slept, when they would not be expecting it. And we thought that after the thawing, we would speak to Khira. We thought that she would hear our warning with more attention than anyone. She's had most of her life to observe the Arnimi, and she lives differently than other barohnas. She has learned to look beyond tradition—in some things at least.

"But we were caught in a storm as we crossed the upper pass from Valley Pentilath. Komas slipped—he fell, and I couldn't reach him. The drop was too sheer. He had fallen too far." Juaren shrugged. "I called and he didn't answer. He didn't move. I waited. The snow fell. The wind blew. It began to get dark. Finally I knew there was nothing I could do except roll rocks down to cover him and hope he was dead when I did it." He raised his head, his voice growing hard. "I could do nothing for him then, but I won't fail him now. When I knew that we would be permitted to go, I went back to where I left him and I pledged him that. There are only a handful of hunters left, and most of them have forgotten everything but taking skins. I'm the only one left who knows the old words. I'm the only one who knows what must be done."

So that was where he had gone in the days before their journey. To renew his pledge to his guild master. His loss was clear in the bleakness of his words. The one person who had accepted him, who had given him place and purpose, was gone. Now he was the only one who remembered that the people must be wakened.

But how? And to what effect? Reyna caught one end of the starsilk and rubbed it against her cheek. He had answered her question, but in doing so he had raised many more. "I'm sorry you lost your master," she said finally, inadequately. "Do you have some idea how to waken the people, if—if we must be the ones to do that?"

"I intended to speak to Khira, but this wasn't the season. She's had too many concerns and she has asked too many concessions from the Council recently. And beyond that, no. I have no idea at all."

Nor did she. None. "You didn't even want to tell me," she said.

He glanced away, frowning. "I wanted to tell you," he said slowly. "Some things become more real when you speak of them. But other things become less real. Particularly—"

Particularly if the person he confided in belittled them. And she had given him little reason to expect a fair hearing. Reyna sighed. "But at least—at least we can talk to each other now," she said tentatively.

"Yes," he said, his head still bowed.

Yet they did not. They sat in silence, each following the direction of his own thoughts, until the door opened. Verra paused in the doorway, studying them in their silence, disappointment touched her features. "I brought you here to talk," she said finally. "I spoke to Commander Cezari just a short time ago. We are going into stasis tomorrow morning, soon after waking time. I know you haven't argued. There is no open dispute between you. But if you can't talk with each other—"

"We have talked," Juaren interposed, rising, nodding as formally as he would have nodded to a juris in her chambers.

Reyna rose too and joined him in the formality of his greeting. "And we have resolved our differences, Verra," she said. "You have our gratitude for bringing us together."

Verra looked from one to the other of them and suddenly flushed with poorly contained pleasure. "You've talked? I thought perhaps I had driven you farther apart, trying to serve as juris."

"No," Reyna assured her. "You've given us each other." At least for the space of the journey she had. Reyna glanced at Juaren, confident he would not contradict her. "If ever I have a valley of my own, I will establish you in offices there." Verra had even found the right setting for their confrontation, a cluttered office much like the chambers from which valley jurises administered their halls. Reyna doubted she herself could ever bring the same sensitivity to resolving a problem between two Arnimi.

The brightness in Verra's cheeks mounted. She patted nervously at her hair, an Arnimi gesture that had always irritated Reyna. "I'll remember that, Reyna Terlath," she said. "I won't forget the offer of an office in your palace. And now, if you have managed to reconcile yourselves, perhaps you would like a tour of the stasis chamber. I'm sure you'll be more comfortable with the process if you understand it."

"Of course," Reyna agreed, amused by the brightness she had brought to Verra's cheeks, when they both knew she would never have a palace of her own or an office to offer. For the first time since she had learned that she could not be a barohna, the bitterness was gone. She had found other concerns, necessary concerns. There was a danger—many dangers—to be studied and a people to be wakened—and Birnam Rauth still to be found, if he was living. She didn't know any better than she had a few minutes ago how they were to achieve any of those things. She didn't even know that they could be achieved. But she no longer felt alone, without purpose or place.

She glanced at Juaren and for the first time saw him smile. She answered with a smile of her own, tentative at first, then certain. Perhaps they neither had a place in Valley Terlath—or any valley. Perhaps he would always be a winter-child and she a palace daughter. But they had a place together, at least for a while.

EIGHT
TSUUKA

Tsuuka stretched in the grass of the clearing grooming herself while Paalan and Kaliir tumbled and growled nearby, baby teeth gnashing. Occasionally she roused herself to slap playfully at one of them or to soothe the other when their sparring became too rough. The grass was warm, the sun bright, and they were fed, all of them, cubs, weanlings and herself. Tsuuka should have had no concern beyond cleansing herself and letting the midday sun dry her fur.

But her languor was as much feigned as the weanlings' ferocity. There was a harsh note in Dariim's chuckling growl today and a half-concealed brightness in her eyes. Not the brightness of mischief or pleasure but of something secretive, something that made her bound recklessly through the trees, frightening away game and shredding white-barked trunks with restless claws. And whatever the secret, Falett didn't share it. That was clear from the way she peered after her sibling, head cocked, teeth bared in an anxious grin.

Restlessly Tsuuka roused herself and called to her weanlings. They gave up their sparring reluctantly, but when Tsuuka had groomed them, they settled down to nap readily enough. She rose and looked over them with distracted eyes, waiting until their breath was soft and regular before she padded away. Their stomachs were full and they had tired themselves. They would sleep now until mid-afternoon, when the shadows of the trees lengthened and reached out to cool the grass.

So she had that long, but for what she didn't know. She paced into the trees. Dariim had darted away again, Falett running after her. Tsuuka dropped to fours and picked up their scent from the soil.

It didn't take long to find them. They were hunched under the brush near the streamside, watching the spinners as they washed freshly spun silent-silks in the running water. Tsuuka saw immediately from the aloof set of Dariim's shoulders, from the half-concealed glint in her eyes that she did not want to be there, sitting quietly. She held herself rigidly, her shoulder not touching her sibling's, and her claws were extended, restlessly shredding the soft soil.

Tsuuka watched them a moment longer, studying the hard shine of their coats, the set of their ears, the new lankiness of their limbs. Dariim was crafty in her stalking already, daring in her attack, and Falett was learning, although more slowly. They would not live much longer under her silks.

But the most perilous days were ahead, the days when the last, keen energy of cubhood drove their maturing bodies and challenge gleamed more brightly than judgment or caution. Falett would not be drawn far from safety. Tsuuka knew that because Falett was much as she herself had been. But Dariim . . .

Tsuuka's eyes narrowed to yellow slits. Dariim had already been drawn away. Today's restlessness told Tsuuka that. Something had blazed its mark in her eyes, and Tsuuka did not even know when it had happened.

She did know her own heart. She had never relished the fact that she felt something for Dariim she did not feel for the others. But today she knew it was true. She did not know what had happened to Maiilin in the heart of the trees so many years ago. She could not guess what had stolen her wit and left an empty husk. But if she herself had been bolder, if she herself had been braver, perhaps it need not have happened.

But she had hidden, and now her only recompense was that her second-born carried Maiilin's spirit. How could she let that rebirth be threatened?

Yet how could she counter the threat when she couldn't even guess its source? Tsuuka lingered in the shadows, wondering, until she heard a shrill of alarm from the other side of the water. She responded automatically. Without thinking, she splashed through the stream and bounded into the trees that lined its bank.

A prickle-hide had emerged from a fresh tunnel. The soil it had thrown aside rose nearby in a cone, still damp. It slowly circled a screaming spinner. The little creature's witless eyes were wide, glazed, as the predator described its slowly narrowing circle. The prickle-hide had already raised its venom-quill. Tsuuka could see the deadly amber drops glistening on its tip.

That gave her pause for only a moment. The prickle-hide had seen her and its venom was deadly, but experience told her the prickle-hide would require precious seconds to renounce the prospect of game and deploy its quill for defense instead. Tsuuka did not grant it those seconds. She sprang immediately, muscles moving fluidly, the fur at the back of her neck softly erect. With practiced claws, she dealt the startled prickle-hide a glancing blow that bowled it to its side. The animal squealed, legs flailing, and tried to regain its feet, but Tsuuka already tore at its vulnerable underbelly. Before the spinner could cease its mindless squealing, the predator was dead.

Dariim and Falett appeared in the next instant, quivering with alertness. Tsuuka broke off the poisoned quill and plunged it into the earth. Then she raised her bleeding prey and shook it. "For you, cubs," she said, the words hissing softly. "Find the sun and make your meal." The unexpected feast would occupy them for a while and give her time to study Dariim's mood.

Falett chuckled happily and, when Dariim held back, took the game herself. Although there was no relish in Dariim's response, she followed as her sibling carried the prickle-hide in search of a sunny spot. When Tsuuka had cleaned her claws, she followed them both.

She always found pleasure in watching her young feed. But today Dariim had little enthusiasm for the unexpected feast. She tore at the meat, but without her usual hoarse mutter of appreciation. And there remained something secret in her eyes, some boldness that was veiled but not dampened.

Tsuuka stretched out nearby, watching. It was plain that Dariim no more wanted to be here than she had wanted to watch the spinners work. It was also plain that her drooping eyelids hid furtiveness as she licked her lips and stretched out in feigned satiety. Falett dispatched the last of the prickle-hide and presented herself to be groomed, grinning and sated. Tsuuka pulled a lazy tongue through the cub's fur and let her own eyes narrow to drowsy slits.

Dariim smoothed her coat perfunctorily, then sank down in apparent sleep. But through her narrowed eyelids, Tsuuka saw the telltale rigidity of her muscles, the quivering of her eyelids. When Falett dozed, Tsuuka tucked her own chin into her fur and let her breath rasp thickly in her throat, but she remained alert beneath the guise of sleep.

She did not need to open her eyes to know when Dariim rose and padded away. Some sixth sense told her that. She waited for moments, then opened her eyes.

Falett slept soundly, the sun warm on her fur. There was no sign of Dariim.

So she had gone to pursue whatever had blazed the mark in her eyes. Growling softly, Tsuuka rose and took her cub's scent.

She remembered some of Maiilin's cubhood ploys, remembered how cleverly Maiilin had outwitted their mother when she had wanted to pursue mischief. There were the feigned sleeps followed by the secret disappearances. There were the abrupt, galloping bursts of speed after game no one else could see. There were the meandering rambles that seemed to lead directly away from her actual destination. There were the long scampers down streambeds, where the running water washed away her scent.

Dariim exercised none of those ploys today beyond the first. Her trail led directly through the trees and toward the heart of the woods. Following, Tsuuka realized with sinking heart that that was no accident. Dariim had found something in the deep trees, just as Maiilin had so many years before. And despite all Tsuuka's warnings, she was pursuing it.

Things no sithi must see. But what could there be in the heart of the trees that was never to be glimpsed? Tsuuka followed Dariim's scent, her thoughts darting without order or reason. The unseen—what was the unseen? It joined thoughts with the spinners and the silks, it directed their activities, but why was it never seen? Was it the thing in the deep trees her mother had warned her about? Or was the unseen something else entirely?

She knew so little. Sometimes questions came to her, but she batted them away unexamined. Because she was afraid of them? Because Maiilin had had questions and had screamed and become a growler? Or simply because questioning brought back memory of Maiilin and with it a burdening sense of her own failure? If she had not hidden that day, if she had gone with Maiilin...

Tsuuka ran through the trees, letting the questions come now. And they were many. How were the spinners, witless and vulnerable, able to create the silks, which spoke so cleverly, so silently in her mind? Did the silks' cleverness come from something the spinners wove into them? Or did they mirror some hidden cleverness of the spinners themselves? And why did the thoughts that joined the spinners, the silks and the unseen become nightmares when they touched sithi minds? Just because sithi were sithi and not spinners or silks? Just because the images that carried information to one mind touched a different mind more darkly?

And what had happened to Maiilin? Could spinners have done that to her? Tsuuka knew that spinners came and went in the heart of the trees. But why would spinners have trussed Maiilin in strings of foul-smelling silk? And how could spinners have quenched her wit? And why? The mysterious things Maiilin had claimed she saw in the cavernous trees, blind, half-formed growing things—perhaps it was true. Perhaps she had seen those things. But what were they?

Tsuuka growled miserably as she ran. If she had gone with Maiilin, perhaps she would know what those things were.

Or perhaps—a sudden chill rippled down her back, raising the fur— perhaps if she had gone with Maiilin, she would be a growler now too. Perhaps both of them would be wandering the verges of the forest, crying when the silks sang.

Black claws closed around her heart. It had happened to Maiilin. It could well have happened to her. But it must not happen to Dariim. Tsuuka ran faster, letting her muscles work to their own rhythm. She was grateful that her heart pumped swiftly with the effort. Otherwise she would have known the beat of its fear.

The trees around her became denser, taller, their trunks stained now with moss and fungus growths. Even the smell of the air became different—damper, closer, heavier. Beneath layers of decomposed leaves, the soil was wet, as if the sun never reached here to dry it. And there was a silence that was as heavy as the air. Here there were no spinners chattering, no sithi chuckling or growling, no scamper of small game. Here there was only stillness.

But the stillness was not absolute. For as Tsuuka ran farther into the trees, she heard a voice in the distance. Her feet missed a beat, making her lurch awkwardly. A silk singing so deep in the trees? There were no bowers here. Although spinners came and went, they did not carry silks with them—not here.

But the song was unmistakable, vivid and clear—and wild. Because this silk sang by sunlight. It tuned its voice on the sun's bright energy and cried out with a feeling she had seldom heard in a silk. Here was no sweetness. Here was no subtlety. Here was no trilling pleasure. Here was protest and triumph and mockery.

Tsuuka slowed, baffled. Dariim's scent was stronger here. She traced it until she reached a place where it led in several directions at once. There she stopped, growling. Obviously Dariim had circled, leaving crossing trails. If she knew which to follow—Tsuuka raised her head and gazed into the trees.

Her throat closed with alarm. A chestnut shadow clung to the heavily mossed trunk of one of the tallest trees. Dariim was scrambling up the tree, claws tearing at the heavy bark, ears laid back. And above her, tangled in the highest branches, was a red silk. It clung to the tree and stretched out for the sun, its song throbbing as if it were sunlight given voice.

A copy-master—someone had set a copy-silk free. Tsuuka recognized the special quality of its voice now. For most of the time, copy-silks were kept hidden, starved of light and breeze and freedom. But sometimes the spinners tied them briefly beside the stream to air after they had used them to make songsilks. There was a special plaint to their song, as if there were memories caught in their silken strands that protested imprisonment.

Tsuuka could not guess why that should be, or why master-silks were not permitted to sing in the moonlight like the songsilks that were made from them.

But now someone had set a copy-silk free and Dariim was stalking it, clawing her way up the moss-flanked tree. When she crept near, making her way precariously from trunk to branch and from branch to still more fragile branch, the silk freed itself and rippled away, singing its scornful song.

Tsuuka caught her breath as narrow branches bowed under Dariim's weight. Thwarted, Dariim picked her way back to safety and peered toward the silk's new perch. Even from the ground, Tsuuka could see the hungry intensity of her gaze, could see the quiver of straining muscles.

She bounded forward, raising her voice angrily, when Dariim bounced to the ground. "What have I told you, what have I said—" The words came in a hissing rush, the same words her mother might have uttered years before, words driven by angry terror. "Have I told you that you are not to come here? Have I told you why? Yet here I find you. Here—"

Dariim spun and faced her with wide-eyed startlement. Momentarily the pupils of her yellow eyes were fixed. She grunted with surprise.

But neither surprise nor her mother's anger penetrated the spell that gripped her. Before Tsuuka could say more, Dariim darted past her and set claws to the tree where the silk clung now.

Impotently Tsuuka watched as she scurried up the slippery trunk. Helplessly she caught her breath as the silk teased her, singing its fiery song from the tip of the most fragile branch, then billowing away as Dariim crept out the swaying branch, claws extended. Agony streaked Tsuuka's thoughts. What must she do when her cub would not listen to her? What must she do when her cub was ensorcelled by a copy-silk? Capture the silk herself?

Another time she would have shrunk from that suggestion. No sithi kept a copy-silk. And no sithi was welcome this deep in the trees. She could feel the unwelcome in the air. There was a secret here that must not be discovered.

But she would not have Dariim's wit quenched as Maiilin's had been. She would not carry that grief.

Growling to give herself courage, she bounded toward the tree where the silk had entangled itself this time, the tallest, the oldest of the trees. She dug angry claws into its bark and felt the slime of moss against her belly as she climbed. There was a foreign odor to this tree. It didn't have the clean, dry smell of the tree where she made her bower. Some secret mustiness breathed from its hollow interior, as if something lived there.

But what could live inside a tree? Something blind? Something half-formed?

There was no time to wonder. The copy-silk rippled from limb to limb, singing a taunting song. Glancing down, Tsuuka saw that Dariim hesitated at the base of the tree. Fleetingly she wondered why her errant cub had not already set claws to bark. Certainly she had not hesitated before.

Then from inside the tree, from the hollow cavern of its interior— from inside the tree came sound and motion. First Tsuuka heard the rising shrill of voices, a sound so concentrated it made her ears ring. Then she felt a boiling resonance, as if tens of bodies swarmed over one another in mindless excitement. She froze, her thoughts ringing wildly, intensifying her confusion. What *could* live inside a tree? Shock loosened her claws and she slid an arm's length down the slippery trunk before anchoring herself again.

By then spinners had begun to boil from the interior of the tree and line themselves along its broad-stretching branches. They were not the fully matured spinners who spun beside the stream. These were frailer, their tiny limbs underdeveloped, their pink flesh transparent. Tsuuka could see blood vessels branching beneath the translucent flesh, could see the shadow of internal organs. She could even see the folds of tiny brains through the thinness of their skulls.

And in some of them she could see something that made her cold, a curving, sharp-pointed organ that grew where the tongue should have been. And their sacs, the sacs of their necks— She stared, her pupils fixed in shock, as her claws loosened and she slipped down the mossy trunk. The spinners continued to shrill. The sound rose and fell, piercing in its intensity, making something deep in her ears flutter as if it were struggling to escape.

When Tsuuka's feet touched ground, she jumped back from the tree, still staring up, mouth open in shock. *Stingers*. Some of the spinners had stingers instead of tongues. And their neck sacs were taut with sulphurous fluid. She could see its color through the transparent flesh.

Stingers and venom—for what purpose? Her mind darted. Were these the spinners that had bound Maiilin? Had they stung her as well? Tsuuka was peripherally aware of Dariim crouched nearby. She bared her sharp cub's teeth in a defiant grimace, her claws kneading the air in a reflex gesture. As Tsuuka stumbled back from the tree, Dariim took a single crouching step forward.

Tsuuka's reaction was spontaneous. Whipping around, she dealt Dariim a blow that knocked her to the ground. Before the cub could bounce up again, Tsuuka flew at her, slapping and growling. Anger, fear, shock—she put them all into the blows she rained on Dariim's startled body. She cuffed and bit until Dariim wriggled away, scrambled to her feet, and fled.

Tsuuka loped after her, howling angrily—howling so loudly she drowned out the shrilling of the spinners and the mocking song of the silk. Running on all fours, she swatted at the heels of the fleeing cub, not troubling herself that the rebukes she uttered were little more than strangled cries.

She chased the cub until Dariim dodged into a marshy growth of brush and eluded her. Tsuuka searched for her, nettled branches tearing at her coat. And Tsuuka listened for her. All she heard was the heaving of her own breath, the splash of her own feet. She could not catch Dariim's scent on the marshy ground, although the smell of fear was distinct beneath the brush.

Perhaps it was her own. At last she gave up. She groped free of the brush and threw herself down, laboring for breath.

When she took her feet again, her mouth was sour and the long muscles of her legs quivered. She longed for the balm of sunlight and she was worried for Paalan and Kaliir, left alone longer than they had ever been alone before. Yet she was reluctant to go back to the clearing when she could not find Dariim. She hesitated, weighing her fear for Dariim against the needs of her other offspring. She had little concern for Falett. When she woke, she would accept her mother's absence with equanimity. But Paalan and Kaliir had seldom been alone. They would cry when they woke and did not find her there to tend them.

Torn, Tsuuka paced through the trees, trying to order her thoughts.

She did not like to leave her weanlings to waken alone. But if they cried and Falett heard, she would go to them. And if she did not, there were other adult sithi who would take a moment to comfort them, however distractedly. Riifika, perhaps, who had given birth to stillborns just a few days ago, who had neither cubs nor weanlings of her own.

There was no one else to return to the heart of the trees and see that Dariim did not try again to retrieve the red silk.

And so Tsuuka returned to the shadowy depths of the grove, stealthily, silently—reluctantly—her ears alert to every sound.

There were scuff marks in the rotted leaves beneath the tall trees. Her scent and Dariim's still clung to the soil. But there was no sign of the spinners who had boiled from inside the eldest tree. There was no sign of the red silk; apparently it had flirted away. And there was no sign that Dariim had returned.

Cautiously Tsuuka eased herself to her haunches in the shadows. She veiled the brightness of her eyes and settled down to watch.

Occasionally she heard the red silk singing in the distance, its voice heralding the sun. Twice she saw it flutter among the trees and briefly entangle itself. She laid back her ears, trying to shut out its song. There was something mocking in its bright tones, yet angry too—and lost, as if it searched for something it could not find.

Yet what could a silk have lost, even a copy-silk? She knew so little. There were so many questions she had never asked. And so many others she had asked but had never heard answers for. She thought fleetingly of her skysilk, with its evasive ways and its distracting song.

The spinners did not emerge from the tree again. Tsuuka crouched, waiting, until the air cooled and darkness began to come. Then she rose, stiffly, and padded away.

She did not find her weanlings crying where she had left them. She did not find Falett searching for her in confusion. When she reached her tree, she found all four of her offspring in their bowers. The weanlings slept quietly, with no sign of disturbance. Falett and Dariim were curled in their silks. Only Dariim opened her eyes when Tsuuka looked in upon them. They gleamed in the dark.

Tsuuka tried to read their expression. Was it abject? Was it defiant? Or was it both at once? Tsuuka held Dariim's gaze, her own stern, until the cub dropped her head and hid her muzzle beneath the silks. Then

Tsuuka silently retreated to her own bower, taking with her no illusions. Dariim was not cowed either by the day's experience or by her mother's displeasure. She was only temporarily dampened.

But tomorrow, the next day—

Tomorrow or the next day she would slip away again. She would resume her stalking of the red silk. Nothing Tsuuka told her, no promise Tsuuka extracted from her would long hold her. Dariim wasn't of an age for caution. She was of an age for testing, and the same qualities that made her a promising fledgling hunter—boldness, curiosity, persistence—would draw her back to the heart of the trees.

Tsuuka stretched out on her silent-silks, cold with that understanding and the helplessness that accompanied it. Only time and wisdom could dissuade Dariim, and she had no way to force those things upon her. All she could do was tell her again that she must not go where she had gone, must not see what she would look for anyway, must not question the very things she would question.

Briefly Tsuuka's eyes lingered upon her own silks. Then she hooded her gaze, sinking deep into thought.

She did not emerge when the moon rose. She did not emerge when she heard Petria's amber silk begin to sing from the trees, when her own silks rippled wistfully in the passing breeze. She did not even emerge from her thoughts when a moving star brightened to brilliance in the sky and discharged a spark that swept sharply downward, a deep sound accompanying its ascent.

She only escaped her troubling thoughts when finally she slept. It was an uneasy sleep, haunted by a mocking red song, the shrill of angry voices, and fear. Because she knew that there was only one way to prevent Dariim from going back to the heart of the trees. That was to go there herself, to take the red silk before Dariim could return for it. And she was afraid.

NINE
REYNA

A forest of white-stalked trees. Chestnut-furred animals with oblique yellow eyes. Bright silks singing in the branches. Those were the things Danior had seen with the pairing stone when Jhaviir's blue silk sang. But Reyna didn't see any of them tonight as she gazed out the open hatch of the Arnimi ship, the starsilk folded under one arm. Instead she saw the moon—there was just one—waning over a featureless plain. She saw a single tree, misshapen. And she saw stars that seemed muted after the brilliance of those she had seen from the *Narsid*.

Undecided, she glanced back at Juaren and Verra. They slept on their couches, Verra pale, cramped, as if her stomach hurt, Juaren frowning in his sleep, shielding his eyes against the ship's dim interior lights. It would be hours before they woke again. The sedative they had taken to counter the discomforts of the transition from stasis assured that. But Reyna's afterdose sat untouched in its sealed cup. She had wakened from stasis with nothing more than a dull ache at her temples and a sense of disorientation.

She could deal with neither of those by pacing the small ship's interior. Memory insisted she had entered stasis only that morning. She could still see the cold pallor of the technician's face as he bent over her. She could still hear his disinterested voice as her consciousness slipped away in carefully measured stages. She even imagined she could hear first the hatch of the Arnimi ship, then the much heavier hatch of the warp-pod thump shut, although she knew she had slipped into stasis before either ship had been sealed.

She knew tens of days had passed since those events, days during which they had crossed broad gaps between stars that weren't even visible from Brakrath. But how could she grasp the reality of the transition by gazing out ports and hatches? And how could she hear the starsilk speak?

Surely she had watched here, surely she had listened here long enough to be confident there was nothing waiting outside the ship. Glancing back again, deciding, she let down the metal ramp and stepped out, easing the ship's outer hatch shut behind her.

Moonlight showed her a broad, flat expanse of terrain grown with low brush, grass, and an occasional discouraged tree. The air touched her face softly, warmer than she expected and heavy with flavors and nuances completely alien. She paused for a moment, doubtfully, testing and weighing. But the ship's hatch would not have opened if there were any element in the air inimical to the human metabolism. Verra had assured her of that.

She picked her way carefully through the ragged grass, stopping to listen with every stop. When she reached the misshapen tree, she stood for moments without moving, testing the night for any unexpected sound. A tiny shadow moved in the air and brushed at her cheek. She jumped back, catching her breath in surprise. An insect that flew? There were none like that on Brakrath. If it were poisonous—

But she wouldn't be driven back to the ship now. She had been confined long enough, and the starsilk couldn't speak to her there. When the tiny shadow returned, she fanned it away and unfolded the starsilk. Stroking it, she shook it out and fed it to the breeze.

It raised its voice immediately, speaking the familiar words. *I can't speak, but the thoughts that leave me go somewhere. Somewhere, and I think they are recorded. If you hear them, come for me. Let me go. Set me free.*

My name is Birnam Rauth and my thoughts are recorded.

Come for me.

She didn't need Verra's translator to understand that much. Before leaving Brakrath, she had listened to the silk until she knew every sharp-edged syllable. But tonight, as the breeze rose, the silk raised a second voice too, one that did not speak but sang.

Startled, Reyna caught the silken fabric, silencing it. She peered around, breath held, hair rising.

She was alone, just as she had been before. There was no sign of any living creature. But in those bare moments, the silk's unexpected song had raised some inexplicable sense of presence. She felt as if someone stood behind her, as if he might touch her, might put his hand on her shoulder.

Her father's voice—her father's voice as well as Birnam Rauth's spoke from the silk. She had expected that. But the silk had never sung before, and briefly she stood as if frozen. Then carefully, she tied the silk to the lowest branch of the malformed tree and stepped back.

The silk raised its voices again. As she stood there, Birnam Rauth spoke his message to the night breeze time and again, the words, their inflection, always the same. At the same time he sang, but Reyna heard no repetition in his wordless song. It was seamless, without stanza or verse, rhyme or meaning.

Even so it spoke things to her, things that stirred deeply. She listened as the moon slowly sank and the breeze grew fitful. Tiny shadows flew before her face. Sometimes she thought she felt the flutter of wings. Once an insect landed on her shoulder and she brushed at it carelessly, preoccupied. Birnam Rauth's song made her think of lonely winters and empty corridors. It made her think of the forces that had driven her here: pride, stubbornness, pain. And it made her realize, shivering, what things she owned beyond consciousness and breath, made her think of the bright legends that lived in her, of the memories she held and of others she might one day hold, whether dark or shining.

After a while, unbidden, a song of her own rose. It was silent, it was inner, it was a song much like the starsilk's—a song of questioning and loneliness. Caught, she sang until the moon sank beneath the horizon. Then, slowly, dazed, she emerged from her trance—and realized with a sharply indrawn breath that she was no longer alone. Eyes watched her from the brush.

Reyna froze, staring directly into them. They were yellow, the pupils vertical and elongated. Their elevation told her their owner stood at least as tall as she did. Reyna stood pillared in ice for the space of a dozen shallow breaths. Then, haltingly, she began to think. Her pike was in the cargo hold and she was not wearing her hunting blade. If the creature that watched was a predator—

But it only watched, eyes unwinking, coming no nearer. Perhaps if she backed toward the ship, slowly, without offering provocation—

But the silk still sang from the tree. She could not leave it. Drawing a deep breath, steeling herself, she stepped forward. She did not fan at the shadowy insects that fluttered at her face in a new flurry. One moved along her arm, tickling her, but she ignored it. With stiff fingers she untied the starsilk.

She did not take time to fold it. She pulled it from the tree, crumpled it under one arm, and stepped back.

She had intended a careful retreat, every motion measured. Instead she felt a pain in her shoulder so sharp, so stinging that she cried out and spun around, slapping wildly. Before she realized what she had done, the creature that watched her took alarm and fled, crashing from the brush and bounding away on four feet.

Stunned, Reyna cupped her stinging shoulder and stared after the fleeing creature. She saw little more than a running shadow. Slowly she dropped her hand. In the palm, crushed, was the insect that had stung her. She stared at it first blankly, then with deepening apprehension. On Brakrath most insects were harmless. But of the few that did sting, several were deadly.

She forgot the creature that had watched from the brush. Numbly, cradling the dead insect in one palm, she stumbled back to the ship. When the hatch closed behind her, she carried the insect to the light and examined it, turning it with cold fingers, not knowing what she looked for. Fragile, jointed legs, filmy wings veined with color—

It was the stinger that made it ugly. Only the stinger. "Verra?" Reyna said weakly, dropping the crushed insect, kneeling beside the couch where the Arnimi woman slept. The starsilk spilled to the floor, unnoticed. "Verra?" A poultice—would a poultice help? But they had brought only Arnimi medicinals, and she didn't know how to use those.

And Verra did not waken. Nor did Juaren when she called to him. He only turned away, pressing his forearm to his eyes as if they hurt. Trembling, Reyna dropped to her own couch. Her shoulder itched violently and her blood raced, drumming in her ears. Her heart jumped so hard at her ribs she felt each beat as a separate blow.

But she could not help herself if she panicked. She closed her eyes and forced herself to draw a series of deep breaths. Then, gingerly, she touched her wrist, measuring her pulse. Surprisingly, it beat little faster than its usual pace.

Unsteadily she reexamined the situation. Perhaps there had been no poison in the sting. She closed her eyes again and forced herself to be completely still for several minutes. Then she stood, carefully, and gazed around the cabin. Juaren slept on his stomach now, his face hidden in the crook of one arm. Verra still huddled as if her stomach hurt. The starsilk was tumbled on the floor, the crushed insect near it.

Carefully Reyna retrieved the weightless body and dropped it in the disposer. The motion did not make her dizzy. Nor was she feverish or nauseated. If there had been poison in the sting, apparently it had affected her only momentarily.

And the creature that had watched her from the brush had not tried to harm her. Nor had she done it harm in turn. But neither Juaren nor Verra would wake, and beyond the ship lay an entire world she didn't know. A world she had journeyed to without even wondering how its strangeness would touch her. Bleakly she lay down again, blinking up at the harsh lights. After a few minutes, when her head began to ache, she unsealed her sedative dose and swallowed it. Then she slept too.

Time passed in slow measure. After a while someone shook her. Someone called her name and tried to force hot brew between her lips. It was the smell of unfiltered air that finally roused her. Juaren bent over her and the ship's hatch stood open. Struggling, she sat. "Verra?" she said numbly.

"She's gone outside to look around. How do you feel?"

"I feel—" But before she could test the stiffness of her muscles, the thickness of her tongue, a more urgent concern came to mind. "Juaren, there's something out there. Outside. I saw it last night."

The pupils of his grey eyes contracted sharply. He straightened, frowning. "You were outside?"

"Yes, while you were asleep. And there was an animal—" She stopped herself. An animal? What did that mean? She had seen watching eyes, then a running form. But she had seen creatures aboard the *Narsid* she would have called animals just a season ago, and Verra had called them human. "I took the starsilk out to sing," she said more slowly. "It—whatever it was—was watching me from the brush. I startled it when—"

Her disjointed account was interrupted by a cry from outside the ship. Reyna stared dumbly as Juaren jumped up and disappeared down the ramp. She sat and forced herself to her feet.

By the time she reached the door, Juaren and Verra were stepping up the ramp, Verra cradling a familiar object in her palm. Her face was pale, her hand trembling.

"It's not poisonous," Reyna assured her quickly. "One of them stung me last night. Here—" She pushed up the sleeve of her tunic and looked with surprise at the red welt on her shoulder. The flesh was tender and hot. At the center of the welt was a core of infection. She touched it gingerly. "It wasn't so bad last night," she said lamely.

Juaren examined the welt. "This is the same kind of insect that stung you?"

Reyna nodded. "I didn't have anything to put on the sting. I thought—I thought it would be all right." At least she had thought that after her initial panic.

Some of the color returned to Verra's face. She stepped to the pharmaceutical cabinet and dropped the dead insect on the counter surface, laughing unsteadily. "I've been too long on Brakrath. I saw the nest in the tree, and I saw insects crawling near it, but it didn't occur to me that they could fly. I'd better treat us both right away."

When she had dabbed Reyna's wound and her own and they had made a quick meal, Verra sat down briefly at her console. "The air analysis was complete before the auto-lock released the door, of course. But there is some additional information the an-system logged in before we were wakened—"

"This place doesn't look anything like what Danior saw when he used the pairing stone," Reyna said doubtfully, gazing out the ship's door. There were no tall trees, no bright silks, only broad expanses of brush and grass.

Verra nodded, tapping at the console, glancing quickly at the data that flickered across the screen. "Danior described the night sky in just enough detail that our ship's system was able to calculate the location

of the forested area he described. It used its own discretion in setting
us down half a day's walk from there. If we were using the skimmer,
we could cover that distance in a matter of minutes. In fact, if we were
to break out the lift-packs—"

Reyna frowned, wondering if her reluctance to use Arnimi equipment
in her search for Birnam Rauth was simply a part of her prejudice. "We
can walk that far," she said.

"Easily," Juaren confirmed. "And we'll learn more on foot."

Verra capitulated without argument. "The lift-packs are fine on unfamiliar terrain if you're using sensory instrumentation to gather basic
data. Since you prefer not to use instrumentation—" She ran a hand
back through her hair. "I do want to take the translator so we'll have
the ability to communicate in Birnam Rauth's dominant tongue."

Reyna glanced at her sharply, wondering if she heard some lack of
conviction in the words. Did Verra doubt they would find Birnam Rauth?
Did she doubt they would even learn what had happened to him here?
Quickly Reyna glanced at Juaren, wondering for the first time what his
expectations were.

And her own? What were her own expectations? She found she did
not want to examine them. Not today. Not with the sense of presence
the silk's song had raised so fresh and haunting.

It was late morning when they locked the ship behind them and made
a wide circle around the misshapen tree. By daylight they could see
papery insect warrens in its spindly upper branches. Reyna clutched her
pike and tried to ignore the crawling of her skin. Her pack weighed
lightly on her back. Verra had persuaded them to bring a single lift-
pack as insurance against emergency. They had bundled their food-
stocks, spare clothing and other necessities together and strapped the
load to the lift-pack. It floated behind them, programmed to follow.

The midday sun was yellow-bright. As they walked, Reyna could
smell the warmth it gave the soil and vegetation. The grass was thick
and darkly green, but the trees they passed were twisted and spindly,
infested with flying insects.

They walked single-file through the grass and brush. Reyna wore
the starsilk at her waist, ends tucked in. She had to discipline herself
not to rub the itching welt on her shoulder. She had to discipline herself

against apprehension too. The land was so broad, so empty.

Juaren at least was at ease, more so than she had seen him before, although he moved watchfully. And lightly. Reyna looked for the print of his boots on the soil and couldn't find it. She found her own prints though, and she found Verra's.

Juaren was the one who sighted the small stream cutting its way between brush and tree-grown banks. He called a halt and they studied the glint of water from a judicious distance.

"I'd like to test it, to see if its drinkable," Verra said doubtfully.

Juaren narrowed grey eyes at the trees that lined the banks. Their frail upper limbs were bowed with insect nests. There was the bright iridescence of wings in the air. He frowned, endorsing Verra's doubt. "What do you think, Reyna?"

Reyna's hand tightened on the pike and her shoulder began to itch again. "If our supplies run out and we don't find water anywhere else—"

"Then we'll take the chance," Verra agreed. She rubbed her arm distractedly.

By mutual consent, they avoided the strand of tree-shaded water that laced across the plain and gave wide berth to the scattered trees. In the early afternoon, when they stopped to eat, Juaren wandered away and returned frowning and distracted. Studying him, Reyna found her own appetite shrinking. If Juaren was disturbed, there must be something here to be wary of. But she saw nothing. And the unfamiliar brightness of the sun, the emptiness of the terrain made her increasingly uneasy. Boarding the *Narsid*, she had worried that she didn't know the language, the customs, the ordinary courtesies of the people she would encounter there.

Here, beyond last night's fleeting glimpse of a running form, there was no sign of habitation. There was only a profound emptiness, as if they had come to a land without legend or history, a land that had no one to articulate the drama of its seasons and give story to its natural features.

Was that why Juaren had grown so silent? Because he felt the emptiness of the land as she did? Reyna studied him uneasily as they resumed their trek. He took the lead, walking briskly, not glancing back. His gaze flickered everywhere, and although there had been desultory conversation earlier, he no longer spoke. He no longer pointed out plant specimens or responded when Reyna or Verra did. Soon they fell into silence too.

Later that afternoon the twisted trees grew in clumps and small groves. Once the wind rose from a clear sky, sweeping a cloud of flying insects toward them. They swatted and fanned until the insects were dispersed.

Soon after that they saw the shadow of the forest on the horizon. Juaren halted abruptly, without word. He gazed toward the tall trees, then studied the horizon in every direction. "I'll go ahead alone," he said finally. The words were distracted, as if they relayed a decision he had made much earlier. "That animal you saw last night, Reyna, and the tracks I've seen today—"

That jarred her. "Tracks?" Was that why he had been so distant? But she had not seen tracks.

He didn't seem to notice her surprise. "There are traces of small game, of course. But the others—they're large, almost as heavy as we are. They move on two limbs some of the time, on four other times. I wouldn't call the print of the front extremities footprints. They're smaller, better articulated, and they have opposing thumbs." He shielded his eyes against the sun, seeming to notice her frown for the first time. "The only animals on Brakrath that have opposed thumbs are humans and minx."

Reyna chilled. She had never encountered a minx, but she had heard tales of their deadly intelligence, of the way they gamed with their prey before striking. Had the creature last night been waiting to play some obscure game with her?

If so, it had not. Instead it had run. "I—I didn't see tracks," she said. "And I don't see why you should go into the trees alone. I—"

"Here—" Without asking, he took the pike from her hand. "Tell me how many signs of game you see from here. Turn a full circle and tell me."

She wanted to argue. This was no fair test; she was not a hunter. Instead she acquiesced, turning completely around, studying the ground intently. She saw nothing.

"That's why I want to go first, alone," he said. Extending her pike, he began to point out disturbed soil, bent grass, a crushed insect imbedded in the dry thatch beneath a clump of brush, all signs so minute she had difficulty seeing them. "I've trained myself to see these things, and I've trained myself to go places where you can't go—not if you want to pass unnoticed. Not if you want to observe without disturbing."

She frowned, knowing what he said was true—and still not liking it. Not liking him to go alone either, to a place they knew so little about. "How long will you be gone?" she asked finally.

"I'll try to be back by moonrise. It may be longer."

"We'll wait here," Verra said, touching Reyna's arm in a reassuring gesture that made Reyna stiffen again.

They both watched as he continued on alone, walking even more briskly then before. At first his path took him nearer the stream. Then he veered away, and soon they could see him no longer. They could only see the shadowy smudge of the forest on the horizon.

Moonrise. How many hours would that be? Juaren had taken the trouble to provide himself with information from the data console before leaving the ship. "How long will he be gone?" Reyna said finally, sorry she had not paid better attention in the last hours before stasis, when Verra had instructed them both in the function of the data console and the use of the translator that made filed information accessible verbally in their own language.

"Five or six hours, I think. It will be dark in two. Are you tired?"

"A little," Reyna admitted.

"Sleep if you want and I'll watch. Then I can catch a nap while you watch."

Reyna hesitated, not wanting to be deferred to. "If you want to sleep first—"

"No, I just want to sit quietly for a while and think my thoughts." Verra touched the controls of the hovering lift-pack and it dropped their possessions gently to the ground.

Understanding, Reyna unpacked bedding and lay down in the grass. She had thoughts to think too. Closing her eyes, she tried to sort the various strands of her mood: doubt, uncertainty, mistrust—of herself, of her own judgment. What if she had brought Juaren and Verra here to no purpose? What if they found no sign of Birnam Rauth? What if they could not learn what had happened to him or how his voice had come to speak from the starsilk? She rolled over, pressing her face to the warm grass, and tried to find some conviction that he was here, perhaps even alive. As she fell asleep, she seemed to hear his song again, lonely and questioning.

. Finally she slept. When she woke, it was dark and she knew immediately that she was alone. She sat and drew a shallow breath, listening over the beat of her heart to the darkness that surrounded her. "Verra?"

There was no answer. Shakily she stood, her heart racing now. "Verra?" The sky was clear, bright with stars, but their light was not sufficient to banish the shadows of the plain. Distractedly she stroked the starsilk, pulling one end free. It murmured as it caught the breeze. "Verra?" she called again, more loudly.

"Reyna—here." The answer was faint, cautious.

Relieved, Reyna picked her way toward the sound. Verra crouched near a clump of brush, bending over a dark shape stretched in the grass. Reyna halted. "What—what is it?" As she stared down, the shape began to take form: a long emaciated body, four limbs, a head thrown sharply back, eyes—she couldn't tell their color—staring and blank. Reluctantly she knelt and touched dark fur. The flesh beneath it hadn't yet begun to cool into rigidity.

"I don't know. But apparently she gave birth recently. She's mammalian, and the milk sacs are engorged. I heard a sound—" Gently Verra picked up one limp limb and stroked the foot.

But it was more hand than foot, Reyna saw, long-fingered, black-clawed, with an oddly jointed thumb. Looking more closely, Reyna saw that the arm was sparsely furred, bare in spots. And there were familiar looking welts, larger than the one on her shoulder, far more angrily infected, some of them abscessed. Carefully she pressed the flesh of the arm. There was no fatty layer. The muscle was wasted. She looked down into the shadowy face. "Is she—could she be human?" There had been humans aboard the *Narsid* who were furred, humans she would not have recognized as such if she had met them on a mountain trail instead of in a ship's corridor.

Verra shook her head. "No. She's not from our family. She's far more like *Chatnus Maior*."

Reyna hesitated, hoping Verra would explain. "Like what?"

"Just a classification. I doubt if it means anything here, unless this is an introduced species. There were strains of *Chatnus—Maior and Minor*—exported at the time of Earthexodus. I suppose it's possible this was one of the worlds they were resettled to. I think it's more likely this is a completely independent form." Slowly Verra stood. "She's not long dead, but I don't think it was her voice I heard."

"Her—her child?" Reyna suggested. "If we're quiet—"

They stood for a while in silence, listening. Once Reyna thought she heard the crackle of brush from the direction of the stream. The sound was not repeated, nor was there any other beyond the sounds that came with the breeze. Finally Verra sighed and said, "Nothing. I'd better sleep if we're to walk any farther after Juaren returns."

"I'll watch," Reyna agreed.

Together they covered the body with dried brush and returned to where they had left their bundles. Verra wrapped herself in her bedding and Reyna sat in the grass, arms around her drawn up knees, more aware than ever of the emptiness of the land. She was able to escape a sharp sense of oppression only by listening—listening intently for a lost voice.

It did not come until long after Verra slept, and then it was so faint Reyna thought at first she had imagined it. Wispy, plaintive—she caught the starsilk in one hand and stood, waiting with held breath for the sound to come again. She heard only the rustle of the grass.

Then, in the distance, she heard the voice again, weakly. Sparing a single glance for Verra, she slipped away, choosing her direction by instinct.

She moved soft-footed in the direction of the stream, and when the plaint came again, it seemed nearer. Reyna hesitated, wanting to answer it, wanting to call out some reassurance. But what could she say to reassure a child who was not human? If she spoke, she might frighten it into total silence.

And if it were not a child, if it were something else, an animal of prey, calling softly—

She refused to consider that. The voice was lost and small. She continued picking her way toward it.

She continued picking her way until she realized that the plaint came from a cluster of trees growing near the stream. She hesitated, imagining the flutter of lacy wings against her face, imagining other things even less benign. She did not know what might live in the shadows. Certainly she did not know that if she met another like the animal that had died, it would recognize her good intentions.

If this were an infant, perhaps it wasn't even the dead animal's offspring. Perhaps it had parents of its own, ready to defend it.

She considered that possibility as her feet carried her forward again. She considered it as she entered the shadow of the trees and fanned at the insects that fluttered softly against her face. She considered it when the whimpering became suddenly very near and she found herself kneeling over not one but two tiny forms. They wriggled helplessly at her feet, pressing weakly against her, apparently drawn to her warmth. She could not see them clearly in the dark, but her probing fingers told her they were smaller than human infants, that they wore coats of soft fur, and that they were pitifully frail. They carried little more spare flesh than the animal Verra had found dead, and their skins were savagely welted.

Reyna fanned angrily at the insects that clouded around her, stifling a cry as one stung her neck. There was no time to wonder if these were orphans or if they had a parent who might return. Quickly she scooped up the tiny creatures and dodged from beneath the trees.

The insects followed her a short distance, stinging again at her neck and arms and at the tiny creatures she carried. When she escaped them, she paused briefly to cradle the tiny creatures more securely. One of them snuggled against her willingly. The other struggled weakly, scratching at her with feeble claws, suddenly coughing as if it would choke. It felt warmer than the other, fever-hot, and its limbs were more frail.

When she reached the place where Verra slept, Reyna knelt and laid the two little creatures on her bedding. Starlight was brighter here, where there were no trees to obstruct it. She examined the creatures, stroking their small limbs, their tiny heads. They were clearly of the same kind as the creature she and Verra had buried under dried brush. And they were surely very young, perhaps only days old. What was she to do with them? What did they need? The smaller one choked again, its tiny limbs drawing up in spasms, and Reyna had the helpless feeling that she could never give it what it needed. She touched the other and it caught her finger in its mouth and began to suck.

Verra woke as she fumbled through the supply bags. "What is it?" Her voice was thick with sleep.

"I found them," Reyna said distractedly. "But I don't know what to do. I don't know what to give them." Medicines? Food? Could they digest human food? Did she dare use the same ointment on their insect bites that she and Verra had used on their own? She rubbed at her fresh bites, wishing she knew.

"You found them?" Verra sat, her voice alert now. She made her way quickly to Reyna's bedding and bent over the two creatures, examining them. "One healthy, or relatively so, one sick," she said. "I think we should separate them. Here—we have some extra blankets. We'd better wrap the smallest and set it aside."

"And not take care of it?" Reyna demanded in alarm. As if she knew how to care for the helpless creature.

"I don't think it can eat, Reyna. And I doubt that we have any medicines that would be helpful. I don't know that we can do much beyond keeping it warm."

"And the other one? I can thicken some water with starch concentrate. Or I can use the protein granules—"

Verra had taken an extra blanket from their bundles and was wrapping the smaller creature in it. "Cubs, I think. On Arnim, these would be cubs."

"You *have* seen animals like them?" Reyna demanded sharply. She watched tensely as the smaller creature began choking again, its tiny body caught in spasms.

"I've seen chatni. A species we imported from Old Earth. There are points of similarity to these creatures." She cradled the creature as it stopped choking and began a gasping struggle for breath. "Why don't you try plain water first. See if it can take it from a spoon or your fingertip. I'll see if this one can take a few drops."

Reyna found her cub could take water from a spoon and licked eagerly at her finger when she first dampened it, then dipped it in protein granules. It seemed to wink up at her from slitted yellow eyes as it sucked her fingertip. And despite its frailty, she thought she caught a sharp-toothed grin on its face when it first tasted starch concentrate.

She became so absorbed in its care that she didn't notice when the air grew cool, when the moon rose. She didn't notice when Verra set aside the smaller cub and briefly bowed her head. Only when her own cub lapsed abruptly into satisfied sleep did she realize that the smaller cub lay still in the same way its mother had earlier.

Verra shrugged, but moonlight caught the glint of tears in her eyes. "There was nothing we could do."

Nothing they could do—and, Reyna realized abruptly, the moon was in the sky. She stood and peered across the silver-lit plain. "Juaren hasn't come back."

"No," Verra said.

Was there nothing they could do about that either? Reyna found her lips suddenly dry. "Do you think one of us should go to find him? If something has happened—"

"I think we should wait right here, as we said we would," Verra said quietly. "He's found his way across the peaks in winter. He'll find his way back here."

"Of course," Reyna echoed, but the words were faint and there was a tremor in her hands as she stroked the sleeping cub. Because if Juaren didn't find his way back, if something happened to him before they had the chance to talk again, if something happened to him on this search she had initiated—

This unwise search? This ill-considered search? Reyna choked back sudden fear. She had known from the beginning that something might happen to her, that she might never find her way back to Brakrath. But if something happened to Juaren or Verra simply because they had accompanied her—

"I thought it would be simple," she said, more to herself than to Verra. "We'd come here, we'd find—whatever there is to find—"

Her voice trailed away. Nothing had been simple at all. They had come and she had listened to Birnam Rauth's song, but she had no idea how to begin her search. She had no idea how to find him. Now Juaren had gone to the forest and hadn't come back, and she held a sleeping cub in her arms, a responsibility she didn't know how to meet. And she didn't even know which of the stars she saw tonight shone on Brakrath or whether it was morning or night in the Valley Terlath. She shook her head mutely.

"It's never simple," Verra assured her. "Never. But Juaren will find his way back, and so will we."

Words. Easy to speak, suddenly painfully difficult to believe. Reyna touched the silk at her waist and understood better some of the things she had heard in Birnam Rauth's song the night before. Her own song was beginning to rise again, silently, full of the same things: doubt, solitude, fear. She listened to it as she cradled the sleeping cub and prayed for Juaren to find his way back.

TEN
REYNA

Later Reyna didn't remember when she abandoned her vigil and fell asleep. The cub woke twice as she sat watching and whimpered until she fed it. The first time it quickly fell asleep again. The second time it squirmed restlessly in her arms, its slit eyes gleaming with some incomprehensible reproach. Instinctively she tucked it closer to the warmth of her body, wondering if its untrained senses told it what strangers their two kinds were. Or was it wakeful simply because she had failed, in all ignorance, to provide something it needed?

How could she guess what it required? Perhaps she had fed it too much, perhaps too little; perhaps the things she had given it were wrong. She wondered—had its mother comforted it by rocking? By petting? By crooning? She tried all those things, jiggling the tiny creature and whispering night-songs to its furred ear. It only squirmed with increased irritability, and Verra shifted in her bedding and muttered a sleepy query.

"It's all right. I'm just trying to get it to sleep."

Verra rose on one elbow, rubbing her eyes. "Maybe its nocturnal. Do you want me to take it for a while?"

Nocturnal? Was that why the tiny eyes seemed to grow brighter and more fretful with the moon? "No. I'll wake you later, if I need to." At least the cub's squirming kept her occupied, kept her from glancing toward the forest every time the grass rustled.

Finally the cub fell into an unwilling sleep, abandoning itself in her arms. Reyna cradled it until her shoulders began to ache. Then she laid it down in her bedding and stretched out beside it. She knew she would not sleep, but she did not want the cub to be cold. It had probably never slept alone before.

Nor did it sleep alone that night. Reyna closed her eyes, trying to ease the anxious frown that made her scalp hurt. And she slept, as abruptly, as totally, as unwillingly as the cub.

Later she realized vaguely that she had abandoned her watch and she fought the drowning-depth of sleep, trying to raise feeble eyelids against it. The effort was beyond her. At some point she was aware of quiet movement in the dark, of the sound of whispered words. Someone threw covers over her bare arms. She tried to burrow into them but her body refused to cooperate even to that small degree.

Later still she realized that a chill dawn lay beyond her closed eyelids and that someone lay close beside her. She roused herself enough to roll over, dragging her covers with her. Juaren slept beside her, cocooned in his own bedding, his hair the only brightness in the grey morning. Relieved, Reyna slept again.

It was almost mid-morning before she roused enough to realize that there was no small, furred body warm beside her. Alarmed, she came fully awake and sat, rubbing her eyes.

The cub was gone. And Verra was gone too, as well as the lift-pack. All that remained were herself, Juaren, and the untidy clutter of their possessions. "Juaren?" Her voice held sleep and panic.

He woke in a way she had never seen anyone wake before. He was soundly asleep when she called. A moment later he was sitting beside her, fully awake, not the faintest cloud of sleep in his eyes. "What is it?"

She didn't know whether to be reassured or alarmed by his immediate alertness. "Verra's gone."

He looked at her uncomprehendingly, then frowned, running his fingers through his hair. "Don't you remember? She told you she was going."

"She told me?" What had Verra told her? When?

"She told you she was lifting back to the ship with the cub. She wants to run a few samples through bioanalysis to get some idea of what its dietary requirements are, which of our foods it can use. She woke you and told you. It was just after dawn. You opened your eyes. You nodded."

"I—I don't remember," Reyna said, alarm turning to a feeling of foolishness. "I didn't even know you had come back. I was—" But did she want to tell him that—that she had been anxious for him? Did she want to tell him she had stared for hours into the dark, willing him to emerge? That there had been a frightening emptiness just below her heart when he had not?

Would he believe those things when he had returned to find her curled in her bedding asleep? Embarrassed, she stared down at her feet. "I was tired," she said.

He nodded, but a moment's distracted frown suggested he caught the discrepancy between words and expression. He hesitated briefly, rubbing his jaw, then stood and cast his bedding aside. "Are you hungry?"

"Yes," she agreed, relieved to change the subject. "Juaren, when you went to the forest—" She smoothed the starsilk against her waist, not certain how to begin. She had so many questions, some of them barely formed. "When you went there—"

Juaren glanced toward the distant trees, his eyes catching light from the mid-morning sun. "It was just as your brother told you. The trees, the silks, the moon—you'll see."

"And the—animals?" Could she call them that? Danior had. But she had seen the slender fingers, the jointed thumb the night before. And she imagined she had seen more than animal cunning in the cub's glinting yellow eyes.

"They're there. In the trees." Juaren brushed at his shining white hair and said again, "You'll see."

So he didn't want to tell her. He wanted her to see with her own eyes. Biting her lip, Reyna bent and rolled her bedding. "Will you tell me, at least—did you hear anything like the starsilk?"

He shrugged, folding his bedding into a compact bundle. "I saw white silks, two of them, but neither of them spoke."

Reyna bit her lip. Was that enough to refresh her doubts? Just the fact that he had not heard Birnam Rauth's voice in the trees? She turned and gazed around, taking the measure of the day. The land did not seem so empty this morning. She heard occasional music in the rustle of the grass, in the rattle of dry brush. The smell of the soil was less foreign. Her eyes had even grown accustomed to the yellow-brightness of the sun. It seemed less harsh than the day before. It seemed warm—welcoming.

Or perhaps it was this opportunity to be alone with Juaren she welcomed. Flushing, Reyna secured her bedding and threw it into the pile of their possessions. "I *am* hungry," she said. "There was that package of food Verra said was special—"

Juaren nodded in quick complicity, apparently sharing her sense of occasion. "Let's open it. Let's see what an Arnimi delicacy tastes like."

They dug through the supplies until they found the carton of colorfully wrapped containers that had been processed on Verra's home-world. There was something unexpected in the bright figures that decorated the wrappings and in the artistry of the food itself, in the contrasting delicacy and piquancy of flavors. "I wonder what the Arnimi do when they eat these things?" Reyna mused as they sampled their way through the carton. Did they smile? Did they laugh and sing? She couldn't imagine a group of Arnimi gathered around a festive table, joined in a celebratory mood. Perhaps only wealthy deviants—as Verra had called herself—knew how to enjoy these foods.

Certainly Reyna and Juaren knew. They sampled every container, making a game of trying to decipher the markings on the packages. Soon they were talking about other meals—about delicacies Juaren and Komas had foraged for in the mountains, about festival foods Reyna had helped prepare in the palace kitchen, about meals taken when they were so hungry even the coarsest food tasted as if it had been prepared for the festival board.

But eventually the meal was done, the carton was repacked, and they both knew the time for laughing was past. They sat in the grass and Reyna glanced toward the dark line that was the forest and said, "I want to learn to track. Like you do." Yesterday had taught her that. She did not want to walk blind again, through this world or any other. She wanted to learn to read the ground, she wanted to learn to use the Arnimi data console, she wanted to learn whatever might be necessary.

Juaren's white brows drew together and he spoke sharply. "Why?"

"I want to see what you see," she said, surprised at his reaction. "I want to know what has passed, the way you did yesterday." She didn't want to feel foolish again—or small, or unprepared.

But he did not seem pleased. He gazed at her with guarded eyes, then glanced away and rubbed his lips with the back of one hand. "You can always ask me. I told you what I saw yesterday, didn't I?"

"Yes, but there are things I need to know for myself. I intended to learn them anyway, before I made my challenge, some of them." Every palace daughter learned to read the prints of the mountain predators from the soil. In the last weeks before she made her challenge, every palace daughter learned to track a breeterlik to its den or a crag-charger to its lair.

"You intended to learn them from shepherds and lens tenders. Not from a hunter."

"Of course. We hardly ever see hunters in the valley. But Wollar would have taken me to Terlath and taught me. He taught Aberra and Tanse."

"Wollar is a herder."

"Then you can teach me better," Reyna said, puzzled. The meal, the laughter, the confidences they had shared seemed forgotten. He held himself stiffly, his gaze remote and unsmiling. She didn't understand his reaction at all. Did he think she was incapable of learning? Did he think a crippled herder, too old to follow the herds, was the best teacher she could ask? She glanced at his set face, confusion turning to baffled anger. "Am I asking you to share secrets of some kind?" she demanded. "Is that why you don't want to teach me?"

Abruptly Juaren stared down at the ground, evading her angry gaze. His forefinger traced an obscure figure in the dirt. He stared at it, lips tight, and finally said, "I didn't say I wouldn't teach you. But—" He frowned, seeming to seek passage around some verbal barrier. Quickly, as if he must hurry the words or not speak them at all, he looked up. "Are you willing to apprentice yourself to me for a full turn of seasons? That's what a master hunter demands of any apprentice. When we go back, when we do whatever things we have to do, will you go to the mountains with me for a year?"

"You—you won't teach me otherwise?" she demanded, as confused by his manner as by his words. "You won't teach me how to read the ground if I won't pledge myself to you as an apprentice?" Was that some rule of his guild? And why was it suddenly so difficult for him to speak?

Juaren shifted uncomfortably, staring down again. "I didn't say that."

Then what *had* he said? Reyna didn't try to hide her exasperation. "*You did*. That's what you did say."

"I didn't say I wouldn't teach you," he insisted, the words abrupt, almost angry. "I only asked if you would go with me for a year when we return to Brakrath." He held himself stiffly, returning her angry stare with a challenging frown, a frown of hard intensity. "I've lived in your palace. I've eaten food from your table. I'm asking if you will live in my palace and eat from my table. For a year."

How could he insist he had not said exactly what she had heard him say? How— And then she understood. Suddenly she understood exactly what he asked and why he asked it so clumsily, and she laughed with surprise. He was asking her to pledge herself to him for a year—not as an apprentice but as a year's mate. And he was distant, he was abrupt because he thought she would refuse. "Tell me," she said quickly, because she saw that her laughter had deepened his frown, "would you have asked me to go with you anyway, even if I hadn't asked you to teach me to track?"

"Yes," he said finally, stiffly aloof, obviously wary of her shift of mood. "I decided that a long time ago."

"That you would ask me?"

"That I wanted to ask you."

Perhaps he had even decided it on wood-smoke night, when they had almost danced together. "And is there a price?" she demanded.

His taut features relaxed slightly. "If so, it's your place to ask it. Not mine."

Her place to ask a price from a hunter. That pleased her. "Then I already have. If you will teach me, I'll—I'll live a year in your palace." The mountains. She needed no time to deliberate. She had never thought of taking a mate. That had always been a consideration for the future, more a duty than a fulfillment. But she could taste the cold air already. She could hear the crackle of their cookfire and smell the savor of the things they would cook. They would talk every day as they had talked

today, laughing, learning all the things they held in common. Learning
their differences too. Perhaps at the end of the year, they would decide
to take another year together. Or perhaps they would separate. And if
her mother objected, if her mother was hurt—

"My mother—" she said unwillingly.

He shook his head. "She'll understand."

Slowly Reyna nodded. She would. Her heart had never been with
Juaren, not for more than a few moments, and then only because Iahn
was in the desert. If they brought back news of Birnam Rauth, if her
father returned to the palace, Juaren would mean no more to Khira than
any other man of the halls. Reyna recognized that and glanced up
quickly. "So I've told you my price."

He smiled with obvious relief. "It's exactly the price I had to offer."
He gazed back in the direction of the ship. "I'll begin paying it now if
you're ready to pledge yourself as my apprentice."

"I'm ready."

He hesitated, frowning. "There are obligations. You must commit
the old words to memory. And you must listen to me in everything."

"Oh? Am I obliged to obey?" She spoke teasingly.

He didn't respond to her manner, only to her words. "No, you're
only obliged to listen—but closely."

"I'll listen," she promised, laughing at his seriousness.

He relaxed and, ranging in a circle from their campsite, they studied
the ground together. Juaren used Reyna's pike to point out minute signs
and she tried to guess what they meant. All too often she could not
even see them until she knelt and frowned hard at the ground. Juaren
waited silently, as if she were a blind person trying to find her way—
as if she must be permitted to find it without intrusive assistance. "I
don't understand how you saw anything yesterday," she said finally,
brushing dirt from her knees. "We were walking so fast."

"When you cipher scrolls, do you stop and study each stroke of every
figure individually?"

"No," she said. "But—"

"It's harder to find the meaning of the text that way. I know because
I read that way before Komas taught me to use my eyes quickly, to let
them be a window to let things in quickly, so my brain can find the
patterns and report them to me. At first you must stop and study every

small sign individually. You must suggest to your brain how to interpret it. But later you must walk quickly, you must look quickly—so you can see things whole, not in parts."

See things whole. She frowned, wondering if that weren't the most important part of the lesson. Wondering when she might begin to put it into practice. Quickly her thoughts veered away in a troubling direction. "Juaren—" He had been to the forest. He had seen the silks in the trees. What did he think of their chances of finding Birnam Rauth alive? Of learning anything about him at all?

But he had turned away, gazing toward the horizon. "Verra's coming."

"I don't see anything."

"You're looking too high. She's traveling near the ground."

Verra joined them within minutes, settling gently to the ground and shrugging out of the lift-pack harness. Reyna was momentarily surprised at the brightness of her eyes, at the flush in her cheeks, as if she had found some welcome freedom in flight. She had devised a sling to hold the cub. It curled against her body, leaving her hands free.

"Is it—is he all right?" she asked quickly. "Did you learn what to feed him?"

Verra nodded briskly, rubbing the tiny creature's back. "More. More of everything we're already giving him. Or her. That's a little inconclusive. But he's metabolizing our food well enough for now. There are some trace elements he'll require in higher concentration, but we have a few days' leeway in providing those. Perhaps we'll be able to foster him out when we reach the forest."

Foster him to one of the creatures who lived in the bowers? Reyna nodded, relieved at that suggestion. Such a tiny creature, yet responsibility for him weighed heavily.

And the cub had begun to squirm again. "Hungry," Verra pronounced. "So am I. Have you eaten?"

"Earlier," Reyna said guiltily. "But there's plenty left." At least she and Juaren had left enough of the special Arnimi delicacies for one person to feast on. "I'll feed him while you eat."

"And then you're both going to learn to use the lift-pack," Verra pronounced. "I decided that on my flight back. It won't do us much good to have emergency transportation if I'm the only one who can use it."

Reyna felt herself stiffen, but Juaren responded by retrieving the pack and studying the controls with unqualified interest. "How long will it take to learn?"

"A few minutes ground-training. Then some practice time. I suppose I should have brought another from the ship so I could air-coach you. But you'll catch on quickly enough. And maybe when you've tried it, you'll want to go back to the ship and issue yourselves packs."

"No," Reyna said automatically. But the suggestion was not so unwelcome as it had been the day before. They would be able to move more quickly, they would be able to see the land better if they used the lift-packs. And it was foolish to reject any device just because it was Arnimi. Not if it would help them find Birnam Rauth.

Or not, she admitted reluctantly, if it would help them exhaust the possibilities of the search more quickly. She took the wriggling cub from Verra and stroked its ears. It immediately caught her finger and began to suck.

They sat in a circle in the grass, she dabbing a mixture of water and concentrate powders into the cub's demanding mouth, Verra poking unsmilingly through her small store of delicacies, Juaren watching them both with silent composure. Finally Verra put the last container aside with a small frown of dissatisfaction.

"I'm sorry we ate so much," Reyna said quickly. "We—we should have left more."

"No," Verra said. She smoothed one of the brightly printed wrappers across her thigh, frowning at it. "You should have saved me some laughter. I'm sure you two laughed when you ate these things."

Reyna stiffened. Did Verra think they had mocked the foods she had gone to such trouble to obtain from the *Narsid*'s stores? "They were good. We tried to guess what would be in the packages before we opened them."

"Without much luck, I imagine. I have one more carton in the hold. When we get back to the ship, we'll dine Arnimi style. Then you'll understand. You're not supposed to enjoy these foods. You're supposed to use them to demonstrate how well you've disciplined your palate."

Reyna frowned, not sure she understood. "How—how would we do that?"

"By not laughing, first of all. By sitting severely, by addressing your entire attention to each bite. By speaking to no one except to find fault with the food."

"But there wasn't anything wrong with the food."

Verra laughed sharply. "Of course there was, although my tongue has gone so stale—or I've spent so much time in the wrong company—that I enjoyed it too. Even the spondiloni, which was overcooked and far too aggressively seasoned."

"Is that what an Arnimi feast is like?" Reyna demanded incredulously. "Do the people come to find what's wrong with the food?" Not for the warmth, not for the companionship, not for the laughing and telling of tales? But to criticize each bite, finding minute fault with it?

Verra laughed. "Let's not call it a feast. Such a good word. We shouldn't contaminate it. And it looks like our small friend has finished his feast. Or hers."

Reyna looked down. The cub had fallen abruptly asleep again. It lay in a posture of abandon in her arms, wearing a sticky mustache, legs sprawling. "You'd better teach Juaren to use the lift-pack first," Reyna suggested.

"Yes. Our ward will wake thinking of his stomach if we move him too soon," Verra agreed.

Whatever her concerns, Reyna found it peaceful to sit in the sun with the cub sleeping in her arms while Juaren glided over the grasslands. Reyna tensed the first time he lifted. But he waved as he swept past and she saw pleasure and concentration in his face and knew Verra had won her point.

It was early afternoon by the time Reyna's turn came. She learned the lift-pack controls easily and then, breathless with fright and anticipation, she looked down and watched her boots slowly lift from the ground. At first, when she hung in the air, she thought she would forget how to use the controls and drift helplessly away. But Verra was calling to her—laughing and waving, running after her—and she managed to manipulate the controls as she had been instructed. Soon she was gliding over the grasslands with the same exhilaration she had seen in Juaren's face.

She practiced until mid-afternoon, occasionally taking turns with Juaren. Then they all gathered again to lay plans. "Moonrise is the best time to go into the trees," Juaren said. He had taken a turn feeding the cub. Now he cradled it, rubbing its ears absently. "We can look around then without disturbing the—what did you call them, Verra?"

"Chatni. It suits them even if it isn't accurate—even if they're something else entirely."

"Yes. We can look around without disturbing the chatni then. They'll be in their bowers. And we'll be able to find our way by moonlight."

"The—the chatni aren't nocturnal?" Reyna demanded.

"Not that I noticed."

So perhaps the cub had been wakeful the night before only because he was hungry. "And the insects—" Unconsciously Reyna rubbed the unhealed welt on her shoulder.

"I saw no sign of them in the forest." Jauren's glance flicked to the lift-pack. "I'll make the run back to the ship this time, Verra. Are there enough packs in the hold for each of us to use one and keep this one for our bedding and supplies?"

"We were issued five." At his questioning look, she went on, "One for utility purposes, one for each of us, one for Birnam Rauth. If we find him."

If. Reyna didn't miss the qualification. But what had she expected? She smoothed the starsilk against her waist and glanced at Juaren, wondering what qualifications he set against the possibility of finding Birnam Rauth—or even of learning what had become of him. His face told her nothing beyond the fact that he was eager to fly again.

She and Verra passed the rest of the afternoon in desultory activity, Verra studying plant specimens, Reyna discovering that the cub could eat more than she had imagined he could hold and that he liked to have his bulging stomach rubbed. When she indulged him, his eyes narrowed to sleepy slits and he grunted with pleasure. Reyna laughed each time he produced the throaty sound.

They ate again when Juaren returned and then, at his advice, napped briefly. Finally it was moonrise and they buckled into the lift-packs, Verra carrying the cub in the sling she had devised. They rose gently from the ground, their shadows trailing behind.

They flew low, skimming grass and brush, avoiding the spindly trees. At first the trees appeared more frequently, growing in clusters and small groves, lining the winding stream. Then as abruptly as if a line had been drawn across the grasslands, the vegetation changed. Both brush and trees disappeared. The stream emerged naked and ran through the grass—and into the shadow of the forest. Into the shadow of tall white trees that grew in straight ranks, the moon sending down silver shafts among them. Their shadows striped the ground, which was deep with leaf mold. The smell under the tall trees was sharp, fresh. Their arching limbs carried sparse dark foliage.

Reyna, Verra and Juaren settled to the ground within the perimeter of the trees. Reyna peered around in awe. She had not expected them to be so tall, she had not expected them to be so straight. She had not expected them to grow in even ranks, as if they were about to march. The moon seemed to shine more brightly here than it had in the grasslands, creating a gridwork of shadows. Following Juaren's lead, she switched off her lift-pack.

"On foot from here," he whispered, and it seemed appropriate that he did not raise his voice.

Because there was something here she had not found in the grasslands. This, she realized, was a place where legends might live—bright, strange legends like none told in the halls of Brakrath. This was a place where the shadows knew tales and the breeze spoke a new, more sibilant tongue.

They had entered a living forest. She knew that despite the silence around them. She knew that despite the unmoving shadows. Juaren and Verra knew it too. Reyna could tell from the careful way Verra set down her feet, from the wary glint of Juaren's eyes when he glanced back at her. The cub had wakened and for once did not squirm and mewl. He peered silently from his sling, his eyes wider than Reyna had ever seen them, his nostrils damply flared. The evening breeze played with them all, wrapping fingers in their hair and soughing through the trees.

Juaren led the way, walking with a light-footed step, as if he knew exactly where he took them. Reyna followed and soon lost all sense of direction. Only the position of the moon told her they walked deeper into the trees rather than skirting the edges of the forest. Occasionally the stream laced across their path and they waded through it. Once they paused for silent moments in a grassy dell. There were no insects in the air and no sign of their papery nests in the trees.

They heard the singing long before they saw the silks in the trees.

It reached them faintly at first, a single voice that shone through the trees like light given voice. They halted, pressing close together, and a tingling chill passed up Reyna's spine. Silently she slipped her hand into Juaren's. The warmth of his fingers was welcome as they continued on, following the sound.

It grew sweeter as they neared it, clearer and less lonely. And the first voice was joined by others, some near, some distant, all singing wordlessly, each voice separate and distinctive. Hearing them, Reyna had a sense of brightness and color, as if she listened to a rainbow given voice. And she had an increasing sense of unreality. Her footsteps seemed to fall away soundlessly, as if she walked without touching the ground, as if the lift-pack still buoyed her.

They pressed farther. They crossed a wide clearing, deep-grown in grass. Early dew dampened Reyna's boots and chilled her feet. She didn't notice because Juaren's hand tightened on hers and with a floating sense of detachment she looked up and saw bowers blossoming in the white-trunked trees beyond the clearing. Their walls were made of tight-stretched silks of every color: amber, yellow, lilac; scarlet, emerald, gold; azure, chartreuse, red. Moonlight fell through the silks and made their colors luminous, living.

Reyna caught her breath, staring up. There were silks in the trees and their colors were so vivid, her sense of reality so distorted that she felt she could rise weightlessly and touch them. She felt she could float among the silks, singing her own song, a song of wordless joy. But Juaren held her hand, anchoring her, and they walked on.

Cautiously they made their way through the singing forest, no one raising any cry against their intrusion. They stopped often to watch the silks ripple against the breeze, fluttering and twisting in the moonlight. Occasionally Reyna saw a long-limbed shadow silhouetted against the silken walls of a bower. From some bowers two or three silks fluttered loose, raising their wordless song. From others none sang. Narrowing her eyes, gazing up, Reyna saw that there were smaller bowers in the upper branches of the trees. The silks that formed their walls were duller than those that enclosed the lower bowers and none of them reached for the breeze. None of them sang.

The trees seemed to grow in broad avenues. They made Reyna think of the stone avenues of Valley Terlath, wide and empty except when the people were coming home from the fields or when the herders drove their flocks to pasture. Juaren guided them from shadow to shadow. Reyna emulated his light-footed step—not difficult when she felt she might easily rise upon the current of silken voices. Verra followed them both, holding the cub close against her chest, one finger tucked into its mouth to quiet it.

Several times as they moved from shadow to shadow they heard the rustle of brush nearby. Once Reyna glanced down and saw winking black eyes peering from a burrow. When her shadow fell across the mouth of the burrow, its inhabitant vanished, throwing back dirt to close the aperture in the ground.

Then two things happened at once, two things that banished Reyna's enchantment and made her skin draw tight. At some sign she did not perceive, Juaren halted, gripping her hand tightly, and pulled her deep into the shadows. She caught her breath, suppressing a startled question, and followed his pointing finger.

A dark-furred creature stood peering down from its bower, moonlight haloing it with light. As clearly as if it were daylight, Reyna saw the creature: oblique yellow eyes, small sharp teeth, pointed ears, and gleaming black claws. And she saw more. She saw the muscle that rippled smoothly beneath the chestnut fur. She saw the acuteness of the eyes, the flare of the nostrils, the prick of the ears—and her thoughts took an instinctive leap.

A hunter—this was not some enchanted creature. This was not a creature that lived on song and light. This was a creature that tore flesh—a predator. That was clear in the sinuous way it moved as it released an amber silk to sing. That was clear in the set of the graceful, compactly formed head upon the long, slender neck, in the gleam of teeth and claws. This was a hunting animal, and it gazed directly at her.

Before Reyna realized that the creature did not see her, did not see any of them, so deeply were they submerged in shadow, the second thing happened. A starsilk raised its voice from the distant trees, singing the lonely song she knew so well—and speaking the words she knew just as well. She froze into breathless immobility as the familiar syllables called through the trees.

Come for me. Let me go. Set me free.

My name is Birnam Rauth and my thoughts are recorded. If you hear them, come for me.

Come for me.

Caught, she listened to the voice that had called her across the stars. She listened to the words that had brought her here—to the words she had not been able to forget or disregard.

Come for me.

Set me free.

She listened and the hair at the back of her neck rose. Her spine chilled and her heart became stone in her chest, crowding out breath. For the first time she felt the full reality of what she heard—felt it in the hollows of her heart, in the pit of her stomach, in the tingling tips of her fingers and toes.

More than a century ago, a man named Birnam Rauth had walked here, down these same tree-grown avenues. A man named Birnam Rauth had left his heelmarks upon this soil. A man named Birnam Rauth, whose voice was her father's voice, whose face, whose eyes were her father's too. Birnam Rauth had stood under these very trees, looking up at the dark-furred hunters in their bowers, listening to the song of the silks. Perhaps he had felt the same floating sense of enchantment she felt now.

If so, his wonder had turned to something else. And now his voice pleaded through the moonlit trees. *I'm held here. I don't know how.*

Set me free.

Reyna drew an aching breath, feeling Birnam Rauth's plea as a pain in her chest. Whatever had befallen him had befallen him here. He had come here to explore. He had been drawn to the forest by the magic of the silks—and he had been trapped, imprisoned...held. Perhaps by dark-furred hunters like the one they stared up at. Perhaps by something else that lived in the forest, something they had not glimpsed yet. Tensely Reyna glanced at the cub. Its yellow eyes were open wide. Did she see something feral in its gaze? Its claws—so tiny, so sharp. It had only milk-teeth, but she knew now what its adult teeth would look like. They would be white and gleaming, tearing-sharp.

Birnam Rauth—his blood ran in her veins, his voice pleaded from the trees. Something had happened to him here. He had come and never returned. And now she, Juaren and Verra walked under the same trees. She, Juaren and Verra opened themselves to the same danger, seen or unseen. The bright colors, the silken songs—they didn't make her senses float now. They made her heart shrink and her breath grow tight in her chest.

ELEVEN
TSUUKA

Tsuuka never toyed with game. When she took prey, she dispatched it quickly, with a clean blow of her claws or a hard shake of her head. Nor did she ever tease her young. She never hid from them and watched to see them cry. She never dawdled fresh meat before their noses and then withdrew it, making them leap and bat hungry claws for it. Nor had she ever torn a neighbor's silk or spoken gruffly to a neighbor's cub or exercised any other form of spite. But tonight she tortured the azure silk—the silk she had chosen to share her most intimate thoughts with—deliberately, knowingly, with calculated cruelty. And she did so without remorse, because any distress she visited upon the silk was small compared to her own.

Stingers... She had gone to the heart of the trees again the night before, moving as a shadow did at moonrise, stretching herself silently across the ground. She met neither sithi nor spinner as she went. Nor did she see any sign of the red master-silk as she took up watch in the dense shadows at the base of a moss-trunked giant. For a long while she crouched there, hearing only the slow rush of her own blood and the woody creaking of heavy branches. Sometimes the shadows seemed to shift and she glanced around uneasily but saw nothing.

Then clouds cleared from the moon and the red silk billowed from some hidden place and flirted through the trees. Tsuuka stared up, breath held, every muscle quivering. The silk rippled through the trees like a streak of fugitive sunlight, too restless to stay long in any one place. Sometimes it clung to distant upper branches. Other times it descended and brushed against mossed trunks, its fiery song deepening to a moan. Tsuuka crouched, aching with sustained alertness, until finally the silk fluttered low and tangled itself in the lower branches of the very tree she hid beneath.

Tsuuka didn't waste the barest fraction of a second in deliberation. She had come to take the silk. Every nerve was primed, every muscle ready. And so she sprang, digging sharp claws into the mossy trunk, bolting up the tree.

Swift as she was, the silk was swifter. Tsuuka's fingertips brushed it, her claws snagged it, but the silk tore itself away, its voice rising angrily. Then, before Tsuuka could pursue it up the tree, wood resonated under her claws and spinners boiled not just from the tree she clung to but from other trees as well. She stared around in shock. She had come so silently. She had waited in such shadowed stillness. She had not moved except in the split seconds of her spring. But spinners shrilled at her from a dozen branches, their witless eyes wide with fury. And among them were the ones she had seen before—spinners with stingers.

Spinners with stingers—and they had matured visibly since the afternoon before. Their tiny limbs were sturdier, their flesh denser. Their stingers had acquired a layer of horn, making the point crueler. Their voices held a new, more vehement warning, mindless and shrill.

Tsuuka stared for bare moments into their depthless eyes. Then instinct moved her and she skidded down the tree, dropped to fours and plunged away. Fear—atavistic fear—drove her so hard she didn't consider where she was running or why. The blood of terror pounded in her ears.

But even as she ran she was aware of the burn of the red master-silk upon her fingertips. She had touched the silk. Her claws had torn it. If she had been an instant swifter— Her thoughts stopped there and swiftly changed course. If she had caught the red silk, would she be running free now? Or would the spinners have spit sticky silk at her, binding her, paralyzing her?

Spinners with stingers. It was so wrong her mind rebelled. Spinners were witless creatures, without guile or defense. They fed on insects and tree-boils, those hard-shelled nodules of sap that formed on tree trunks wherever bark-borers did their work. They had neither claws nor teeth—nor any other defense. Confronted with danger, all they could do was scream until some sithi heard and came to repel the aggressor.

At least that was the reality Tsuuka had always known. Spinners were weak and sithi strong, spinners helpless, sithi their protectors. But now she had run in terror from spinners—not once but twice.

Who could tell her why? She considered that as she climbed back to her own bower and dropped to her silent-silks to groom away the lingering smell of fear. No matter which of the older sithi she went to, she would hear the same rote warning: she must never go to the heart of the trees; there was something there no sithi must glimpse. That was how her mother had admonished her, and that was how she had admonished her own cubs in turn, understanding the warning no better than her mother had.

But her azure silk, her skysilk—she gazed up at it stretched tight among its sisters. Her silk was born of the spinners. It shared thoughts with them and with the unseen. If there was any agency in the forest that could give her answers, it was the silk.

If it would. If it would listen to her questions and not try to trill them away on the breeze. She growled softly, smoothing down her rumpled fur. She knew what she could expect if she approached it with the usual ceremony in the familiar confines of her bower. She had asked it questions before, and it had evaded them—sweetly, softly, reasonably, leaving her placated but vaguely unsatisfied. But if she took it to some unfamiliar place, if she let it feel her claws—

Because she would not be evaded this time. Nor would she be lulled by silent whispers or meaningless melodies. Ignorance and fear had robbed her of Maiilin; they would not rob her of Dariim as well.

She considered the matter the next day as she watched her cubs play and she laid her plans. That night—*this night*—she approached the azure silk silently at moonrise. She loosed it from the bower poles, refusing to identify herself, ignoring its increasingly agitated queries. The silk knew well enough who she was. It was only her uncharacteristic silence that made it shiver with doubt. That and the fact that she had loosened both its ends, as she had never done before. All around her, its sister silks knew something was amiss and they strained at their poles, trying to find slack to tune their anxious voices. She hardened herself against their silent confusion.

The skyswath bundled under one arm, Tsuuka glanced cursorily into Paalan and Kaliir's bower. They snored softly in a tangle of furred limbs. She peered in upon Dariim and Falett, silencing their evening-whispers with a meaningful growl. Then she slipped to the ground and carried the swath through the forest, speaking silently as she went. *You are going to tell me things tonight, skyswath. I have been ignorant long enough. Now I will learn. You will teach me tonight.*

She could scarcely number the things she must know. Each time she reckoned up a roster of her questions, she discovered others beyond them and upbraided herself. How could she have lived so long in the forest and remained so ignorant? Why had she never looked beyond the lazy routine of hunting and sunning and training her cubs? Why hadn't she shared Maiilin's curiosity?

But Maiilin was a growler now, wit and memory dead. Tsuuka shivered with sudden cold, digging black claws into the skyswath.

She carried the swath to a place she knew where six young trees grew in a closely spaced circle. The forest was silent there. No bowers blossomed for a wide distance around. Tsuuka stepped into the enclosure of trees and shook the azure silk free. Then, before the breeze could take it, she lashed it to the strongest of the six white trunks. She caught its ends, wrapping one around either hand and pulling them tight. *You are going to answer my questions, skyswath,* she said. *Because if you do not, I will leave you here, tied like this. I will leave you alone in this deserted place, without your sisters, with no company but your own.*

Or if your response displeases me, I will do more. I will untie you and throw you on the ground. You are no master-silk. You can rise little higher than the breeze will carry you. If you don't answer me, I'll throw you down and let you crawl on your belly until a bark-shredder or a grass-pup finds you and takes you to line its den. There will be no one here to hear you cry.

There will be no one here to save you and restore you to the trees, silk. Just as no one can restore my sibling's wit.

Just as no one can restore my ignorance, now that I have begun to ask questions.

She felt the silk throb in her hand; she heard the whisper of a plea in her mind. Slowly, slowly she eased the pressure on the taut ends, giving the silk carefully measured slack. *Tell me why there are spinners with stingers in the heart of the trees, silk.*

The silken voice came softly, diffidently, disregarding her question. *Tsuuka? Are you Tsuuka, daughter of Mirala, sibling of Maiilin?*

You know well who I am, silk, Tsuuka said without patience, snapping at the silk, briefly pulling it taut again.

Yes—yes, you are Tsuuka, hunter of the forest, the silk said anxiously when she let it speak again. *You are Tsuuka, who stalks so skillfully, Tsuuka who pounces so lightly. You are—*

Tsuuka snapped again at the silk, this time holding it taut for a longer time. *Silk, I have asked a question, the first of many. And I have told you what I will do if you do not answer. Why do you waste time making talk that amounts to nothing?*

The silk seemed to recoil. *Tsuuka, hunter, tell me please—what other talk do you expect of me? I am not a master-silk with thought and will of its own, drawn from the life-silk of the preserved. I am only a songsilk, little better than a silent-silk.*

You have never called yourself little better than a silent-silk before.

But I speak truly now, Tsuuka, because you have asked and you are the hunter of my bower. You are the one who commanded the spinners to give me life. You are the one who ordered that I have voice. You are the one for whom I sing.

Then use your voice and sing answers for me! Releasing her claws, Tsuuka flexed them, scratching at the slippery fabric. *You have just said something I have never heard before: that the master-silks draw thought and will from the life-silk of the preserved.*

They do, the silk responded wispily. *Tsuuka, they do. That is why they must be secured so carefully. Because they are precious and rare and their making is difficult. The spinners must find special substances to feed themselves with before they can create a master-silk. Then the work is painstaking and long. And when it is done the swath must be mated for three days and three nights with the life-silk of the preserved selected to give it awareness and thought.*

But once all this is done, once the master-silk is created, it has a will of its own characteristic to its kind and separate from the will of the preserved selected to animate it. And its will is to fly in the trees ripping itself on high branches and scarring its filaments by taking too much sun. Left to its own, it soon becomes so worn it carries only a garbled memory of what it took from the life-silk.

You are confusing me, skyswath. What is a life-silk? What is the preserved? Is it a living thing? Is it the thing you call the unseen? I know none of these things. Why have you never spoken of them to me?

The silk shuddered lightly. *How can I answer so many questions, Tsuuka? I am only a songsilk. You have taken me from my sisters, and I must hear their voices. I must sing my song. That is what I was made for—to soothe and please you, not to trouble you with these things.*

Tonight this is your song. What is the preserved? What is the unseen? You've told me so little, silk, that I don't even know how spinners are born. I don't know if they have young they hide in their nests until they are grown. I don't know if they have weanlings they suckle. Among the sithi, there was an estrus cycle. When the season came, those sithi who were ready to bear young chose mates from among their neighbors and petted and coddled them until their bodies underwent the mating change and produced the fertilizing agent. Tsuuka had never observed any such behavior among the spinners. Nor had she ever seen a spinner who appeared immature—before she had climbed the mossy tree.

She growled, suddenly full of chagrin. She who called herself the swiftest and the best, she who boasted the keenness of her senses— there were so many things she had failed to observe, just as there were so many things she had failed to question.

We are the spinners' only offspring, the silk said with soft regret. *My sister silks and I are the children of their glands. They have no young but us.*

How could that be? Tsuuka's forebrow creased, drawing her ears erect. The spinners created the silks—she had seen that. But to call the silks their offspring, to say they had no others—

Tsuuka's grip on the silk tightened. *Are you telling me tales, silk? If the spinners have no offspring but you, why are there always spinners working by the streamside and feeding in the trees? Where do they come from?*

Do you insist upon knowing, Tsuuka?

I insist, silk. With a growl.

The silk murmured a self-effacing plaint. *You are a hunter, as swift as the best, yet you concern yourself with these small matters. Matters so insignificant . . .*

Tell me these small matters!

The silk sighed. *If you must know, Tsuuka. The spinners hatch from the bulb-well. The unseen seeds them there and feeds and tends them until their membranes rupture. Then they take their final feeding from her and they go into the forest to live and to bring food to her in turn. Because they are her offspring and that is the way of it. The spinners feed the unseen and the unseen feeds the new bulbs as they grow.*

So the spinners were the offspring of the unseen. But what was the unseen? Who was the unseen? Tsuuka growled in perplexity. So many questions to be asked. Which were the right ones? *I have seen spinners coming and going in the heart of the trees, silk—where I thought nothing lived.* It was a question, even though she didn't express it so.

The silk recognized it readily enough. *Must you know these things, Tsuuka? We keep them secret because they are so insignificant. They are so uninteresting to a sithi hunter.*

I must know, silk. Be certain of that.

The silk writhed with poorly concealed distress. *Then I will tell you. You are correct. The unseen lives there where the oldest trees grow. The bulb-wells are found in the hollows of the trees. The spinners come and go because they must carry digest to the unseen in their feeding sacs. They nourish her so that she can nourish those who depend upon her.*

The new hatching of spinners. *Then the unseen—the unseen is what no sithi must ever glimpse.*

No sithi must see her, the silk agreed.

And my sibling—Maiilin—

I know it hurts you to speak of your sibling, Tsuuka, the silk said softly.

It hurts me, and I must know. You will tell me. Because if she did not learn what had happened to Maiilin, how could she prevent the same thing from happening to Dariim?

The silk's voice fell to a bare whisper. *I was not spun then, Tsuuka. You had not commanded the spinners to give me life because you were no more than a cub. If I had had voice then, if I had had words to warn you with—*

But you did not.

I did not. And your sibling did not listen to the warning your mother gave her. She thought no harm would come to her because she had gone to the deep trees before without harm. She had looked into the bulb-well.

Let me tell you, Tsuuka—there are *times when a cub can run and climb and hunt there. There are even times—brief times—when she can look down into the bulb-well and see the bulbs rooted to its walls— because at those times the unseen is sheltered in her pulp-bed at the bottom of the well, safe from sight.*

But there are other times when no sithi must walk near those trees, and that was the time your sibling chose to go there.

And so it was spinners who turned her to a growler, Tsuuka said. *Spinners with stingers.*

The silk throbbed silently against the chill air. When she spoke, her voice was wispy, apologetic. *They are called escorts—because they escort the unseen and her successor when they leave the bulb-well. They escort them at times like the one when your sibling chose to visit the deep forest. And you have guessed right. It was their sting that made her a growler, although it was not intended to do that. It was only intended to protect the unseen.*

Against Maiilin? Tsuuka demanded with a growl of anger. *Maiilin didn't go there to do harm. She only went there—*

She only went there because youth and thirst for adventure drove her. You know our nature, silk. We are deadly to game but never to the spinners. Never to you.

You are the protectors of our kind. You make the forest safe so the spinners can go freely and gather food for the unseen, the silk acknowledged meekly. *But there is only one unseen. In this entire quarter of the forest, which stretches so far, there is only one, and only she can seed the bulb-well. Only she can create a successor when she feels her seed sacs begin to dry. Only she can join all our thoughts and direct our lives. And she is not a spinner, my hunter. Not in nature, not in appearance. We dare not rely upon chance and the judgment of a cub—or of any other creature—when she must leave her well. We trust her protection to the instinct of the escorts. They have but one instinct and only she can moderate it, if she is strong enough to do so. Often when the unseen nears the end of her time, she is too weak to do more than trust to the escorts to fulfill their protective function.*

To sting. To paralyze. To deaden—the body for minutes, the mind forever. Tsuuka bowed her head, releasing the skyswath, leaning slack-limbed against a white-trunked tree and letting the weight of responsibility slip from her shoulders. Maiilin's destruction had been only chance. Because only chance had taken them to the deep trees on that day, at that time. She could not have saved her sibling. If she had been brave, if she had not hidden, she would be a growler too.

Slowly Tsuuka raised her head. Moonlight fell silver-bright beyond the circle of trees, but the azure silk did not catch the breeze and reach for it. It hung abjectly. *Silk,* Tsuuka said, realizing she could not stop with her own vindication, realizing what else she must ask next, *tell me one thing more. How can I capture the red master-silk and save my cub from being turned to a growler?*

The silk caught enough breeze to shiver violently. *Tsuuka, my hunter, you cannot. No sithi can own a master-silk. It draws life directly from the life-silk. It carries the full memory of the preserved from which it was drawn—all her joys, all her fears, all the things she learned in the seasons of her life. You cannot tie a master-silk to your bower poles and bid it to sing in harmony with my sister silks and me. It will not. Its voice is no more harmonious than the starsilk's voice. It—*

Silk, I don't care now for harmony, Tsuuka interrupted impatiently. Nor did she care that the silk spoke again of things she didn't understand: the life-silk, the preserved. *If I do not take the master-silk, my cub will go for it again—and again and again. Can you promise me that no harm will come to her in the hunt?*

Tsuuka, hunter—I am just a songsilk. I cannot raise my arms without the help of the breeze. I cannot speak without moonlight. My voice and my awareness come from the master-silk I was bathed with but I carry only the faint voice of thought. I am less than any other creature of my kind except the silent-silks.

Can you promise me? Tsuuka insisted.

I can promise you that if your cub goes to hunt the silk she will meet the escorts. And it will be sooner rather than later. Because the unseen has already remarked the drying of her seed sacs and she has given her successor her last feeding, the one that rouses her from dormancy and stimulates her to maturity. Soon the successor will be ready. Then she must make the pilgrimage from the bulb-well where she hatched to the one where she will seed her own bulbs. And the unseen must emerge to spin her life-silk before her awareness can be preserved in it. That can't be done in the darkness of the well. At both those times, no creature—sithi or other—must go to the heart of the trees. Because the escorts have only one instinct, Tsuuka—to protect the unseen and her successor, and through them all our species.

Apprehension sank black claws into the soft tissue of Tsuuka's heart. Successor, life-silk, unseen... She could not guess the nature of any of them. She could not imagine how they looked or what scent they carried. But she had seen the stingered escorts, and she had seen what they could do. *When—when will these things happen, silk?* Her fingers were cold, her inner voice faltering.

Soon is all I can tell you, Tsuuka, the silk said abjectly. *The time is soon.*

And so Tsuuka knew, as she had known before, that there was only one thing to do. She must capture the red silk herself.

Tonight? Must she go for it tonight? She stroked her fur, trying to find courage. What if she went and did not return? What was to become of her weanlings? Falett and Dariim could look after themselves. Paalan and Kaliir could not. She must provide against the possibility that she might not return.

Bleakly Tsuuka thought of Riifika, whose cubs had been stillborn so recently. If she was to hunt the red silk, she must wake Riifika and ask her to care for Paalan and Kaliir in the event she did not return: to feed and groom them, to discipline and train them, to see them safely to their own tree.

Because if she did not come back from the heart of the trees, she would not sun herself with her offspring again. She would not watch them tear meat, she would not hear their chuckles and growls, she would not monitor their cub games and sparring bouts.

Silk— she said weakly. But she could not ask the skyswath for courage. She had to find that herself.

Tsuuka? Are you Tsuuka?

Yes, I am Tsuuka, and I must go again to the heart of the trees. She said it more to herself than to the silk. Then, before the silk could object, she untied it and folded it beneath one arm.

Her senses seemed overcharged as she made her way back through the trees, as if the energy she dared not invest in thought concentrated in her senses instead. She saw every dark-veined leaf and every white-limned trunk separately, the shattered components of a larger reality. Each scuff of the soil, each animal scent made the hair rise at the back of her neck. She detected the distinctive odor of a grass-puppy and followed its trail to a cluster of bushes. She found the spoor of a bark-shredder and saw a disturbance of the earth where a prickle-hide had dragged some tiny prey to its burrow. Every sensory clue impinged upon her, demanding its brief moment of attention.

Her thoughts were so scattered, her awareness so fragmented that she was unprepared for what occurred next. As she neared the stream, she caught an unfamiliar scent on the soil—sharp, alien, distinctive. Tsuuka froze, nostrils flaring, mouth open. Looking down, she saw the print of feet—but feet like none she had seen before. There were three pairs of them, as long as her own feet and broader. None of them bore the mark of toes. None bore any sign of claws. Stunned, she stared down at them, quelling her first irrational alarm, reassuring herself that this was not the deep forest. These were not the prints of the unseen. There were no escorts waiting here to quench her wit.

But something had passed this way, something that had never entered this quarter of the forest before.

And before she could decide what she must do, she heard its voice nearby—low, controlled, the syllables sharp and unfamiliar. She listened, struck by recognition, paralyzed by it.

The starvoice— The syllables were unfamiliar. The voice itself was different in timbre, in pitch. But this was unmistakably the same kind of voice that spoke from the starsilk.

Slowly Tsuuka's frozen wits thawed and she began to think coherently. There were strangers in the forest, strangers of the same breed as the stranger who spoke from the starsilk. Why? How had they come here? Her blood surged with alarm. Her weanlings, her cubs—

Her mind urged caution, but alarm was stronger and it drove her forward. The murmur of voices and the mark of feet guided her until she found the intruders clustered beside the stream, two standing, the third sitting, bending over a small bundle. Tsuuka stiffened as she slipped near, concealing herself in shadow, and heard a familiar whimper—the whimper of a newborn.

Her pupils flared so sharply she felt the pull of tiny muscles. Three intruders, at once alike and different from one another. One bulkier, more muscular than the others. One—the one who sat—as slight as an adolescent cub, with glossy fur that streamed over her shoulders and down her back. Their features were strange and bare. Their claws were broad, blunt and pink. By moonlight she saw the flash of equally blunt teeth.

Cold gripped her, the cold of uncertainty and fear. What kind of prey did they tear with those teeth? How did they sharpen such awkwardly shaped claws and what use did they make of them? *Why were they here—and why did they have a sithi cub?*

More perplexing still, what must she do? Slip away and rouse her neighbors? Send her own cubs to hide? Who had the intruders stolen the newborn from? Why did it whimper so irritably? Had it been one of her own, she would have called it a milk-cry. But perhaps the intruders had injured it. With one hand she kneaded the skyswath, wishing she could call up its familiar voice for counsel.

Then Tsuuka stiffened as the creature who sat holding the newborn stood. She turned, moonlight falling full upon her, and Tsuuka saw two things. The cub she held was frail and welted with insect stings; it had come from the grasslands, where nightflyers fed. And the slightest intruder wore a familiar band of white at her waist.

Tsuuka bared her teeth in a startled grimace. The intruders had come from the grasslands and they had a starsilk. Where had they obtained it? Who had they taken it from? None of the sithi who lived in the grasslands had silks. No spinners lived there to spin them. And the newborn—

Before she could find answers to any of those perplexities, Tsuuka realized that some unspoken communication had passed among the intruders. At a signal from one of them, all three raised their heads and peered into the shadows where she stood. None spoke, none moved, as strange, round-pupiled eyes found hers. A slow breath rasping in her throat, Tsuuka measured the tension of their limbs against hers. Moonlight glanced off the unfurred surfaces of their faces and exposed a stiffness that could only be fear.

She tried to tear her eyes from theirs and could not. Nor could they evade her staring gaze. Tense, silent, they stared at each other over the short space that separated them. Then the slightest intruder did something entirely unexpected. She stepped forward, her eyes never wavering from Tsuuka's, and extended the frail newborn with both hands. When the newborn caught Tsuuka's scent, its slit eyes widened and it began to squirm.

It wasn't courage that made Tsuuka step forward to take the wriggling cub. It was simple instinct. The cub was squirming so vigorously Tsuuka thought the creature would drop it. She took it only to keep it from harm.

She had not thought either of offering the blue silk in exchange for the newborn. But one of the hands she extended for the cub held the silk and the intruder misunderstood. She relinquished the cub, hesitated, and then with trembling fingers slipped the silk from Tsuuka's grasp. She stepped back quickly, stroking the silk, still watching Tsuuka tensely.

Tsuuka felt a warning growl rise in her throat. But the intruder's round-eyed fear dampened it. That and some quality she saw in the intruder's eyes, some kinship of intelligence. Their two gazes held for moments longer. Then Tsuuka took a single step back into the shadows. The intruder followed suit, retreating swiftly without turning her back. When she stood beside her companions again, all three disappeared quickly into the streamside shadows.

Tsuuka stared for a long time at the place where they had stood, ignoring the hungry whimper of the newborn. She gazed at the print of their feet and tried to understand what had happened, what it meant. She had given the intruder her skysilk, however unwillingly. Just as unwillingly she had taken custody of a grassland cub. She stood listening, wondering if she heard the skysilk calling her, wondering if she heard its anxious voice.

But that was illusion, and she must harden herself against it. She must not let this diversion distract her. There were intruders in the forest but they had not offered harm. The master-silk did, and she must capture it. She must not hesitate and lose courage.

She pulled the squirming newborn close, hissing so loudly in its ear that it twitched, and set out toward Riifika's bower, her heart as heavy as an orphaned cub's.

TWELVE
REYNA

An hour's walk upstream from the spot where they had encountered the chatni, the stream broadened and became shallow, cutting its way between towering trees. The air was heavy with shadow and the smell of dampness. There was no sign of bowers in the trees. Juaren examined the ground by moonlight and found only the prints of small animals. "The chatni don't come here. This looks like the best place for us to sleep."

Reyna sank gratefully into her bedding, her mind ringing with impressions: Birnam Rauth's voice calling through the trees, the creature they had met beside the stream, the glint of its eyes and the tearing-sharpness of its teeth—and balanced against those, something in its gaze that went beyond a predator's shrewdness. Something that suggested a creature that reasoned, however alien its thought processes might be.

The fact that the creature had offered her the blue songsilk in exchange for the cub supported her feeling that she had seen intelligence in its eyes—but an intelligence bounded by different perimeters than her own, an intelligence that must be measured against different standards. And what did that mean? That the chatni offered no danger? Or that she, Juaren and Verra must be doubly wary now that the creatures knew they were in the forest?

Reyna slept uneasily, rousing herself often to listen to the silence of the trees. She kept her hunting blade and her pike beside her.

Light seeped dimly through the tall trees when a scuffling sound nearby woke her. She caught a sharp breath and rose to one elbow, closing anxious fingers around her pike, then blinked in surprise. A tiny, pink-faced creature had emerged from the brush and stared at her with the immobility of shock. Startled, she returned its stare. From a distance, she might have mistaken it for an undersized human infant: pink and bare, with chubby limbs and round face. It stood on two dimpled legs, its bald head tottering unsteadily on its fat neck.

But the resemblance did not bear close examination. The creature's skin was strangely textured, its mouth broad and lipless, and what appeared to be rolls of fat on the neck and abdomen were instead bulging sacs.

Filled with what? Reyna could not guess. It was the creature's eyes that held her, round and dark and vacant, as if they accepted images without comprehending them. "Juaren," she said softly. He slept with his covers pulled over his head. "Juaren!" Carefully, moving deliberately, she turned back her bedding.

She got no farther before the creature reacted. Its eyes widened, its tiny, three-fingered fists clutched, and it emitted a shrill scream, feet firmly planted.

Verra and Juaren woke immediately, snatching at their own weapons. When their initial shock passed, they lowered weapons, glancing at one another in bewilderment. "Where did it come from?" Juaren demanded when the creature continued to shrill.

"I woke up and found it here. It just—I think it just stumbled across us." Reyna had to shout over the creature's din. The sound was like an alarm, strident and penetrating.

Juaren grunted with irritation. "I'm ready for it to stumble away." He rose to his knees, looming over the creature, and clapped his hands.

The creature's eyes flared, becoming still larger, still darker, still more witless. It started so violently it almost toppled backward. For a moment its voice faltered. When Juaren clapped again, it emitted a brief yelping cry. Then, shrilling, it turned and fled, tottering awkwardly on fat pink legs.

Reyna listened to the fading scream, hearing no answering cry from the brush or the trees. Reluctantly, rubbing her eyes, she left the warmth of her bedding and studied the tiny creature's tracks. They were three-toed—familiar. "I don't see others like it here," she said. "But last night, downstream—"

"The ground was covered with tracks like this in the area where we met the chatni. They apparently congregate near the water—but not this far upstream." Juaren joined her, searching the ground in a widening circle. "A few old tracks," he concluded finally. "They don't come here often or in numbers. And they're obviously not dangerous."

That much seemed clear. In fact the tottering pink creature might have amused her if it hadn't screamed with such mindless stridence. Reyna rubbed her arms, trying to warm them. The morning was chill and grey, uninviting. Verra shivered in her blankets, looking no more eager for the day than Reyna felt. Her teeth chattering, Reyna sat and thrust her bare feet back into her bedding to warm them.

But Juaren didn't seem to notice the grey light or the morning chill. He brushed a brisk hand through his white hair. "I want to look a little farther into the trees. I won't be long."

Reyna glanced up in alarm. "Do you think—" Did he think he should go alone? At this hour?

Apparently he did. "I won't be long," he repeated.

Reyna nodded reluctantly. When he had slipped away into the trees, she followed Verra's example, sliding all the way back into her bedding. She curled up, still trying to rub warmth into her arms, but found neither sleep nor comfort. Some vagrant sense of responsibility prodded her. They knew almost nothing about the forest. They didn't know that the chatni were friendly or that there were no other predators. Yet she had let Juaren go into the trees alone, without even his lift-pack.

Perhaps he didn't need the doubtful protection of her company. Perhaps he wouldn't welcome her if she followed him. She knew she could not walk as lightly or watch as quietly as he could. Perhaps she would never train herself to that degree. But finally, hardening herself against the morning chill, she crawled out of her bedding. She splashed her face from the stream, shuddered, and pulled on a clean shift. In deference to the cold, she added a pair of trousers, tucking them into her boots with stiff fingers. Then she gathered up the two lift-packs and shook Verra awake. "Juaren forgot his lift-pack. I'm taking it to him."

The Arnimi woman nodded sleepily and burrowed deeper into her covers.

Wearing one lift-pack, carrying the other, Reyna pressed her fledgling tracking skills into service. The trail Juaren left as he moved downstream was faint, uneven. Sometimes, for short distances, it disappeared entirely. When that happened, Reyna paused and glanced back in the direction she had come, relieved that she had the stream to guide herself by, relieved that there was no wind to make brush rustle and branches sigh, relieved that the forest was still. If she encountered a chatni or if she lost herself trying to find Juaren—

Eventually, of course, she did. She followed the faint track of his boots away from the stream, into the trees, and lost it entirely. Dismayed, she turned a full circle, peering at undisturbed layers of leaf mold. There was no mark, no disturbance, nothing to guide her— nothing to suggest which direction he had taken from this point. She stared at the ground helplessly, as if it had betrayed her.

What must she do? Return to the campsite? Wait for Juaren there? An unattractive option. Surely if she searched in a broad radius from his last discernible print, she would pick up his trail again. Or so she told herself. And if not, at least she would be no more lost than she was now.

Purposefully, decided, she drew a large X in the soil with the toe of her boot. She walked one broad circle around it, then another, studying the soil.

She found nothing. But she continued to search, refusing to admit for a long time that her third and broadest circle had become loose and wandering, that she had lost her own mark as well as Juaren's trail.

Finally, discouraged, beginning to be frightened, she halted and gazed up. The sky was uniformly grey—no help. Nor could she guide herself by the slope of morning shadows. Without sun or moon, there were only vaguely defined pools of grey beneath the trees. And as she stood counseling herself against the first shrill promptings of panic, she realized that somehow all the trees had changed. They had become alike. She stood among endless ranks of identical, sparsely leafed white shafts.

She fingered the controls of her lift-pack, gazing around in growing fright, trying to decide what she must do next. To activate the pack and glide rapidly, randomly through the trees searching for the stream was to admit that she had lost herself.

To fail to do so when she had indeed lost herself was foolish.

Still, stubbornly, she stumbled on, trying to complete her circle—until the moment when Juaren materialized soundlessly from the early morning shadows, making her start with surprise. He pressed one finger to his lips. "Over here."

Reyna sighed with relief but he seemed not to notice. Gratefully, she followed him.

He led her back to the stream, to a point where it had contracted to a narrow strand and looped back upon itself, creating a narrow peninsula. White-trunked saplings grew there and pink creatures like the one that had run from them earlier swarmed up the slender trees, chattering noisily.

"Feeding," Juaren whispered. "There are bubbles of sap on the trunks—you've seen them. They have a brittle shell. If you pierce it, they're full of liquid. Here—" He turned, surveying the trees behind them, finding one of the amber-shelled nodules. He drove the point of his knife through the shell and amber liquid ran down the tree's trunk. "Sticky," he said. "It will seal itself in just a moment. As nearly as I can tell, they lick until the shell dissolves and then fill the sacs at their necks with the fluid."

"Can we go nearer? Without frightening them?"

"We can try. Here—"

They slipped forward cautiously, hiding themselves in the shadows a short distance from the streambank. The creatures shinnied up and down the smooth trunks readily, hugging them with plump pink limbs. They fed until their sacs bulged. Then they tottered away, chattering among themselves, occasionally uttering small shrills.

Reyna didn't become aware until the tittering voices died in the trees that Juaren's shoulder touched hers, that her hand had found its way to his. She pulled away immediately, unaccountably embarrassed, and he dropped her hand with a surprised frown. "I—I thought you might need your lift-pack," she said quickly, wishing she knew some way to turn back the warm tide that rose to her face. It made her feel awkward, as if she had something to hide. "I brought it."

Juaren found his poise more quickly than she found hers. "Good. I want to go up to the treetops. Come with me?"

She gazed up uncertainly, wondering whether he invited her to accompany him in a reconnaissance of the forest or in something else. Did it matter when she had already agreed to go to the mountains with him? She spoke crisply to hide confusion. "Of course."

He strapped into his pack without further comment, then stood for a moment listening to the forest. "Slowly. We don't want to get tangled in the trees."

Reyna nodded, and when he touched his controls, she lifted from the ground after him. They rose side by side, the lift-packs making an almost inaudible rushing sound. They wove between wide-reaching branches, pushing aside foliage, until finally they hovered above the canopy of trees. Reyna glanced down and quelled a moment's dizzy disorientation. Trees stretched below them as far as she could see. The clouds had begun to lift and the sky was faintly stained with color. She wheeled around, peering through the screening foliage. Far below, she saw the glint of water. "If we follow the stream—"

"Our camp isn't far, just a few minutes to the north." Juaren nodded, indicating the direction. "And our ship—"

"Where is it?" she said quickly, realizing that they had drifted together again, and his hand had found hers. Before he could answer, she said, "I—I was lost this morning. A few minutes ago." She frowned, immediately annoyed with herself, wondering what impulse made her tell him that. Was she trying to place some claim of helplessness on him? Or was she only trying to explain, in some circuitous way, why she didn't withdraw her hand? But why withdraw her hand when she had already promised to be his year's mate when they returned to Brakrath?

Perhaps because Brakrath lay stars away and she had never considered taking even a season's mate until yesterday.

Self-consciously she realized that he studied her, guessing at each mood as it played across her face—saying nothing. Abruptly she kicked her legs and touched her controls, drawing him swiftly after her above the treetops. Air rushed at them, tugging at their hair. The quick, decisive motion gave her courage to ask the question she hadn't asked before, the central question of their presence here. "Do you think he's here? Do you think we'll find him?"

Juaren tapped at the controls of his pack, reversing their direction, spinning her around. He pulled her swiftly through the air after him, legs trailing, then drifted to a halt. "Birnam Rauth?"

"Yes," she said breathlessly. Her hair swirled around her shoulders. Strands of it veiled her face. She pushed it aside, not daring to look down. The trees must be spinning. "Do you think we'll learn what happened to him?" she pressed.

Juaren's grey eyes held hers, offering her nothing more telling than her own reflection. "I knew you were lost," he said finally. "I thought if I left you alone, you would find your way again."

But she hadn't. And he hadn't answered her question, an evasion that was clearly deliberate. She sighed, knowing it was no use insisting. What could he tell her except that he did not expect to find Birnam Rauth? That he had come for his own reasons—to learn what lay beyond Brakrath—and that pressing the search for Birnam Rauth was the price he paid for his passage. "I'm—I'm glad you didn't laugh at me," she said softly.

His fingers played at the lift-pack controls again. They swung in a wide arc, then turned sharply and spun back again. When they glided to a halt, his eyes glinted. "Then you won't laugh at me, will you?"

"About what?" The words were faint. Something squeezed tight in her chest, something leaped in her stomach as he swung her again, sharply, without warning. Was he deliberately trying to frighten her? To prevent her from laughing? At what? She brushed the hair from her face with clumsy fingers.

His eyes narrowed and took a hard intensity. "You won't laugh when I ask you to teach me to cipher."

She looked at him in surprise, catching her breath. "To cipher? You already know how to cipher." Every child of the halls learned to do that in his eighth year.

"I know how to read simple-stroke," he said. "I learned that much before I apprenticed myself to Komas. So I can read the breeding records, the harvest rolls, the seed charts. But that's not what I want to read."

"That's all anyone reads," she protested. "Except the barohna and her daughters and the history keepers. And the juris, of course." The people of the halls had no need to consult the library scrolls. The histories recorded there were kept alive by word of mouth in the halls. They were chanted and sung at the festival table. They were whispered to the youngest children as bedtime tales. Everyone knew them—the old stories, the new ones.

"That's not all I want to read," he persisted, and she saw from the hardening lines around his eyes that he had thought long about what he said next. "Do you remember what you told me when I asked why you wanted to learn to track? I want the same thing you want. I want to know what has passed. And I don't want to know it just from tales and songs. I want to hold the earliest scrolls in my hands. I want to touch the parchment and smell the ink and understand the figures—and everything behind them. I want to know what kind of hands wrote them. And then I want to write histories of my own. No hunter has written his story since the early days. I want to write mine and Komas'. And whatever price you want to set—"

Price? She winced under the pressure of his hand, not wanting to talk about prices. Because she understood now what he wanted. He wanted to look behind the familiar tales. He wanted to touch the past, to grasp its scent and its texture. He wanted to track the legendary figures from flesh to the place where myth claimed them. Because what was sung and whispered in the halls was legend. Only the scrolls exposed the human flesh behind it. *Kirsa, who had discovered that dreams hatched from broken shells. Tima, who had realized that the early timers would find humanity only in change. Noa, first of the guardians to stand watch over the redmanes. Niabi, the first barohna, who had found her power only to see her lover fall in ashes at her feet.*

"I'll teach you," she said. "I'll teach you everything I know."

"And the price?" His hand still gripped hers, tightly.

She gazed into the rising sun, then pivoted and said as lightly as she could. "You'll probably have to apprentice yourself to me for a winter. You'll probably have to pledge to spend a full winter in my palace."

Where else, after all, was he to find parchment and pens and tables to spread them upon?

"Only a winter?" he demanded, responding to the teasing tone of her voice.

"Maybe longer. Can you stay away from the mountains in winter?"

"If I can't, we'll pack writing tools in our packs and go find the snow."

"We'll go," she laughed. "And you can write your story in the snow pack with a pike." But they could do none of those things until they had fulfilled his promise to Komas, she realized, her mood changing with the thought. They could do nothing until they found a way to waken the people.

And they could not do that until they had returned safely from their search. Reyna gazed down over the forest, the momentary lightness of her mood slipping away. The trees below stretched so far they might be endless. And Juaren believed their search was futile. Reyna touched her temples, wondering if her belief was any stronger than his. "I left Verra sleeping. We'd better get back."

They followed the stream north and settled through the trees to their campsite. Packs and supplies lay where they had dropped them the night before. All three rolls of bedding had been neatly bundled and stacked beside the supplies and Verra was gone. They found a few carefully incised figures in the damp soil of the streambank.

Reyna ciphered them aloud. "She wants us to wait here. She's gone to follow the stream farther north." She gazed upstream, frowning. "She took her lift-pack."

Juaren nodded, unworried. "Did you eat yet?"

"No."

Another time they might have laughed and talked while they made their meal. But a shadow had come between them since they had returned to the ground. Perhaps it was the specter of Birnam Rauth. Perhaps it was the unspoken recognition of the things they must accomplish before she could teach Juaren to cipher the library scrolls, before they could go to the mountains together.

Reyna ate slowly, not tasting the food. When she finished, she stared down at her empty bowl and realized she had not even taken time this

morning to tie the starsilk at her waist. Frowning, she rinsed her bowl
in the stream and went to her pack.

The blue silk was folded with the white, forgotten. She stroked it
thoughtfully, then took it to where Juaren sat. "Do you want to wear
this?"

His eyes flickered with interest. "Let's hear it first." Setting aside
his bowl, he tied the blue silk to the slender trunk of a sapling.

The breeze was a long time coming. Then it moved gently among
the trees, tossing their branches lightly. The blue silk shivered and
reached out feebly, raising silken hands to the dappled morning sunlight.
The song it sang was brief and disturbing, a sound that made Reyna
think of unshed tears. She listened and was suddenly cold. "I—I think
we should give it back," she faltered, turning to Juaren. "Back to the
chatni." Did he hear the same bereavement in the silk's song that she
did?

Apparently he did. He nodded slowly. "Yes." He stood and untied
the blue silk. "I'll put it in the pack until we find a way."

They sat silently for a while, waiting for Verra, listening to the
silence of the forest and the sporadic morning breeze. Occasionally
Reyna thought of the song the blue silk sang and shivered. Finally,
when Verra did not appear, Juaren rose and walked along the streambank, gazing down into the shallow water. He picked up a twig and
incised random figures in the damp soil.

Eventually Reyna roused herself and joined him. They found tiny
creatures in the shallow water and insects that hid beneath the occasional
rocks. They examined plant specimens, trying to decide what conditions
each required to grow. Once they found a tiny blue flower blooming
from a cavity in the trunk of a tree. They studied it breathlessly, as if
it might wither under their scrutiny.

When Reyna heard the light rush of Verra's lift-pack, she was surprised to look up and see that it was mid-morning. Verra settled through
the trees and touched ground in a flurry of white silks. She wore several
starsilks at her waist, their silken arms fluttering. She also wore an
emerald silk coiffed into a turban, concealing her greying hair. Its clear,
vivid tone made the sparkle of her eyes and the color in her cheeks
brighter. "Did you think I had deserted you?" she demanded and then

went on without waiting for an answer. "I went up for a quick reconnaissance and flew a little farther than I intended. Have you two taken a good look over the forest?"

"We—we went up for a while. Where did you find those? Did you take them from the chatni?"

Verra caught the white silks and wound them loosely around one hand. "No, but someone did. Did you see the burned area to the southeast? I don't know enough about local growth cycles to guess when it happened, but the trees are just beginning to reestablish themselves. They're fighting their way up through a heavy growth of brush."

Juaren was immediately interested. "We didn't go that far."

"I've realized all along that commerce ships of some kind—perhaps only shuttles; perhaps larger craft—must have made groundfall here to gather the silks the trader ship brought to Brakrath. After I managed to wake myself this morning, I decided to use instrumentation to see if I could find some unexplained radiation that might indicate where they had landed." She tapped her waist, where an instrument pouch bulged beneath the silks, and said quickly. "You'll be pleased, Reyna. I never took it out of the case. When I sighted the burn area, I took one quick float over it and spotted what caused the ignition: a craft substantially smaller than the one that came down on Brakrath but similar in certain other details. I doubt it had independent warp capabilities. It was probably a surface shuttle, and apparently it was loaded and prepared to return to the mother-ship when it failed in lift-off, fell and ignited. The wreckage is pretty sketchy. I couldn't find any sign of a crew. If they survived the crash, they were probably retrieved by another shuttle.

"The only sign of cargo was one fire-resistant carton that had been thrown clear of the wreckage and not retrieved. I pried it open and found silks. These. And this—" Quickly she lifted the emerald turban from her head and unwound it. She stepped into a patch of dappled sunlight and drew the emerald silk back and forth through the air.

There was nothing sad in its fluttering song. The emerald silk raised a clear, bright voice—as clear, as bright as Verra's eyes as she listened to it. She swept it back and forth briefly, intent upon its song, then tied it around her forehead, letting the ends hang free. The effect was rakish, at odds with the austerity of the black uniform she wore. "I want to pick up other colors later. Perhaps for my children. Although—" She caught the emerald streamers in one hand, frowning.

"Don't you think they would like them?" Reyna probed when the Arnimi woman didn't go on. She had difficulty imagining any other Arnimi winding a silk around her head and taking its brightness into her eyes.

Verra didn't respond for several moments. Then she spoke briskly, untying the white silks at her waist. "We'd better give some thought to how we want to structure the day. What we want to do with it."

"I'd like to see the wreckage," Juaren said quickly. "And if we can observe the chatni without disturbing them—" He hesitated, frowning with a new thought. "The instrument you were going to use to find where the trade ships made groundfall—would it help us find Birnam Rauth's ship?"

"Mmmmm. Questionable, after this length of time. But I brought another instrument that could be helpful. I doubt he set down in the forest, since he didn't have a ground party to clear a landing site for him. We'll probably have to scout the less heavily wooded areas around the perimeters of the forest. And it's possible he made landing at a substantial distance, as we did. In that case, a visual search could be quite time-consuming. But with this instrument, we could survey entire blocks of area at a time." She raised a questioning eyebrow. "Reyna?"

Reyna frowned down at the ground, realizing that both Verra and Juaren expected her to object to using an Arnimi instrument in the search. Realizing too that they had given much more thought to the mechanics of the search than she had. Reluctantly she said, "How—how would your instrument find the ship?"

"It's a metal locator. A very basic instrument. If you wish, I'll let you carry it yourself. I can teach you how to read it in just a few moments. In a place like this, where there are no metal products in use aside from what we're carrying ourselves, we can set the ranging parameters wide. We can eliminate days of search."

And perhaps days of danger. Reyna frowned, looking beyond her reluctance, surprised at what she found there: sharp unease at the prospect of finding Birnam Rauth's ship, of learning from it what had become of him. She stroked the starsilk, wondering suddenly if she could bear to listen to its song once she knew why Birnam Rauth had never come back from this land. Wondering if she could bear to wear the silk or even to keep it then.

Wondering too if, in fact, she would ever know what had happened to him.

And Verra was handing her the other starsilks, the ones she had retrieved from the wrecked trader. They shimmered in the Arnimi woman's hands, alive in some way Reyna didn't understand, needing only light and breeze to tune their urgent voices.

"Juaren—" she said and was immediately ashamed of the weakness in her voice. But she could not take the starsilks, could not touch them. It was enough that she wear this one—on the day when they might find what was left of Birnam Rauth's ship.

"I'll wear one," Juaren said quickly. "I'll carry the others in my pack. Unless you want one, Verra."

"No. Reyna?"

Reyna looked up and realized with surprise that neither of them saw her assent—her capitulation—in her face. They had to ask. She studied them both, then nodded, forcing crispness to her voice. "Yes, show me how to use the instrument."

THIRTEEN
REYNA

The Arnimi instrument was an unwelcome weight on Reyna's wrist, but she listened carefully to Verra's instructions and repeated them to herself as they lifted above the trees. Verra's green silk sang in the sunlight, its loose ends fluttering. Juaren wore his starsilk as Reyna wore hers, tied at his waist, ends tucked in. Trees passed below, tall shafts supporting broad platforms of branches. Occasionally they glimpsed the brightness of silk in the lower branches. Sometimes they saw small clearings far below, carpeted in green. Once Reyna saw chatni sunning themselves and she gazed down, wondering if they would look up. They did not.

She watched the lazy way her shadow trailed over the treetops, sometimes following her, sometimes running ahead as they changed direction. Then the trees grew patchy and gave way to ragged brush, and her shadow plummeted.

"Here—" Verra said, descending. "We're entering the burn area. Make this a practice run, Reyna. See if you can lead us to the trader without making a visual scan. We'll go in low. Remember what I told you—press the blue pane for a broad radius reading, then narrow the scan radius as we get closer."

Reyna followed Verra's instructions, and the instrument's indicator screen glowed. Frowning, Reyna studied the visual display—a series of concentric circles, a flickering red brightness shimmering in one quadrant of the outermost circle.

"There—you have it already," Verra said, hovering near.

"That?" The flickering light? She had expected something more substantial, something that hinted more closely at the solidity of the mass of the fallen trade ship.

"That's it. Change your direction of flight—make small corrections, no abrupt changes—as you have to until it stands still. When that happens, continue straight on course and narrow the radius. We won't be able to center the mass until you've set the final radius."

Reyna nodded distractedly. The flickering light had already begun to move, retreating around the screen. Staring down at the display, Reyna made a slight change of direction, leading the way just above the tops of the scattered white-trunked saplings that fought the heavy brush for light and space. The flickering brightness continued to shift. Reyna watched the indicator screen with increasing concentration, becoming only peripherally aware of Juaren and Verra flanking her, matching speed and direction to hers as she methodically altered her course. If she could find the correct course, if she could make the elusive red light stand still . . . She glanced up, taking her direction from the sun, and altered course again.

"When you have the mass centered in the display, Reyna—"

When she had the mass centered, she had only to glance down at the ground. The wrecked ship would be there. Reyna nodded distractedly, realizing that the flickering brightness had not shifted for several seconds, for half a minute, for a full minute—that she had found the correct course. She pressed the next colored pane in sequence, narrowing the scan radius. The flickering light began to shift again, but more slowly. A series of small corrections and it stood still again.

Finally the flickering brightness settled at the center of the indicator. After a moment's blank surprise, Reyna looked down and saw a twisted metal shape glinting dully from the brush. She laughed aloud, surprising herself.

"*Cantro ci!*" Verra said, settling toward the ground.

Reyna eased herself out of the air, avoiding a tangle of brush. "What?"

"*Cantro ci!* One of the least favored expletives in the Arnimi language. It means I'm trying to find some fault with the way you handled that and I can't—to my great annoyance." Verra touched ground, the green silk settling upon her shoulders.

Reyna laughed again. "You can't find anything wrong with the way I did the job, so you're angry with me instead?"

Verra shrugged, catching at the tails of her silk. "Sounds that way, doesn't it? Do you want to look inside the ship? It's pretty well burned out."

A passing glance at the charred interior was enough for Reyna. She had no desire to prod burned controls and charred furnishings. She withdrew, catching a deep breath and gazing up into the brightness of the sun. Then, while Verra and Juaren examined the wreckage, she looked around for sign of the container of silks.

She found it several hundred paces from the wreckage, a trunk of some tough material she didn't recognize, its lid ajar. Inside were silks of every color—cool and slippery against her fingertips. They were crushed tightly together, but when she selected a sunny yellow one and shook it free, it was smooth and uncreased. Standing, she tied it to a slender sapling and let its ends hang free.

When the breeze caught it, the silk sang in a high, sweet voice. Unconsciously Reyna stroked the starsilk, sorry it could not sing a song as brightly, as mindlessly joyous as this one. When she turned and saw Verra and Juaren approaching, deep in discussion, she took the yellow silk from the tree and tied it at her waist, letting the ends float free.

Before they left the wreckage of the trader, Verra chose a rainbow of silks and slipped them into the small pouch she carried. Juaren sorted through the container and selected an icy blue swath. Reyna wondered briefly what he saw in it as he tied it at his waist. The winter sky? The face of the glacier that ground its way through the mountains far to the north of Valley Terlath? But the swath's song, when they flew again, was neither cold nor implacable. It trilled brightly in the sunlight, joining its voice harmoniously with the voices of the green and yellow silks.

Reyna listened to the three fluttering voices and wished she could sing with them, wished she could sing away the gathering tension of her mood. Because she had used the Arnimi instrument successfully. She had located the fallen trader. And now they were flying in search of Birnam Rauth's ship. She activated the instrument as they left the burn area, watching the small screen for some sign of a second metal mass.

At Verra's advice, they flew above the trees to the perimeter of the forest. By the time she saw the grasslands ahead, Reyna realized that a hesitant light flickered at the edge of the small indicator screen. But Verra shook her head. "Our own ship. If you want to home on it for practice—"

Reyna did not. Another practice run would not resolve the tension that made her frown down at the screen and then peer narrowly at the sun, trying to decide which way she must lead the search first. It would not release the tautness of muscles that already made her scalp ache. She hovered briefly, one hand winding the yellow songsilk tight, and then chose to fly northward along the edge of the forest.

In places the boundary of the forest was sharply defined. Tall white trees grew to a certain point and abruptly stopped, giving way to scrub and grass. In other places the trees straggled out into the grasslands, sometimes standing solitary among marshy reeds, sometimes marching in distinct lines toward the eastern horizon. Occasionally they intergrew with the twisted trees of the grasslands. Once Reyna looked down and saw a tattered silk clinging to the branches of a white-trunked sapling. The sun had washed it pale. She circled the tree and saw that the silk had not been tied there, that the wind had tangled it in the branches.

So it was a clue to nothing. No one had hung it there as a sign.

No one had left a sign of any kind, in fact. The land seemed as empty today as it had when she first saw it. Grass, brush, trees—they existed only for themselves.

Yet each time they touched ground, Juaren pointed out the prints of small animals. Occasionally they found the distinctive track of a chatni. And they flew on, silks singing at their waists, songs that grew wilder and sweeter in the warm early afternoon sunlight.

They ate at mid-afternoon, quickly rifling the small pouches they carried. Juaren wandered away when he had eaten and eventually returned with a small frown of dissatisfaction.

Reyna felt the same dissatisfaction. There had been no flicker of the Arnimi instrument, and soon they would have to turn back to the stream, where they had left their bedding and supplies, or to their own ship.

She frowned into the eastern sky, frustrated by its emptiness. "Maybe we're searching too close to the trees," she said slowly, thinking aloud. Their own ship had shown as a hesitant flicker at the outer edge of the indicator screen that morning. If Birnam Rauth's ship lay much farther from the edge of the forest than their own, the instrument would not have picked it up.

Juaren nodded, carefully gathering the scraps of his meal and burying them. "If we fly back the way we came, but to the east, perhaps as far to the east as our own ship lies—"

"Then we'll have the start of a grid pattern," Verra agreed. "And if we find nothing today, at least we'll be in position to build upon the pattern tomorrow."

But they had not flown long into the east before Reyna knew they would not have to search the next day—not for Birnam Rauth's ship. A flicker of red had appeared on the instrument screen, and even as she stared down at it, licking suddenly dry lips, it became brighter, like a beacon. Without thinking, she caught the ends of the yellow silk and tucked them in, silencing the silk's trilling voice. Then, quickly, she took her bearings from the sun, prepared to begin making gradual alterations of course.

Only two small alterations were necessary. After that the red flicker did not shift. She narrowed the scan radius twice, three times, and maintained course.

It was almost anticlimactic when the mass centered and Reyna looked down at the craft that stood in the tall grass below. It was larger than their own ship, its finish duller, its lines heavier. It sat at the center of a ring of solitude, closed against weather and time. Except for the grasses that grew high against its hull, it might have landed the morning before. Reyna glanced quickly at Juaren, at Verra, and saw they waited for her to touch ground first.

She dropped, extending booted toes, and settled in the shadow of the craft. She felt no laughing triumph this time as she deactivated the Arnimi instrument. She felt only disbelief. "This—this is the one? This is the ship?" An empty question. What other ship could it be?

"It's the correct model, it carries the correct markings," Verra assured her.

Birnam Rauth's ship. Reyna stepped forward and placed her fin-

gertips against the sun-warmed metal of its hull. Birnam Rauth's ship—
and she felt nothing but distant bewilderment. This was the shell that
had brought him here. But what could it tell her now, a century later?
And why had that century left no mark on its metal hull? Why did the
ship wait here so matter of factly, as if Birnam Rauth might come
walking back across the grasslands at dusk? Frowning, she shrugged
out of her lift-pack and circled the craft.

The hatch did not open easily. It had been closed too long. Seals
had aged. But it yielded eventually and Verra and Juaren stood aside
while Reyna ventured first into the ship's interior.

A yielding surface underfoot, the stale smell of air trapped too long
in an enclosed space—and lights. They glowed alive when Reyna
stepped through the interior hatchway. At the same time a familiar voice
spoke. But her heart missed no more than a beat. Her trip aboard the
Narsid had taught her that walls could speak. And she recognized the
tone of the words that came from the recessed speakers, if not their
meaning. Her father had welcomed her to the dining table often enough
in much the same tone.

Still she hesitated, wondering. Were these words Birnam Rauth had
recorded to welcome himself? Or had he expected someone else to step
aboard his ship?

Who could have stepped aboard his ship here?

And why hadn't he come back? Back to his empty couch, back to
the papers and miscellaneous possessions that were strewn around the
interior of the craft. Back to all the things she recognized and the others
she couldn't put a name to. Reyna turned a slow circle, taking a cursory
inventory: a loosely bound volume, its open pages covered with finely
lined sketches; eating utensils, a clean platter, and two knives with
metal blades; a tumbled pile of silks, their colors dull, muted; a mug
that might have held water; several articles of clothing, tossed casually
on the floor; implements, tools, instruments—Birnam Rauth hadn't
shared her father's penchant for order.

Or perhaps he had cultivated some other, less obvious form of order.
Reyna pressed her temples and stared around, feeling suddenly helpless.
She had found Birnam Rauth's ship but what did it have to tell her?
That he had been here, that he was here no longer. But could it tell her
where he had gone? Why he hadn't come back to resume the com-

monplaces of his life? Why he wouldn't walk back across the grasslands tonight?

Juaren and Verra lingered at the inner hatch, watching her. With a flash of irritation at her own helplessness, Reyna stepped to the work-counter and flipped the pages of the volume Birnam Rauth had left open.

Chatni—he had filled the loosely bound pages with sketches of chatni. They gazed down from their bowers with the predator alertness she had seen the night before. They stalked small woods creatures. They sunned themselves in the grass. They groomed each other, they played, they fed their cubs. Birnam Rauth had captured grace, humor, and a lanquid intelligence with his sketching tool. And she realized, studying his work, that he had not done so by keeping a cautious distance between himself and his subjects. His sketches were filled with detail, with characterization. Flipping through the volume, she began to recognize individuals. Near the end of the book, she found a birth sequence and knew that he had been there, that he had witnessed the birth. Perhaps he had even assisted at it.

Also near the end of the book she found a self-portrait—a deft caricature of a man who hovered at the transition point between human and chatni. Birnam Rauth grinned up at her with sharp white teeth, his ears pointed and lightly furred. She stared into the laughing eyes, then laughed herself, until she turned the page and found a chatni gazing up at her with human eyes. This time there was no humor, no laughter. The chatni tilted its sleek head and seemed about to speak, about to ask some question that could never be answered.

Whose question had Birnam Rauth captured in those eyes—the chatni's or his own? Disturbed, Reyna closed the volume. Without thinking, she loosed the starsilk's ends and let them hang free. Slowly she turned. Verra and Juaren still watched from the hatchway, as if they required her permission to trespass upon Birnam Rauth's domain.

"There's another sketch book there, on the floor beside his couch," Verra said softly, nodding. "And voy-caps on the work-counter. His equipment is Ptachidarki—the same capping equipment my mother used for her genealogical studies when I was young. If it's still functional, I'll be able to show you how to operate it."

Reyna turned distractedly. A second loosely bound sketch volume was half lost beneath tumbled bedding. She retrieved it, flipping through it absently, Forest scenes. Small animals. Creatures like the one that had screamed at them that morning—climbing, feeding, washing silks in the stream. "Voy-caps?"

"For oral recording. He probably kept note of his studies on caps. But I don't see any sign of a portable capping unit. Only the player and the stationary capper. If he had a portable capper, he may have been carrying it when—when he left here."

For the last time.

"Do you want me to show you how to use the equipment?"

A tactful probe. And Verra still stood carefully in the hatchway, not intruding. Reyna held the sketch volume close and tried to understand why Verra's diplomatic suggestion rankled—why she didn't want to listen to Birnam Rauth's recordings, why she didn't want to open cabinets and inventory his possessions, why she only wanted to go back to the stream and listen to the trees.

It was too much. The ship sitting untouched in the grasslands, the casual disorder of the cabin, the sketch book lying open on the workcounter—Birnam Rauth's environment was alive. It waited for him. And standing in the cabin where he had eaten, where he had slept, Reyna's bewilderment was turning to loss.

She needed time—time to accept what she found here: Birnam Rauth's humanity. His kinship. All the other things that had been only abstractions until now, although she had thought she felt their full weight from the beginning.

"Why—why don't you go ahead and listen to the recordings, Verra," she said carefully, aware of the sudden fragility of her composure. "I want to look through his sketch books."

"Of course." More tactful words. And Verra stood aside and carefully did not see Reyna's painfully contained agitation.

Reyna found a place in the grass where brush partially obscured her view of Birnam Rauth's ship. She sat, dropping the sketch books beside her, and put her head on her knees. The sun warmed her back. It pressed against her flesh like a weight. But she did not cry, and after a while, distractedly, she began to wonder why.

Because the time was not right? Because they had only found an empty ship? Or because what her mother called strong-mindedness would not let her. The search was only half begun; this was not the moment for weakness. Sighing, she took up the second sketch book and flipped its pages.

The forest passed before her eyes, all its secret places recorded: empty clearings carpeted with flowers, streamside caves, individual trees, some white and smooth-trunked, others mossy, somber, as if the deepest of all the secrets of the forest lived among them. They stood like giants, the caverns in their trunks as impenetrably shadowed as the rock caverns Birnam Rauth had found beside the stream. Reyna passed her fingertips lightly over the loose pages, wishing she could feel what Birnam Rauth had felt when he probed these secrets, when he recorded them. If she had scroll and pen—

But what good would it do her to sketch the empty ship, the living disorder of its interior? Those were the secrets she must probe, and she must use means more potent than a pen.

And what good would it do her to sit here, thinking thoughts that led nowhere?

Finally she stood, heavily, and returned to the ship.

She did not understand immediately what she heard when she stepped through the inner hatch. Two voices came from the wall speakers, one Birnam Rauth's but speaking in a hissing tongue she knew immediately was not Carynese. The other voice was softer, airier. Listening to it— to the utterly alien quality of it—Reyna felt herself stiffen and chill. She realized belatedly that Verra sat with her translator on her knees but did not use it.

Juaren glanced up distractedly as Reyna settled beside him on the couch. "Chatni," he said softly at her questioning look. "He's talking with a chatni."

"He learned their language?" But that was obvious, because surely the tongue that came from the wall speakers had not originated with any human race. Reyna couldn't imagine herself speaking it. And as she listened, she was not certain that Birnam Rauth spoke it well. His words had a different, sharper rhythm than the chatni's. When the chatni spoke, the sounds rushed together with an airy lack of definition. Nor could he reproduce some of the sibilants or the occasional punctuating growls.

They listened silently, absorbed, until abruptly the two voices stopped speaking. Verra stood from her stool, briskly, and popped a small metal capsule from an unimposing box that sat on the work-counter. "His own Class Five," she said softly. "He found his own Class Five." Seeing Reyna's questioning look, she explained. "A classification—a non-human race corresponding closely enough to ours in intelligence, physiology and psychology that verbal communication is possible. And I don't know which would be more remarkable—if we were to prove that the chatni were descended from exported Terran *Chatnus* or if we were to prove that they were not."

Reyna frowned, disturbed by the speculative brightness of Verra's eyes. "We're not here to prove either of those things."

For a moment Verra didn't seem to understand her sharpness. Then she nodded distractedly. "No, of course not." She turned back to the counter. "He's numbered some of his caps. Others he apparently generated without ever putting them into any particular order. Shall we listen to the random recordings first? Or would you prefer to audit the sequential recordings now and leave the others for later?"

Reyna approached the work-counter and studied the three tall transparent capsule containers unenthusiastically. "How long will it take to listen to all of these?"

"Days."

Days of listening, when there was a search to be made? Reyna frowned, dissatisfied with the prospect. "Do we have to stay here? Can we listen to these somewhere else?"

"Mmmmm. The player is fully portable. It's operating on ship's power now, but it should function on standard wafers. Were you thinking of going back to our own ship?"

"No—to the forest," Reyna said. "To the place where we stayed last night." She felt as much at home there as anywhere. And she did not want to eat here, to sleep here. The couch, the work-counter, all the cabin's mute furnishings—everything here was waiting for Birnam Rauth. They were intruders.

"Of course," Verra said. "Give me a few minutes to disconnect the unit and see if he has a travel case for it."

"We won't damage it, moving it?"

"Not unless we're careless. And I don't intend to be."

And in fact they were careful. Verra, the most experienced flyer, carried the case holding the cap player when they lifted away from the grasslands. Juaren carried the containers of capsules, and Reyna brought Birnam Rauth's sketch books. She let the yellow silk flutter as they flew, but the bright pleasure of its song did not touch her.

Days of sitting, days of listening—but how else were they to know where to search next? She stroked the starsilk, discouraged.

Shadows were settling under the trees when they reached the streamside. Their supplies and bedding waited, undisturbed. Verra extricated a portable cooking unit from one of her packs, but Juaren gathered wood and made a fire instead. They gathered close to it while they ate, shoulders almost touching, yet isolated within their thoughts.

Finally Verra spoke. "If you don't want to listen to the caps, Reyna, if you want to look in some other direction—"

Reyna glanced up at the Arnimi woman, surprised that she had read her thoughts so clearly. "If I knew another direction to take, if we had some trail to follow—" she said softly. The print of boots, broken branches, crushed blades of grass—

But of course broken branches and crushed blades had healed by now. The print of boots had faded. Reyna took up the first sketch book and opened it to Birnam Rauth's self-portrait. She gazed down at it, trying to see with his eyes. She had come here to meet her challenge, and he was her prey. And Juaren had told her yesterday, when he instructed her in the first rules of tracking, that she must learn her prey's mind. That she must learn its habits, its appetites, its vagaries and whims. Because only then could she successfully find and follow its trail.

Was there no way to learn about Birnam Rauth except by listening to the recorded capsules? She stroked the starsilk again, freeing its ends, drawing them through her fingers, and found an answer.

The starsilk had touched her with a sense of Birnam Rauth's presence the first night they had spent here. Now she needed to touch his presence again, not—she realized—by a methodical auditing of the capsules but by listening again to his song, by losing herself in it—by stepping outside her own mind and into his. Slowly she stood, tucking the sketch books under one arm. "Why don't you listen to the caps, Verra? And tell me if you hear something you think might be important. I—I need to be alone. I need to be by myself for a while."

She saw concern in Verra's face, sudden guarded stiffness in Juaren's. Impulsively she touched his arm. "I won't be far," she said. "I won't be long."

But she wasn't sure he understood as she hurried away into the trees. She found a grassy hollow near the stream and sat for a while, frowning and undecided, wanting to go back, wanting to explain that her sudden need to be alone wasn't a rejection. But surely he understood that. Finally, unhappily, she rose and tied the starsilk to a branch.

The silk hung dim and white in the deepening shadows, catching at the occasional breeze. Its song was as muted as the dusk, and the smoky quality of its voice, the growing gloom of early night settled upon Reyna like a trance. She let herself sink into it, let herself be drawn away from the concerns of daylight and reason.

The silk sang and she sang her own song, silently—a song that held much the same loneliness, much the same want, much the same occasional baffled anger. She sang, and while she did so, she listened to herself with silent detachment, trying to understand what she heard. Because the things she felt were kin to the things Birnam Rauth had felt, and they would lead her to an understanding of him.

She sang until the moon rose and the silk's voice brightened. Then, letting her own voice die, she looked down at her lap. She held the sketch volumes there, her fingers resting lightly upon their covers. Nodding as if she had received an instruction, she opened them, keeping the first on her lap, spreading the second on the ground beside her. Idly, without direction, her fingers began to turn the pages.

The starsilk sang and her fingers sought both volumes randomly, yet she always came back to the same scene: a dark-mossed tree that stood somewhere in the forest, mystery in its cavernous hollows.

Was this the mystery that had compelled Birnam Rauth? Was this the mystery that had made a prisoner of him? Was this where he wanted her to go to learn what had happened to him?

She sat looking down at the shadowy sketch and listening to the silk's song. Now she felt that Birnam Rauth stood near. Now she felt that his hand touched her shoulder. Was he summoning her? Or did he only want her to listen tonight? Did he only want her to begin to understand, however poorly?

She listened until the moon had crossed half the sky, until the trees held it in upraised arms and her eyelids were heavy. Then, nodding as if she had posed herself a question, as if she had found its answer, she stood. Carefully she untied the starsilk and fastened it around her waist again, ends tucked under. She took up the sketch books and walked back through the moonlit forest. The shadows of the trees fell in broad grids, guiding her.

When she reached the place where she had left Juaren and Verra, she saw that Verra was already rolled in her bedding asleep. Juaren sat cross-legged on the ground a distance away, head bowed, white hair shining in the moonlight. He had tied his own starsilk to a tree and it spoke and sang to him. Reyna hesitated briefly, watching, listening. Slowly she realized that the silk spoke different words than the one she wore at her waist, although its song was the same, restless, poignant, sometimes thwarted and angry. When she stepped nearer, she saw that Juaren wore Verra's translator plugged into his ears. He sat with eyes closed, intent upon what he heard.

She dropped to the ground beside him, and after a while she knew that he guessed that she was there. He didn't open his eyes, he didn't speak, but the tension of his body changed. It altered to accommodate her presence.

Finally he took the plugs from his ears and set the translator aside. His face was without expression—carefully without expression, as if he had deliberately purged his features of whatever he felt. Standing, he took the starsilk from the tree and tied it at his waist. Then he extended one hand, wordlessly helping Reyna to her feet.

"Juaren," she said hesitantly, worried that he hadn't spoken, worried at the distance in his eyes, "earlier—this evening—"

He nodded absently. "I know."

She frowned, beginning to be disturbed by the way he held himself, by the careful impassivity of his features. Why wouldn't he look at her? Why did he still seem to listen to the silk, even though he had tied it at his waist and carefully tucked the ends under? What had he heard in the silk's song, or in its words? "I had to be alone," she said, pressing his hand, trying to cross the distance his distraction set between them. "It wasn't—I didn't go because I didn't want to be with you. I didn't—"

"You went because you needed to be alone," he said, still looking past her. At what? What did he see beyond her shoulder? "And I worried because I didn't want you to be alone—not here, not in the dark. But I understood. I have to be alone sometimes too."

He understood. But why did he speak with such detachment? Reyna drew a hand across her eyes, suddenly tired. The day had been long. Her back ached and her eyelids were heavy. She did not want to ask Juaren now what the starsilk had said. She did not want to tell him about the hollow tree and its shadowed mystery. This was not the time to tell him she thought they would learn there what had happened to Birnam Rauth. This was the time to sleep. "Aren't you tired?" she said.

He turned and finally he met her eyes. His gaze was mirror-like, reflective—betraying nothing. But his voice was gentle. "Aren't you?"

"Yes," she said shakily, relieved at what she heard in his tone. "I'm very tired."

"Then we should go to bed."

Go to bed and rehearse the things she would ask him in the morning, the things she would tell him. Juaren pulled his bedding near hers, and soon she thought, from the quietness of his breath, from the still shadows the moon painted on his face, that he slept. Relaxing, she surrendered her own concerns and slept too.

But briefly. Perhaps Juaren made some sound as he rose, created some involuntary disturbance of twig or stone as he moved away into the dark. Reyna turned restlessly, pulling her bedding close—and woke to the certain realization that she was alone. Verra still slept a distance away, but Juaren had abandoned his bedding. He was gone.

She stared for long moments at the emptiness beside her, trying to reach past alarm to put some order to her thoughts. Where had he gone? The moon was waning and he had said he was tired. Why had he lulled her into thinking that he slept and then left her? If he needed to be alone now, tonight, why hadn't he told her, as she had told him? Was he afraid she would worry, as he had? She sat, rubbing her eyes. The starsilk—she remembered how intently he had listened to the starsilk.

She remembered the guarded stiffness of his face afterward. Was that why he had slipped away? Because of something he had heard from the starsilk?

If she knew what the starsilk had said to him . . . Its message had been different than the one her silk carried. She knew that much. If he had not taken it with him—

But he had. She slumped back to her bedding, hugging herself against the cold. What must she do? Let him go, as he had earlier let her go? Track him—when the moon was setting and shadows were deepening under the trees? Crawl back into her bedding and wait, anxiously?

She crouched there, undecided, her arms growing cold, until she remembered that Verra had brought several starsilks back from the wrecked trader. Juaren had taken one and folded the others into his pack. If he had left his pack— Quickly Reyna extricated herself from her bedding and padded across the campsite.

Juaren's pack was piled with the supplies, and the other silks, three of them, were folded inside it. Hands shaking, Reyna slipped them from the pack. She paused to pull on her boots. Then she slipped into the trees, leaving Verra sleeping.

The breeze was sporadic, but its first burst told her that two of the silks carried the same message hers did. The third one spoke differently, its tone calmer, the words distant, almost disinterested. Quickly Reyna folded the first two silks away and slipped back to camp to search for the translator. If she could teach herself to use it, if she could learn what Birnam Rauth had said on this second silk—

But she did not find the translator. Juaren had left his pack but taken the lift-pack and translator with him.

Why? Where had he gone? Leadenly, mechanically, Reyna returned to where the silk hung. She sat and waited until the breeze came again, until the silk repeated its incomprehensible words. At the same time it sang, its song touching her with Birnam Rauth's presence as her own silk had. She bowed her head and he stood beside her. She could not understand the words he said. But they touched her with something deeper, something crueler than the cold of night. They touched her with a cold that bruised her, making her body stiffen and her bones ache. Because they touched her with a growing conviction.

Juaren had not slipped away in the dark because he wanted to be alone. He had slipped away because the silk had directed him somewhere—and he had chosen to go alone.

He had chosen to go alone because there was danger and he thought he was better equipped to deal with it than she was.

He had gone alone to learn what had happened to Birnam Rauth. But if Birnam Rauth had died—where? in the dark heart of the forest? among the cavernous trees?—Juaren could die too, no matter how lightly he walked, no matter how carefully he watched, no matter how closely he listened.

Slowly, frightened, Reyna stood. She could hesitate no longer. Juaren had gone alone, and no matter how carefully considered his reasons, she could not permit it. Because he could as readily die as she. And who would write his story and Komas' then? Who would winter with her in the mountains? Who would cut figures on streambanks and spin above the trees?

She paused only to tuck away the extra starsilks and, on impulse, to find the azure silk and tie it at her waist. Then she took up her pike, shrugged into her lift-pack, and slipped away into the trees.

FOURTEEN
TSUUKA

Tsuuka groomed her weanlings with special attention that night, and they stretched themselves luxuriantly under her tongue and grunted with drowsy pleasure, suspecting nothing. But when she went to Falett and Dariim, they lay wide-eyed in their silks watching for her, Falett anxiously, Dariim with guarded wariness. And Tsuuka knew they guessed she was leaving them. They had guessed it sometime during the day.

She growled softly, realizing with sinking heart that she should not have waited. She should have returned to the heart of the trees that dawn, while her cubs still slept. But Riifika had wanted the day to lie with the grassland cub, accustoming herself. So Tsuuka had stolen the opportunity to sun herself with her cubs and weanlings again, to feed and groom them a last time before going back to the heart of the trees.

Shadows lay ahead. She had wanted that last brightness. Now she saw it reflected in Dariim's eyes, mocking her.

"My cubs—" she said, but what had she to say beyond that? She didn't know the words for parting, and a last admonition would not find its mark. Falett would listen with anxious attention, but Dariim had already armored herself against wise words. The blaze of the red silk was in her eyes. Tsuuka gazed at her with a helplessness that approached anger. That she should care so much for one cub when they all needed her—

Impulsively she bent to smooth Falett's fur and said softly in her ear, "Tall trees and a full stomach, my good cub." What more could she wish her firstborn when she could not love her as fiercely as she loved her sibling?

And perhaps she would capture the red silk tonight without harm. Perhaps tomorrow she would watch her weanlings tumble in the grass just as she had today. Perhaps one day she would see Falett take her first grass-pup and choose a tree to share with her sibling.

Perhaps—a taunting word. Tsuuka's eyes shimmered and she turned from the bower before tears could spill over. She took no parting from Dariim. How could she part sweetly from a cub who wore rebellion in her eyes, never guessing its price? Climbing down her tree, Tsuuka dropped to the ground and padded away into the dark.

Shadows followed her. It had been too many nights since she had taken song-dreams. Nightmares clawed at the weakened barriers of her mind. But she had no time to take song-dreams now, nor did she have her skysilk to guide her. The other silks—scarlet, amber, lilac, yellow; chartreuse, crimson, emerald—none of them could lead her into the song-dreams as the azure silk could. She who was so sleek, she who was so swift—tonight she was prey.

Thoughts—the nightmares were only the shadows of thoughts that passed in the air. Tsuuka reminded herself of that as she padded through the trees, trying to find comfort in it. Had she been insensitive to the nightmares, she could never have shared thoughts with a songsilk.

Had she been insensitive to the nightmares, she would not feel the hair rising at the back of her neck now. She would not imagine that she heard ghost-feet on the forest floor. She would not see insubstantial bodies curling in the air before her, vanishing when she raised irritable claws to tear them. She shook her head, annoyed with her own weakness. The nightmares could not catch her unless she slept. And tonight she would not sleep.

Yet she had no plan for what she would do. She had tried before to catch the red silk and failed. Now, the azure silk said, a dangerous time was coming, a time when the unseen and her successor must leave their hidden places. The escorts were alert, poised against any intrusion. How was she to capture the elusive red silk without being stung? Could it hear her thoughts as the songsilks did? Could she plead with it to give up its freedom to her?

But no sithi had ever kept a master-silk. And why should this one surrender to her? If she could impress it with her need, it would already be in her hands.

Would she know any better what to do if she understood the things the skysilk had said: that the master-silk carried the memory of the preserved, drawn directly from its life-silk? She clawed bitterly at the soil. She did not understand and she could ask the skysilk no more questions. She had traded it, however unintentionally, for a grassland cub. It would take her precious nights to build rapport with another silk.

And to even think of building rapport with a master-silk—she shook herself impatiently.

She drank briefly at the stream, then sat with her eyes half-lidded, thinking—and while she thought, drifting across the hazy boundary into somnolence. The forest was silent. The moon had not risen. No silks sang. There was no sound but her own heartbeat—*and the nearly inaudible scuff of feet in the brush behind her*. But when she jumped up and spun around, heart racing, there was nothing there. Not a tree-mole. Not a bark-shredder.

Not Dariim, following her.

But her fur was damp. Her breath was shallow and quick. Her eyes darted nervously, as if they had a life of their own. The shadows—

The shadows were taking form. They were rising from beneath the trees, spreading wings of black silk, wings that reached to enfold her, *wings*—

Tsuuka shook herself, uttering an angry growl. Nightmares—she had let herself doze and the nightmares had overtaken her. Instinctively she threw herself into the cold-running stream. The shock made her gasp, made her eyes start. It also brought her fully awake again and the black wings retreated and spread themselves back under the trees.

It took her time after that to groom herself dry. She monitored the state of her wakefulness carefully as she did so. She had slept so little the night before. Fatigue ached so heavily in her limbs. It would be easy to slip back into a half-waking state.

Instead, as the moon rose, she found herself moving into a state of heightened awareness, as if her senses had sharpened to compensate for her fatigue. When she was dry she stood and listened to the distant song of silks. Their early evening chorus seemed to glow through the trees, light given voice. She stood and gazed into the trees, expecting to see a shining brilliance.

But the forest was dark.

And time had passed, precious time ... Goading herself, Tsuuka fell to all fours to cover ground more quickly.

Her senses trembled with alertness as she ran. The forest floor was littered with scents. They lay like fallen leaves, cluttering her path. Here a treemole had paused to urinate. There a groundfowl had escorted her young from one clump of brush to another. A bark-shredder had paused here and touched this trunk with saliva, testing the acidity of the bark. Spinners had left their scent too. And the intruders—

Encountering the sharpness of their day-old scent, she came to an unwilling halt and sniffed the ground. Her nose had not been so keen the night before. She had not differentiated the scent of one intruder from another then. But tonight she found that there were three individual trails, interwoven. She paused, inhaling through nose and mouth at once, then hissing involuntarily at the offensive sharpness of the mingled scents. Questions rose unbidden. Had the starvoice walked on two feet once just as the intruders did, leaving a scent on the forest floor? If so, where had he come from? Where had the intruders come from? Would they be starvoices too one day? She had never heard a whisper of creatures like them in the forest. Why were they here now?

Tsuuka came erect, a new thought making her grunt. The intruders had living bodies much like her own. She had seen them. She had felt the heat of the smallest intruder's fingertips. Their individual scents were in her nostrils now. Had the starvoice had just such a body once too—fleshly, real, as precious to him as her body was to her? And if he had and yet had been captured in silk, to sing from her bower poles—

Then the unseen had a living body too.

She shook herself, letting that thought settle into place. Wasn't that what the azure silk had tried to tell her? That the unseen lived for a time and then was somehow preserved and captured in silk so that master-silks could be made from her life-silk—and songsilks from the master-silks? Yet she had not fully understood, not as she found herself understanding now. She had imagined the unseen to be a shadowy presence—a presence somehow mysteriously threatening.

But the escorts had not been created to guard a dangerous insubstantiality. There was no need to guard the invulnerable. A prickle-hide didn't carry quills because his body was tough-armored but because his flesh was tender. A sithi did not stand guard over her newborns because her newborns were dangerous to her older cubs—but because her newborns were helpless against their heedless older siblings.

And the unseen, she realized with the scent of the intruders in her nostrils, was not only flesh. She was a progenitor of songsilks, or would be when she had been preserved. Someday silks would carry something of her awareness, something of her vitality, but twice removed.

This was what her silk had tried to tell her the night before. That the escorts guarded the unseen because she was made of tender flesh—and because there was no other in this quarter of the forest who could seed the bulbs from which the spinners hatched. If the unseen was harmed, there would be no spinners to spin silks and no silks for sithi bowers. And insects would nest in the forest as they did in the grasslands.

Tsuuka stared up at the moon, putting those thougts in order, examining the new perspective they gave her. Their lives were interwoven. The sithi protected the spinners from predators. The spinners protected the sithi from insect wounds and in turn nourished the unseen so that there could be more spinners and more silks. And the silks brought song into the lives of the sithi and protected them from nightmares—which were no more than thoughts that threw shadows upon their uncomprehending minds.

But there was more. Her skysilk had saved her from nightmares, but surely she had given something in return. Her silks could not run, could not play, could not taste cold water and fresh meat—not for themselves. But they did those things through her each night when she went to her bower and shared the events of her day with them. They walked the forest upon her feet. They saw the trees with her eyes. They stretched in the grass at their ease and felt the warm sun on her fur.

Was that why they sang in the moonlight? Because they tasted the joy of life through her senses? How else were they to taste it, after all, bound as they were to the poles? How was the unseen to taste it, hidden in her bulb-well, toiling over her unhatched spinners?

And the thoughts that passed between the silks and the unseen—whose were those thoughts? Surely many of them were simply sithi thoughts, sithi experiences, but translated into the silent idiom that joined silks, spinners and the unseen. What else had a silk to tell the unseen but the tales told it by its sithi companion?

What would a nightmare be if she met it waking? Perhaps she would discover that it was nothing more than her own thoughts and experiences, but translated into some other system of images—the system of images by which the silks and the unseen spoke to one another.

Slowly Tsuuka dropped to fours again, absorbed by her thoughts, wondering what she had gained from thinking them.

At least the nightmares seemed less pressing as she continued through the trees. They were little more than mist in the air. And she was no longer distracted by the over-keenness of her senses.

She did not permit those things to make her careless as she approached the heart of the trees. When she entered the place where the trees stood tallest, where their trunks were most thickly hoared with moss, she moved with deliberation, watching, listening with every step.

There was a special, waiting silence under the tallest trees tonight. She felt it immediately, felt its weight. And, yes, there were nightmares here, shadowy thoughts spreading like dormant wings under the trees. They were concentrated here, she guessed, because this was the realm of the unseen. This was the place toward which the silks' thoughts were directed. This was the heart of the trees.

But many of these are my thoughts, she reminded herself. *Many of these are my own thoughts and the thoughts of other sithi I know. These are the events of our day. The silks have put them into another form and addressed them here to the unseen so she can understand all the business of the forest, so she can better direct the spinners in their feeding and spinning.*

But Tsuuka knew there must be alien thoughts here too, thoughts that had never originated with any sithi—thoughts that originated with the unseen instead and were addressed by her to the spinners and the silks. And Tsuuka still could not imagine the true nature of the unseen.

To toil for a lifetime in the musty hollow of a tree, never glimpsing sunlight, never tasting the breeze...

Yet what harm could the unseen's thoughts hold for her? She occupied a necessary place in the scheme of their mutual life. She was a hunter, protector of spinners, master of silks. There would be no thoughts inimical to her here—only thoughts alien in their form.

And if she could address her thoughts directly to the unseen, if she could plead to have the red silk... Hadn't her skysilk told her the unseen could temper the activity of the escorts? Perhaps she could do other things too. Perhaps she could direct the red silk to give itself to her. Tsuuka closed her eyes and tried to address herself to the unseen, tried to project what she felt to the fleshly creature hidden here in the heart of the trees. Her emotions were of an aching intensity. She focused upon the loss she had experienced years ago, upon the loss she could experience again. She tried to show the unseen the brightness of her cub's eyes—the brightness that must not be quenched. She thought of the streaking red silk and its taunting song. She offered the unseen all the reasons why she must have the silk to carry back to her bower.

She put the full force of feeling behind her thoughts, but there was no answering change in the air. The winged shadows did not lighten. They continued to lie black and heavy under the trees. And the red silk did not appear, delivering itself to her.

Finally she hunched against the nearest tree, hugging herself against the sting of her own helplessness. How could she speak with the unseen without her skysilk? Even if she could find the right form for her thoughts, what guarantee did she have that the unseen had time or strength to care for her troubles—or that the unseen was capable of persuading the red silk to give itself into captivity?

Tsuuka sat that way, hunched and helpless, until she began to be angry with herself. Then she drove sharp claws into her arms and raised her head, forcing herself to consider what she must do next. The moon looked down upon silence. The red silk was not to be seen.

It remained in its hiding place then, and she did not know where that could be, except that it was near. Near enough that she would hear it sing when it emerged, near enough that she could try again to stalk and capture it.

Yet she was tired. Her muscles ached with the need for sleep. They would betray her if she didn't have it. She dug thoughtful claws into the soil, wondering. Now that she fully understood the nightmares, could she sleep without being torn by them?

She could only try. Experimentally Tsuuka hunched herself small again, losing herself in the shadow of a clump of brush, and closed her eyes. Deliberately she let alertness slip away, let the nightmare images draw near. They touched her, darkly, and she drew a slow breath and instructed her heart not to race. Slowly, carefully, she released herself into their slow-moving vortex, letting herself spin without resistance among them. Soon she slept, only peripherally aware of the occasional twitch of her limbs or grunt of her breath.

It was not a sound that woke her later, when the moon had set and the first bare hint of dawn touched the sky. It was not a movement. It was simply the pressure of two agonized eyes. They peered at her from the nearby shadows, wide with terror—Dariim's eyes.

Tsuuka shook herself alert, her breath catching, making her heart race. She had guessed Dariim would not stay in her silks. She had expected her to come here, tonight or some other night. But what had she found that had put terror in her eyes? And Falett—

The silence under the trees was so carefully poised, Tsuuka was reluctant to break it by taking her feet, by padding across the forest floor to where Dariim crouched. She did so expecting the trees to shrill with alarm. But there was only the soft sound of her own feet. And then her own voice. "Where have you left your sibling, cub?"

Dariim looked up stiffly, as if the muscles of her neck had cramped with fear. Her fur was damp, her pupils small and quivering. She licked her lips. "Back—she went back. She wouldn't come here."

"But you would. I told you not to come, but you did. For a silk you know you cannot own." Tsuuka saw that for once she had the advantage over this headstrong cub, because Dariim was afraid while she was not.

"My silk—it's my silk." The words were faint but stubborn. They brought a rising gleam to Dariim's yellow eyes.

"It is a master-silk. No sithi can own a master-silk. They're kept hidden except when they're needed to give voice to songsilks." Tsuuka reached to touch her, to stroke her ears, but Dariim drew back, rigid and trembling. "Don't you know that?"

"It's my silk," Dariim repeated. The muscles of her back and shoulders had begun to twitch. She shook herself with angry impatience. "Mine."

Tsuuka gazed at her, slowly understanding what she saw, slowly understanding the rigidity and the terror. "You came for the silk, but you've found nightmares, my cub," she said softly. Tsuuka understood about the nightmares now. She understood that if she threw herself unresisting into their pit, she could float there, unharmed, while she slept. But tonight Dariim felt darkness clawing for her and she understood nothing.

"Here—they're here," Dariim said, shaking herself again. Her fur was matted, her eyes drowning. "I can see them. I can see them moving in the shadows. But I can't catch them. You're the swiftest hunter in the forest and I'm your cub, but I can't catch them."

Tsuuka grunted. It was like Dariim to try to catch a nightmare. Another time she could tell her about them, about what they were and why they lay so heavily under the trees here. But Dariim would not understand any of those things tonight, no matter how carefully they were explained to her. Tsuuka saw that in the constriction of her pupils, in the convulsive shudder of her limbs.

Tonight she must either give herself to the full terror of the nightmares or she must take song-dreams. There was no other way.

Yet there was no silk to give her song-dreams. She had chosen the red silk, but it was hiding in the trees. To find another, to establish rapport with a silk that did not know her temperament or her mind, when the nightmares already held her in terror—

But there was a silk that knew those things. Tsuuka grunted softly, realizing that. The azure silk knew Dariim—through her. The azure silk had caught glimpses of Dariim from birth. The azure silk had watched the development of her character, the trend of her temperament. And the azure silk knew Tsuuka's concern for her secondborn.

If she could find the intruders, if she could take back her skysilk from them—

It was a possibility that made Tsuuka's eyes gleam and her ears rise erect. She had caught the intruders' scent earlier. If she could follow it to them—

This time Tsuuka did not let Dariim draw away from her. She held her firmly by the shoulders and said to her with all the conviction she could muster, "You are ready for your first song-dreams, my cub. But you can't take them here. Your silk has hidden itself and won't be found. So you must come with me. You must help me search out my skysilk and when we find it, it will give you song-dreams."

Dariim tried to pull away, shaking her head stubbornly. "My own silk—" she insisted.

"You will never capture your silk if you aren't strong. And how can you be strong with the nightmares clawing at you, pulling your muscles tight, making them tremble? You must take song-dreams first. Then you will be ready to hunt your silk again."

That was deception of course. When Dariim had taken her first song-dreams, she would only be ready to sleep. And while she slept, Tsuuka would return to the heart of the trees alone. "We must find my skysilk, cub, and your nose is even keener than mine. There is a scent in the forest tonight, a new scent, a strange scent. I think it will lead us to my silk."

It took her minutes longer to persuade the cub, even though Dariim was confused and trembling with a fear she did not understand. When she was persuaded, she wandered unevenly through the trees, distracted by every scent. Tsuuka tried to direct her back toward the stream, where she had found the scent of the intruders earlier. But Dariim circled feverishly, twitching, grunting, sometimes poking her nose into the shadows, then starting violently and leaping away. Tsuuka followed, resigning herself to a long search. At least she had persuaded Dariim from the heart of the trees. At least they had left the worst danger behind.

Yet their wandering course had not led them far from the deep trees when Dariim stiffened and stared down at the forest floor in astonishment. She bared her teeth, inhaling through both nose and mouth, then raised her head, eyes shimmering dizzily. "Here," she said. "Here there is something strange."

The scent of the intruders, and it was fresh. Tsuuka joined her cub, studying it. Two of them had passed this way, the small one who had given her the grassland cub—the small one who had taken her skysilk—and one other, she couldn't guess which. "You are a hunter, cub," Tsuuka said softly—and was surprised to feel her heart leap expectantly.

Her blue silk, she was hungry for the song of her blue silk. Now perhaps she would have it.

They followed the trail, pausing often to watch, to listen. In the end, it was their ears that found the intruders first. Tsuuka heard the first hard edge of their voices when she raised her head from examining a cluster of brush. She caught Dariim's arm, pulling her down. The sky was chill grey with impending dawn. "Do you hear?" she hissed. "Do you hear the starvoices?"

Dariim cocked her head, her eyes glistening and intent. "There—I hear them there."

Tsuuka nodded, but her gaze lingered briefly upon her cub and wariness made the flesh at the back of her neck draw tight. With every step they took from the heart of the trees, Dariim was less troubled by the nightmares. Her eyes were brighter, her muscles less rigid. Perspiration was slowly drying from her fur, leaving it glossy again. If the fear fell away entirely and she decided to return for her prey—

"Lead me to them, cub, and we will find my skysilk," Tsuuka said softly. "But quietly. You have never seen anything like them. Watch and you will see how strange they are."

The intruders stood together in a small clearing, their heads bent together. The sound of their voices was urgent, impatient—or did starvoices always sound that way? Tsuuka and Dariim approached silently and peered from the shadows. Dariim's pupils danced giddily at the sight of the intruders. "Do you see, cub, how strange they are?"

Dariim's lower jaw sagged, exposing her teeth in all their cub-sharpness. "They have never been here before."

"But you have heard a voice like theirs when my starsilk sings," Tsuuka reminded her. "And there—there is my skysilk." The smaller intruder, who was little taller, little heavier than Dariim, wore it at her waist. "There is the silk you will take your first song-dreams from. And then you will be swift and strong when you return to hunt your firesilk."

Dariim dabbed at her lips with a delicate tongue. "Their teeth are so strange," she whispered, clutching Tsuuka's arms. "And their claws—"

"Their claws are blunt. We have nothing to fear from those. But the sharpened stick the smaller one carries, we must be wary of that.

And if you will look at the larger one—he carries a single tooth at his waist. See how it gleams." Tsuuka did not find it hard to imagine what damage the intruder could do with that sharp-bladed tooth. Her own mother had carried such a tooth, but chipped from stone, in her elder years, when her own teeth had failed her.

Dariim had begun to tremble again, but this time with eagerness. "You are the best hunter in the forest, but you have never taken game so large as this," she hissed.

Tsuuka stiffened. "We are not taking game now, cub. We are only taking the skysilk. And how we will do that—" She didn't know. That was the baffling truth. Spring from the shadows and bowl the intruders over with a swift swipe of their claws? It seemed wrong when she remembered that the intruders had carried a helpless cub from the grasslands and entrusted it to her. It seemed wrong when she remembered the kinship she had glimpsed in the smaller intruder's eyes the night before. It seemed wrong when she remembered how many empty nights the starsilk had filled for her.

Step from the shadows and ask for her silk then? Ask as she would ask another sithi? But she did not speak the starvoice language. She did not think she could make her tongue do the things theirs did. She didn't have blunt teeth to collect words behind. Her teeth were sharp; they cut her words into hisses.

She growled softly with frustration. Would the intruders understand if she demanded the silk in her own language? Sometimes the starsilk used a few words of sithi. Perhaps the intruders knew her language.

The one thing she could not do was turn back, not with Dariim watching fervidly to see what she would do. Tsuuka considered alternatives again, swiftly, then stood, decided. "Come, we will do the boldest thing we have ever done, cub. We will walk up to these intruders and ask them for what we want."

That took Dariim's breath, but only momentarily. Then she was all eagerness.

Tsuuka deliberately rattled brush to warn the intruders of their approach. She knew they had heard when their voices abruptly died. They presented her with a tensely waiting silence when she stepped forward, Dariim her shadow.

They were as they had been the night before, the two of them. One tall and muscular, with shining white fur that he wore in a cap, the other slight, her darker fur streaming down her back. Both their faces were stiff with surprise and the remnant of whatever argument they had with each other—if indeed it was an argument. They seemed to require precious moments to believe what they saw. But the larger did not take his shining tooth from his waist, and the smaller did not wield her sharpened stick in any threatening way.

Tsuuka spoke softly at first, not wanting to frighten them. "Starvoices, I have given you my skysilk in error. Its sisters cry. Their song has an emptiness. I must restore the skysilk to my bower." She glanced from one to the other, alert for some sign that they understood.

She was startled when they did—when the smaller intruder immediately laid aside her stick, untied the skysilk from her waist, and offered it on her extended hands. The intruder's face was tense, her eyes round. She seemed to hold her breath. The larger intruder's hand fell but hovered clear of the hilt of his tooth. Tsuuka hesitated for a moment, evaluating the danger, then touched Dariim's shoulder. "Take it, cub." If Dariim wanted to do bold deeds, here was one—one she would not guess was entirely safe. Because who would suppose that creatures like these would understand her request and honor it so readily?

Dariim's eyes glinted and Tsuuka felt the tension of her muscles beneath the shining fur. Her first step was hesitant. Then she sprang forward boldly and snatched the skysilk, whipping it in the air as she jumped back with it.

The intruders drew back instinctively. For a moment they stared at each other and no one made a sound. Then the smaller intruder said something that sounded almost questioning.

But she did not say it in sithi. Tsuuka took the skysilk from Dariim's clutching fingers. She pressed it against her face, eager for its cool touch. "You have restored the harmony of my bower," she said in a grateful whisper. Then she drew Dariim back into the shadows with her.

She waited tensely, clutching Dariim's arm, to see if the intruders would follow. But they did not. They stared after her, then slipped away just as they had the night before, their faces becoming pale ovals against the darkness, then disappearing.

Tsuuka tied the silk at her waist, wearing it as the intruder had. Then she slipped forward and briefly took up the intruders' scent. Their trail led now in the direction of the heart of the trees. She peered in the direction they had taken, puzzled, momentarily touched by an uneasiness she could not name.

But she had no time to examine that unformed apprehension. Dariim bobbed with excitement, chuckling under her breath. Tsuuka saw unwillingly that there was no sign of nightmare upon her now. And soon the sun would rise. Dariim must be safely sleeping by then or she would not sleep at all.

The heart of the trees . . . The intruders were going to the heart of the trees.

"My cub, come," she said, frowning. "We must choose a tree so you can learn what song-dreams are and how strong and alert they can make you."

Dariim chuckled aloud at that, giddy with the success of her brave deed. "But mother, see now—see what I've done. I'm already strong. The nightmares are gone."

"No," Tsuuka said firmly. "They are paler here. But if you go back to the heart of the trees, they will be heavy and dark. Because that is the place where they are most concentrated. Someday I will tell you why. Tonight you must obey me because I know what is best." All spoken with a quiet certainty she did not feel, because she was not at all confident Dariim would obey. Not with the giddiness of her exploit upon her and the terror of the nightmares fading. "Come, cub."

Dariim's resistance showed itself in her trailing footsteps, in the defiant brightness of her eyes as she gazed back toward the heart of the trees. But occasionally as they scampered back through the forest, she touched the azure silk. Then the brightness of her eyes became different, both anticipatory and anxious.

So she was cowed by the prospect of this new experience. That made it easier to insist that she come. She would never willingly betray her fear with open reluctance.

Tsuuka looked for a tree in its prime, one that stood tall and broad but would not creak and wake Dariim when she slipped away later. "Here," she said when she found one that satisfied her. "You must choose the branch. It must be high so the skysilk can find light from below the horizon."

"And you will stay with me?" Dariim probed, gazing up the tall stalk of the tree.

"How else will I be able to instruct my silk to give you song-dreams?" Tsuuka said and was relieved to see no sign that Dariim detected her evasion. Now if only she could set aside the unease she had felt since parting with the intruders—

It refused to be forgotten. It forced itself to her attention again, taking explicit form this time. The intruders were going to the heart of the trees—where the unseen lived. The unseen, who was vulnerable flesh— the unseen without whom there would be no spinners and no silks in this quarter of the forest. Tsuuka's hand closed on her skysilk, so cool, so slippery. Did the intruders know that the unseen was fragile? That she must not be injured? Or did they go there hunting her with their sharpened stick and polished tooth?

Chill stiffened Tsuuka's muscles. She had wondered what prey the intruders might seek with their blunt teeth and dull claws. If the unseen were as fragile as she feared—and who could tell her whether the escorts' stings would deter the intruders? She shuddered, gazing up at Dariim, who already clawed her way up the tree. She wanted to go after the intruders, wanted to be certain of their intent.

Surely there was time to see her cub sleeping. Surely—

But there was no time at all. Because as Tsuuka put reluctant claws to the bark, a dim, fiery song rose from the direction the intruders had taken. Tsuuka stiffened, recognizing it immediately despite the distance. It was the song of the red silk. She glanced up, alarmed, and saw Dariim staring into the darkness, teeth bared. Then, with no warning, Dariim's body streaked past her, dropping toward the ground.

Her own response was almost as swift. The red silk had come from hiding. It sang its taunting song again and Dariim was galloping after it, not even pausing to glance back. Tsuuka dropped to the ground too, fell to all fours, and surged after Dariim.

The red silk, the unseen, the intruders—Tsuuka'a heart drummed against her rib cage; her blood pulsed to a dizzy rhythm. She didn't know what use her claws would find tonight. She didn't know who they must defend, the unseen, her cub, or herself. But the jarring leap of her heart, the choking shortness of her breath told her she soon would know.

FIFTEEN
REYNA

It was easier to find Juaren that night than it had been in the morning. Easier in the dark forest than it had been in the daylight one. Not because Reyna had become so much more expert in tracking; she stumbled through the trees almost blindly, guided more by instinct than by the occasional bootmark she found on the soil. But because she blundered loudly, not trying to hide the fact that she was lost— begging him to hear her and to turn back. She tripped on a swollen root, she rattled through a patch of brush, she clambered over a fallen tree—and Juaren stood on a small rise, as still as moonlight, looking down at her.

She halted, catching her breath involuntarily, frozen by the expression in his eyes. Was it displeasure? Unwelcome? Or something else— consternation? Certainly he was not pleased to see her. For a moment she could not speak. "You forgot to tell me you were going," she said finally. "I heard something. I woke up and you were gone."

His face changed, but only to become more masklike. "I thought you were tired. I thought you needed to sleep."

"No," she said, disturbed by the contrast between words and expression, the one concerned, the other unrevealing. "You *waited* until I was asleep. Then you slipped away. Because you wanted to go alone."

Juaren sighed deeply, his hands closing to fists, his face changing again—the mask falling away to reveal the concern behind it. "I wanted to go alone," he said. "Yes. Because the place where I'm going—is dangerous. I may go there and come back. I may not. I don't understand completely. I won't understand until I've seen. And I won't fail you as I've failed the others."

"Fail me?" She stared at him blankly, unprepared for those words, for the hard edge they brought to his voice, the pain they brought to his face. And his hands—she did not want to look at his hands. If his nails were cutting crescents in the flesh, she did not want to see.

"I failed my mother by being born while she took wintersleep. I failed Komas by not pulling him back up the mountain—"

"You couldn't reach him," she said, surprised. How could he blame himself for that? Or for his own birth?

"I failed him. But I won't fail you. If only one of us is to go back to Brakrath, it will be you."

"No—" she said involuntarily. A thought she had never considered. One she would not consider now.

"Yes. No one on Brakrath cares that I've gone. And no one will listen when I go back, not if I go alone. I'm a winter-child and a hunter, not a person to be listened to.

"But you are a barohna's daughter. Your mother, your father, all the people of Valley Terlath are waiting for you to come back. And when you do, they will listen to you. They will listen when you tell them what you've seen, what you know, what you've learned.

"I've made you my apprentice. I've given you the old words. Now you must treat them as your pledge. You must accept my guidance as your guild master and let me go alone."

"You call yourself my master?" she said in surprise, not certain if she was more bewildered or frightened by the things he said. *If only one of them was to go back . . .*

"You asked to become my apprentice. You agreed to certain obligations. One of them is to listen to me."

Yes, she had apprenticed herself to him, and he had warned her that there were obligations—and she had laughed. Now she raised a shaky hand to her temples, realizing she should never have laughed. Not when Juaren spoke of his guild. He had made his guild his family, his valley, his life—because for too many years he had had nothing else.

Slowly she released a long breath, trying to find an answer he would understand. "All right. I have listened," she said finally. "But you've made a palace daughter your apprentice, Juaren. Just a palace daughter. I came here to meet my challenge, and if I don't, I'll always be a palace daughter. I'll never be more, no matter how many pledges I take."

"You're more already," he said without hesitation.

"Maybe you see more. Maybe Verra does. But I don't," she insisted. "If I don't meet my challenge, if I hide in my bed while you go to learn what happened to Birnam Rauth, I'll be a child for the rest of my life. I'll never tell anyone about the things we've seen. I'll never raise my voice. I'll never waken anyone. It won't be my place to do that. Because I will be no one—as surely as if I had never left my mother's palace. And then—then you will have failed me truly." She said the last words reluctantly, as if she were putting her knife to him. Because she understood him better tonight than she ever had before. She understood how deeply he pledged his loyalty when once he pledged it—and how concerned he was not to fail in the pledge.

"No."

"Yes. You want to protect me. But how can I be anything but a child if I let you do it? I want to know what your silk told you. I want to know where you're going. And I want to go with you." Strong words, words that made her tremble. She had to go with him, for all the reasons she had given him. But she knew she could not move as unobtrusively as he could. She knew her reactions were not as swift as his. She knew she might distract him at the wrong moment. She knew she might place his life at risk—more at risk than if he went alone.

But she hadn't come here to wait in her bed. "There's a tree—a hollow tree—" she began.

Juaren's eyes flashed. One hand fell to the silk at his waist. Huskily he said, "How do you know that?"

"Birnam Rauth is my kin," she said. "I guessed it from listening to his silk."

His eyes narrowed. "No. I've heard the message your silk carries—"

"I guessed it from the song—and from something I saw in one of his sketch books." And from Birnam Rauth himself, standing at her shoulder in the dark. Could she tell Juaren that? "There's a tree he sketched several times. It—it attracted him."

"Yes," he said slowly, waiting for her to go on.

But she had nothing more to tell. "Let me hear the silk," she said.

His hand touched the starsilk, almost protectively. He stared down at the forest floor, then looked up, capturing her gaze, refusing to release it. "Reyna, there were times when Komas went alone into the ice caverns and I waited outside. That was my part of the hunt—to be ready if he blundered into a breeterlik, if he needed help or had wounds to be treated."

She caught his arm and pressed it, almost tenderly. "I won't wait outside, Juaren."

His lips tightened. He stared down at the ground again, describing a slow pattern with the toe of one boot. Finally he said, "I'll show you how to use the translator."

He carried it at his waist, concealed beneath the starsilk. He tied the starsilk to a tree and had Reyna sit, the translator in her lap, earplugs in her ears. When the breeze caught the silk, fluttering its loose ends, a genderless voice spoke in her ear.

"...clearer now. I was disoriented at first, but I've begun to remember details now. I've begun to remember why I went there. Or came here. It's hard to believe I have a physical location, something that could be marked on a chart of the forest. I have no sense of my body—and I think I know the reason for that. But I still have my thoughts, and if I understand correctly what's happened, some of them are being recorded, in some form. Maybe someday someone will hear them, someone who can decipher them—someone who will be interested in what I've found here.

"It's not unique, I suppose. I can find parallels to other species. But this is my own discovery, so I have a certain proprietorial pride—especially since I won't make any discoveries after this one."

Reyna shifted, struck by the dispassionate choice of words, struck too by the methodical way he laid out his observations so that she could understand them.

She could understand them, but she could not believe them. Not immediately, not as she listened in the darkened forest. Sithi—that was the name Birnam Rauth gave the chatni. And the details Birnam Rauth had gathered so carefully through the sithi, through the silks they shared thoughts with, through observation—she found it hard to believe that the silks that sang so eloquently in the trees had been spun by the chattering creatures she and Juaren had watched feeding that morning. She found it hard to believe that the songsilks derived at least a part of their consciousness from other creatures who were years or even decades dead—the preserved. She found it hard to believe that Birnam Rauth had dared go to the deep trees to try to glimpse something his sithi companion and her silk had told him must never be seen.

Something fragile. Something dangerous. Something born wise— the unseen, Birnam Rauth called it—that saw the light of day only twice in the year of its life: once when it made its way from the tree where it had hatched to the tree where it would perform its life work, and later when it made its way from that tree to spin its life-silk and to die.

Life-silks, master-silks, songsilks; spinners, escorts, the unseen and the preserved—and all of them of a single family. But the preserved were no more than the living wills of the creatures whose consciousness was lodged in the life-silks. And there were countless life-silks hidden here in the forest—as many as there had been years since the beginning of their time. Some of them were long forgotten, their filaments inter- grown with the wood fibers of the trees where they hid. Some had slipped away into the soil and dissociated into individual filaments. Others were fresher, newer, and these were still used, through the agency of the master-silks, to lend awareness to the songsilks.

No, she believed none of it. But when Birnam Rauth's narrative ended abruptly mid-word, then began to repeat itself, Reyna looked up and thought she saw filmy silks swirling from the white-barked trees. She shook her head sharply, dismissing that perception, and reached with numb hands to remove the earplugs.

"He's here. Hidden. In one of the trees," she said unwillingly. But could she say that Birnam Rauth was alive? Was that a fair description of his state? Birnam Rauth had eventually guessed himself what had happened. The unseen had studied him—his mind, his thoughts, his physiology—through the sithi and the silks. She had found a uniqueness in him that was at once precious, perplexing and threatening, a challenge to her inbred wisdom. So when he had come to the deep woods, when he had intruded upon this most closely held inviolability, when he had tried to see what was not to be seen, she had directed the escorts to capture him. He didn't remember how it had happened; he thought he had exercised more than reasonable care. But the escorts had taken him, and then, because the unseen had not wanted to destroy him, she had spun a life-silk to cradle his awareness and his will.

No, she had not killed him. Not in her view. Because hers was a wisdom far different than human wisdom. She had simply preserved him and hidden him away for her successors to study, to try to understand. She and her kind were vulnerable, a vulnerability that fed their secretiveness and their vigilance. If there were more like Birnam Rauth, they must be prepared to deal with them.

"He's here," Reyna repeated. "Somewhere."

"Yes," Juaren agreed. "When we were flying over the forest today, I noticed a place where the trees were taller, older. The heart of the trees, he called it. The place where the forest lives. He's there."

And they were near that place now. If she closed her eyes, Reyna could feel it beat, that heart of wood. She could feel its rhythm in her bones. For a moment she entertained a craven thought: now we know what happened to him; now we can go back.

But of course they couldn't. Somewhere there was a silk that contained the remnant of Birnam Rauth's consciousness. They could not turn back until they found it. Slowly she stood and took Juaren's starsilk from the tree. "Do you know how to find the heart of the trees?"

"We've taken the right direction. Look—you can see that the trees are older here than they were beside the stream."

The trees were older, taller, darker. Reyna gazed around, seeing that, wondering if these trees sheltered life-silks. There were some with open hollows, some with healed wounds, a few standing dead and empty. But were they empty? Shivering, she remembered the escorts, the stingered spinners Birnam Rauth had described. Remembered what they could do to any creature who became too curious. How would they know which trees they could search, which they dared not?

"If you want to sleep, then come back tomorrow—" Juaren said.

"No." If she left now, how would she find the courage to return? "Which—which direction must we take? To the oldest trees?"

"This way."

She followed, trying to walk as lightly as he did—trying to walk as if the soil were alive and could feel her step. The moon had set, leaving the forest dark except for the distant sparkle of sunlight. Reyna saw it sometimes between wide branches when she glanced up.

The trees became older as they walked. She saw that in their size and in the roughness of their bark. Moss and fungus padded their massive trunks. Their foliage was sparse, carried on branches that reached tall against the sky, and there were wounds in their trunks where lower branches had torn away.

Briefly they paused and talked. When they went on, Reyna felt the presence of life in the trees—life both fragile and timeless. The dark-mossed trunks, the soil underfoot—they seemed strung with living filaments, filaments informed with an awareness that had survived from a time so ancient she could not imagine it. She could almost hear silent songs in the air. She could almost hear—

But the crackle of brush was not a sound from some ancient time. Reyna caught Juaren's arm and together they stared in the direction of the sound.

Two sithi stepped from the shadows, one adult, one younger, no taller, no heavier than Reyna. Reyna stared blankly at their approach. She had given no thought to encountering sithi tonight. She had been too preoccupied. Anxiously she saw that the adult had unsheathed her claws, although she didn't brandish them. The younger hung behind the older, half-crouched, and from the glint of her eyes she was both frightened and excited. Reyna stared in fascination at the sharpness of her teeth, at the smooth motion of muscles beneath her chestnut fur.

She had no time to wonder what they would do. The older stepped forward. Could it be the sithi they had encountered the night before, the one they had traded the grassland cub to? She seemed to recognize them. And she spoke in the hissing, growling language Reyna had heard Birnam Rauth try to speak.

She spoke, but what did she say? The sithi's yellow glance flickered to the blue silk Reyna had tied at her waist. She wet her lips, tentatively.

Her ears stood erect. Her brow was deeply creased, making her expression almost quizzical.

Did she want the silk? Had she regretted trading it away? Remembering the sad song the silk had sung, Reyna trusted to instinct. Quickly she untied the silk and offered it.

She knew she had guessed correctly immediately. The adult sithi's pupils shimmered wide and she spoke softly to the younger. The cub took a single hesitant step forward, then snatched at the silk and sprang back. The adult sithi took the silk from her, touching it almost reverently, then spoke again, softly, in a whisper.

"You gave your silk to me and then you missed it," Reyna said, knowing it was true—and knowing the sithi could not possibly understand her words. Then Juaren touched her arm and drew her back into the shadows, and she was surprised to find that she was shaking.

The reaction passed quickly, although Reyna glanced back over her shoulder often as they continued through the trees. And she listened for the pad of feet.

Soon the shadows grew increasingly dense and the trees crowded together, their trunks broad, deep with increasingly cavernous hollows. The air smelled different, damper, mustier, as if the cleansing breeze could not move among the close-grown trees.

"Your pike—may I have it?"

They had not spoken since encountering the sithi. Reyna hesitated, yielding the weapon doubtfully. "What are you going to do?"

For answer Juaren began to tap lightly at hollow trunks as they picked their way among the forest giants. "If there's something here—"

"Juaren—" she said apprehensively, then bit back the protest. If there was something here, they must find it. Somehow. And did she have any better idea than his?

And there was something. Something near. As Juaren tapped at the trees, Reyna held her breath and felt its presence. She felt the beating of its heart in the very heaviness of the air. She felt the waiting quality of the shadows. She felt anticipation. "It's almost dawn," she said. Almost imperceptibly the sky had begun to lighten.

"Soon."

A creature that saw daylight only twice ... When would the unseen emerge from its bulb-well to spin its life-silk and die? When would the successor it had carefully nourished leave to enter the tree where it would make its own well? Was this the season? Had Birnam Rauth said? Reyna couldn't remember.

"Juaren—" But before she could ask, Juaren tapped lightly at one of the aged giants—and jumped back, pulling her with him, as an indistinguishable shape billowed from the tree's interior and rippled through the air. Briefly it swirled around them, slapping them with silken arms, as if it were angry. Then it rushed away, and as it rose through the trees, it began to sing, loudly, almost fiercely.

Reyna fell back against a moss-cushioned trunk, startled. A life-silk? Had they frightened a life-silk from hiding? How would they know? Birnam Rauth had seen only master-silks and songsilks and the duller silks that lay silently in sithi bowers. She knew a songsilk could not rush through the air as this silk did, returning again to flutter angrily at their faces, then disappearing high into the branches. And she had never heard a songsilk sing so loudly or so impatiently. She stared up. It was impossible to tell if the silk had color, but its voice was like an angry splash of red against the silence of the forest.

The silence of the forest? Reyna had no time to shed her startlement gradually. Because Juaren had caught her arm again, pulling her back against the trunk of the nearest tree. And there were running feet and the rattle of brush. Reyna turned and stared as the two sithi came bolting through the trees, running on all fours, their stride long, rocking, muscular. The adult wore the blue silk tied at her waist, ends flying. It warbled weakly as she ran.

Seeing Reyna and Juaren, the cub jumped aside skittishly and hissed before running on. The adult briefly broke stride, baring her teeth in an unmistakable snarl. Reyna's fingers bit so hard into the bark of the tree that she felt moss pack beneath her nails. Only the lift-pack she wore on her back kept her from pressing herself flat against the tree.

The lift-pack—at least they had lift-packs. How high could the sithi jump? She touched the lift-pack controls strapped to her left wrist. "Juaren—"

"The silk." He had released her. He stared briefly after the sithi and the silk. Then he was running. "They're trying to catch the silk."

"Wait!" she cried, panic-stricken. But the sithi were gone, bounding into the pre-dawn shadows. And abruptly, with no explanation, Juaren was gone too. Reyna stood frozen, trying to understand. There was a silk loose in the trees, singing an angry song. The sithi were pursuing it and Juaren had gone after them. And she stood here alone, as if she had lost command of her legs.

She touched the starsilk at her waist. She touched the controls of her lift-pack. Slowly, not understanding what was happening, she moved away from the tree that shadowed her and took herself in the direction the others had taken. The darkness of night had become the grey of earliest morning. The strange half-light, the looming trees and the deep shadows that attended them gave Reyna a sense of unreality as she pushed her way through the forest. She felt as if she groped her way through a dream, trying to find its symbols and their meanings while she still slept. "Juaren!" It hardly seemed her own voice. "Juaren!"

Then there were other voices, drowning hers. Shrill voices, angry voices—Reyna froze again, momentarily immobilized by shock. The creature that had discovered them sleeping that morning, the spinner— she heard tens of them screaming from the trees. And the sound came from the direction Juaren had taken. Had the sithi alarmed the spinners? Had Juaren?

Or were these the voices of spinners at all? Did the escorts scream too? Birnam Rauth had said they were nothing more than spinners with stingers.

Reyna ran then. Ran into the unreal pallor of early morning. Ran through the ancient trees, the musty smell of them making her choke for breath. Ran until she found herself in a place where the trees stood so ancient, so moss-choked, their hollows so cavernous, that she felt she had made her way into a nightmare.

Perhaps it was a nightmare. Because now she saw the creatures that screamed, and they were not spinners. They were no larger than spinners. They were no less plump, no less infantile. But they wagged horny stingers in the air, their limbs pumping and straining with anger, their eyes depthless and virulent at once. She could barely hear the taunting song of the silk over their voices.

She could barely hear the scream of the adult sithi. But the sithi was indeed screaming. Reyna rocked to a halt, staring around with half-seeing eyes, trying to find the sense of the scene.

The runaway silk—she could see it more clearly now; it was as red as its song—clung to the withered lower branch of one of the ancient trees. The sithi cub plunged up the tree's trunk, eyes glinting, ears laid flat against its skull, teeth bared in a covetous grin. Escorts boiled from the hollow of the tree, from the hollows of neighboring trees, and shrilled, brandishing their stingers. And the adult sithi crouched on the forest floor, screaming with an anguish more punishing than any Reyna had ever seen. Remembering what Birnam Rauth had said the sting of an escort could do to a bright-eyed cub, Reyna understood the older sithi's anguish. It touched her too, making her breath short, making her stomach tight.

She didn't know why the red silk flew free or why the cub hunted it. But she knew immediately that she couldn't stand here and watch the cub stung. And she couldn't stand here and watch the older sithi sacrifice herself trying to defend the cub. Almost without thinking Reyna touched the controls of her lift-pack. It wasn't until she drifted into the air that she realized Juaren already floated in the shadows nearby, pike raised, fending back escorts that scrambled across the wide branches toward the silk. The tiny creatures flailed their stingers in rage, three-fingered fists knotted, toes clinging to the heavily mossed branches. Juaren extended the pike, keeping a safe distance from their wagging stingers, prodding their chubby legs, driving them back.

But only temporarily. Reyna could see that. Tens more of the creatures pressed behind the nearest ones, pushing at them. When one of the creatures lost its grip on the slippery moss and fell, the others seemed not to notice. They drove forward, clutching after the pike now with three-fingered hands.

There was no way Reyna could shout to Juaren, no way to make herself heard. And what had she to say, with the adult sithi suddenly springing and clawing her way up the tree, her fur damp, her eyes slitted, her ears laid flat? Juaren was safe. Even if he could not hold the escorts back, he had only to maneuver away from reach of their stingers. But the sithi had no lift-packs. Watching them claw their way up the tree, Reyna acted upon impulse, without thinking. She fingered her controls and ascended rapidly to the branch where the silk clung.

The silk had tangled itself in a cluster of dried twigs, singing defiantly. It required only a fraction of a second to sense Reyna's presence, to guess her intention as she snatched for it. Too late, it struggled, trying to extricate itself from pointed twigs and streak away. In its fury it caught and tore instead.

And Reyna captured it. She closed fingers around the silk and was immediately startled by the strength she felt in it, the will. It writhed in her grasp, slapping silken arms at her, as she tugged it free of the branch. Instinctively she held it at arm's length, clutching it tight in one fist, afraid it would try to wrap strangling arms around her neck.

The sithi cub blinked up in startled disbelief. Reyna dropped quickly, giving the cub no time to decide she intended to steal its prize and to mount a second offensive. Keeping careful range from the cub's razor claws, she held the struggling silk within reach.

Yellow eyes drew to distrustful slits. Facial muscles slackened, then stretched taut. Then, so swiftly Reyna didn't have time to flinch, clawed fingers snatched the silk. The cub turned and scrambled down the tree, clutching the silk, leaping to the ground at the same time that the older sithi sprang down from the tree.

At first Reyna thought the cry she heard was the older sithi's. The sithi spun when she touched ground, her anguish turning to fury. She slapped the startled cub's face and, when the cub fled, raced after it, swatting and biting. Muscles bunching under her sweat-dampened coat, she chased the cub away into the trees.

And the cry continued, then abruptly ceased. Reyna's feet touched ground and she turned and looked up. Her breath choked away at what she saw. Juaren had not followed her. He still hung in the air. The pike had fallen from his hands and he was thrashing helplessly against white strings that tangled around his arms and legs.

White strings spit by the shrilling escorts. They ejected the sticky strands at him from every direction, and with the involuntary thrashing of his limbs, he wrapped the strands around him. Reyna stared up, paralyzed, capable of only one useless thought. *Birnam Rauth hadn't warned them of this.*

But Birnam Rauth had remembered so little of what happened to him in the heart of the trees. He had not remembered being immobilized by strings of sticky silk. He had not remembered struggling and then slumping into unconsciousness. He had not remembered being reeled in by the escorts and swiftly lashed to the trunk of a mossy tree, head sagging, arms hanging limp. As Reyna watched helplessly, all those things happened to Juaren.

And when they had happened, when he hung immobile, the shrilling chorus of the escorts died. The heart of the woods was suddenly silent again as many tens of depthless eyes turned to Reyna. She stared up. Her hands had closed to painful fists. Her mouth was parchment-dry. Her breath came in painful gulps, as if silken strands bound her too. But the escorts made no motion toward her. They stood with their tiny hands fisted, their eyes unwinking.

As if they had been ordered to watch her. As if they had been ordered to record her image. Reyna licked her lips, to no effect. Her tongue was dry too, cottony. The unseen—Birnam Rauth said the unseen directed the activities of the spinners and to some extent the activities of the escorts too. Now, for some reason, she had directed them to stare at Reyna, to record her movements.

Reyna laughed, a half-hysterical sound, entirely involuntary. What did the unseen see through all those unwinking eyes? A strange and frightened creature, with all the wildness of despair in her eyes? Or simply a creature so alien the unseen could read nothing from its face, from its posture? Nothing but a momentarily leashed threat.

Reyna shuddered, trying to bring herself under control. She could not yield to hysteria now. Juaren was helpless. She was the only person who could help him.

But when she tried to think what to do, what she *could* do that would have any effect, she thought of nothing. Experimentally she stepped forward, reaching for the pike Juaren had dropped.

The escorts responded immediately, crouching and screaming, stingers wagging. Reyna caught a sharp breath and took an involuntary step back. Obviously she wasn't to be permitted to retrieve the pike. And what could she do if she did retrieve it? It hadn't saved Juaren. He had wielded the pike, and now he hung helpless in the tree.

Briefly Reyna squeezed her eyes shut, pressing her temples with trembling fingers, trying to force some thought to the surface. She didn't dare take even a single step forward. And she didn't dare use her lift-pack to lift toward the tree where Juaren hung in silken bonds. Because if the escorts spit their paralyzing web at her too, if she found herself as helpless as Juaren already was, then there would be no help for either of them.

Go back to the stream? Wake Verra? She pressed harder at her temples, wondering what Verra could do. And what if she ran back to the stream to fetch Verra and returned to find that Juaren had been hidden away in her absence, tucked out of reach in some musty hollow?

There were tens of them large enough to hold him. Tens of them large enough to conceal him while the unseen did whatever she chose to do. Would she spin a life-silk to contain his thoughts, as she had done with Birnam Rauth? Was she curious about him? Did she consider him precious and rare enough to preserve? Reyna shuddered violently, wondering what had become of Birnam Rauth's body. Had it died slowly in a clinging net of silk after the unseen spun his life-silk? Had he been permitted to starve, unconscious and helpless?

She was going to fail Juaren. She was going to fail him in just the way he thought he had failed his mother and his guild master. She was going to stand helplessly while he died. The certainty was like a blow. It took her breath. It left her tearful and stunned.

And depthless eyes continued to stare. *The unseen—the unseen was watching her through the eyes of the escorts.* That certainty came slowly, coldly, making her dizzy with helpless anger. She raised her head and glared up at the tiny creatures that lined the trees.

What do you expect to see? she demanded silently, fiercely. *What do you expect me to do? Just walk away? Didn't you learn anything from Birnam Rauth? Didn't you learn anything about us from him? Didn't you learn that we cherish our bodies? And each other?*

But how could she vent her anger at something she couldn't see? Something whose nature and dimensions she couldn't even imagine? The unseen was here, hidden somewhere nearby. Poised, waiting, watching through tens of eyes. Did her heart, if she had one, beat with the same fear that Reyna's did? Was she hurting with fear? How must this encounter look to her?

It must look as if strange creatures had come thrusting into the most vulnerable heart of her sanctuary. It must look as if their presence threatened not just her but the entire web of life that depended upon her. It must look as if her choices were to destroy those creatures or to risk being destroyed herself, with all her offspring and all her kind.

But we didn't come here for that, Reyna found herself pleading silently, as if the unseen could hear her thoughts, as if she could understand them. *We didn't come here to harm you. We didn't come here to hurt you. Let my mate go and we'll leave. We'll leave now.*

The trees gave no sign that anyone heard. The escorts continued to stare down at her. They crouched on their limbs, as if they had settled into place for a long vigil.

What else did they have to do but to maintain this vigil? That was their entire function—to protect the unseen. *Let my mate go and we'll never tell anyone about this place. We'll never tell anyone that you live here.* Foolish—it was foolish and useless to try to talk to a creature she couldn't see, a creature whose nature she couldn't comprehend. Still, with aching-cold fingers, Reyna untied the starsilk from her waist and held it free. *Listen—you know this voice. This man is my kin, and by now you know he wouldn't have harmed you—no more than we will harm you.*

Reyna felt certain of that. Birnam Rauth had come to the heart of the trees to observe the unseen, never to harm her. And surely, if the unseen and all her predecessors had studied him, they recognized that— with whatever alien wisdom they used to recognize any truth.

The starsilk clung to her fingers and sang with the passing breeze. It sang a song the unseen must have heard before. But there was no sign that the song tore at the unseen, that it even touched her. Slowly Reyna lowered her head. The bitterness of tears rose to her eyes and spilled over onto her cheeks. They were acid, etching their paths in her flesh. Her mood changed.

There were weapons and implements in their ship. Verra had shown her them. Flame-throwers, chopping blades, weapons that cast projectiles through the air so swiftly no one could dodge them. And other, more obscure weapons. Vengefully Reyna thought of those things. If she left Juaren here and went for them, she might never see him again. She might never find where the escorts hid him in her absence. But she could do the very things the unseen must fear most. She could cut the escorts down. She could burn them where they perched. She could torch the heart of the trees. She could make the unseen feel her grief, if not her need.

She could destroy something as rare, as precious as Juaren himself. She could denude the forest. She could quench its spirit and its song.

She shuddered with those thoughts and knew she would never obey them. Was sorry she had even briefly entertained them.

She was too preoccupied to hear the sithi approach. Nor did she notice when the creature's shadow fell at her feet. When the sithi touched her arm, closing slender fingers upon it, Reyna started violently and uttered a half-strangled scream.

She spun, staring into the sleekly furred face, expecting to see bared teeth, finding instead something she didn't believe at first: comprehension.

That startled her more than hostility or aggression. The sithi saw what had happened and understood what Reyna felt. It understood that Juaren was caught and that she was grieving and angry and helpless—entirely helpless. Reyna shivered, trying to put her thoughts in order. How did the sithi understand those things? Did their dissimilarity hide some basic likeness? Were they more of a kind than she had thought?

There were things she and Juaren had understood too. They had understood that the sithi cub intended to have the red silk. They had understood the danger of its quest. They had understood the older sithi's helpless anguish. Had they not understood those things, Juaren would be free now.

Did the sithi understand that too? The creature had released her arm. With a tentative hand, it stroked the starsilk. Its brows drew together, as if it wanted to question her.

Reyna scrubbed the back of one hand across her face, not knowing any way to answer that unasked question. Not knowing any way to speak with this creature who observed her helplessness with obvious sympathy.

Except perhaps in song. And was that such a foolish thought? Reyna knew from what Birnam Rauth had said that the sithi shared some silent communication with the silks. If she sang like a silk, sang her own song—

What else did she have to do? It wasn't as if she had alternatives. Trembling, Reyna held the starsilk to the breeze again. When it began to sing, she sang too, but aloud, as she never had before. She sang all the things she wanted the sithi to understand. She sang of her own world, where the mysteries that lived in the forest were different from the mysteries that lived here. She sang of people she had cared for and land she loved. She sang of the sun shining from her mother's sunthrone. She sang of the mountains, where she had intended to walk with Juaren. She sang of the stories he could not write if he died here, of the children he could not father, of the apprentices he could not teach. She sang of the pain of failing—in her quest for the throne, in her challenge, in her need to save Juaren from death.

She sang promises too. Pledges and vows, these directed more at the unseen than the sithi. Pledges that if Juaren were allowed to go free, she would search no more for Birnam Rauth. That they would leave and forget his lonely song. That if Juaren were freed, they would turn from the heart of the trees and never try to see what must not be seen. That they would return to their ship and to their own world.

She sang pledges that hurt. Pledges that burned as she gave them voice. Because she knew that if Juaren were freed, if they were permitted to go, Birnam Rauth's song would always torment her. She could fold the starsilk and hide it in the most obscure corner of the palace. She could bury it or burn it, and she would still hear its song. For all the days of her life.

Yet she offered Birnam Rauth for Juaren. She offered to leave him entombed forever if Juaren could be freed. And she didn't even know the use of her song. She didn't know if the sithi understood. She didn't know if the unseen even heard it.

Those things comprised the conscious stanzas of her song. Her song spoke from another level too, from a deeper level. Her song spoke from the place where pain lived, where loneliness lived, where duty and hope and trust struggled daily for life.

After a while she realized that the sithi's blue silk sang along with the starsilk. That the sithi stood with her head thrown back, her eyes pressed shut, as if she somehow sang through her silk. Reyna wondered—could the sithi speak to the unseen through her silk? Could she plead Reyna's cause as she understood it?

How did she understand it? The sithi stood with hands rigidly outstretched, claws digging at the air. Her brow was creased, her ears erect, quivering. Reyna drew a tremulous breath, pressed her eyes shut, and resumed her own song.

Slowly, after a while, she realized that something had changed. There was a shifting, a rustling, a stirring. And then there was a return of stillness. She bit at her lip, afraid to open her eyes, afraid of what the stillness meant, afraid of what she would see.

At last she did look, the hardest thing she had yet done, because all her hope lay in the first reluctant glance.

She saw what she hadn't dare believe she would ever see. The escorts had withdrawn. The branches were bare. It was fully daylight and Juaren looked down at her with dazed eyes.

She felt nothing in that moment. There was no time for it, no time to let the intensity of her emotions unfold. And there was no time to hesitate. No time to wonder if the escorts would emerge from hiding again if she lifted to where Juaren hung, slipped his knife from his belt, and sawed with trembling hands at the strands of silk that held him prisoner. She simply did those things, feeling nothing, but laughing while tears streamed down her face.

"Can you manage your controls?" she demanded when Juaren hung by just two strands of silk. He hadn't spoken, but he looked at her with recognition.

He nodded stiffly, as if he were uncertain of his strength. "Yes." It was more question than answer.

"What can you do?" she probed, praying that he had not been left witless like a too-curious sithi cub, stung by escorts—but he had not been stung. He had only been swaddled in sticky silk. And now she had cut the dried strands away, frowning at their lingering odor.

For a moment he gazed at her blankly. "I can use my pack controls," he said finally, with forced distinctness. "I can press the buttons."

"Which buttons will you press to go to the ground?" she insisted.

Again he was briefly blank. "The—the button nearest my palm."

"Yes." Relieved, she brushed the tears from her eyes and severed the last strands of silk.

When they reached the ground, the sithi had slipped away into the trees, leaving them alone. Alone where the trees held musty shadows, alone where life-silks hid. Alone in a place that waited for them to go.

They used their packs to make their way back through the forest. They drifted just above the ground, and sometimes she had to guide Juaren when he seemed lost or confused. Sometimes he forgot where they were and let his eyelids fall shut and then she woke him. But at other times he knew her and spoke sense to her.

Verra was awake when they returned. She looked up with quick concern, then guided them to their beds. "Sleep. You need sleep, both of you," she said. "Tell me about it later. Whatever it was." Kind words. Rational words. Only the deep crease of her brow admitted to all the questions she wanted to ask.

The reaction didn't come until Reyna shed her pack and slipped into her bedding. Then her teeth began to chatter and her entire body to shake. Quickly Verra fetched her own bedding and swaddled her in it. She prepared hot brew and forced her to drink it. Even so it took time for Reyna to throw off the helpless shivering. She hugged herself, aware that Juaren watched her from his own bed, still trying to understand what had happened.

"Birnam Rauth?" he said huskily.

Reyna shuddered, wishing she did not have to look down into the hollow pit of her grief, however briefly. "We had to leave him," she said as matter of factly as she could. "We had to leave him there. And I promised not to go back."

Drawing a trembling breath, she stretched both hands out before her. They were slender, fragile, the hands of a palace daughter. She had not changed. She had met her challenge, and she had both succeeded and failed in it. She had brought Juaren safely from the heart of the woods, but she had left Birnam Rauth. And none of it had changed her.

Quickly she slipped down into her bedding, hiding herself there from all the things she still held at abeyance: a relief so profound she didn't think her soul could hold it, a grief of the same magnitude. Tomorrow. Tomorrow was time enough to examine those feelings. Tomorrow was time enough to touch them and to let them touch her. Perhaps by then she could accept both her success and her failure. Perhaps by then she could place them in perspective and accept the fact that she could not have had the one without the other.

She pressed her eyes shut and willed herself to sleep.

SIXTEEN
REYNA

Reyna slept without dreaming, as if all thought, all experience had fallen away, leaving her empty even of sorrow. It was midday when Verra shook her. "Reyna."

"No." Reyna turned away, burrowing deeper into her bedding, not ready to wake. Sleep had not even begun to heal her. Her body still ached, her eyes still burned, and the wound of her failure would be raw for a long time, perhaps for all her life. Juaren had not died, but she had left Birnam Rauth somewhere in the heart of the trees and she was pledged not to return for him. "No."

But Verra was insistent. "Reyna—there's someone here for you. I'm sure it's you he wants, from the way he stares at you."

Reyna caught a sobbing breath and pushed irritably at her bedding. Someone to see her? She sat, pulling one hand through her hair, prepared to be angry—with Verra for wakening her with a ruse, with herself for responding.

She sat and she saw who had come to see her. A spinner stood beside the stream. It gazed at her stolidly as if it had been instructed to wait there until she woke. Its round eyes were vacant. Its chubby legs were bowed. It held a parcel almost as large as itself. When it realized that

Reyna had wakened, it dropped the parcel and waddled rapidly away, shrilling once in retreat.

Surprised, still half-sleeping, Reyna stared at the parcel it had dropped. The outer wrapper was of ivory silk, stained by time and rain. "Verra—" she said uncertainly. How had the spinner found her here? And what had it brought?

"You don't have your boots on. Let me get it for you." The Arnimi woman stepped quickly to the streambank and retrieved the bundle, placing it in Reyna's hands.

It was not heavy. Its contents compressed easily under her probing fingers. And it appeared to have been hidden away for a very long time. Reyna stared down at it, biting her lip, her fingertips tingling with a first stunning intimation of what the parcel might contain.

Juaren had wakened and was sitting cross-legged on his bedding, watching with an intent frown. Verra bent near. Reyna looked at them both, licking dry lips. Then, afraid to wait, afraid to build expectations that might only crumble, she pulled the wrappings from the bundle.

She caught her breath, realizing with her first glimpse of the contents that she had guessed correctly. Realizing with her first glimpse how well the unseen had understood her song. Or how well the sithi had understood and translated it through her blue songsilk.

Hesitantly, as if her nails might tear it, Reyna drew a sheer white silk from the bundle. It was longer than her starsilk, wider, and it appeared infinitely more delicate. But she saw immediately that there were tough filaments woven through it, and she guessed from the first touch that this was no fragile silk. This was a silk that would endure through many centuries—and many legends.

Standing, she shook out the silk, hoping it would not struggle as the red silk had, hoping it would not try to escape her. Could she bear it if she had found Birnam Rauth and he only wanted to be free? Only wanted to flirt away through the trees as the red silk had?

He did not. The silk moved of its own accord in the light breeze, first swirling around her, then lacing itself loosely around her shoulders and one arm, clinging there lightly. She could feel its life and its will in its silken touch. She could almost feel the processes of its thought as it spoke in the voice she already knew so well.

Verra quickly fetched the translator and it repeated Birnam Rauth's first words for them in its own genderless voice. "Who are you? I can tell you're human. Who are you?"

Reyna drew a long breath, catching her lower lip in her teeth, her eyes suddenly burning with tears of joy. She touched the silk with wondering fingertips. It was hard to believe this had happened. It was hard to believe this was real. She had made a choice. She had renounced her search. But through the agency of the sithi and the unseen, Birnam Rauth was here, speaking to her. She had understood the sithi's anguish and the unseen's vulnerability, and they in turn had understood her.

They had done more than understand. They had reached out, both of them. She had traveled across the stars on her quest, and it had been fulfilled not because she had used wit, not because she had used force, but because she had made herself understood to two alien creatures.

She laughed aloud, giddily. Lessons. There were lessons in this. She had learned some of them last night. She was learning some of them now. And there were many others she must yet consider. But this wasn't the time. Quickly she took the translator from Verra and adjusted it. "I'm Reyna Terlath," she said. "I'm daughter of your son, and I came here because you called."

"Daughter? Of my son? You heard my call?"

"I heard it," she said. And now she was ready to hear many things, to see many things, to do many things—some she had never even considered before.

But there were matters more urgent than that today. She felt the warmth of Juaren's shoulder against hers. She felt the heat of the midday sun on her hair. She felt the pleasure of Verra's smile. And she felt the first stirring of Birnam Rauth's comprehension—that he was free, that he was among kin, that someone had come for him. Quickly she tried to guess the full state of his mind. She tried to guess what things he would want most to taste today, with his first freedom.

Warmth. Light. Breeze. The touch of human hands. Quickly she rose and walked barefoot to a place where sunlight fell unobstructed through the trees, to a place where the breeze could curl easy fingers around them. She summoned Juaren to her side. "Here—hold your arm here, so he can touch you."

The sharing of warmth; the sharing of joy; the sharing of freedom—
and later, when those things had been done, they would have stories
to tell each other and a journey to make.

Many stories.

A long journey.

SEVENTEEN
REYNA

The first thing Reyna saw when she woke was Juaren. He had framed himself in the window casement, and he sat with knees drawn up, arms wrapped around them, watching her without expression. Midmorning sunlight touched his hair. Reyna sat, pulling her covers with her, briefly confused. Pitted stone walls, time-faded hangings, the friendly disorder of piled scrolls, a forgotten inkstand—

Home. They had reached home, arriving in the darkest hours of Kimira's night. The Arnimi had met their ship and delivered them to the plaza in their aircar. Servants had met them there, solemnly, awed, and conducted them to Reyna's chambers, offering food and drink and someone to chant in the corridor while they found sleep. But Reyna had looked up and seen her mother silhouetted at the window of the watchtower. And she had asked simply that they be left to sleep.

Because there was much business to be conducted the next day. Greetings, reconciliations, requests—intentions to be stated and defended. And changes to be met. It seemed to Reyna that their journey had occupied only a portion of a season, even though they had spent a full double hand of days aboard the *Pitric* on their return journey. But each of the servants who met them was visibly changed. Nivan's shoulders were more stooped. Neddica's eyes squinted from a deeper webwork of wrinkles. And Ondic, who had been a year short of her first majority when they left, now wore the blue-embroidered headband of a second-year apprentice.

Changes. Reyna lay for a moment, meeting Juaren's waiting gaze, and wondered what things had not changed in their absence. Then she got up, shrugged into the clean shift that lay across the back of her chair—she wondered idly how long it had been waiting there—and went to the door.

"Daughter? Are you ready for your meal?" It was Nivan, and she knew from the absence of the specially carved pendant he wore when engaged upon the barohna's business that he had stationed himself there as a friend rather than as her mother's runner. A very old friend, one who had seen Reyna and her sisters through childhood and smiled benignly even on the rare occasions when they had run wild in the corridors.

She turned back. "Juaren—do you want to eat before we meet with my mother?"

Juaren unfolded from the window casement, shaking his head.

Reyna nodded agreement. They had many things to discuss with Khira. Their first meal would taste sweeter with that behind. "Nivan, would you tell my mother we would like to speak with her before we eat? We have—news."

"She is already waiting in the throneroom. She has said she will see no petitioners and no guild monitors until she has first spoken with you."

"And with my year's mate. Would you run for me then and tell her we're coming?"

Nivan went immediately, walking more stiffly than she remembered. Reyna turned back, aware of rising tension—tension Juaren clearly shared. He stroked his ice-blue songsilk and then stepped to the bureau drawer where they had left the bundled life-silk.

Birnam Rauth spoke immediately when they roused him. "Did you sleep well, granddaughter? Juaren?"

Only a faint touch of irony marred his already carefully-trained Brakrathi—irony Reyna guessed he used to mask his occasional unease with his dependence upon her senses and Juaren's. Because while he heard, while within certain limits he felt, he did not see or taste or smell—

except through them. And the situation was new enough to him, and to them, that sometimes it stung. "Very well, my grandfather," she replied, meeting his irony with a generous portion of her own. "Will you be worn or will you be carried when you meet my mother?"

"I'll be carried if you can pack me back into my wrappings without crushing my old grey beard."

"You know we're always careful of your beard," she said dryly. "And your tired bones. A man of your years—"

"A man of my years—" he echoed with an invisible smile, wry and deprecating.

She felt as if she had known him for a very long time. She felt as if she had known him all her life. Carefully Reyna folded his silk and rewrapped it. Then she took the hand Juaren offered her and they stepped into the hall.

There were a surprising number of servants in the upper corridors this morning, all assiduously sweeping and trimming, careful not to glance up too obviously as Reyna and Juaren passed. There were monitors too and people from every possible guild and occupation. The trenchers were here, the canners, the weavers, the scribers. There were shepherds and cooks. Creche workers had somehow found errands to bring them to the palace, all their charges trailing behind them, eyes wide. Altogether it was surprising how many people had found business in the palace corridors on the very morning of Reyna's return.

Of course none stared or pointed. None spoke. None did more than smile and offer an unobtrusive nod. Reyna returned their carefully restrained greetings, wondering what they would say among themselves later about the palace daughter who had gone so far to meet her challenge—and returned still only a palace daughter. She guessed there were legends building already.

With her mother's help, she and Juaren must use those legends, just as they must use the ones they intended to build more directly. These people, so innocently smiling, with eyes that had never looked beyond their own isolated world, these people, who didn't even guess they were sleeping—

But she followed those thoughts no further. Because they had descended the staircase and they approached the throneroom. And there, standing a little apart from the others, was her father.

Reyna caught Juaren's arm, for a moment not believing. They had arrived in the dark hours of night. How had her father ridden here from the desert so quickly? But that was impossible. It took a message days to travel to her uncle's glass-paned city. Yet here was her father—like an act of magic, he was here.

Apparently it seemed an act of magic to him that she was here. He gazed at her for long moments, blankly, as if he did not entirely trust his eyes. Then his brows rose and he was smiling, hurrying toward her with arms extended.

He smelled the way he always had. He felt the way he always had. And she came no farther up his shoulder than she ever had. "How long have you been here?" she demanded breathlessly when he released her. "Did you just come? Did you hear—" But what could he have heard except that they were due to arrive? They had sent ahead no other news.

"I've been here all along—since the season after you left."

She gazed up at him disbelievingly. "You came—"

He shrugged, as wryly as Birnam Rauth might have. "How long did you think I could leave your mother here alone? No matter what I told her when I left. No matter what I told myself. The palace is a lonely place when your kin have scattered. Too lonely for a barohna with all the responsibilities of the throne and the people." He shrugged again. "And my brother's clan-kin kept offering me wives—more wives than I've ever wanted. Some of them were offered rather—forcefully."

Black-eyed wives who wore double-edged knives even to the dining table? Reyna blinked in momentary surprise, wondering how forcefully Danior's mate had been offered. "So you told your brother goodbye."

"And I came home. Just in time to welcome Sonel." He glanced briefly at Juaren, as if evaluating him, then turned and bent. When he straightened he held a fragile two-year-old with auburn hair and glinting amber eyes. "I suppose now that you've traveled, Reyna, you've had time to think about some of our customs. About the fact that you're one of the few palace daughters ever to know her father, ever to pull his hair or spit food on his shoulder. Others seldom even learn their father's name. Of course that is the custom."

"I—" But Reyna saw he didn't really address his observations to her. It was to Juaren that he spoke. And it was into Juaren's arms that he placed the child.

So this was her sister, Juaren's child—the next barohna of Valley Terlath. Father and child studied each other with well-matched reserve and Reyna felt unexpected tears sting her eyelids. "So this is the sister we will teach next winter while you and my mother go to the winter palace," she said, touching the child's fragile hand. This was the sister she and Juaren would tend and tell stories to while everyone else in the valley slept. This was the sister they must prepare to assume the sunthrone. The sister who must one day understand all the things they had learned about Brakrath and the universe.

"The very one," her father agreed, smiling, suddenly embracing her again. "Reyna, you're the first of my daughters I've known as an adult, and you've become the person I hoped."

Heady praise. Praise so unexpected, so disconcerting Reyna hardly noticed when he drew them into the throneroom, hardly noticed when the tall doors closed, shutting out all the people who had watched their reunion. Reyna stood briefly dazed by the brightness of mirrors and throne, by the dark figure caught at the center of their light. It took her moments to realize that Khira was not alone and that Khira was not as she and Juaren had left her: lonely and drawn. Instead she talked animatedly with Verra, glancing up from their conversation with a welcoming smile as they approached.

"My daughter—" She stepped down from the throne, away from the focused light of the mirrors. The hands she extended to Reyna were warm, strong. "I hear from my friend that you have come back well. And I have just had the pleasure of granting a wish for her."

Reyna glanced quickly at Verra as Khira took the throne again. "You're going back to Arnim now? To see your children?"

Verra caught at the tail of the green songsilk she wore as a headband, twisting it around her fingers. "No, no. I'm taking an office in the palace—that same office you offered me once. I'm going to be an adviser to the throne. I'm sure there will be questions I can answer, even if I have to pose them myself." She smiled at Reyna's obvious surprise. "Didn't I tell you I was a rebel? What properly taught Arnimi would ever have thought of traveling all the way back across the stars just to see her children? When she's contributed nothing to the shaping of them except a few body cells? I've decided to do the kind thing and not embarrass them with my interest."

Reyna found she was not entirely surprised. Verra's eyes had seldom brightened when she spoke of her children. Instead they had darkened. And her status as a member of the Arnimi party—did she intend to renounce that as well? Certainly she had hinted often enough of her dissatisfaction. "Your commander—"

"My commander is going to tell me when I discard my uniform this afternoon that I can only make a fool of myself, never a Brakrathi."

So she did intend to renounce her people. "And you'll tell him—"

"I'll tell him that I'm continuing the unfortunate work my parents undertook. I'm making a human of myself. He won't understand, of course. But he has accepted the hospitality of Khira's palace for a number of years. He won't dare take the prescribed disciplinary measures."

Reyna nodded, deciding she didn't even want to know what those measures might be. Perhaps they involved eating day after day from a silent dinner table, flanked by dour companions. Perhaps they involved wearing an austere uniform for thirty years longer. Perhaps they involved never listening to the land and the people, only to instruments. Without the assistance of the Arnimi and their equipment, she and Juaren could never have found Birnam Rauth. But she guessed she would never feel anything more for them than strained tolerance. "Remind me and I'll make ink for your stand, Verra," she said. "I have a formula—one of my own."

"Do it," Verra said, clasping her hand.

Then they could put it off no longer. They must speak to her mother. They must place their intentions before her. Reyna glanced quickly at Juaren. He had set the child down. He addressed a tense glance at Reyna.

"My mother—" she said.

But she didn't have her mother's attention. The child did. She was climbing to Khira's lap, tugging at her gown, pressing her bare limbs against the inviolable stone of the throne. And Khira, instead of reminding her that she must stand beside the throne and never leave the print of her hands upon it, only pulled her up and cradled her and stroked her hair.

Because of course, Reyna realized, Sonel was the one daughter her mother could give her heart to. Sonel was the one daughter whom she need not hold lightly. When Sonel went to the mountain, she would return.

"My mother—" she said again, when the child was settled in Khira's lap. "There are things we have seen, things we must discuss with you and later with all the people of the valleys. I don't know if you know the hunter's pledge, I don't know if you have any idea how many peoples live beyond Brakrath, I don't know if you understand how poorly we're prepared to meet them—"

She stopped, for a moment uncertain. Much depended upon her mother's support. If she and Juaren went from valley to valley to tell the story of their journey, if they took Birnam Rauth to tell his stories as well, and the Council of Bronze forbade the people to listen—

They required her mother's support. She was the only one of them who could speak to the Council, who could present their case and present it strongly. But Reyna could not read her expression. It had grown remote, thoughtful. "My mother—" she began again.

But Khira silenced her with a raised hand. "The child," she said to Iahn. "She's hidden herself in the alcove again. Would you bring her?"

Another child? Whose? Reyna bit her lip, disturbed by the interruption, wondering if she should try to override it. The Council must permit the people to hear Birnam Rauth's stories of all the people and places that lay beyond Brakrath. His was the voice that could rouse them, his the tales that could wake them.

"A moment, my daughter," Khira said. "There is a child—"

Reyna's father went quickly to the alcove off the throneroom, where scrolls were stored. They heard him speak coaxingly. Finally he emerged leading a child by the hand.

Reyna knew immediately that this was no Brakrath child. She was not fragile and auburn-haired like a palace daughter. Nor was she blonde and sturdy like a daughter of the halls. She was slender and pale with hair so light it was almost like silver. Her face was thin, as if she had been starved, and her eyes were huge—huge and dark and frightened. She looked around at them all with a shrinking gaze and spoke incomprehensibly to Iahn.

"Who—who is she?" Reyna demanded. But she had already half-guessed, remembering the stories she had heard of the winter her father had come to Brakrath.

"The Arnimi tell us she's named Cilka Fynn—or the woman she was imaged from was named that, a long time ago. The field monitors found her three days ago, wandering in the fields, crying and hungry."

Reyna tongued dry lips. "The Benderzic—"

"The Benderzic left her to study our land. Just as they left Iahn once."

The Benderzic had left this child—was she properly called a Fynn-image?—to probe their society, to learn their language, their customs, to discover their resources, their strengths and weaknesses. Because the Benderzic expected that information to be valuable one day. "She's so small," Reyna protested. The child could not be five.

"Who observes more closely or learns more quickly than a child? And who is less likely to be considered a threat? The Benderzic have left this one, and one day they will return for her. Even if they aren't able to take her from us, their attention is upon us. They will find ways to evaluate us, eventually. So my daughter—" Now it was Khira who hesitated, who seemed uncertain. "My daughter, you and Juaren have seen things no other Brakrathi have seen. You know better than any of us—except Verra—what waits out there, beyond our skies. The Council doesn't know of this child yet. I will tell them when session is called at season's end. And I will tell them something else too. The people must know. The people must begin to understand that the universe doesn't end here, that they cannot sleep while the Benderzic gather information to bid away. The people—"

"The people must be wakened," Juaren said softly. "They've been sleeping. They've been dreaming. Now they must wake and see what the morning brings."

"Yes," Khira said, looking at him directly for the first time, obviously relieved that he understood. "And you—you are the people to waken them."

Reyna laughed softly, touching Juaren's arm, feeling the tension ebb from him. So her mother wanted them to do the very thing they had intended to do. She formally requested them to do it. She would defend the necessity of it to the Council.

It was the end of a long journey and the beginning of another. Silently Reyna numbered some of the lessons she had learned: that it didn't matter who held the sunthrone of Valley Terlath, so long as someone did. That with understanding, she became as tall as her mother, as ageless as the throne, as resilient as the silk she held in her hand—and all with no apparent change. That with understanding, she became a woman with a place—in the mountains, in the valley, in her own eyes. And the more she increased her understanding, the more secure she would be in all those things.

So there were many more lessons to be learned and now was the time to begin learning them. Smiling, she offered the bundle that held the life-silk to Juaren, so he could remove the wrappings.

"My mother, my father, my sister, there is someone you must meet."

BIRNAM RAUTH

A nd so he was free again. He ate light and drank breeze, taking strength from them both. He sang when he wanted, sometimes silently, sometimes aloud. He bathed himself in sunlight by day and starlight by night. He eavesdropped with less and less compunction upon the thoughts of anyone who stepped near. Sometimes when they did not step near enough, he went to them and lightly wrapped silken arms around them so he could use all the complex structures of their bodies to remember more clearly what it was to be human. They never seemed to be frightened by him when he did that. Some of them considered themselves honored.

He had learned many things from this last, long exploration. He had learned to find humanity in alien creatures. He had discovered the alien in himself. And he had learned that sometimes the alien and the human are so far separated by perception and experience that it is difficult to speak across the gap.

He had also learned that being imprisoned for a century in the hollow of a tree had not made him a sage. It had only helped him learn to accept solitude and loss. But at least in the loss of his body, he had acquired the ability to move freely from human mind to human mind, gathering impressions and information he could never have gathered by more clumsy means. So perhaps one day he would be a sage after all.

It was not an ambition he had ever aspired to. To see, to probe, to give his curiosity full reign, yes. To speak with an ancient's wisdom, when he still felt young and hungry for understanding—no.

But when he traveled with Reyna and Juaren, when he spoke to the awed people who gathered to hear the tales of his star journeys—to hear of the strange, benign peoples and creatures he had known, to hear of other peoples and creatures who were not benign at all—he put on a sage's manner. Like Reyna, like Juaren, he knew the need to spur these people to look beyond their own fields and halls, to begin to think of their strengths and weaknesses.

He knew because he had reached into Iahn's mind. He had reached deeply, far past that day when Iahn had stood as a boy on a strange world and wondered why a white silk spoke with a familiar voice. In looking, he had looked into the very face of the Benderzic. He had reached into Cilka's mind too and looked into that same face. And somewhere, scattered across tens and hundreds of little-known worlds, there were others like the child Iahn had been, like the child Cilka was—tools the Benderzic used with no more feeling than if they were made of wood or metal.

The Benderzic would have just as much feeling for the trusting people of Brakrath and for their rich world.

So when Birnam Rauth spoke to those people he put on a sage's manner, he plundered their open minds for every clue to their under-standing, and he vowed to shake them until they woke, blinking and confused, to the world that lay beyond their own skies.